Freeman Wills Crofts was born in Dublin in 1879 and died in 1957. He worked for a Northern Irish railway company as an engineer, writing in his spare time. In 1929 he moved to England and turned to writing detective fiction full-time.

His plots reveal his mathematical training and he specialised in the seemingly unbreakable alibi and the intricacies of railway timetables. He also loved ships and trains and they feature in many of his stories.

Crofts' best-known character is Inspector Joseph French, a detective who achieves his results through dogged persistence.

Raymond Chandler praised Crofts' plots, calling him 'the soundest builder of them all'.

FREEMAN WILLS CROFTS

The Cask

HOUSE OF
STRATUS

This edition published in 2001 by House of Stratus, an imprint of
House of Stratus Ltd, Thirsk Industrial Park, York Road, Thirsk,
North Yorkshire, YO7 3BX, UK.
Also at: House of Stratus Inc., 2 Neptune Road, Poughkeepsie, NY 12601, USA.

www.houseofstratus.com

Typeset, printed and bound by House of Stratus.

A catalogue record for this book is available from the British Library
and the Library of Congress.

ISBN 1-84232-384-9

To

DR ADAM A C MATHERS,

IN APPRECIATION OF HIS KINDLY
CRITICISM AND HELP

CONTENTS

PART 1: LONDON

PART 2: PARIS

PART 3: LONDON AND PARIS

PART 1

London

A STRANGE CONSIGNMENT

Mr Avery, managing director of the Insular and Continental Steam Navigation Company, had just arrived at his office. He glanced at his inward letters, ran his eye over his list of engagements for the day, and inspected the return of the movements of his Company's steamers. Then, after spending a few moments in thought, he called his chief clerk, Wilcox.

'I see the *Bullfinch* is in this morning from Rouen,' he said. 'I take it she'll have that consignment of wines for Norton and Banks?'

'She has,' replied the chief clerk, 'I've just rung up the dock office to inquire.'

'I think we ought to have it specially checked from here. You remember all the trouble they gave us about the last lot. Will you send some reliable man down? Whom can you spare?'

'Broughton could go. He has done it before.'

'Well, see to it, will you, and then send in Miss Johnson and I shall go through the mail.'

The office was the headquarters of the Insular and Continental Steam Navigation Company, colloquially known as the I and C, and occupied the second floor of a large block of buildings at the western end of Fenchurch Street. The Company was an important concern, and owned a fleet of some thirty steamers ranging front 300 to 1000 tons burden, which traded between London and the smaller Continental ports. Low freights were their speciality, but they did not drive their boats, and no attempt was made to compete with the more expensive routes in the matter of speed. Under these circumstances they did a large trade in all kinds of goods other than perishables.

Mr Wilcox picked up some papers and stepped over to the desk at which Tom Broughton was working.

'Broughton,' he said, 'Mr Avery wants you to go down at once to the docks and check a consignment of wines for Norton and Banks. It came in last night from Rouen in the *Bullfinch*. These people gave us a lot of trouble about their last lot, disputing our figures, so you will have to be very careful. Here are the invoices, and don't take the men's figures but see each cask yourself.'

'Right, sir,' replied Broughton, a young fellow of three-and-twenty, with a frank, boyish face and an alert manner. Nothing loath to exchange the monotony of the office for the life and bustle of the quays, he put away his books, stowed the invoices carefully in his pocket, took his hat and went quickly down the stairs and out into Fenchurch Street.

It was a brilliant morning in early April. After a spell of cold, showery weather, there was at last a foretaste of summer in the air, and the contrast made it seem good to be alive. The sun shone with that clear freshness seen only after rain. Broughton's spirits rose as he hurried through the busy streets, and watched the ceaseless flow of traffic pouring along the arteries leaning to the shipping.

His goal was St Katherine's Docks, where the *Bullfinch* was berthed, and, passing across Tower Hill and round two sides of the grim old fortress, he pushed on till he reached the basin in which the steamer was lying. She was a long and rather low vessel of some 800 tons burden, with engines amidships, and a single black funnel ornamented with the two green bands that marked the Company's boats. Recently out from her annual overhaul, she looked trim and clean in her new coat of black paint. Unloading was in progress, and Broughton hurried on board, anxious to be present before any of the consignment of wine was set ashore.

He was just in time, for the hatches of the lower forehold, in which the casks were stowed, had been cleared and were being lifted off as he arrived. As he stood on the bridge deck waiting for the work to be completed he looked around.

Several steamers were lying in the basin. Immediately behind, with her high bluff bows showing over the *Bullfinch's* counter, was the *Thrush*, his Company's largest vessel, due to sail that afternoon for Corunna and Vigo. In the berth in front lay a Clyde Shipping Company's boat bound for Belfast and Glasgow and also due out that afternoon, the smoke from her black funnel circling lazily up into the clear sky. Opposite was the *Arcturus*, belonging to the I and C's rivals, Messrs Babcock and Millman, and commanded by 'Black Mac,' so called to distinguish him from the Captain M'Tavish of differently coloured hair, 'Red Mac,' who was master of the same Company's *Sirius*. To Broughton these boats represented links with the mysterious, far-off world of romance, and he never saw one put to sea without longing to go with her to Copenhagen, Bordeaux, Lisbon, Spezzia, or to whatever other delightful-sounding place she was bound.

The fore-hatch being open, Broughton climbed down into the hold armed with his notebook, and the unloading of the casks began. They were swung out in lots of four fastened together by rope slings. As each lot was dealt with, the clerk noted the contents in his book, from which he would afterwards check the invoices.

The work progressed rapidly, the men straining and pushing to get the heavy barrels in place for the slings. Gradually the space under and around the hatch was cleared, the casks then having to be rolled forward from the farther parts of the hold.

A quartet of casks had just been hoisted and Broughton was turning to examine the next lot when he heard a sudden shout of 'Look out, there! Look out!' and felt himself seized roughly and pulled backwards. He swung round and was in time to see the four casks turning over out of the sling and falling heavily to the floor of the hold. Fortunately they had only been lifted some four or five feet, but they were heavy things and came down solidly. The two under were damaged slightly and the wine began to ooze out between the staves. The others had had their fall broken and neither seemed the worse. The men had all jumped clear and no one was hurt.

'Upend those casks, boys,' called the foreman, when the damage had been briefly examined, 'and let's save the wine.'

The leaking casks were turned damaged end up and lifted aside for temporary repairs. The third barrel was found to be uninjured, but when they came to the fourth it was seen that it had not entirely escaped.

This fourth cask was different in appearance from the rest, and Broughton had noted it as not belonging to Messrs Norton and Banks' consignment. It was more strongly made and better finished, and was stained a light oak colour and varnished. Evidently, also, it did not contain wine, for what had called their attention to its injury was a little heap of sawdust which had escaped from a crack at the end of one of the staves.

'Strange looking cask this. Did you ever see one like it before?' said Broughton to the I and C foreman who had pulled him back, a man named Harkness. He was a tall, strongly built man with prominent cheekbones, a square chin and a sandy moustache. Broughton had known him for some time and had a high opinion of his intelligence and ability.

'Never saw nothin' like it,' returned Harkness. 'I tell you, sir, that there cask 'as been made to stand some knocking about.'

'Looks like it. Let's get it rolled back out of the way and turned up, so as to see the damage.'

Harkness seized the cask and with some difficulty rolled it close to the ship's side out of the way of the unloading, but when he tried to upend it he found it too heavy to lift.

'There's something more than sawdust in there,' he said. 'It's the 'eaviest cask ever I struck. I guess it was its weight shifted the other casks in the sling and spilled the lot.'

He called over another man and they turned the cask damaged end up. Broughton stepped over to the charge hand and asked him to check the tally for a few seconds while he examined the injury.

As he was returning across the half-dozen yards to join the foreman, his eye fell on the little heap of sawdust that had fallen out of the crack, and the glitter of some bright object showing through it caught his attention. He stooped and picked it up. His amazement as he looked at it may be imagined, for it was a sovereign!

He glanced quickly round. Only Harkness of all the men present had seen it.

'Turn the 'eap over, sir,' said the foreman, evidently as surprised as the younger man, 'see if there are any more.'

Broughton sifted the sawdust through his fingers, and his astonishment was not lessened when he discovered two others hidden in the little pile.

He gazed at the three gold coins lying in his palm. As he did so Harkness gave a smothered exclamation and, stooping rapidly, picked something out from between two of the boards of the hold's bottom.

'Another by gum!' cried the foreman in low tones, 'and another!' He bent down again and lifted a second object from behind where the cask was standing. 'Blest if it ain't a blooming gold mine we've struck.'

Broughton put the five sovereigns in his pocket, as he and Harkness unostentatiously scrutinised the deck. They searched carefully, but found no other coins.

'Did you drop them when I dragged you back?' asked Harkness.

'I? No, I wish I had, but I had no gold about me.'

'Some of the other chaps must 'ave then. Maybe Peters or Wilson. Both jumped just at this place.'

'Well, don't say anything for a moment. I believe they came out of the cask.'

'Out o' the cask? Why, sir, 'oo would send sovereigns in a cask?'

'No one, I should have said; but how would they get among the sawdust if they didn't come out through the crack with it?'

'That's so,' said Harkness thoughtfully, continuing, 'I tell you, Mr Broughton, you say the word and I'll open that crack a bit more and we'll 'ave a look into the cask.'

The clerk recognised that this would be irregular, but his curiosity was keenly aroused and he hesitated.

'I'll do it without leaving any mark that won't be put down to the fall,' continued the tempter, and Broughton fell.

'I think we should know,' he replied. 'This gold may have been stolen and inquiries should be made.'

The foreman smiled and disappeared, returning with a hammer and cold chisel. The broken piece at the end of the stave was entirely separated from the remainder by the crack, but was held in position by one of the iron rings. This piece Harkness with some difficulty drove upwards, thus widening the crack. As he did so, a little shower of sawdust fell out and the astonishment of the two men was not lessened when with it came a number of sovereigns, which went rolling here and there over the planks.

It happened that at the same moment the attention of the other men was concentrated on a quartet of casks which was being slung up through the hatches, the nervousness caused by the slip not having yet subsided. None of them therefore saw what had taken place, and Broughton and Harkness had picked up the coins before any of them turned round. Six sovereigns had come out, and the clerk added them to the five he already had, while he and his companion unostentatiously searched for others. Not finding any, they turned back to the cask deeply mystified.

'Open that crack a bit more,' said Broughton. 'What do you think about it?'

'Blest if I know what to think,' replied the foreman. 'We're on to something mighty queer anyway. 'Old my cap under the crack till I prize out that there bit of wood altogether.'

With some difficulty the loose piece of the stave was hammered up, leaving a hole in the side of the barrel some six inches deep by nearly four wide. Half a capful of sawdust fell out, and the clerk added to it by clearing the broken edge of the wood. Then he placed the cap on the top of the cask and they eagerly felt through the sawdust.

'By Jehoshaphat!' whispered Harkness excitedly, 'it's just full of gold!'

It seemed to be so, indeed, for in it were no fewer than seven sovereigns.

'That's eighteen in all,' said Broughton, in an awed tone, as he slipped them into his pocket. 'If the whole cask's full of them it must be worth thousands and thousands of pounds.'

They stood gazing at the prosaic-looking barrel, outwardly remarkable only in its strong design and good finish, marvelling if beneath that commonplace exterior there was indeed hidden what to them seemed a fortune. Then Harkness crouched down and looked into the cask through the hole he had made. Hardly had he done so when he sprang back with a sudden oath.

'Look in there, Mr Broughton!' he cried in a suppressed tone. 'Look in there!'

Broughton stooped in turn and peered in. Then he also recoiled, for there, sticking up out of the sawdust, were the fingers of a hand.

'This is terrible,' he whispered, convinced at last they were in the presence of tragedy, and then he could have kicked himself for being such a fool.

'Why, it's only a statue,' he cried.

'Statue?' replied Harkness sharply. 'Statue? That ain't no statue. That's part of a dead body, that is. And don't you make no mistake.'

'It's too dark to see properly. Get a light, will you, till we make sure.'

When the foreman had procured a hand lamp Broughton looked in again and speedily saw that his first impression was correct. The fingers were undoubtedly those of a woman's hand, small, pointed, delicate, and bearing rings which glinted in the light.

'Clear away some more of the sawdust, Harkness,' said the young man as he stood up again. 'We must find out all we can now.'

He held the cap as before, and the foreman carefully picked out with the cold chisel the sawdust surrounding the fingers. As its level lowered, the remainder of the hand and the wrist gradually became revealed. The sight of the whole only accentuated the first impression of dainty beauty and elegance.

Broughton emptied the cap on to the top of the cask. Three more sovereigns were found hidden in it, and these he pocketed with the others. Then he turned to re-examine the cask.

It was rather larger than the wine barrels, being some three feet six high by nearly two feet six in diameter. As already mentioned, it was of unusually strong construction, the sides, as shown by the broken stave, being quite two inches thick. Owing possibly to the difficulty of bending such heavy stuff, it was more cylindrical than barrel shaped, the result being that the ends were unusually large, and this no doubt partly accounted for Harkness' difficulty in upending it. In place of the usual thin metal bands, heavy iron rings clamped it together.

On one side was a card label, tacked round the edges and addressed in a foreign handwriting: 'M. Léon Felix, 141 West Jubb Street, Tottenham Court Road, London, W, via Rouen and long sea,' with the words 'Statuary only' printed with a rubber stamp. The label bore also the sender's name:

'Dupierre et Cie, Fabricants de la Sculpture Monumentale, Rue Provence, Rue de la Convention, Grenelle, Paris.' Stencilled in black letters on the woodwork was 'Return to' in French, English, and German, and the name of the same firm. Broughton examined the label with care, in the half-unconscious hope of discovering something from the handwriting. In this he was disappointed, but, as he held the hand-lamp close, he saw something else which interested him.

The label was divided into two parts, an ornamental border containing the sender's advertisement and a central portion for the address. These two were separated by a thick black line. What had caught Broughton's eye was an unevenness along this line, and closer examination showed that the central portion had been cut out, and a piece of paper pasted on the back of the card to cover the hole. Felix's address was therefore written on this paper, and not on the original label. The alteration had been neatly done, and was almost unnoticeable. Broughton was puzzled at first, then it occurred to him that the firm must have run out of labels and made an old one do duty a second time.

'A cask containing money and a human hand – probably a body,' he mused. 'It's a queer business and something has got to be done about it.' He stood looking at the cask while he thought out his course of action.

That a serious crime had been committed he felt sure, and that it was his duty to report his discovery immediately he was no less certain. But there was the question of the consignment of wines. He had been sent specially to the docks to check it, and he wondered if he would be right to leave the work undone. He thought so.

The matter was serious enough to justify him. And it was not as if the wine would not be checked. The ordinary tallyman was there, and Broughton knew him to be careful and accurate. Besides, he could probably get a clerk from the dock office to help. His mind was made up. He would go straight to Fenchurch Street and report to Mr Avery, the managing director.

'Harkness,' he said, 'I'm going up to the head office to report this. You'd better close up that hole as best you can and then stay here and watch the cask. Don't let it out of your sight on any pretext until you get instructions from Mr Avery.'

'Right, Mr Broughton,' replied the foreman, 'I think you're doing the proper thing.'

They replaced as much of the sawdust as they could, and Harkness fitted the broken piece of stave into the space and drove it home, nailing it fast.

'Well, I'm off,' said Broughton, but as he turned to go a gentleman stepped down into the hold and spoke to him. He was a man of medium height, foreign-looking, with a dark complexion and a black pointed beard, and dressed in a well-cut suit of blue clothes, with white spats and a Homburg hat. He bowed and smiled.

'Pardon me, but you are, I presume, an I and C official?' he asked, speaking perfect English, but with a foreign accent.

'I am a clerk in the head office, sir.' replied Broughton.

'Ah, quite so. Perhaps then you can oblige me with some information? I am expecting from Paris by this boat a cask containing a group of statuary from Messrs Dupierre of that city. Can you tell me if it has arrived? This is my name.' He handed Broughton a card on which was printed: 'M. Léon Felix, 141 West Jubb Street, Tottenham Court Road, W.'

Though the clerk saw at a glance the name was the same as that on the label on the cask, he pretended to read it with care while considering his reply. This man clearly was the consignee, and if he were told the cask was there he would doubtless claim immediate possession. Broughton could think of no excuse for refusing him, but he was determined all the same not to let it go. He had just decided to reply that it had not yet come to light, but that they would keep a look out for it, when another point struck him.

The damaged cask had been moved to the side of the hold next the dock, and it occurred to the clerk that anyone standing on the wharf beside the hatch could see it. For all he knew to the contrary, this man Felix might have watched their whole proceedings, including the making of the hole in the cask and the taking out of the sovereigns. If he had recognised his property, as was possible, a couple of steps from where he was standing would enable him to put his finger on the label and so convict Broughton of a falsehood. The clerk decided that in this case honesty would be the best policy.

'Yes, sir,' he answered, 'your cask has arrived. By a curious coincidence it is this one beside us. We had just separated it out from the wine barrels owing to its being differently consigned.'

Mr Felix looked at the young man suspiciously, but he only said: 'Thank you. I am a collector of *objets d'art*, and am anxious to see the statue. I have a cart here and I presume I can get it away at once?'

This was what Broughton had expected, but he thought he saw his way.

'Well, sir,' he responded civilly, 'that is outside my job and I fear I cannot help you. But I am sure you can get it now if you will come over to the office on the quay and go through the usual formalities. I am going there now and will be pleased to show you the way.'

'Oh, thank you. Certainly,' agreed the stranger.

As they walked off, a doubt arose in Broughton's mind that Harkness might misunderstand his replies to Felix, and if the latter returned with a plausible story might let the cask go. He therefore called out – 'You understand then, Harkness, you are to do nothing till you hear from Mr Avery,' to which the foreman replied by a wave of the hand.

The problem the young clerk had to solve was threefold. First, he had to go to Fenchurch Street to report the matter to his managing director. Next, he must ensure that the cask was kept in the Company's possession until that gentleman had decided his course of action, and lastly, he wished to accomplish both of these things without raising the suspicions either of Felix or the clerks in the quay office. It was not an easy matter, and at first Broughton was somewhat at a loss. But as they entered the office a plan occurred to him which he at once decided on. He turned to his companion.

'If you will wait here a moment, sir,' he said, 'I'll find the clerk who deals with your business and send him to you.'

'I thank you.'

He passed through the door in the screen dividing the outer and inner offices and, crossing to the manager's room, spoke in a low tone to that official.

'Mr Huston, there's a man outside named Felix for whom a cask has come from Paris on the *Bullfinch* and he wants possession now. The cask is there, but Mr Avery suspects there is something not quite right about it, and he sent me to tell you to please delay delivery until you hear further from him. He said to make any excuse, but under no circumstances to give the thing up. He will ring you up in an hour or so when he has made some further inquiries.'

Mr Huston looked queerly at the young man, but he only said, 'That will be all right,' and the latter took him out and introduced him to Mr Felix.

Broughton delayed a few moments in the inner office to arrange with one of the clerks to take up his work on the *Bullfinch* during his absence. As he passed out by the counter at which the manager and Mr Felix were talking, he heard the latter say in an angry tone – 'Very well, I will go now and see your Mr Avery, and I feel sure he will make it up to me for this obstruction and annoyance.'

'It's up to me to be there first,' thought Broughton, as he hurried out of the dock gates in search of a taxi. None was in sight and he stopped and considered the situation. If Felix had a car waiting he would get to Fenchurch Street while he, Broughton, was looking round. Something else must be done.

Stepping into the Little Tower Hill Post Office, he rang up the head office, getting through to Mr Avery's private room. In a few words he explained that he had accidentally come on evidence which pointed to the commission of a serious crime, that a man named Felix appeared to know something about it, and that this man was about to call on Mr Avery, continuing – 'Now, sir, if you'll let me make a suggestion, it is that you don't see this Mr Felix immediately he calls, but that you let me into your private office by the landing door, so that I don't need to pass through the outer office. Then you can hear my story in detail and decide what to do.'

'It all sounds rather vague and mysterious,' replied the distant voice, 'can you not tell me what you found?'

'Not from here, sir, if you please. If you'll trust me this time, I think you'll be satisfied that I am right when you hear my story.'

'All right. Come along.'

Broughton left the post office and, now when it no longer mattered, found an empty taxi. Jumping in, he drove to Fenchurch Street and, passing up the staircase, knocked at his chief's private door.

'Well Broughton,' said Mr Avery, 'sit down there.'

Going to the door leading to the outer office he spoke to Wilcox. 'I've just had a telephone call and I want to send some other messages. I'll be engaged for half an hour.' Then he closed the door and slipped the bolt. 'You see I have done as you asked and I shall now hear your story. I trust you haven't put me to all this inconvenience without a good cause.'

'I think not, sir, and I thank you for the way you have met me. What happened was this,' and Broughton related in detail his visit to the docks, the mishap to the casks, the discovery of the sovereigns and the woman's hand, the coming of Mr Felix and the interview in the quay office, ending up by placing the twenty-one sovereigns in a little pile on the chief's desk.

When he ceased speaking there was silence for several minutes, while Mr Avery thought over what he had heard. The tale was a strange one, but both from his knowledge of Broughton's character as well as from the young man's manner he implicitly believed every word he had heard. He considered the firm's position in the matter. In one way it did not concern them if a sealed casket, delivered to them for conveyance, contained marble, gold, or road metal, so long as the freight was paid. Their contract was to carry what was handed over to them from one point to another and give it up in the condition they received it. If anyone chose to send sovereigns under the guise of statuary, any objection that might be raised concerned the Customs Department, not them.

On the other hand, if evidence pointing to a serious crime came to the firm's notice, it would be the duty of the firm to acquaint the police. The woman's hand in the cask might or might not indicate a murder, but the suspicion was too strong to justify them in hiding the matter. He came to a decision.

'Broughton,' he said, 'I think you have acted very wisely all through. We will go now to Scotland Yard, and you may repeat your tale to the authorities. After that I think we will be clear of it. Will you go out the way you came in, get a taxi, and wait for me in Fenchurch Street at the end of Mark Lane.'

Mr Avery locked the private door after the young man, put on his coat and hat, and went into the outer office.

'I am going out for a couple of hours, Wilcox,' he said.

The head clerk approached with a letter in his hand.

'Very good, sir, A gentleman named Mr Felix called about 11.30 to see you. When I said you were engaged, he would not wait, but asked for a sheet of paper and an envelope to write you a note. This is it.'

The managing director took the note and turned back into his private office to read it. He was puzzled. He had said at 11.15 he would be engaged for half an hour. Therefore Mr Felix would only have had fifteen minutes to wait. As he opened the envelope he wondered why that gentleman could not have spared this moderate time, after coming all the way from the docks to see him. And then he was puzzled again, for the envelope was empty!

He stood in thought. Had something occurred to startle Mr Felix when writing his note, so that in his agitation he omitted to enclose it? Or had he simply made a mistake? Or was there some deep-laid plot? Well, he would see what Scotland Yard thought.

He put the envelope away in his pocket-book and, going down to the street, joined Broughton in the taxi. They rattled along the crowded thoroughfares while Mr Avery told the clerk about the envelope.

'I say, sir,' said the latter, but that's a strange business. When I saw him, Mr Felix was not at all agitated. He seemed to me a very cool, clear-headed man.'

It happened that about a year previously the shipping company had been the victim of a series of cleverly planned robberies, and, in following up the matter, Mr Avery had become rather well acquainted with two or three of the Yard Inspectors. One of these in particular he had found a shrewd and capable officer, as well as a kindly and pleasant man to work with. On arrival at the Yard he therefore asked for this man, and was pleased to find he was not engaged.

'Good morning, Mr Avery,' said the Inspector, as they entered his office, 'what good wind blows you our way today?'

'Good morning, Inspector. This is Mr Broughton, one of my clerks, and he has got a rather singular story that I think will interest you to hear.'

Inspector Burnley shook hands, closed the door, and drew up a couple of chairs. 'Sit down, gentlemen,' he said. 'I am always interested in a good story.'

'Now, Broughton, repeat your adventures over again to Inspector Burnley.'

Broughton started off and, for the second time, told of his visit to the docks, the damage to the heavily built cask, the finding of the sovereigns and the woman's hand, and the interview with Mr Felix. The Inspector listened gravely and took a note or two, but did not speak till the clerk had finished, when he said – 'Let me congratulate you, Mr Broughton, on your very clear statement.'

'To which I might add a word,' said Mr Avery, and he told of the visit of Mr Felix to the office and handed over the envelope he had left.

'That envelope was written at 11.30,' said the Inspector, 'and it is now nearly 12.30. I am afraid this is a serious matter, Mr Avery. Can you come to the docks at once?'

'Certainly.'

'Well, don't let us lose any time.' He threw a London directory down before Broughton. 'Just look up this Felix, will you, while I make some arrangements.'

Broughton looked for West Jubb Street, but there was no such near Tottenham Court Road.

'I thought as much,' said Inspector Burnley, who had been telephoning. 'Let us proceed.'

As they reached the courtyard a taxi drew up, containing two plain-clothes men as well as the driver. Burnley threw open the door, they all got in, and the vehicle slid quickly out into the street.

Burnley turned to Broughton. 'Describe the man Felix as minutely as you can.'

'He was a man of about middle height, rather slightly and elegantly built. He was foreign-looking, French, I should say, or even Spanish, with dark eyes and complexion, and black hair. He wore a short, pointed beard. He was dressed in blue clothes of good quality, with a dark green or brown Homburg hat, and black shoes with light spats. I did not observe his collar and tie specially, but he gave me the impression of being well dressed in such matters of detail. He wore a ring with some kind of stone on the little finger of his left hand.'

The two plain-clothes men had listened attentively to the description, and they and the Inspector conversed in low tones for a few moments, when silence fell on the party.

They stopped opposite the *Bullfinch's* berth and Broughton led the way down.

'There she is,' he pointed, 'if we go to that gangway we can get down direct to the forehold.'

The two plain-clothes men had also alighted and the five walked in the direction indicated. They crossed the gangway and, approaching the hatchway, looked down into the hold.

'There's where it is,' began Broughton, pointing down, and then suddenly stopped.

The others stepped forward and looked down. The hold was empty. Harkness and the cask were gone!

2

INSPECTOR BURNLEY ON THE TRACK

The immediate suggestion was, of course, that Harkness had had the cask moved to some other place for safety, and this they set themselves to find out.

'Get hold of the gang that were unloading this hold,' said the Inspector.

Broughton darted off and brought up a stevedore's foreman, from whom they learnt that the forehold had been emptied some ten minutes earlier, the men having waited to complete it and then gone for dinner.

'Where do they get their dinner? Can we get hold of them now?' asked Mr Avery.

'Some of them, sir, I think. Most of them go out into the city, but some use the night watchman's room where there is a fire.'

'Let's go and see,' said the Inspector, and headed by the foreman they walked some hundred yards along the quay to a small brick building set apart from the warehouses, inside and in front of which sat a number of men, some eating from steaming cans, others smoking short pipes.

'Any o' you boys on the *Bullfinch's* lower forehold?' asked the foreman, 'if so, boss wants you 'alf a sec.'

Three of the men got up slowly and came forward.

'We want to know, men, said the managing director, 'if you can tell us anything about Harkness and a damaged cask. He was to wait with it till we got down.'

'Well, he's gone with it,' said one of the men, 'less 'n 'alf an hour ago.'

'Gone with it?'

'Yes. Some toff in blue clothes an' a black beard came up an' give 'im a paper, an' when 'e'd read it 'e calls out an' sez, sez 'e, " 'Elp me swing out this 'ere cask," 'e says. We 'elps 'im an' 'e puts it on a 'orse dray – a four-wheeler. An' then they all goes off, 'im an' the cove in the blue togs walkin' together after the dray.'

'Any name on the dray?' asked Mr Avery.

'There was,' replied the spokesman, 'but I'm blessed if I knows what it was. 'Ere Bill, you was talking about that there name. Where was it?'

Another man spoke.

'It was Tottenham Court Road, it was. But I didn't know the street, and I thought that a strange thing, for I've lived off the Tottenham Court Road all my life.'

'Was it East John Street?' asked Inspector Burnley.

'Ay, it was something like that. East or West. West, I think. An' it was something like John. Not John, but something like it.'

'What colour was the dray?'

'Blue, very fresh and clean.'

'Anyone notice the colour of the horse?'

But this was beyond them. The horse was out of their line. Its colour had not been observed.

'Well,' said Mr Avery, as the Inspector signed that was all he wanted, 'we are much obliged to you. Here's something for you.'

Inspector Burnley beckoned to Broughton.

'You might describe this man Harkness.'

'He was a tall chap with a sandy moustache, very high cheekbones, and a big jaw. He was dressed in brown dungarees and a cloth cap.'

'You hear that,' said the Inspector, turning to the plain-clothes men. 'They have half an hour's start. Try to get on their track. Try north and east first, as it is unlikely they'd go west for fear of meeting us. Report to headquarters.'

The men hurried away.

'Now, a telephone,' continued the Inspector. 'Perhaps you'd let me use your quay office one.'

They walked to the office, and Mr Avery arranged for him to get the private instrument in the manager's room.

He rejoined the others in a few minutes.

'Well,' he said, 'that's all we can do in the meantime. A description of the men and cart will be wired round to all the stations immediately, and every constable in London will be on the lookout for them before very much longer.'

'Very good that,' said the managing director.

The Inspector looked surprised.

'Oh no,' he said, 'that's the merest routine. But now I'm here I would like to make some other inquiries. Perhaps you would tell your people that I'm acting with your approval, as it might make them give their information more willingly.'

Mr Avery called over Huston, the manager.

'Huston, this is Inspector Burnley of Scotland Yard. He is making some inquiries about that cask you already heard of. I'll be glad if you see that he is given every facility.' He turned to the Inspector. 'I suppose there's nothing further I can do to help you? I should be glad to get back to the City again, if possible.'

'Thank you, Mr Avery, there's nothing more. I'll cruise round here a bit. I'll let you know how things develop.'

'Right. Goodbye then, in the meantime.'

The Inspector, left to his own devices, called Broughton and, going on board the *Bullfinch*, had the clerk's story repeated in great detail, the actual place where each incident happened being pointed out. He made a search for any object that might have been dropped, but without success, visited the wharf and other points from which the work at the cask might have been overlooked, and generally made himself thoroughly familiar with the circumstances. By the time this was done the other men who had been unloading the forehold had returned from dinner, and he interviewed them, questioning each individually. No additional information was received.

The Inspector then returned to the quay office.

'I want you,' he asked Mr Huston, 'to be so good as to show me all the papers you have referring to that cask, waybills, forward notes, everything.'

Mr Huston disappeared, returning in a few seconds with some papers which he handed to Burnley. The latter examined them and then said – 'These seem to show that the cask was handed over to the French State Railway at their Rue Cardinet Goods Station, near the Gare St Lazare, in Paris, by MM. Dupierre et Cie, carriage being paid forward. They ran it by rail to Rouen, where it was loaded on to your *Bullfinch*.'

'That is so.'

'I suppose you cannot say whether the Paris collection was made by a railway vehicle?'

'No, but I should think not, as otherwise the cartage charges would probably show.'

'I think I am right in saying that these papers are complete and correct in every detail?'

'Oh yes, they are perfectly in order.'

'How do you account for the cask being passed through by the Customs officials without examination?'

'There was nothing suspicious about it. It bore the label of a well-known and reputable firm, and was invoiced as well as stencilled, "Statuary only." It was a receptacle obviously suitable for transporting such goods, and its weight was also in accordance. Unless in the event of some suspicious circumstance, cases of this kind are seldom opened.'

'Thank you, Mr Huston, that is all I want at present. Now, can I see the captain of the *Bullfinch*?'

'Certainly. Come over and I'll introduce you.'

Captain M'Nabb was a big, rawboned Ulsterman, with a hooked nose and sandy hair. He was engaged in writing up some notes in his cabin.

'Come in, sir, come in,' he said, as Huston made the Inspector known. 'What can I do for you?'

Burnley explained his business. He had only a couple of questions to ask.

'How is the trans-shipment done from the railway to your boat at Rouen?'

'The wagons come down on the wharf right alongside. The Rouen stevedores load them, either with the harbour travelling crane or our own winches.'

'Would it be at all possible for a barrel to be tampered with after it was once aboard?'

'How do you mean tampered with? A barrel of wine might be tapped, but that's all could be done.'

'Could a barrel be changed, or completely emptied and filled with something else?'

'It could not. The thing's altogether impossible.'

'I'm much obliged to you, captain. Good day.'

Inspector Burnley was nothing if not thorough. He questioned in turn the winch drivers, the engineers, even the cook, and before six o'clock had interviewed every man that had sailed on the *Bullfinch* from Rouen. The results were unfortunately entirely negative. No information about the cask was forthcoming. No question had been raised about it. Nothing had happened to call attention to it, or that was in any way out of the common.

Puzzled but not disheartened, Inspector Burnley drove back to Scotland Yard, his mind full of the mysterious happenings, and his pocket-book stored with all kinds of facts about the *Bullfinch*, her cargo, and crew.

Two messages were waiting for him. The first was from Ralston, the plain-clothes man that he had sent from the dock in a northerly direction. It read: 'Traced parties as far as north end of Leman Street. Trail lost there.'

The second was from a police station in Upper Head Street: 'Parties seen turning from Great Eastern Street into Curtain Road about 1.20 p.m.'

'H'm, going north-west, are they?' mused the Inspector taking down a large scale map of the district. 'Let's see. Here's Leman Street. That is, say, due north from St Katherine's Docks, and half a mile or more away. Now, what's the other one?' – he referred to the wire – 'Curtain Road should be somewhere here. Yes, here it is. Just a continuation of the same line, only more west, say, a mile and a half from the docks. So they're going straight, are they, and using the main streets. H'm, H'm. Now I wonder where they're heading to. Let's see.'

The Inspector pondered. 'Ah, well,' he murmured at last, 'we must wait till tomorrow,' and, sending instructions recalling his two plain-clothes assistants, he went home.

But his day's work was not done. Hardly had he finished his meal and lit one of the strong, black cigars he favoured, when he was summoned back to Scotland Yard. There waiting for him was Broughton, and with him the tall, heavy-jawed foreman, Harkness.

The Inspector pulled forward two chairs. 'Sit down, gentlemen,' he said, when the clerk had introduced his companion, 'and let me hear your story.'

'You'll be surprised to see me so soon again, Mr Burnley,' answered Broughton, 'but, after leaving you, I went back to the office to see if there were any instructions for me, and found our friend here had just turned up. He was asking for the chief, Mr Avery, but he had gone home. Then he told me his adventures, and as I felt sure Mr Avery would have sent him to you, I thought my best plan was to bring him along without delay.'

'And right you were, Mr Broughton. Now, Mr Harkness, I would be obliged if you would tell me what happened to you.'

The foreman settled himself comfortably in his chair.

'Well, sir,' he began, 'I think you're listening to the biggest fool between this and St Paul's. I 'ave been done this afternoon, fairly diddled, an' not once only, but two separate times. 'Owever, I'd better tell you from the beginning.

'When Mr Broughton an' Felix left, I stayed an' kept an eye on the cask. I got some bits of 'oop iron by way o' mending it, so that none o' the boys would wonder why I was 'anging around. I waited the best part of an hour, an' then Felix came back.

' " Mr 'Arkness, I believe?" 'e said.

' "That's my name, sir," I answered.

' "I 'ave a letter for you from Mr Avery. P'raps you would kindly read it now," 'e said.

28

'It was a note from the 'ead office, signed by Mr Avery, an' it said that 'e 'ad seen Mr Broughton an' that it was all right about the cask, an' for me to give it up to Felix at once. It said too that we 'ad to deliver the cask at the address that was on it, an' for me to go there along with it and Felix, an' to report if it was safely delivered.

' "That's all right, sir," said I, an' I called to some o' the boys, an' we got the cask swung ashore an' on to a four-wheeled dray Felix 'ad waiting. 'E 'ad two men with it, a big, strong fellow with red 'air an' a smaller dark chap that drove. We turned east at the dock gates, an' then went up Leman Street an' on into a part o' the city I didn't know.

'When we 'ad gone a mile or more, the red-'aired man said 'e could do with a drink. Felix wanted 'im to carry on at first, but 'e gave in after a bit an' we stopped in front o' a bar. The small man's name was Watty, an' Felix asked 'im could 'e leave the 'orse, but Watty said "No," an' then Felix told 'im to mind it while the rest of us went in, an' 'e would come out soon an' look after it, so's Watty could go in an' get 'is drink. So Felix an' I an' Ginger went in, an' Felix ordered four bottles o' beer an' paid for them. Felix drank 'is off, an' then 'e told us to wait till 'e would send Watty in for 'is, an' went out. As soon as 'e 'ad gone Ginger leant over an' whispered to me, "Say, mate, wot's 'is game with the blooming cask? I lay you five to one 'e 'as something crooked on."

' "Why," said I, "I don't know about that." You see, sir, I 'ad thought the same myself, but then Mr Avery wouldn't 'ave written wot it was all right if it wasn't.

' "Well, see 'ere," said Ginger, "maybe if you an' I was to keep our eyes skinned, it might put a few quid in our pockets."

' " 'Ow's that?" said I.

29

' " 'Ow's it yourself?" said 'e. "If 'e 'as some game on wi' the cask 'e'll not be wanting for to let any outsiders in. If you an' me was to offer for to let them in for 'im, 'e'd maybe think we was worth something."

'Well, gentlemen, I thought over that, an' first I wondered if this chap knew there was a body in the cask, an' I was going to see if I couldn't find out without giving myself away. Then I thought maybe 'e was on the same lay, an' was pumping me. So I thought I would pass it off a while, an' I said: "Would Watty come in?"

'Ginger said "No," that three was too many for a job o' that kind, an' we talked on a while. Then I 'appened to look at Watty's beer standing there, an' I wondered 'e 'adn't been in for it.

' "That beer won't keep," I said. "If that blighter wants it 'e'd better come an' get it."

'Ginger sat up when 'e 'eard that.

' "Wot's wrong with 'im?" 'e said. "I'll drop out an' see."

'I don't know why, gentlemen, but I got a kind o' notion there was something in the air, an' I followed 'im out. The dray was gone. We looked up an' down the street, but there wasn't a sign of it nor Felix nor Watty.

' "Blow me, if they 'aven't given us the slip," shouted Ginger. "Get a move on. You go that way an' I'll go this, an' one of us is bound to see them at the corner."

'I guessed I was on to the game then. These three were wrong 'uns, an' they were out to get rid o' the body, an' they didn't want me around to see the grave. All that about the drinks was a plant to get me away from the dray, an' Ginger's talk was only to keep me quiet till the others got clear. Well, two o' them 'ad got quit o' me right enough, but I was blessed if the third would.

' "No, you don't, ol' pal," I said. "I guess you an' me'll stay together." I took 'is arm an' 'urried 'im on the way 'e 'ad wanted to go 'imself. But when we got to the corner there wasn't a sign o' the dray. They 'ad given us the slip about proper.

'Ginger cursed an' raved, an' wanted to know 'oo was going to pay 'im for 'is day. I tried to get out of 'im 'oo 'e was an' 'oo 'ad 'ired 'im, but 'e wasn't givin' anything away. I kept close beside 'im, for I knew 'e'd 'ave to go 'ome sometime, an' I thought if I saw where 'e lived it would be easy to find out where 'e worked, an' so likely get 'old o' Felix. 'E tried different times to juke away from me, an' 'e got real mad when 'e found 'e couldn't.

'We walked about for more than three hours till it was near five o'clock, an' then we 'ad some more beer, an' when we came out o' the bar we stood at the corner o' two streets an' thought wot we'd do next. An' then suddenly Ginger lurched up against me, an' I drove fair into an old woman that was passing, an' nearly knocked 'er over. I caught 'er to keep 'er from falling – I couldn't do no less – but when I looked round, I'm blessed if Ginger wasn't gone. I ran down one street first, an' then down the other, an' then I went back into the bar, but never a sight of 'im did I get. I cursed myself for every kind of a fool, an' then I thought I'd better go back an' tell Mr Avery anyway. So I went to Fenchurch Street, an' Mr Broughton brought me along 'ere.'

There was silence when the foreman ceased speaking, while Inspector Burnley, in his painstaking way, considered the statement he had heard, as well as that made by Broughton earlier in the day. He reviewed the chain of events in detail, endeavouring to separate out the undoubted facts from what might be only the narrator's opinions. If the two men were to be believed, and Burnley had no reason for doubting either, the facts about the discovery and removal of the cask were clear, with one exception. There seemed to be no adequate proof that the cask really did contain a corpse.

'Mr Broughton tells me he thought there was a body in the cask. Do you agree with that, Mr Harkness?'

'Yes, sir, there's no doubt of it. We both saw a woman's hand.'

'But might it not have been a statue? The cask was labelled "Statuary," I understand.'

'No, sir, it wasn't no statue. Mr Broughton thought that at first, but when 'e looked at it again 'e gave in I was right. It was a body, sure enough.'

Further questions showed that both men were convinced the hand was real, though neither could advance any grounds for their belief other than that he 'knew from the look of it.' The Inspector was not satisfied that their opinion was correct, though he thought it probable. He also noted the possibility of the cask containing a hand only or perhaps an arm, and it passed through his mind that such a thing might be packed by a medical student as a somewhat gruesome practical joke. Then he turned to Harkness again.

'Have you the letter Felix gave you on the *Bullfinch*?'

'Yes, sir,' replied the foreman, handing it over.

It was written in what looked like a junior clerk's handwriting on a small-sized sheet of business letter paper. It bore the I and C's ordinary printed heading, and read:

5th April, 1912

Mr Harkness,
on s.s. *Bullfinch*,
St Katherine's Docks.

Re Mr Broughton's conversation with you about cask for Mr Felix.

I have seen Mr Broughton and Mr Felix on this matter, and am satisfied the cask is for Mr Felix and should be delivered immediately.

On receipt of this letter please hand it over to Mr Felix without further delay.

As the Company is liable for its delivery at the address it bears, please accompany it as the representative of the Company, and report to me of its safe arrival in due course.

For the I and C S N Co. Ltd.,

X Avery,
per X X,
Managing Director.

The initials shown 'X' were undecipherable and were apparently written by a person in authority, though curiously the word 'Avery' in the same hand was quite clear.

'It's written on your Company's paper anyway,' said the Inspector to Broughton. 'I suppose that heading is yours and not a fake?'

'It's ours right enough,' returned the clerk, 'but I'm certain the letter's a forgery for all that.'

'I should imagine so, but just how do you know?'

'For several reasons, sir. Firstly, we do not use that quality of paper for writing our own servants; we have a cheaper form of memorandum for that. Secondly, all our stuff is typewritten: and thirdly, that is not the signature of any of our clerks.'

'Pretty conclusive. It is evident that the forger did not know either your managing director's or your clerks' initials. His knowledge was confined to the name Avery, and from your statement we can conceive Felix having just that amount of information.'

'But how on earth did he get our paper?'

Burnley smiled.

'Oh, well, that's not so difficult. Didn't your head clerk give it to him?'

'By Jove! sir, I see it now. He got a sheet of paper and an envelope to write to Mr Avery. He left the envelope and vanished with the sheet.'

'Of course. It occurred to me when Mr Avery told me of the empty envelope. I guessed what he was going to do, and therefore I hurried to the docks in the hope of being before him. And now about that label on the cask. You might describe it again as fully as you can.'

'It was a card about six inches long by four high, fastened on by tacks all round the edge. Along the top was Dupierre's name and advertisement, and in the bottom right-hand corner was a space about three inches by two for the address. There was a thick, black line round this space, and the card had been cut along this line so as to remove the enclosed portion and leave a hole three inches by two. The hole had been filled by pasting a sheet of paper or card behind the label. Felix's address was therefore written on this paper, and not on the original card.'

'A curious arrangement. How do you explain it?'

'I thought perhaps Dupierre's people had temporarily run out of labels and were making an old one do again.'

Burnley replied absently, as he turned the matter over in his mind. The clerk's suggestion was of course possible. In fact, if the cask really contained a statue, it was the likely one. On the other hand, if it held a body, he imagined the reason was further to seek. In this case he thought it improbable that the cask had come from Dupierre's at all and, if not, what had happened? A possible explanation occurred to him. Suppose some unknown person had received a statue from Dupierre's in the cask and, before returning the latter, had committed a murder. Suppose he wanted to get rid of the body by sending it somewhere in the cask. What would he do with the label? Why, what had been done. He would wish to retain Dupierre's printed matter in order to facilitate the passage of the cask through the Customs, but he would have to change the written address. The Inspector could think of no better way of doing this than by the alteration that had been made. He turned again to his visitors.

'Well, gentlemen, I'm greatly obliged to you for your prompt call and information, and if you will give me your addresses, I think that is all we can do tonight.'

Inspector Burnley again made his way home. But it was not his lucky night. About half-past nine he was again sent for from the Yard. Someone wanted to speak to him urgently on the telephone.

3

THE WATCHER ON THE WALL

At the same time that Inspector Burnley was interviewing Broughton and Harkness in his office, another series of events centring round the cask was in progress in a different part of London.

Police Constable Z 76, John Walker in private life, was a newly-joined member of the force. A young man of ideas and of promise, he took himself and his work seriously. He had ambitions, the chief of which was to become a detective officer, and he dreamed of the day when he would have climbed to the giddy eminence of Inspector of the Yard. He had read Conan Doyle, Austin Freeman, and other masters of detective fiction, and their tales had stimulated his imagination. His efforts to emulate their heroes added to the interest of life and, if they did not do him very much good, at least did him no harm.

About half-past six that evening, Constable Walker, attired in plain clothes, was strolling slowly along the Holloway Road. He had come off duty shortly before, had had his tea, and was now killing time until he could go to see the second instalment of that thrilling drama, 'Lured by Love,' at the Islington Picture House. Though on pleasure bent, as he walked he kept on practising observation and deduction. He had made a habit of noting the appearance of the people he saw and trying to deduce their histories and, if he did not succeed in this so well as Sherlock Holmes, he hoped he would some day.

He looked at the people on the pathway beside him, but none of them seemed a good subject for study. But as his gaze swept over the vehicles in the roadway it fell on one which held his attention.

Coming along the street to meet him was a four-wheeled dray drawn by a light brown horse. On the dray, upended, was a large cask. Two men sat in front. One, a thin-faced, wiry fellow was driving. The other, a rather small-sized man, was leaning as if wearied out against the cask. This man had a black beard.

Constable Walker's heart beat fast. He had always made it a point to memorise thoroughly the descriptions of wanted men, and only that afternoon he had seen a wire from Headquarters containing the description of just such an equipage. It was wanted, and wanted badly. Had *he* found it? Constable Walker's excitement grew as he wondered.

Unostentatiously he turned and strolled in the direction in which the dray was going, while he laboured to recall in its every detail the description he had read. A four-wheeled dray – that was right; a single horse – right also. A heavily made, iron-clamped cask with one stave broken at the end and roughly repaired by nailing. He glanced at the vehicle which had now drawn level with him. Yes, the cask was well and heavily made and iron clamped, but whether it had a broken stave he could not tell. The dray was painted a brilliant blue and had a Tottenham Court Road address. Here Constable Walker had a blow. This dray was a muddy brown colour and bore the name, John Lyons and Son, 127 Maddox Street, Lower Beechwood Road. He suffered a keen disappointment. He had been getting so sure, and yet – It certainly looked very like what was wanted except for the colour.

Constable Walker took another look at the reddish brown paint. Curiously patchy it looked. Some parts were fresh and more or less glossy, others dull and drab. And then his excitement rose again to fever heat. He knew what that meant.

As a boy he had had the run of the small painting establishment in the village in which he had been brought up, and he had learnt a thing or two about paint. He knew that if you want paint to dry very quickly you flat it – you use turpentine or some other flatting instead of oil. Paint so made will dry in an hour, but it will have a dull, flat surface instead of a glossy one. But if you paint over with flat colour a surface recently painted in oil it will not dry so quickly, and when it does it dries in patches, the dry parts being dull, the wetter ones glossy. It was clear to Constable Walker that the dray had been recently painted with flat brown, and that it was only partly dry.

A thought struck him and he looked keenly at the mottled side. Yes, he was not mistaken. He could see dimly under the flat coat, faint traces of white lettering showing out lighter than the old blue ground. And then his heart leaped for he was sure! There was no possible chance of error!

He let the vehicle draw ahead, keeping his eye carefully on it while he thought of his great luck. And then he recollected that there should have been four men with it. There was a tall man with a sandy moustache, prominent cheekbones, and a strong chin; a small lightly made, foreign-looking man with a black beard and two others whose descriptions had not been given. The man with the beard was on the dray, but the tall, red-haired man was not to be seen. Presumably the driver was one of the undescribed men.

It occurred to Constable Walker that perhaps the other two were walking. He therefore let the vehicle draw still farther ahead, and devoted himself to a careful examination of all the male foot-passengers going in the same direction. He crossed and recrossed the road, but nowhere could he see anyone answering to the red-haired man's description.

The quarry led steadily on in a north-westerly direction, Constable Walker following at a considerable distance behind. At the end of the Holloway Road it passed through Highgate, and continued out along the Great North Road. By this time it was growing dusk, and the constable drew slightly closer so as not to miss it if it made a sudden turn.

For nearly four miles the chase continued. It was now nearly eight, and Constable Walker reflected with a transient feeling of regret that 'Lured by Love' would then be in full swing. All immediate indications of the city had been left behind. The country was now suburban, the road being lined by detached and semi-detached villas, with an occasional field bearing a 'Building Ground to Let' notice. The night was warm and very quiet. There was still light in the west, but an occasional star was appearing eastwards. Soon it would be quite dark.

Suddenly the dray stopped and a man got down and opened the gate of a drive on the right-hand side of the road. The constable melted into the hedge some fifty yards behind and remained motionless. Soon he heard the dray move off again and the hard, rattling noise of the road gave place to the softer, slightly grating sound of gravel. As the constable crept up along the hedge he could see the light of the dray moving towards the right.

A narrow lane branched off in the same direction immediately before reaching the property into which the dray had gone. The drive, in fact, was only some thirty feet beyond the lane and, so far as the constable could see, both lane and drive turned at right angles to the road and ran parallel, one outside and the other inside the property. The constable slipped down the lane, thus leaving the thick boundary hedge between himself and the others.

It was nearly though not quite dark, and the constable could make out the rather low outline of the house, showing black against the sky. The door was in the end gable facing the lane and was open, though the house was entirely in darkness. Behind the house, from the end of the gable and parallel to the lane, ran a wall about eight feet high, evidently the yard wall, in which was a gate. The drive passed the hall door and gable and led up to this gate. The buildings were close to the lane, not more than forty feet from where the constable crouched. Immediately inside the hedge was a row of small trees.

Standing in front of the yard gate was the dray, with one man at the horse's head. As the constable crept closer he heard sounds of unbarring, and the gate swung open. In silence the man outside led the dray within and the gate swung to.

The spirit of adventure had risen high in Constable Walker, and he felt impelled to get still closer to see what was going on. Opposite the hall door he had noticed a little gate in the hedge, and he retraced his steps to this and with infinite care opened it and passed silently through. Keeping well in the shadow of the hedge and under the trees, he crept down again opposite the yard door and reconnoitred.

Beyond the gate, that is on the side away from the house, the yard wall ran on for some fifty feet, at the end of which a cross hedge ran between it and the one under which he was standing. The constable moved warily along to this cross hedge, which he followed until he stood beside the wall.

In the corner between the hedge and the wall, unobserved till he reached it in the growing darkness, stood a small, openwork, rustic summerhouse. As the constable looked at it an idea occurred to him.

With the utmost care he began to climb the side of the summerhouse, testing every foothold before trusting his weight on it. Slowly he worked his way up until, cautiously raising his head, he was able to peep over the wall.

The yard was of fair length, stretching from where he crouched to the house, a distance of seventy or eighty feet, but was not more than about thirty feet wide. Along the opposite side it was bounded by a row of out-offices. The large double doors of one of these, apparently a coach house, were open, and a light shone out from the interior. In front of the doorway and with its back to it stood the dray.

The coachhouse being near the far end of the yard, Constable Walker was unable to see what was taking place within. He therefore raised himself upon the wall and slowly and silently crawled along the coping in the direction of the house. He was aware his strategic position was bad, but he reflected that, being on the south-east side of the yard, he had dark sky behind him, while the row of trees would still further blacken his background. He felt safe from observation, and continued till he was nearly opposite the coachhouse. Then he stretched himself flat on the coping, hid his face, which he feared might show white if the lantern shone on it, behind the dark sleeve of his reddish brown coat, and waited.

He could now see into the coachhouse. It was an empty room of fair size with whitewashed walls and a cement floor. On a peg in the wall hung a hurricane lamp, and by its light he saw the bearded man descending a pair of steps which was placed in the centre of the floor. The wiry man stood close by.

'That hook's all right,' said the bearded man, 'I have it over the tie beam. Now for the differential.'

He disappeared into an adjoining room, returning in a moment with a small set of chain blocks. Taking the end of this up the steps, he made it fast to something above. The steps were then removed, and Constable Walker could just see below the lintel of the door, the hook of the block with a thin chain sling hanging over it.

'Now back in,' said the bearded man.

The dray was backed in until the cask stood beneath the blocks. Both men with some apparent difficulty got the sling fixed, and then pulling on the chain loop, slowly raised the cask.

'That'll do,' said the bearded man when it was some six inches up. 'Draw out now.'

The wiry man came to the horse's head and brought the dray out of the building, stopping in front of the yard gate. Taking the lantern from its hook and leaving the cask swinging in mid-air, the bearded man followed. He closed the coach house doors and secured them with a running bolt and padlock, then crossed to the yard gates and began unfastening them. Both men were now within fifteen feet of Constable Walker, and he lay scarcely daring to breathe.

The wiry man spoke for the first time.

' 'Alf a mo,' mister,' he said, 'what abaht that there money?'

'Well,' said the other, 'I'll give you yours now, and the other fellow can have his any time he comes for it.'

'I don't think,' the wiry man replied aggressively. 'I'll take my pal's now along o' my own. When would 'e 'ave time to come around 'ere looking for it?'

'If I give it to you, what guarantee have I that he won't deny getting it and come and ask for more?'

'You'll 'ave no guarantee at all abaht it, only that I just tells yer. Come on, mister, 'and it over an' let me get away. And don't yer go for to think two quid's goin' for to settle it up. This ain't the job wot we expected when we was 'ired, this ain't. If you want us for to carry your little game through on the strict q.t., why, you'll 'ave to pay for it, that's wot.'

'Confound your impertinence! What the devil do you mean?'

The other leered.

'There ain't no cause for you to swear at a poor workin' man. Come now, mister, you an' me understands other well enough. You don't want no questions asked. Ten quid apiece an' me an' my pal we don't know nothin' abaht it.'

'My good man, you've gone out of your senses. I have nothing to keep quiet. This business is quite correct.'

The wiry man winked deliberately.

'That's orl right, mister, I know it's quite c'rrect. And ten quid apiece'll keep it that way.'

There was silence for a moment, and the bearded man spoke: 'You suspect there is something wrong about the cask? Well, you're wrong, for there isn't. But I admit that if you talk before Thursday next I'll lose my bet. See here, I'll give you five pounds apiece and you may have your mate's.' He counted out some coins, chinking them in his hands.

'You may take it or leave it. You won't get anymore, for then it would be cheaper for me to lose the bet.'

The wiry man paused, eyeing the gold greedily. He opened his mouth to reply, then a sudden thought seemed to strike him. Irresolutely he stood, glancing questioningly at the other. Constable Walker could see his face clearly in the light of the lantern, with an evil, sardonic smile curling his lips. Then, like a man who, after weighing a problem, comes to a decision, he took the money and turned to the horse's head.

'Well, mister,' he said, as he put his vehicle in motion, 'that's straight enough. I'll stand by it.'

The bearded man closed and bolted the yard gates and disappeared with his lantern into the house. In a few seconds the sounds of the receding wheels on the gravel ceased and everything was still.

After waiting a few minutes motionless, Constable Walker slipped off the coping of the wall and dropped noiselessly to the ground. Tiptoeing across to the hedge, he passed silently out of the little gate and regained the lane.

4

A MIDNIGHT INTERVIEW

The constable paused in the lane and considered. Up to the present he felt he had done splendidly, and he congratulated himself on his luck. But his next step he did not see clearly at all. Should he find the nearest police station and advise the head constable, or should he telephone, or even go to Scotland Yard? Or more difficult still, should he remain where he was and look out for fresh developments?

He paused irresolutely for some fifteen minutes pondering the situation, and had almost made up his mind to telephone for instructions to his own station, when he heard a footstep slowly approaching along the lane. Anxious to remain unseen, he rapidly regained the small gate in the hedge, passed inside, and took up a position behind the trunk of one of the small trees. The sounds drew gradually nearer. Whoever was approaching was doing so exceedingly slowly, and seemed to be coming on tiptoe. The steps passed the place where the constable waited, and he could make out dimly the form of what seemed to be a man of medium height. In a few seconds they stopped, and then returned slowly past the constable, finally coming to a stand close by the little gate. It was intensely still, and the constable could hear the unknown yawning and softly clearing his throat.

The last trace of light had gone from the sky and the stars were showing brightly. There was no wind but a sharpness began to creep into the air. At intervals came the disconnected sounds of night, the bark of a dog, the rustle of some small animal in the grass, the rush of a motor passing on the high road.

The constable's problem was settled for him for the moment. He could not move while the other watcher remained. He gave a gentle little shiver and settled down to wait.

He began reckoning the time. It must, he thought, be about half-past eight o'clock. It was about eight when the dray had turned into the drive and he was sure half an hour at least must have passed since then. He had leave until ten and he did not want to be late without authority, though surely, under the circumstances, an excuse would be made for him. He began to picture the scene if he were late, the cold anger of the sergeant, the threat to report him, then his explanation, the sudden change of manner...

A faint click of what seemed to be the entrance gate of the drive recalled him with a start to his present position. Footsteps sounded on the gravel, firm, heavy footsteps, walking quickly. A man was approaching the house.

Constable Walker edged round the tree trunk so as to get it between himself and any light that might come from the hall door. The man reached the door and rang.

In a few seconds a light appeared through the fanlight, and the door was opened by the bearded man. A big, broad-shouldered man in a dark overcoat and soft hat stood on the steps.

'Hallo, Felix!' cried the newcomer heartily. 'Glad to see you're at home. When did you get back?'

'That you, Martin? Come in. I got back on Sunday night.'

'I'll not go in, thanks, but I want you to come round and make up a four at bridge. Tom Brice is with us, and he has brought along a friend of his, a young solicitor from Liverpool. You'll come, won't you?'

The man addressed as Felix hesitated a moment before replying.

'Thanks, yes. I'll go, certainly. But I'm all alone and I haven't changed. Come in a minute till I do so.'

'And, if it's a fair question, where did you get your dinner if you're all alone?'

'In town. I'm only just home.'

They went in and the door was closed. Some few minutes later they emerged again and, pulling the door behind them, disappeared down the drive, the distant click of the gate signifying their arrival at the road. As soon as this sounded, the watcher in the lane moved rapidly, though silently, after them, and Constable Walker was left in undisputed possession.

On the coast becoming clear he slipped out on to the lane, walked down it to the road and turned back in the direction of London. As he did so a clock struck nine.

Entering the first inn he came to, he called for a glass of ale and, getting into conversation with the landlord, learnt that he was near the hamlet of Brent, on the Great North Road, and that Mr Felix's house was named St Malo. He also inquired his way to the nearest public telephone, which, fortunately, was close by.

A few minutes later he was speaking to Scotland Yard. He had to wait for a little time while Inspector Burnley, who had gone home, was being fetched, but in fifteen minutes he had made his report and was awaiting instructions.

The Inspector questioned him closely about the position of the house, finally instructing him to return to his post behind the tree and await developments.

'I will go out with some men now, and will look for you by the little gate in the hedge.'

Constable Walker walked rapidly back, and as he did so the same clock struck ten. He had been gone exactly an hour. In the meantime, Inspector Burnley got a taxi and, after a careful examination of his route and the district on a large-scale map, started for St Malo with three other men. He called on his way at Walpole Terrace, Queen Mary Road, where Tom Broughton lived, and delighted that young man by inviting him to join the party. On the way, he explained in detail the lie of the house and grounds, where he wanted each man to stand, and what was to be done in various eventualities. The streets were full of people and motoring was slow, but it was still considerably before eleven when they entered the Great North Road.

They ran on till the Inspector judged they were not far from the house, when the car was run up a side road and the engine stopped. The five men then walked on in silence.

'Wait here,' whispered Burnley, when they had gone some distance, and slipped away into the dark. He found the lane, walked softly down it until he came to the little gate, slipped inside and came up to Constable Walker standing behind his tree.

'I'm Inspector Burnley,' he whispered. 'Has anyone come in or out yet?'

'No, sir.'

'Well, wait here until I post my men.'

He returned to the others and, speaking in a whisper, gave his directions.

'You men take up the positions I explained to you. Listen out for a whistle to close in. Mr Broughton, you come with me and keep silent.'

The Inspector and his young acquaintance walked down the lane, stopping outside the little gate. The other three men posted themselves at various points in the grounds. And then they waited.

It seemed to Broughton that several hours must have passed when a clock in the distance struck twelve. He and the Inspector were standing beside each other concealed under the hedge. Once or twice he had attempted whispered remarks, but Burnley was not responsive. It was rather cold and the stars were bright. A light breeze had risen and it rustled gently through the hedge and stirred the branches of the trees. An insistent dog was barking somewhere away to the right. A cart passed on the road, the wheels knocking on their axles annoyingly. It took ages to get out of earshot, the sounds coming in rotation through nearly a quarter of the compass. Then a car followed with a swift rush, the glare of the headlights glancing along through the trees. And still nothing happened.

After further ages the clock struck again – one. A second dog began barking. The breeze freshened, and Broughton wished he had brought a heavier coat. He longed to stamp up and down and ease his cramped limbs. And then the latch of the road gate clicked and footsteps sounded on the gravel.

They waited motionless as the steps came nearer. Soon a black shadow came into view and moved to the hall door. There was a jingling of keys, the rattling of a lock, the outline of the door became still darker, the shadow disappeared within and the door was closed.

Immediately Burnley whispered to Broughton: 'I am going now to ring at the door, and when he opens it I will flash my light in his face. Take a good look at him and if you are sure – absolutely positive – it is Felix, say "yes," just the one word "yes". Do you understand?'

They went in through the small gate, no longer taking any precautions against noise, walked to the door, and Burnley knocked loudly.

'Now, remember, don't speak unless you are sure,' he whispered.

A light flickered through the fanlight and the door was opened. A beam from the Inspector's dark lantern flashed on the face of the man within, revealing the same dark complexion and black beard that had attracted Constable Walker's attention. The word 'Yes' came from Broughton and the Inspector said: 'Mr Léon Felix, I am Inspector Burnley from Scotland Yard. I have called on rather urgent business, and would be glad of a few minutes' conversation.'

The black-bearded man started.

'Oh, certainly,' he said, after a momentary pause, 'though I don't know that it is quite the hour I would have suggested for a chat. Will you come in?'

'Thanks. I'm sorry it's late, but I have been waiting for you for a considerable time. Perhaps my man might sit in the hall out of the cold?'

Burnley called over one of his men who had been stationed near the summerhouse,

'Wait here till I speak to Mr Felix, Hastings,' he said, giving him a sign to be ready if called on. Then, leaving Broughton outside with Constable Walker and the other men, he followed Felix into a room on the left of the hall.

It was fitted up comfortably though not luxuriously as a study. In the middle of the room stood a flat-topped desk of modern design. Two deep, leather-covered armchairs were drawn up on each side of the fireplace, in which the embers still glowed. A tantalus stood on a small side table with a box of cigars. The walls were lined with bookshelves with here and there a good print. Felix lighted a reading lamp which stood on the desk. He turned to Burnley.

'Is it a sitting down matter?' he said, indicating one of the armchairs. The Inspector took it while Felix dropped into the other.

'I want, Mr Felix,' began the detective, 'to make some inquiries about a cask which you got from the steamer *Bullfinch* this morning – or rather yesterday, for this is really Tuesday – and which I have reason to believe is still in your possession.'

'Yes?'

'The steamboat people think that a mistake has been made and that the cask that you received was not the one consigned to you, and which you expected.'

'The cask I received is my own property. It was invoiced to me and the freight was paid. What more do the shipping company want?'

'But the cask you received was not addressed to you. It was invoiced to a Mr Felix of West Jubb Street, Tottenham Court Road.'

'The cask was addressed to me. I admit the friend who sent it made a mistake in the address, but it was for me all the same.'

'But if we bring the other Mr Felix – The West Jubb Street Mr Felix – here, and he also claims it, you will not then, I take it, persist in your claim?'

The black-bearded man moved uneasily. He opened his mouth to reply, and then hesitated. The Inspector felt sure he had seen the little pitfall only just in time.

'If you produce such a man,' he said at last, 'I am sure I can easily convince him that the cask was really sent to me and not to him.'

'Well, we shall see about that later. Meantime, another question. What was in the cask you were expecting?'

'Statuary.'

'You are sure of that?'

'Why, of course I'm sure. Really, Mr Inspector, I'd like to know by what right I am being subjected to this examination.'

'I shall tell you, Mr Felix. Scotland Yard has reason to believe there is something wrong about that cask, and an investigation has been ordered. You were naturally the first person to approach, but since the cask turns out not to be yours, we shall – '

'Not to be mine? What do you mean? Who says it is not mine?'

'Pardon me, you yourself said so. You have just told me the cask you expected contained statuary. We know the one you received does not contain statuary. Therefore you have got the wrong one.'

Felix paled suddenly, and a look of alarm crept into his eyes. Burnley leant forward and touched him on the knee.

'You will see for yourself, Mr Felix, that if this matter is to blow over we must have an explanation of these discrepancies. I am not suggesting you can't give one. I am sure you can. But if you refuse to do so you will undoubtedly arouse unpleasant suspicions.'

Felix remained silent, and the Inspector did not interrupt his train of thought.

'Well,' he said at length, 'I have really nothing to hide, only one does not like being bluffed. I will tell you, if I can, what you want to know. Satisfy me that you are from Scotland Yard.'

Burnley showed his credentials, and the other said, – 'Very good. Then I may admit I misled you about the contents of the cask, though I told you the literal and absolute truth. The cask is full of plaques – plaques of kings and queens. Isn't that statuary? And if the plaques should be small and made of gold and called sovereigns, aren't they still statuary? That is what the cask contains, Mr Inspector. Sovereigns. £988 in gold.'

'What else?'

'Nothing else.'

'Oh, come now, Mr Felix. We knew there was money in the cask. We also know there is something else. Think again.'

'Oh, well, there will be packing, of course. I haven't opened it and I don't know. But £988 in gold would go a small way towards filling it. There will be sand or perhaps alabaster or some other packing.'

'I don't mean packing. Do you distinctly tell me no other special object was included?'

'Certainly, but I suppose I'd better explain the whole thing.'

He stirred the embers of the fire together, threw on a couple of logs and settled himself more comfortably in his chair.

5

FELIX TELLS A STORY

'I am a Frenchman, as you know,' began Felix, 'but I have lived in London for some years, and I run over to Paris frequently on both business and pleasure. About three weeks ago on one of these visits I dropped into the Café Toisson d'Or in the rue Royale, where I joined a group of acquaintances. The conversation turned on the French Government lotteries, and one of the men, a M. Le Gautier, who had been defending the system, said to me, "Why not join in a little flutter?" I refused at first, but afterwards changed my mind and said I would sport 500 francs if he did the same. He agreed, and I gave him £20 odd as my share. He was to carry the business through in his name, letting me know the result and halving the profits, if any. I thought no more about the matter till last Friday, when, on my return home in the evening, I found a letter from Le Gautier, which surprised, pleased, and annoyed me in equal measure.'

Mr Felix drew a letter from a drawer of his writing table and passed it to the Inspector. It was in French, and though the latter had a fair knowledge of the language, he was not quite equal to the task, and Mr Felix translated. The letter ran as follows:

Rue de Vallorbes, 997,
Avenue Friedland,
Paris
Thursday, 1st April, 1912

MY DEAR FELIX,

I have just had the most wonderful news! *We have won!* The lottery has drawn trumps and our 1000 francs has become 50,000 – 25,000 francs each! I shake both your hands!

The money I have already received, and I am sending your share at once. And now, old chap, do not be very annoyed when I tell you I am playing a little trick on you. I apologise.

You remember Dumarchez? Well, he and I had an argument about you last week. We were discussing the ingenuity and resource of criminals in evading the police. Your name happened to be mentioned, and I remarked what a splendid criminal a man of your inventive talents would make. He said "No," that you were too transparently honest to deceive the police. We got hot about it and finally arranged a little test. I have packed your money in a cask, in English sovereigns – there are 988 of them – and am booking it to you, carriage paid, by the Insular and Continental Steam Navigation Company's boat from Rouen, due in London about Monday, 5th April. But I am addressing it to "M. Léon Felix, 141 West Jubb Street, Tottenham Court Road, London, W," and labelling it "Statuary only," from Dupierre et Cie, the monumental sculptors of Grenelle. It will take some ingenuity to get a falsely addressed and falsely described cask away from the steamer officials without being suspected of theft. That is the test. I have bet Dumarchez an even

5000 francs that you will do it. He says you will certainly be caught.

I send you my best congratulations on the greatness of your coup, of which the visible evidence goes to you in the cask, and my only regret is that I shall be unable to be present to see you open it.

With profound apologies,

Yours very truly,

ALPHONSE LE GAUTIER

PS – Please excuse the typewriter, but I have hurt my hand.

'I don't know whether pleasure at the unexpected windfall of nearly £1000, or annoyance at Le Gautier's test with the cask was my strongest emotion. The more I thought of this part of it, the more angry I became. It was one thing that my friends should amuse themselves by backing their silly theories, it was quite another that I should be the victim and scapegoat of their nonsense. Two things obviously might lead to complications. If it came out that a cask labelled "Statuary" contained gold, suspicion would be aroused, and the same thing would happen if anyone discovered the address to be false. The contents of the cask might be questioned owing to the weight – that I did not know; the false address might come to light if an advice note of the cask's arrival was sent out, while there was always the fear of unforeseen accidents. I was highly incensed, and I determined to wire early next morning to Le Gautier asking him not to send the cask, and saying I would go over and get the money. But to my further annoyance I had a card by the first post which said that the cask had already been despatched.

'It was clear to me then that I must make arrangements to get it away as soon as possible after the boat came in, and before inquiries began to be made. I accordingly made my plans and, as I did so, my annoyance passed away and I got interested in the sporting side of the affair. First I had a few cards of the false address printed. Then I found an obscure carting contractor, from whom I hired a four-wheeled dray and two men, together with the use of an empty shed for three days.

'I had found out that the Steam Navigation boat would be due on the following Monday, and on the preceding Saturday I brought the men and the dray to the shed and prepared them for what I wanted done. To enlist their help and prevent them becoming suspicious, I gave the former a qualified version of Le Gautier's story. I told them I had made a bet and said I wanted their help to pull it off. A certain cask was coming in by the Rouen boat, addressed to a friend of mine, and he had bet me a large sum that I could not get this cask from the steamer people and take it to my house, while I held that I could. The point was to test the effectiveness of the ordinary business precautions. In order, I told the men, that no real trouble should arise and that I should not, in the event of failure, be charged with theft, my friend had given me a written authorisation to take the cask. This I had written out previously and I showed it to them. Finally, I promised them two pounds each if we succeeded.

'I had got a couple of pots of quick-drying blue and white paint, and I altered the lettering on the dray to that of the address my Paris friend had put on the cask. I am skilful at this kind of work and I did it myself.

'On Monday morning we drove to the docks, and I found the *Bullfinch* had just come in with the Paris goods aboard.

She was discharging casks from the forehold, and I strolled along the wharf and had a look at the work. The casks coming ashore were wine casks, but I noticed one at the side of the hold, over which one of the dockers and a young man who looked like a clerk were bending. They seemed very engrossed, and of course I wondered, "Is this my cask, and have they discovered the gold?" I spoke to the young man, found that the cask was mine, and asked him if I could get it away at once.

'He was quite polite, but would not help me, referring me to the quay office and offering to take me there and find a clerk to attend to me. As we were leaving he called out to the man at the cask, "You understand, Harkness, to do nothing till you hear from Mr Avery."

'At the wharf office the young man left me in the outer office while he went, as he said, to get the proper clerk for my work. But he returned with a man that was evidently the manager, and I knew at once that something was wrong. This opinion was confirmed when the manager began raising objection after objection to letting the cask go.

'Some judicious questions elicited the fact that "Mr Avery" was the managing director in the head office in Fenchurch Street. I left the wharf office, sat down on some boxes, and thought out the situation.

'It was clear that something had aroused the suspicions of the clerk and the docker, Harkness, and the former's remark to the latter to do nothing without instructions from Mr Avery seemed to mean that the matter was to be laid before that gentleman. To "do nothing" evidently meant to hold on to the cask. If I were to get my property it was clear I must see to the supplying of those instructions myself.

'I went to Fenchurch Street and asked for Mr Avery. Fortunately for me he was engaged. I said I could not wait, and asked for a sheet of paper and envelope on which to write him a note. By the simple expedient of sealing and addressing the empty envelope, I thus provided myself with a sheet of paper bearing the firm's heading.

'I dropped into a bar and, ordering some ale, borrowed a pen and ink. Then I composed a letter from Mr Avery to Harkness, instructing him to hand over the cask at once to me.

'While I was writing this it occurred to me that if this man's suspicions were really seriously aroused, he would probably follow the cask and thus trace me to my house. I lost another quarter of an hour pondering this problem. Then an idea occurred to me, and I added a paragraph saying that as the Navigation Company had contracted to deliver the cask at an address in the city, he, Harkness, was to accompany it and see that it reached its destination safely.

'I wrote the letter in the round hand of a junior clerk, signing it "The I and C S N Co., Ltd, per" in the same hand, and "Avery" with an undecipherable initial in another kind of writing, with another "per," and then two not very clear initials. I hoped in this way to mislead Harkness, if he happened to know the genuine signature.

'It was my design to get Harkness away from the ship with the cask and my own men, when I hoped to find some way of giving him the slip. This I eventually did by instructing one of the men to clamour for a drink, and the other, a man named Watty, to refuse to leave the horse when I invited the party to a bar for some beer. On the plea of relieving Watty, I left Harkness and the other man drinking in the bar, and slipped away with Watty and the dray. Then he and I went back to the shed and I ran a coat of paint over the dray, restoring it to its original brown and painting out the fictitious name. In the evening we brought the dray home, timing ourselves to arrive here after dark, and unloaded the cask in one of the out houses, where it now is.'

When Felix ceased speaking, the two men sat in silence for several minutes while Burnley turned the statement over in his mind. The sequence of events was unusual, but the story hung together, and, as he went over it in detail, he could see no reason why it should not, from Felix's point of view, be true. If Felix believed his friend's letter, as he appeared to, his actions were accounted for, and if the cask really contained a statue, the letter might explain the whole thing. On the other hand, if it held a corpse, the letter was a fraud, to which Felix might or might not be party.

Gradually, as he pondered, the matter shaped itself into three main considerations.

First, there was Felix's general bearing and manner. The Inspector had a long and varied experience of men who told the truth and of men who lied, and all his instincts led him to believe this man. He was aware that such instincts are liable to error – he had himself erred on more than one occasion in the past – yet he could not overlook the fact that Felix's bearing, as far as his impression went, was that of a sincere and honest man. Such a consideration would not be a decisive factor in his conclusion, but it would undoubtedly weigh.

Secondly, there was Felix's account of his actions in London. Of the truth of this the Inspector had already received considerable independent testimony. He reviewed the chain of events and was surprised to find how few statements of Felix were unsupported. His first visit to the

Bullfinch had been described in almost similar terms by Broughton and by Huston in the wharf office. His call at the Fenchurch Street office and the ruse by which he obtained the shipping company's headed notepaper had been testified to by Mr Avery and his chief clerk, Wilcox. His description of the letter he had written to Harkness was certainly accurate from the Inspector's own knowledge. His account of the removal of the cask and the shaking off of Harkness was in agreement with the statement of the latter and finally, Felix's description of the removal of the cask to its present resting place was fully corroborated by Constable Walker.

There was practically no part of the statement unsupported by outside evidence. In fact, Inspector Burnley could not recall any case where so much confirmation of a suspect's story was forthcoming. Weighing the matter point by point, he came to the deliberate conclusion that he must unreservedly believe it.

So much for Felix's actions in London. But there was a third point – his actions in Paris, culminating in the letter of his friend. The letter. That was the kernel of the nut. Was it really written under the circumstances described? Had Le Gautier written it? Was there even such a man as Le Gautier? All this, he thought, it should not be difficult to find out. He would get some more information from Felix and if necessary slip across to Paris and put the statements to the test. He broke the silence.

'Who is M. Le Gautier?'

'Junior partner in the firm of Le Gautier, Fils, wine merchants, in the rue Henri Quatre.'

'And M. Dumarchez?'

'A stockbroker.'

'Can you give me his address?'

'I don't know his home address. His office is, I think, in the Boulevard Poissonière. But I could get you the address from M. Le Gautier.'

'Please give me an account of your relations with these gentlemen.'

'Well, I have known them both for years and we are good friends, but I cannot recall ever having had any money transactions with either until this matter of the lottery.'

'The details of that mentioned in the letter are correct?'

'Oh, perfectly.'

'Can you remember where precisely the conversation about the lottery took place?'

'It was in the ground floor room of the café, at the window to the right of the entrance, looking inwards.'

'You say other gentlemen were present?'

'Yes, a group of us were there and the conversation was general.'

'Was your arrangement to enter the lottery heard by the group?'

'Yes, we had quite a lot of good-natured chaff about it.'

'And can you remember who were present?'

Mr Felix hesitated.

'I'm not sure that I can,' he said at last. 'The group was quite a casual one and I only joined it for a few moments. Le Gautier was there, of course, and a man called Daubigny, and Henri Boisson, and, I think, Jaques Rôget, but of him I'm not sure. There were a number of others also.'

Felix answered the questions readily and the Inspector noted his replies. He felt inclined to believe the lottery business was genuine. At all events inquiries in Paris would speedily establish the point. But even if it was all true, that did not prove that Le Gautier had written the letter. A number of people had heard the conversation, and anyone could have written it, even Felix himself. Ah, that was an idea! Could Felix be the writer? Was there any way of finding that out? The Inspector considered and then spoke again.

'Have you the envelope this letter came in?'

'Eh?' said Felix, 'the envelope? Why, no, I'm sure I haven't. I never keep them.'

'Or the card?'

Felix turned over the papers on his desk and rummaged in the drawers.

'No,' he answered, 'I can't find it. I must have destroyed it too.'

There was then no proof that these communications had been received by Felix. On the other hand there was no reason to doubt it. The Inspector kept an open mind as he turned again to the letter.

It was typewritten on rather thin, matt-surfaced paper and, though Burnley was not an expert, he believed the type was foreign. Some signs of wear were present which he thought might identify the typewriter. The n's and the r's were leaning slightly to the right, the t's and the e's were below alignment, and the l's had lost the horizontal bar at the top of the downstroke. He held the paper up to the light. The watermark was somewhat obscured by the type, but after a time he made it out. It was undoubtedly French paper. This, of course, would not weigh much, as Felix by his own statement, was frequently in Paris, but still it did weigh.

The Inspector read the letter again. It was divided into four paragraphs and he pondered each in turn. The first was about the lottery. He did not know much about French lotteries, but the statements made could at least be verified.

With the help of the French police it would be easy to find out if any drawings and payments had recently been made, and he could surely get a list of the winners. A winner of 50,000 francs, living in or near Paris, should be easily traced.

The second and third paragraphs were about the bet and the sending of the cask. Burnley turned the details over in his mind. Was the whole story a likely one? It certainly did not strike him as such. Even if such an unusual bet had been made, the test was an extremely poor one. He could hardly believe that a man who could invent the plan of the cask would not have done better. And yet it was undoubtedly possible.

Another idea entered the Inspector's mind. He had, perhaps, been thinking too much of the £988, and too little of the woman's hand. Suppose there really was a corpse in the cask. What then?

Such an assumption made all the circumstances more serious and explained partly the sending of the cask, but it did not, so far as the Inspector could see, throw light on the method of doing so. But when he came to the fourth paragraph he saw that it might easily bear two meanings. He read it again:

> I send you my best congratulations on the greatness of your coup, of which the visible evidence goes to you in the cask, and my only regret is that I shall be unable to be present to see you open it.

This seemed at first sight obviously to mean congratulations on winning the lottery, the 'visible evidence' of which, namely £988 in gold, was in the cask. But did it really mean this? Did a more sinister interpretation not also offer itself? Suppose the body was the 'visible evidence'? Suppose the death was the result, possibly indirect, of something that Felix had done. If money only was being sent, why should Le Gautier experience regret that he could not see the cask opened? But if a corpse was unexpectedly hidden there, would not that statement be clarified? It certainly looked so. One thing at least seemed clear. If a corpse had been sent to Felix, he must know something of the circumstances leading up to it. The Inspector spoke again: 'I am obliged for your statement, Mr Felix, which, I may be allowed to say, I fully accept so far as it goes. But I fear you have not told me everything?'

'I have told you everything material.'

'Then I am afraid we are not in agreement as to what is material. At all events, it all goes back to my original question, "What is in the cask?" '

'Do you not accept my statement that it is money?'

'I accept your statement that you believe it to be money. I do not necessarily accept your authority for that belief.'

'Well,' said Felix, jumping up, 'the cask's in the coach house and I see there is nothing for it but to go and open it now. I did not want to do so tonight, as I did not want to have all that gold lying loose about the house, but it's clear nothing else will satisfy you.'

'Thank you, Mr Felix, I wanted you to make the suggestion. It is, as you say, the only way to settle the matter. I'll call Sergeant Hastings here as a witness and we'll go now.'

In silence, Felix got a lantern and led the way. They passed through a back door into the yard and paused at the coach house door.

'Hold the light, will you, while I get the keys.'

Burnley threw a beam on the long running bolt that closed the two halves of the door. A padlock held the handle down on the staple. Felix inserted a key, but at his first touch the lock fell open.

'Why, the thing's not fastened!' he cried, 'and I locked it myself a few hours ago!'

He removed the padlock and withdrew the running bolt, swinging the large door open. Burnley flashed in the lantern.

'Is the cask here?' he said.

'Yes, swinging there from the ceiling,' answered Felix, as he came over from fastening back the door. Then his jaw dropped and he stared fixedly.

'My heavens!' he gasped, in a strangled tone, 'it's gone! The cask's gone!'

6

THE ART OF DETECTION

Astonished as Burnley was himself at this unexpected development, he did not forget to keep a keen watch on Felix. That the latter was genuinely amazed and dumbfounded he could not doubt. Not only was his surprise too obviously real to be questioned, but his anger and annoyance at losing his money were clearly heartfelt.

'I locked it myself. I locked it myself,' he kept on repeating. 'It was there at eight o'clock, and who could get at it since then? Why, no one but myself knew about it. How could anyone else have known?'

'That's what we have to find out,' returned the Inspector. 'Come back to the house, Mr Felix, and let us talk it over. We cannot do anything outside until it gets light.

'You may not know,' he continued, 'that you were followed here with your cask by one of our men, who watched you unloading it in the coach house. He waited till you left with your friend Martin, a few minutes before nine. He then had to leave to advise me of the matter, but he was back at the house by ten. From ten till after eleven he watched alone, but since then the house has been surrounded by my men, as I rather expected to find a gang instead of a single man. Whoever took the cask must therefore have done so between nine and ten.'

Felix stared at his companion open-mouthed.

'By Jove!' he said. 'You amaze me. How in thunder did you get on my track?'

Burnley smiled.

'It is our business to know these things,' he answered, 'I knew all about how you got the cask away from the docks also.'

'Well, thank Heaven! I told you the truth.'

'It was the wise thing, Mr Felix. I was able to check your statements as you went along, and I may say I felt really glad when I heard you were going to be straight. At the same time, sir, you will realise that my orders prevent me being satisfied until I have seen the contents of the cask.'

'You cannot be more anxious to recover it than I am, for I want my money.'

'Naturally,' said Burnley, 'but before we discuss the matter excuse me a moment. I want to give my fellows some instructions.'

He went out and called the men together. Sergeant Hastings and Constable Walker he retained, the rest he sent home in the car with instructions to return at eight o'clock in the morning. To Broughton he bade 'Good night,' thanking him for his presence and help.

When he re-entered the study Felix made up the fire and drew forward the whisky and cigars.

'Thank you, I don't mind if I do,' said the detective, sinking back into his chair. 'Now, Mr Felix, let us go over everyone that knew about the cask being there.'

'No one but myself and the carter, I assure you.'

'Yourself, the carter, myself, and my man Walker – four to start with.'

Felix smiled. 'As far as I am concerned,' he said, 'I left here, as you appear to know, almost immediately after the arrival of the cask and did not return till after one o'clock. All of that time I was in the company of Dr William Martin and a number of mutual friends. So I can prove an alibi.'

Burnley smiled also.

'For me,' he said, 'I am afraid you will have to take my word. The house was watched by Walker from ten o'clock, and we may take it as quite impossible that anything could have been done after that hour.'

'There remains therefore the carter.'

'There remains therefore the carter, and, as we must neglect no possibilities, I will ask you to give me the address of the cartage firm and any information about the man that you may have.'

'John Lyons and Son, 127 Maddox Street, Lower Beechwood Road, was the contractor. The carter's name, beyond Watty, I don't know. He was a rather short, wiry chap, with a dark complexion and small black moustache.'

'And now, Mr Felix, can you not think of any others who may have known about the cask?'

'There was no one,' replied the other with decision.

'I'm afraid we can't assume that. We certainly can't be sure.'

'Who could there be?'

'Well, your French friend. How do you know he didn't write to others beside you?'

Felix sat up as if he had been shot.

'By Jove!' he cried, 'it never entered my head. But it's most unlikely – most unlikely.'

'The whole thing's most unlikely as far as that goes. Perhaps you are not aware that someone else was watching the house last evening?'

'Good God, Inspector! What do you mean?'

'Someone came to the lane shortly after your arrival with the cask. He waited and heard your conversation with your friend Martin. When you and your friend left, he followed you.'

Felix passed his hand over his forehead. His face was pale. 'This business is too much for me,' he said. 'I wish to heaven I was out of it.'

'Then help me to get you out of it. Think. Is there anyone your friend knows that he might have written to?'

Felix remained silent for some moments.

'There is only one man,' he said at length in a hesitating voice, 'that I know he is friendly with – a Mr Percy Murgatroyd, a mining engineer who has an office in Westminster. But I don't for one moment believe he had anything to say to it.'

'Let me have his name and address, anyway.'

'4 St John's Mansions, Victoria Street,' said Felix, on referring to an address book.

'You might write it down, if you please, and sign it.'

Felix looked up with a smile.

'You generally write notes yourself, I should have thought?'

Burnley laughed.

'You're very quick, Mr Felix. Of course it's your handwriting I want also. But I assure you it's only routine. Now please, think. Is there anyone else?'

'Not a living soul that I know of.'

'Very well, Mr Felix. I want to ask just one other question. Where did you stay in Paris?'

'At the Hotel Continental.'

'Thanks, that's everything. And now, if you will allow me, I will take a few winks here in the chair till it gets light, and if you take my advice you will turn in.'

Felix looked at his watch.

'Quarter-past three. Well, perhaps I shall. I'm only sorry I cannot offer you a bed as the house is absolutely empty, but if you will take a shakedown in the spare room – ?'

'No, no, thanks very much, I shall be all right here.'

'As you wish. Good night.'

When Felix had left, the Inspector sat on in his chair smoking his strong black cigars and thinking, He did not sleep, though he remained almost motionless, only at long intervals rousing up to light another cigar, and it was not until five had struck that he got up and looked out of the window.

'Light at last,' he muttered, as he let himself quietly out of the back door into the yard.

His first care was to make a thorough search in the yard and all the outhouses to ensure that the cask was really gone and not merely hidden in some other room. He was speedily satisfied on this point.

Since it was gone it was obvious that it must have been removed on a vehicle. His next point was to see how that vehicle got in, and if it had left any traces. And first as to the coach house door.

He picked up the padlock and examined it carefully. It was an ordinary old-fashioned four-inch one. The ring had been forced open while locked, the hole in the opening end through which the bolt passes being torn away. Marks showed that this had been done by inserting some kind of lever between the body of the lock and the staple on the door, through which the ring had been passed. The Inspector looked round for the lever, but could not find it. He therefore made a note to search for such a tool, as if it bore marks which would fit those on the door, its evidence might be important.

There was next the question of the yard gate. This opened inwards on two halves, and was fastened by a wooden beam hinged through the centre to the edge of one of the half gates. When it was turned vertically the gates were free, but when horizontally it engaged with brackets, one on each half gate, thus holding them closed. It could be fastened by a padlock, but none was fitted. The gate now stood closed and with the beam lying in the brackets.

The Inspector took another note to find out if Mr Felix had locked the beam, and then stood considering. It was clear the gate must have been closed from the inside after the vehicle had gone out. It must have been opened similarly on the latter's arrival. Who had done this? Was Felix lying, and was there someone else in the house?

At first it seemed likely, and then the Inspector thought of another way. Constable Walker had climbed the wall. Why should not the person who opened and shut the gate have also done so? The Inspector moved slowly along the wall scrutinising it and the ground alongside it.

At first he saw nothing out of the common, but on retracing his steps he noticed, about three yards from the gate, two faint marks of mud or dust on the plaster. These were some six feet from the ground and about fifteen inches apart. On the soft soil which had filled in between the cobble stones in this disused part of the yard, about a foot from the wall and immediately under these marks, were two sharp-edged depressions, about two inches long by half an inch wide, arranged with their longer dimensions in line. Someone had clearly used a short ladder.

Inspector Burnley stood gazing at the marks. It struck him they were very far apart for a ladder. He measured the distance between them and found it was fifteen inches. Ladders, he knew, are about twelve.

Opening the gate he went to the outside of the wall. A grass plot ran alongside it here and the Inspector, stooping down, searched for corresponding marks. He was not disappointed. Two much deeper depressions showed where the ends of the ladder-like apparatus had sunk into the softer ground. These were not narrow like those in the yard, but rectangular and of heavier stuff, three inches by two, he estimated. He looked at the plaster on the wall above, but it was not till he examined it through his lens that he was satisfied it bore two faint scratches, corresponding in position to the muddy marks on the opposite side.

A further thought struck him. Scooping up a little soil from the grass, he went again into the yard and compared with his lens the soil and the dry mud of the marks on the plaster. As he had anticipated, they were identical.

He could now dimly reconstruct what had happened. Someone had placed a peculiar kind of ladder against the outside of the wall and presumably crossed it and opened the gate. The ladder had then been carried round and placed against the inside of the wall, but, probably by accident, *opposite end up*. The outside plaster was therefore clean but scraped, while that on the inside bore traces of the soil from the ends that had stood on the grass. In going out after barring the gate, he imagined the thief had pulled the ladder after him with a cord and passed it over the wall.

The Inspector returned to the grass and made a further search. Here he found confirmation of his theory in a single impression of one of the legs of the ladder some two feet six out from the wall. That, he decided, had been caused by the climber throwing down the ladder when leaving the yard. He also found three footmarks, but, unfortunately, they were so blurred as to be valueless.

He took out his notebook and made a sketch with accurate dimensions showing what he had learnt of the ladder – its length, width, and the shape of the legs at each end. Then bringing out the steps Felix had used to hang the chain blocks, he got on the wall. He examined the cement coping carefully, but without finding any further traces.

The yard, being paved, no wheel or footmarks were visible, but Burnley spent quite a long time crossing and recrossing it, examining every foot of ground in the hope of finding some object that had been dropped. Once before, in just such another case, he had had the luck to discover a trouser button concealed under some leaves, a find which had led to penal servitude for two men. On this occasion he was disappointed, his search being entirely unsuccessful.

He went out on the drive. Here were plenty of marks, but try as he would he could make nothing of them. The surface was covered thickly with fine gravel and only showed vague disturbances with no clear outlines. He began methodically to search the drive as he had done the yard. Every foot was examined in turn, Burnley gradually working down towards the gate. After he left the immediate neighbourhood of the house the gravel became much thinner, but the surface below was hard and bore no marks. He continued perseveringly until he got near the gate, and then he had some luck.

In the lawn between the house and the road some work was in progress. It seemed to Burnley that a tennis or croquet ground was being made. From the corner of this ground a recently filled in cut ran across the drive and out to the hedge adjoining the lane. Evidently a drain had just been laid.

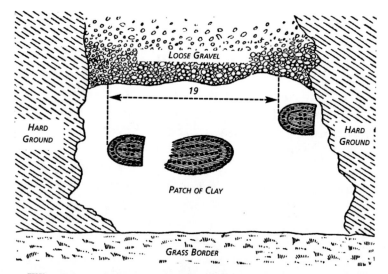

Where this drain passed under the drive the newly filled ground had slightly sunk. The hollow had been made up in the middle with gravel, but it happened that a small space on the lane side which had not gone down much was almost uncovered, the clay showing through. On this space were two clearly defined footmarks, pointing in the direction of the house.

I have said two, but that is not strictly correct. One, that of a workman's right boot with heavy hobnails, was complete in every detail, the clay holding the impression like plaster of Paris. The other, some distance in front and to the left and apparently the next step forward, was on the edge of the clay patch and showed the heel only, the sole having borne on the hard.

Inspector Burnley's eyes brightened. Never had he seen better impressions. Here was something tangible at last. He bent down to examine them more closely, then suddenly sprang to his feet with a gesture of annoyance.

'Fool that I am,' he growled, 'that's only Watty bringing up the cask.'

All the same he made a careful sketch of the marks, showing the distance between them and the size of the clay patch. Watty, he felt sure, would be easy to find through the carting establishment, when he could ascertain if the footsteps were his. If it should chance they were not, he had probably found a useful clue to the thief. For the convenience of the reader I reproduce the sketch.

Burnley turned to go on, but his habit of thinking things out reasserted itself, and he stood gazing at the marks and slowly pondering. He was puzzled that the steps were so close together. He took out his rule and remeasured the distance between them. Nineteen inches from heel to heel. That was surely very close. A man of Watty's size would normally take a step of at least thirty inches, and carters were generally long-stepping men. If he had put it at thirty-two or thirty-three inches he would probably be nearer the thing. Why, then, this short step?

He looked and pondered. Then suddenly a new excitement came into his eyes and he bent swiftly down again.

'Jove!' he murmured. 'Jove! I nearly missed that! It makes it more like Watty and, if so, it is conclusive! Absolutely conclusive!' His cheek was flushed and his eyes shone.

'That probably settles that hash,' said the evidently delighted Inspector. He, nevertheless, continued his methodical search down the remainder of the drive and out on to the road, but without further result.

He looked at his watch. It was seven o'clock.

'Two more points and I'm through,' he said to himself in a satisfied tone.

He turned into the lane and walked slowly down it, scrutinising the roadway as he had done the drive. Three separate times he stopped to examine and measure footmarks, the third occasion being close by the little gate in the hedge.

'Number one point done. Now for number two,' he muttered, and returning to the entrance gate stood for a moment looking up and down the road. Choosing the direction of London he walked for a quarter of a mile examining the gateways at either side, particularly those that led into fields. Apparently he did not find what he was in search of, for he retraced his steps to where a crossroad led off to the left and continued his investigations along it. No better luck rewarding him, he tried a second crossroad with the same result. There being no other crossroads, he returned to the lane and set out again, this time with his back to London. At the third gateway, one leading into a field on the left-hand side of the road, he stopped.

It was an ordinary iron farm gate set in the rather high and thick hedge that bounded the road. The field was in grass and bore the usual building ground notice. Immediately inside the gate was a patch of low and swampy looking ground, and it was a number of fresh wheel marks crossing this patch that had caught the Inspector's attention.

The gate was not padlocked, and Burnley slipped the bolt back and entered the field. He examined the wheel marks with great care. They turned sharply at right angles on passing through the gate and led for a short distance along the side of the fence, stopping beside a tree which grew in the hedge. The hoof marks of a horse and the prints of a man's hobnailed boots leading over the same ground also came in for a close scrutiny.

It was a contented-looking Burnley that turned out of the field and walked back to St Nab. He was well satisfied with his night's work. He had firstly succeeded in getting a lot of information out of Felix, and had further turned the latter into a friend anxious to help in the clearing up of the mystery. And though an unexpected check had arisen in the disappearance of the cask, he felt that with the information he had gained in the last three hours it would not be long before he had his hands on it again.

As he approached the door Felix hailed him.

'I saw you coming up,' he said. 'What luck?'

'Oh, not so bad, not so bad,' returned the other. 'I'm just going back to the city.'

'But the cask? What about it?'

'I'll start some inquiries that may lead to something.'

'Oh, come now, Inspector, don't be so infernally close. You might tell me what you've got in your mind, for I can see you have something.'

Burnley laughed.

'Oh, well,' he said, 'I don't mind. I'll tell you what I found; you see what you make of it.

'First, I found your coach house padlock had been forced with a lever. There was nothing of the kind lying about, therefore whatever theory we adopt must account for this lever's production and disposal. It may quite likely bear marks corresponding to those on the padlock, which evidence might be valuable.

'I then found that your visitor had arrived at the yard gate with a vehicle and had climbed the wall with the aid of a very peculiar ladder. He had, presumably, opened the gate and, after loading up the cask and drawing his vehicle out on to the drive, had closed the gate, leaving by the same means. There is evidence to show that he lifted the ladder over after him, probably pulling it up by a cord.

'I have said the ladder was a peculiar one. Here is a sketch of its shape so far as I could learn it. You will see that it is short and wide with the ends shaped differently.

'I may remind you, in passing, how easy it would have been to load up the cask in spite of its weight. All that was necessary was to back the vehicle under it and lower out the differential pulley, a thing a man could do with one hand.

'I examined the drive, but could find nothing except at one place where there was a most interesting pair of footmarks. You must really see these for yourself, and if you will stroll down now I will point them out. There is reason to believe they were made by Watty when he was approaching the house with the dray, but I cannot be positive as yet.

'I then examined the lane and I found in three places other footmarks by the same man. Finally, about 200 yards along the main road to the north, I found wheel marks leading into a grass field beside which he had walked.

'Now, Mr Felix, put all these things together. You will find them suggestive, but the footmarks on the drive are very nearly conclusive.'

They had by this time reached the marks.

'Here we are,' said Burnley. 'What do you think of these?'

'I don't see anything very remarkable about them.'

'Look again.'

Felix shook his head.

'See here, Mr Felix. Stand out here on the gravel and put your right foot in line with this first print. Right. Now take a step forward as if you were walking to the house. Right. Does anything occur to you now?'

'I can't say that it does, unless it is that I have taken a very much longer step.'

'But your step was of normal length.'

79

'Well then, conversely, the unknown must have taken a short one.'

'But did he? Assume it was Watty, as I think it must have been. You were with him and you saw him walking.'

'Oh, come now, Inspector. How could I tell that? He didn't normally take very short steps or I should have noticed it, but I couldn't possibly say that he never took one.'

'The point is not essential except that it calls attention to a peculiarity in the steps. But you must admit that while possible, it is quite unlikely he would take a step of that length – nineteen inches as against a probable thirty-three – without stumbling or making a false step.'

'But how do you know he didn't stumble?'

'The impression, my dear sir, the impression. A false step or a stumble would have made a blurred mark or shown heavier on one side than the other. This print shows no slip and is evenly marked all over. It was clearly made quite normally.'

'That seems reasonable, but I don't see how it matters.'

'To me it seems exceedingly suggestive though, I agree, not conclusive. But there is a nearly conclusive point, Mr Felix. Look at those prints again.'

'They convey nothing to me.'

'Compare them.'

'Well, I can only compare the heels and there is not much difference between them, just as you would expect between the heels of a pair of boots.' Felix hesitated. 'By Jove! Inspector,' he went on, 'I've got you at last. They're the same marks. They were both made by the same foot.'

'I think so, Mr Felix; you have it now. Look here.' The Inspector stooped. 'The fourth nail on the left hand side is gone. That alone might be a coincidence, but if you compare the wear of the other nails and of the leather you will see they are the same beyond doubt.'

He pointed to several little inequalities and inaccuracies in the outline, each of which appeared in both the marks.

'But even if they are the same, I don't know that I see what you get from that.'

'Don't you? Well, look here. How could Watty, if it was he, have produced them? Surely only in one of two ways. Firstly, he could have hopped on one foot. But there are three reasons why it is unlikely he did that. One is that he could hardly have done it without your noticing it. Another, that he could never have left so clear an impression in that way. The third, why should he hop? He simply wouldn't do it. Therefore they were made in the second way. What was that, Mr Felix?'

Felix started.

'I see what you're after at last,' he said. 'He walked up the drive twice.'

'Of course he did. He walked up first with you to leave the cask. He walked up the second time with the empty dray to get it. If the impressions were really made by Watty that seems quite certain.'

'But what on earth would Watty want with the cask? He could not know there was money in it.'

'Probably not, but he must have guessed it held something valuable.'

'Inspector, you overwhelm me with delight. If he took the cask it will surely be easy to trace it.'

'It may or it may not. Question is, Are we sure he was acting for himself?'

'Who else?'

'What about your French friend? You don't know whom he may have written to. You don't know that all your actions with the cask may not have been watched.'

'Oh, don't make things worse than they are. Trace this Watty, won't you?'

'Of course we will, but it may not be so easy as you seem to think. At the same time there are two other points, both of which seem to show he was at least alone.'

'Yes?'

'The first is the watcher in the lane. That was almost certainly the man who walked twice up your drive. I told you I found his footmarks at three points along it. One was near your little gate, close beside and pointing to the hedge, showing he was standing there. That was at the very point my man saw the watcher.

'The second point concerns the horse and dray, and this is what leads me to believe the watcher was really Watty. If Watty was listening up the lane where were these? If he had a companion the latter would doubtless have walked them up and down the road. But if he was alone they must have been hidden somewhere while he made his investigations. I've been over most of the roads immediately surrounding, and on my fourth shot – towards the north, as I already told you – I found the place. It is fairly clear what took place. On leaving the cask he had evidently driven along the road until he found a gate that did not lead to a house. It was, as I said, that of a field. The marks there are unmistakable. He led the dray in behind the hedge and tied the horse to a tree. Then he came back to reconnoitre and heard you going out. He must have immediately returned and brought the dray, got the cask, and cleared out, and I imagine he was not many minutes gone before my man

Walker returned. What do you think of that for a working theory?'

'I think it's conclusive. Absolutely conclusive. And that explains the queer-shaped ladder.'

'Eh, what? What's that you say?'

'It must have been the gangway business for loading barrels on the dray. I saw one hooked on below the deck.'

Burnley smote his thigh a mighty slap.

'One for you, Mr Felix,' he cried, 'one for you, sir. I never thought of it. That points to Watty again.'

'Inspector, let me congratulate you. You have got evidence that makes the thing a practical certainty.'

'I think it's a true bill. And now, sir, I must be getting back to the Yard.' Burnley hesitated and then went on: 'I am extremely sorry and I'm afraid you won't like it, but I shall be straight with you and tell you I cannot – I simply dare not – leave you without some kind of police supervision until this cask business is cleared up. But I give you my word you shall not be annoyed.'

Felix smiled.

'That's all right. You do your duty. The only thing I ask you is to let me know how you get on.'

'I hope we'll have some news for you later in the day.'

It was now shortly after eight, and the car had arrived with the two men sent back the previous evening. Burnley gave them instructions about keeping a watch on Felix, then with Sergeant Hastings and Constable Walker he entered the car and was driven rapidly towards London.

7

THE CASK AT LAST

Inspector Burnley reached Scotland Yard, after dropping Constable Walker at his station with remarks which made the heart of that observer glow with triumph and conjured up pictures of the day when he, Inspector Walker, would be one of the Yard's most skilled and trusted officers. During the run citywards Burnley had thought out his plan of campaign, and he began operations by taking Sergeant Hastings to his office and getting down the large-scale map.

'Look here, Hastings' he said, when he had explained his theories and found what he wanted. 'Here's John Lyons and Sons', the carriers where Watty is employed, and from where the dray was hired. You see it's quite a small place. Here close by is Goole Street, and here is the Goole Street Post Office. Got the lie of those? Very well. I want you, when you've had your breakfast, to go out there and get on the track of Watty. Find out first his full name and address, and wire or phone it at once. Then shadow him. I expect he has the cask, either at his own house or hidden somewhere, and he'll lead you to it if you're there to follow. Probably he won't be able to do anything till night, but of that we can't be certain. Don't interfere or let him see you if possible, but of course don't let him open the cask if he has not already done so, and under no circumstances allow him to take anything out of it. I will follow you out and we can settle further details. The Goole Street Post Office will be our headquarters, and you can advise me there at, say, the even hours of your whereabouts. Make yourself up as you think best and get to work as quickly as you can.'

The sergeant saluted and withdrew.

'That's everything in the meantime, I think,' said Burnley to himself, as with a yawn he went home to breakfast.

When some time later Inspector Burnley emerged from his house, a change had come over his appearance. He seemed to have dropped his individuality as an alert and efficient representative of Scotland Yard and taken on that of a small shopkeeper or contractor in a small way of business. He was dressed in a rather shabby suit of checks, with baggy knees and draggled coat. His tie was woefully behind the fashion, his hat required brushing, and his boots were soiled and down at heel. A slight stoop and a slouching walk added to his almost slovenly appearance.

He returned to the Yard and asked for messages. Already a telephone had come through from Sergeant Hastings: 'Party's name, Walter Palmer, 71 Fennell Street, Lower Beechwood Road.' Having had a warrant made out for the 'party's' arrest, he got a police motor with plain-clothes driver, and left for the scene of operations.

It was another glorious day. The sun shone out of a cloudless sky of clearest blue. The air had the delightful freshness of early spring. Even the Inspector, with his mind full of casks and corpses, could not remain insensible of its charm. With a half sigh he thought of that garden in the country which it was one of his dearest dreams some day to achieve. The daffodils would now be in fine show and the primroses would be on, and such a lot of fascinating work would be waiting to be done among the later plants...

The car drew up as he had arranged at the end of Goole Street and the Inspector proceeded on foot. After a short walk he reached his objective, an archway at the end of a block of buildings, above which was a faded signboard bearing the legend, 'John Lyons and Son, Carriers.' Passing under the arch and following a short lane, he emerged in a yard with an open-fronted shed along one side and a stable big enough for eight or nine horses on the other. Four or five carts of different kinds were ranged under the shed roof. In the middle of the open space, with a horse yoked in, was a dray with brown sides, and Burnley, walking close to it, saw that under the paint the faint outline of white letters could be traced. A youngish man stood by the stable door and watched Burnley curiously, but without speaking.

'Boss about?' shouted Burnley.

The youngish man pointed to the entrance. 'In the office,' he replied.

The Inspector turned and entered a small wooden building immediately inside the gate. A stout, elderly man with a grey beard, who was posting entries in a ledger, got up and came forward as he did so.

'Morning,' said Burnley, 'have you a dray for hire?'

'Why, yes,' answered the stout man. 'When do you want it and for how long?'

'It's this way,' returned Burnley. 'I'm a painter, and I have always stuff to get to and from jobs. My own dray has broken down and I want one while it's being repaired. I've asked a friend for the loan of his, but he may not be able to supply. It will take about four days to put it right.'

'Then you wouldn't want a horse and man?'

'No, I should use my own.'

'In that case, sir, I couldn't agree, I fear. I never let my vehicles out without a man in charge.'

'You're right in that, of course, but I don't want the man. I'll tell you. If you let me have it I'll make you a deposit of its full value. That will guarantee its safe return.'

The stout man rubbed his cheek.

'I might do that,' he said. 'I've never done anything like it before, but I don't see why I shouldn't.'

'Let's have a look at it, anyway,' said Burnley.

They went into the yard and approached the dray, Burnley going through the form of examining it thoroughly.

'I have a lot of small kegs to handle,' he said, 'as well as drums of paint. I should like to have that barrel loader fixed till I see if it's narrow enough to carry them.'

The stout man unhooked the loader and fixed it in position.

'Too wide, I'm afraid,' said the Inspector, producing his rule. 'I'll just measure it.'

It was fifteen inches wide and six feet six long. The sides were of six by two material, with iron-shod ends. One pair of ends, that resting on the ground, was chisel-pointed, the other carried the irons for hooking it on to the cart. The ends of these irons made rectangles about three inches by two. Burnley looked at the rectangles. Both were marked with soil. He was satisfied. The loader was what Watty had used to cross the wall.

'That'll do all right,' he said. 'Let's see, do you carry a box for hay or tools?' He opened it and rapidly scanned its contents. There was a halter, a nosebag, a small coil of rope, a cranked spanner, and some other small objects. He picked up the spanner.

'This, I suppose, is for the axle caps?' he said, bending down and trying it. 'I see it fits the nuts.' As he replaced it in the box he took a quick look at the handle. It bore two sets of scratches on opposite sides, and the Inspector felt positive these would fit the marks on the padlock and staple of the coach house door, had he been able to try them.

The stout man was regarding him with some displeasure. 'You weren't thinking of buying it?' he said.

'No, thanks, but if you want a deposit before you let me take it, I want to be sure it won't sit down with me.'

They returned to the office, discussing rates. Finally these were arranged, and it was settled that when Burnley had seen his friend he was to telephone the result.

The Inspector left the yard well pleased. He had now complete proof that his theories were correct and that Watty with that dray had really stolen the cask.

Returning to Goole Street he called at the Post Office. It was ten minutes to twelve, and there being no message for him he stood waiting at the door. Five minutes had not elapsed before a street arab appeared, looked him up and down several times, and then said: 'Name o' Burnley?'

'That's me,' returned the Inspector. 'Got a note for me?'

'The other cove said as how you'd give me a tanner.'

'Here you are, sonny,' said Burnley, and the sixpence and the note changed owners. The latter read: 'Party just about to go home for dinner. Am waiting on road south of carrier's yard.'

Burnley walked to where he had left the motor and getting in, was driven to the place mentioned. At a sign from him the driver drew the car to the side of the road, stopping his engine at the same time. Jumping down, he opened the bonnet and bent over the engine. Anyone looking on would have seen that a small breakdown had taken place.

A tall, untidy-looking man, in threadbare clothes and smoking a short clay, lounged up to the car with his hands in his pockets. Burnley spoke softly without looking round

– 'I want to arrest him, Hastings. Point him out when you see him.'

'He'll pass this way going for his dinner in less than five minutes.'

'Right.'

The loafer moved forward and idly watched the repairs to the engine. Suddenly he stepped back.

'That's him,' he whispered.

Burnley looked out through the back window of the car and saw a rather short, wiry man coming down the street, dressed in blue dungarees and wearing a grey woollen muffler. As he reached the car, the Inspector stepped quickly out and touched him on the shoulder, while the loafer and the driver closed round.

'Walter Palmer, I am an inspector from Scotland Yard. I arrest you on a charge of stealing a cask. I warn you anything you say may be used against you. Better come quietly, you see there are three of us.'

Before the dumbfounded man could realise what was happening, a pair of handcuffs had snapped on his wrists and he was being pushed in the direction of the car.

'All right, boss, I'll come,' he said as he got in, followed by Burnley and Hastings. The driver started his engine and the car slipped quietly down the road. The whole affair had not occupied twenty seconds and hardly one of the passers-by had realised what was taking place.

'I'm afraid, Palmer, this is a serious matter,' began Burnley. 'Stealing the cask is one thing, but breaking into a man's yard at night is another. That's burglary and it will mean seven years at least.'

'I don't know what you're talking abaht, boss,' answered the prisoner hoarsely, licking his dry lips, 'I don't know of no cask.'

'Now, man, don't make things worse by lying. We know the whole thing. Your only chance is to make a clean breast of it.'

Palmer's face grew paler but he did not reply.

'We know how you brought out the cask to Mr Felix's about eight o'clock last night, and how, when you had left it there, you thought you'd go back and see what chances there were of getting hold of it again. We know how you hid the dray in a field close by, and then went back down the lane and waited to see if anything would turn up. We know how you learnt the house was empty and that after Mr Felix left you brought the dray back. We know all about your getting over the wall with the barrel loader, and forcing the coach house door with the wheel-cap wrench. You see, we know the whole thing, so there's not the slightest use in your pretending ignorance.'

During this recital the prisoner's face had grown paler and paler until it was now ghastly. His jaw had dropped and great drops of sweat rolled down his forehead. Still he said nothing.

Burnley saw he had produced his impression and leant forward and tapped him on the shoulder.

'Look here, Palmer,' he said. 'If you go into court nothing on earth can save you. It'll be penal servitude for at least five, and probably seven, years. But I'm going to offer you a sporting chance if you like to take it.' The man's eyes fixed themselves with painful intentness on the speaker's face. 'The police can only act if Mr Felix prosecutes. But what Mr Felix wants is the cask. If you return the cask at once, unopened, Mr Felix might – I don't say he will – but he might be induced to let you off. What do you say?'

At last the prisoner's self-control went. He threw up his manacled hands with a gesture of despair.

'My Gawd!' he cried hoarsely. 'I can't.'

The Inspector jumped.

'Can't?' he cried sharply. 'What's that? Can't? What do you mean?'

'I don't know where it is. I don't, I swear. See 'ere, boss,' the words now poured out of his mouth in a rapid stream, 'I'll tell you the truth, I will, swelp me Gawd. Listen to me.'

They had reached the City and were rapidly approaching Scotland Yard. The Inspector gave instructions for the car to be turned and run slowly through the quieter streets. Then he bent over to the now almost frantic man.

'Pull yourself together and tell me your story. Let's have the whole of it without keeping anything back, and remember the truth is your only chance.'

Palmer's statement, divested of its cockney slang and picturesque embellishments was as follows:

'I suppose you know all about the way Mr Felix hired the dray,' began Palmer, 'and painted it in the shed, and about my mate Jim Brown and me?' The Inspector nodded, and he continued: 'Then I don't need to tell you all that part of it, only that Jim and I from the first were suspicious that there was something crooked about the whole business. Mr Felix told us he had a bet on that he could get the cask away without being caught, but we didn't believe that, we thought he was out to steal it. Then when he told us that stevedore fellow was to be fixed so he couldn't follow us, we were both quite sure it was a do. Then you know how Felix and I left Jim and him in the bar and went back to the shed and repainted the dray? You know all that?'

'I know,' said Burnley.

'We waited in the shed till it was getting on towards dusk, and then we got the cask out to Felix's, and left it swinging in a set of chain blocks in an outhouse. Well, sir, I asked more than twice the pay he'd promised, and when he gave it without a word I was certain he was afraid of me. I thought, "There's some secret about that cask and he'd be willing to pay to have it kept quiet." And then it occurred to me that if I could get hold of it, I could charge him my own price for its return. I didn't mean to steal it. I didn't, sir, honest. I only meant to keep it for a day or two till he'd be willing to pay a reward.'

The man paused.

'Well, you know, Palmer, blackmail is not much better than theft,' said Burnley.

'I'm only telling you the truth, sir; that's the way it was. I thought I'd try and find out what part of the house Felix slept in and if there were others about, so as to see what chances there'd be of getting the dray up again without being heard, so I hid it in a field as you know, and went up the lane. I don't think I would have done anything only for Felix going away and saying the house was empty. Then it came over me so strongly how easy everything would be with the coast clear and the cask swinging in the chain blocks. The temptation was too strong for me, and I went back and got in as you said. I suppose you must have been there all the time watching me?'

The Inspector did not reply, and Palmer went on: 'It happened that for some time I had been going to change my house. There was an empty one close by I thought would suit. I'd got the key on Saturday and looked over it on Sunday. The key was still in my pocket, for I hadn't had time to return it.

'I intended to drive the dray down the lane behind this house and get the cask off it, then run round and get in from the front, open the yard door, roll the cask in, lock up again and return the dray to the yard. I would make an excuse with the landlord to keep the key for a day or two till I could get the money out of Felix.

'Well, sir, I drove down the lane to the back of the house, and then a thing happened that I'd never foreseen. I couldn't get the cask down. It was too heavy. I put my shoulder to it, and tried my utmost to get it over on its side, but I couldn't budge it.

'I worked till the sweat was running down me, using anything I could find for a lever, but it was no good, it wouldn't move. I went over all my friends in my mind to see if there was anyone I could get to help, but there was no one close by that I thought would come in, and I was afraid to put myself in anyone's power that I wasn't sure of. I believed Jim would be all right, but he lived two miles away and I did not want to go for him for I was late enough as it was.

'In the end I could think of no other way, and I locked the house and drove the dray to Jim's. Here I met with another disappointment. Jim had gone out about an hour before, and his wife didn't know where he was or when he'd be in.

'I cursed my luck. I was ten times more anxious now to get rid of the cask than I had been before to get hold of it. And then I thought I saw a way out. I would drive back to the yard, leave the cask there on the dray all night, get hold of Jim early in the morning, and with his help take the cask back to the empty house. If any questions were asked I would say Felix had given me instructions to leave it overnight in the yard and deliver it next morning to a certain address. I should hand over ten shillings and say he had sent this for the job.

'I drove to the yard, and then everything went wrong. First, the boss was there himself, and in a vile temper. I didn't know till afterwards, but one of our carts had been run into by a motor lorry earlier in the evening and a lot of damage done and that had upset him.

' "What's this thing you've got?" he said, when he saw the cask.

'I told him, and added that Felix had asked me to take it on in the morning, handing him the ten shillings.

' "Where is it to go?" he asked.

'Now this was a puzzler, for I hadn't expected there'd be anyone there to ask questions and I had no answer ready. So I made up an address. I chose a big street of shops and warehouses about four miles away – too far for the boss to know much about it, and I tacked on an imaginary number.

' "133 Little George Street," I answered.

'The boss took a bit of chalk and wrote the address on the blackboard we have for such notes. Then he turned back to the broken cart, and I unyoked the horse from the dray and went home.

'I was very annoyed by the turn things had taken, but I thought that after all it would not make much difference having given the address. I could go to the empty house in the morning as I had arranged.

'I was early over at Jim's next morning and told him the story. He was real mad at first and cursed me for all kinds of a fool. I kept on explaining how safe it was, for we were both sure Felix couldn't call in the police or make a fuss. At last he agreed to stand in with me, and it was arranged that he would go direct to the empty house, while I followed with the cask. He would explain his not turning up at the yard by saying he was ill.

'The boss was seldom in when we arrived, but he was there this morning, and his temper was no better.

' "Here, you," he called, when he saw me, "I thought you were never coming. Get the big grey yoked into the box cart and get away to this address" – he handed me a paper – "to shift a piano."

' "But the cask," I stammered.

' "You mind your own business and do what you're told. I've settled about that."

'I looked round. The dray was gone, and whether he'd sent it back to Felix or to the address I'd given, I didn't know.

'I cursed the whole affair bitterly, particularly when I thought of Jim waiting at the house. But there was nothing I could do, and I yoked the box cart and left. I went round by the house and told Jim, and I never saw a madder man in all my life. I could make nothing of him, so I left him and did the piano job. I just got back to the yard and was going for dinner when you nabbed me.'

When the prisoner had mentioned the address in Little George Street, Burnley had given a rapid order to the driver, and the statement had only just been finished when the car turned into the street.

'No. 133, you said?'

'That's it, sir.'

No. 133 was a large hardware shop. Burnley saw the proprietor.

'Yes,' the latter said, 'we have the cask, and I may say I was very annoyed with my foreman for taking it in without an advice note or something in writing. You can have it at once on your satisfying me you really are from Scotland Yard.'

His doubts were quickly set at rest, and he led the party to his yard.

'Is that it, Palmer?' asked Burnley.

'That's it, sir, right enough.'

'Good. Hastings, you remain here with it till I send a dray. Get it loaded up and see it yourself to the Yard. You can then go off duty. You, Palmer, come with me.'

Re-entering the car, Burnley and his prisoner were driven to the same destination, where the latter was handed over to another official.

'If Mr Felix will consent not to prosecute,' said Burnley as the man was being led off, 'you'll get out at once.'

The Inspector waited about till the dray arrived, and, when he had seen with his own eyes that the cask was really there, he walked to his accustomed restaurant and sat down to enjoy a long deferred meal.

8

THE OPENING OF THE CASK

It was getting on towards five when Inspector Burnley, like a giant refreshed with wine, emerged once more upon the street. Calling a taxi, he gave the address of St Malo, Great North Road.

'Now for friend Felix,' he thought, as he lit a cigar. He was tired and he lay back on the cushions, enjoying the relaxation as the car slipped dexterously through the traffic. Familiar as he was with every phase of London life, he never wearied of the panorama of the streets, the ceaseless movement, the kaleidoscopic colours. The sights of the pavement, the sound of pneus upon asphalt, the very smell of burnt petrol – each appealed to him as part of the alluring whole he loved.

They passed through the Haymarket and along Shaftesbury Avenue, turned up Tottenham Court Road, and through Kentish Town out on the Great North Road. Here the traffic was less dense and they made better speed. Burnley removed his hat and allowed the cool air to blow on his head. His case was going well. He was content.

Nearly an hour had passed before he rang the bell at St Malo. Felix opened the door, the visage of Sergeant Kelvin, his watchdog, appearing in the gloom at the back of the hall.

'What luck, Inspector?' he cried, when he recognised his visitor.

'We've got it, Mr Felix. Found it a couple of hours ago. I've got a taxi here, and, if convenient for you, we'll go right in and open the thing at once.'

'Right. I'm sure I am ready.'

'You come along too, Kelvin,' said the Inspector to his subordinate, and when Felix had got his hat and coat the three men walked up to the taxi.

'Scotland Yard,' called Burnley, and the car swung round and started citywards.

As they sped swiftly along, the Inspector gave an account of his day to his companion. The latter was restless and excited, and admitted he would be glad to get the business over. He was anxious about the money, as it happened that a sum of £1000 would just enable him to meet a mortgage, which otherwise would press rather heavily upon him. Burnley looked up sharply when he heard this.

'Did your French friend know that?' he asked.

'Le Gautier? No, I'm sure he did not.'

'If you take my advice, Mr Felix, you won't count too much on the cask. Indeed, you should prepare yourself for something unpleasant.'

'What do you mean?' exclaimed Felix. 'You hinted that you thought the cask contained something besides the money. What was it?'

'I'm sorry I can't answer you. The thing was only a suspicion, and we shall learn the truth in so short a time it's not worth discussion.'

Burnley having to make a call on some other business, they returned by a different route, coming down to the river near London Bridge. Already the day was drawing in, and yellow spots of light began to gleam in the windows of the palace hotels, and from the murky buildings on the south side. On the comparatively deserted Embankment they made good speed, and Big Ben was chiming the quarter after seven as they swung into the Yard.

'I'll see if the Chief's in,' said Burnley, as they reached his office. 'He wanted to see the cask opened.'

The great man was just getting ready to go home, but decided to wait on seeing the Inspector. He greeted Felix politely.

'Singular set of circumstances, Mr Felix,' he said, as they shook hands. 'I trust they will remain only that.'

'You're all very mysterious about it,' returned Felix. 'I have been trying to get a hint of the Inspector's suspicions but he won't commit himself.'

'We shall see now in a moment.'

Headed by Burnley, they passed along a corridor, down some steps and through other passages, until they emerged in a small open yard entirely surrounded by a high, window-pierced building. Apparently in the daytime it acted as a light well, but now in the growing dusk it was itself illuminated by a powerful arc lamp which threw an intense beam over every part of the granolithic floor. In the centre stood the cask, on end, with the damaged stave up.

The little group numbered five. There were the Chief, Felix, Burnley, Sergeant Kelvin, and another nondescript-looking man. Burnley stepped forward.

'This cask is so exceedingly strongly made,' he said, 'I've got a carpenter to open it. I suppose he may begin?'

The Chief nodded, and the nondescript man advancing set to work and soon lifted out the pieces of wood from the top. He held one up.

'You see, gentlemen, it's nearly two inches thick, more than twice as heavy as an ordinary wine cask.'

'That'll do, carpenter. I'll call you if I want you again,' said Burnley, and the man, touching his cap, promptly disappeared.

The four men drew closer. The cask was filled up to the top with sawdust. Burnley began removing it, sifting it carefully through his fingers.

'Here's the first,' he said, as he laid a sovereign on the floor to one side. 'And another! And another!'

The sovereigns began to grow into a tiny pile.

'There's some very uneven-shaped thing here,' he said again. 'About the centre the sawdust is not half an inch thick, but it goes down deep round the sides. Lend a hand, Kelvin, but be careful and don't use force.'

The unpacking continued. Handful after handful of dust was taken out and, after being sifted, was placed in a heap beside the sovereigns. As they got deeper the operation became slower, the spaces from which the tightly packed dust was removed growing narrower and harder to get at. Fewer sovereigns were found, suggesting that these had been placed at the top of the cask after the remainder of the contents had been packed.

'All the sawdust we can get at is out now,' Burnley said presently, and then, in a lower tone, 'I'm afraid it's a body. I've come on a hand.'

'A hand? A body?' cried Felix, his face paling and an expression of fear growing in his eyes. The Chief moved closer to him as the others bent over the cask.

The two men worked silently for some moments and then Burnley spoke again, – 'Lift now. Carefully does it.'

They stooped again over the cask and, with a sudden effort lifted out a paper-covered object and laid it reverently on the ground. A sharp 'My God!' burst from Felix, and even the case-hardened Chief drew in his breath quickly.

It was the body of a woman, the head and shoulders being wrapped round with sheets of brown paper. It lay all bunched together as it had done in the cask. One dainty hand, with slim, tapered fingers protruded from the paper, and stuck stiffly upwards beside the rounded shoulder.

The men stopped and stood motionless looking down at the still form. Felix was standing rigid, his face blanched, his eyes protruding, horror stamped on his features. The Chief spoke in a low tone, – 'Take off the paper.'

Burnley caught the loose corner and gently removed it. As it came away the figure within became revealed to the onlookers.

The body was that of a youngish woman, elegantly clad in an evening gown of pale pink cut low round the throat and shoulders, and trimmed with old lace. Masses of dark hair were coiled round the small head. On the fingers the glint of precious stones caught the light. The feet were cased in silk stockings, but no shoes. Pinned to the dress was an envelope.

But it was on the face and neck the gaze of the men was riveted. Once she had clearly been beautiful, but now the face was terribly black and swollen. The dark eyes were open and protruding, and held an expression of deadly horror and fear. The lips were drawn back showing the white, even teeth. And below, on the throat were two discoloured bruises, side by side, round marks close to the windpipe, thumb-prints of the animal who had squeezed out that life with relentless and merciless hands.

When the paper was removed from the dead face, the eyes of Felix seemed to start literally out of his head.

'God!' he shrieked in a thin, shrill tone. 'It's Annette!' He stood for a moment, waved his hands convulsively, and then, slowly turning, pitched forward insensible on the floor.

The Chief caught him before his head touched the ground. 'Lend a hand here,' he called.

Burnley and the sergeant sprang forward and, lifting the inanimate form, bore it into an adjoining room and laid it gently on the floor.

'Doctor,' said the Chief shortly, and the sergeant hurried off. 'Bad business, this,' resumed the Chief. 'He didn't know what was coming?'

'I don't think so, sir. My impression has been all through that he was being fooled by this Frenchman, whoever he is.'

'It's murder now, anyway. You'll have to go to Paris, Burnley, and look into it.'

'Yes, sir, very good.' He looked at his watch. 'It's eight o'clock. I shall hardly be able to go tonight. I shall have to take the cask and the clothing, and get some photos and measurements of the corpse and hear the result of the medical examination.'

'Tomorrow will be time enough, but I'd go by the nine o'clock train. I'll give you a personal note to Chauvet, the chief of the Paris police. You speak French, I think?'

'Enough to get on, sir.'

'You shouldn't have much difficulty, I think. The Paris men are bound to know if there are any recent disappearances, and if not you have the cask and the clothing to fall back on.'

'Yes, sir, they should be a help.'

Footsteps in the corridor announced the arrival of the doctor. With a hasty greeting to the Chief, he turned to the unconscious man.

'What happened to him?' he asked.

'He has had a shock,' answered the Chief, explaining in a few words what had occurred.

'He'll have to be removed to hospital at once. Better get a stretcher.'

The sergeant disappeared again and in a few seconds returned with the apparatus and another man. Felix was lifted on to it and borne off.

'Doctor,' said the Chief, as the former was about to follow, 'as soon as you are through with him I wish you'd make an examination of the woman's body. It seems fairly clear what happened to her, but it would be better to have a postmortem. Poison may have been used also. Burnley, here, is going to Paris by the nine o'clock in the morning to make inquiries, and he will want a copy of your report with him.'

'I shall have it ready,' said the doctor as, with a bow, he hurried after his patient.

'Now, let's have a look at that letter.'

They returned to the courtyard and Burnley unpinned the envelope from the dead woman's gown. It was unaddressed, but the Chief slit it open and drew out a sheet of folded paper. It bore a single line of typing:

'Your £50 loan returned herewith with £2 10s. 0d. interest.'

That was all. No date, address, salutation, or signature. Nothing to indicate who had sent it, or whose was the body that had accompanied it.

'Allow me, sir,' said Burnley.

He took the paper and scrutinised it carefully. Then he held it up to the light.

'This is from Le Gautier also,' he continued. 'See the watermark. It is the same paper as Felix's letter. Look also at the typing. Here are the crooked n's and r's, the defective l's and the t's and e's below alignment. It was typed on the same machine.'

'Looks like it certainly.' Then, after a pause: 'Come to my room for that letter to M. Chauvet.'

They traversed the corridors and the Inspector got his introduction to the Paris police. Then returning to the little yard, he began the preparations for his journey.

First he picked up and counted the money. There was £31 10s. in English gold and, having made a note of the amount, he slipped it into his pocket as a precaution against chance passers-by. With the £21 handed by Broughton to Mr Avery, this made the £52 10s. referred to in the typewritten slip. Then he had the body moved to the dissecting-room and photographed from several points of view, after which it was stripped by a female assistant. The clothes he went through with great care, examining every inch of the material for maker's names, initials, or other marks. Only on the delicate cambric handkerchief was his search rewarded, a small A B being embroidered amid the tracery of one corner. Having attached a label to each garment separately, as well as to the rings from the fingers and a diamond comb from the luxuriant hair, he packed them carefully in a small portmanteau, ready for transport to France.

Sending for the carpenter, he had the end boards of the cask replaced, and the whole thing wrapped in sacking and corded. Labelling it to himself at the Gare du Nord, he had it despatched to Charing Cross with instructions to get it away without delay.

It was past ten when his preparations were complete, and he was not sorry when he was free to go home to supper and bed.

PART 2

Paris

9

M. LE CHEF DE LA SÛRETÉ

At 9.0 a.m. next morning the Continental express moved slowly out of Charing Cross station, bearing in the corner of a first-class smoking compartment, Inspector Burnley. The glorious weather of the past few days had not held, and the sky was clouded over, giving a promise of rain. The river showed dark and gloomy as they drew over it, and the houses on the south side had resumed their normal dull and grimy appearance. A gentle breeze blew from the south-west, and Burnley, who was a bad sailor, hoped it would not be very much worse at Dover. He lit one of his strong-smelling cigars and puffed at it thoughtfully as the train ran with ever-increasing speed through the extraordinary tangle of lines south of London Bridge.

He was glad to be taking this journey. He liked Paris and he had not been there for four years, not indeed since the great Marcelle murder case, which attracted so much attention in both countries. M. Lefarge, the genial French detective with whom he had then collaborated had become a real friend and he hoped to run across him again.

They had reached the outer suburbs and occasional fields began to replace the lines of little villas which lie closer to the city. He watched the flying objects idly for a few minutes, and then with a little sigh turned his attention to his case, as a barrister makes up his brief before going into court.

He considered first his object in making the journey. He had to find out who the murdered woman was, if she was murdered, though there appeared little doubt about that. He had to discover and get convicting evidence against the murderer, and lastly, he had to learn the explanation of the extraordinary business of the cask.

He then reviewed the data he already had, turning first to the medical report which up till then he had not had an opportunity of reading. There was first a note about Felix. That unhappy man was entirely prostrated from the shock and his life was in serious danger.

The Inspector had already known this, for he had gone to the ward before seven that morning in the hope of getting a statement from the sick man, only to find him semiconscious and delirious. The identity of the dead woman could not, therefore, be ascertained from him. He, Burnley, must rely on his own efforts.

The report then dealt with the woman. She was aged about five-and-twenty, five feet seven in height and apparently gracefully built, and weighing a little over eight stone. She had dark hair of great length and luxuriance, and eyes with long lashes and delicately pencilled brows. Her mouth was small and regular, her nose slightly retroussé and her face a true oval. She had a broad, low forehead, and her complexion appeared to have been very clear, though dark. There was no distinguishing mark on the body.

'Surely,' thought Burnley, 'with such a description it should be easy to identify her.'

The report continued:

'There are ten marks about her neck, apparently fingermarks. Of these eight are together at the back of the neck and not strongly marked. The remaining two are situated in front of the throat, close together and one on each side of the windpipe. The skin at these points is much bruised and blackened, and the pressure must therefore have been very great.

'It seems clear the marks were caused by some individual standing in front of her and squeezing her throat with both hands, the thumbs on the windpipe and the fingers round the neck. From the strength necessary to produce such bruises, it looks as if this individual were a man.

'An autopsy revealed the fact that all the organs were sound, and there was no trace of poison or other cause of death. The conclusion is therefore unavoidable that the woman was murdered by strangulation. She appears to have been dead about a week or slightly longer.'

'That's definite, anyway,' mused Burnley. 'Let's see what else we have.'

There was the woman's rank in life. She was clearly well off if not rich, and probably well born. Her fingers suggested culture, they were those of the artist or musician. The wedding ring on her right hand showed that she was married, and living in France. 'Surely,' thought the Inspector again, 'the Chief is right. It would be impossible for a woman of this kind to disappear without the knowledge of the French police. My job will be done when I have seen them.'

But supposing they did not know. What then?

There was first of all the letter to Felix. The signatory, M. Le Gautier, assuming such a man existed, should be able to give a clue. The waiters in the Toisson d'Or Café might know something. The typewriter with the defective letters was surely traceable.

The clothes in which the corpse was dressed suggested another line of attack. Inquiry at the leading Paris shops could hardly fail to produce information. And if not there were the rings and the diamond comb. These would surely lead to something.

Then there was the cask. It was a specially made one, and must surely have been used for a very special purpose. Inquiry from the firm whose label it had borne could hardly be fruitless.

And lastly, if all these failed, there was left advertisement. A judiciously worded notice with a reward for information of identity would almost certainly draw. Burnley felt he was well supplied with clues. Many and many a thorny problem he had solved with far less to go on.

He continued turning the matter over in his mind in his slow, painstaking way, until a sudden plunge into a tunnel and a grinding of brakes warned him they were coming into Dover.

The crossing was calm and uneventful. Before they passed between the twin piers at Calais the sun had burst out, the clouds were thinning, and blue sky showing in the distance.

They made a good run to Paris, stopping only at Amiens, and at 5.45 precisely drew slowly into the vast, echoing vault of the Gare du Nord. Calling a taxi, the Inspector drove to a small private hotel he usually patronised in the rue Castiglione. Having secured his room, he re-entered the taxi and went to the Sûreté, the Scotland Yard of Paris.

He inquired for M. Chauvet, sending in his letter of introduction. The Chief was in and disengaged, and after a few minutes delay Inspector Burnley was ushered into his presence.

M. Chauvet, Chef de la Sûreté, was a small, elderly man with a dark, pointed beard, gold-rimmed glasses, and an exceedingly polite manner.

'Sit down, Mr Burnley,' he said in excellent English, as they shook hands. 'I think we have had the pleasure of co-operating with you before?'

Burnley reminded him of the Marcelle murder case.

'Ah, of course, I remember. And now you are bringing us another of the same kind. Is it not so?'

'Yes, sir, and a rather puzzling one also. But I am in hopes we have enough information to clear it up quickly.'

'Good, I hope you have. Please let me have, in a word or two, the briefest outline, then I shall ask you to go over it again in detail.'

Burnley complied, explaining in half a dozen sentences the gist of the case.

'The circumstances are certainly singular,' said the Chief. 'Let me think whom I shall put in charge of it with you. Dupont is perhaps the best man, but he is engaged on that burglary at Chartres.' He looked up a card index. 'Of those disengaged, the best perhaps are Cambon, Lefarge, and Bontemps. All good men.'

He stretched out his hand to the desk telephone.

'Pardon me, sir,' said Burnley. 'I don't want to make suggestions or interfere in what is not my business, but I had the pleasure of co-operating with M. Lefarge in the Marcelle case, and if it was quite the same I should very much like to work with him again.'

'But excellent, monsieur. I hear you say that with much pleasure.'

He lifted his desk telephone, pressing one of the many buttons on its stand.

'Ask M. Lefarge to come here at once.'

In a few seconds a tall, clean-shaven, rather English-looking man entered.

'Ah, Lefarge,' said the Chief. 'Here is a friend of yours.'

The two detectives shook hands warmly.

'He has brought us another murder mystery and very interesting it sounds. Now, Mr Burnley, perhaps you would let us hear your story in detail.'

The Inspector nodded, and beginning at the sending of the clerk Tom Broughton to check the consignment of wine at the Rouen steamer, he related all the strange events that had taken place, the discovery of the cask, and the suspicions aroused, the forged note, the removal of the cask, the getting rid of Harkness, the tracing and second disappearance of the cask, its ultimate recovery, its sinister contents, and finally, a list of the points which might yield clues if followed up. The two men listened intently, but without interrupting. After he had finished they sat silently in thought.

'In one point I do not quite follow you, Mr Burnley,' said the Chief at last. 'You appear to assume that this murdered woman was a Parisienne. But what are your reasons for that?'

'The cask came from Paris. That is certain, as you will see from the steamship's documents. Then the letter to Felix purports to be from a Parisian, a M. Le Gautier, and both it and the note pinned to the body were typed on French paper. Further, the label on the cask bore the name of a Paris firm.'

'It does not seem to me very conclusive. The cask admittedly came from Paris, but might not Paris have been only the last stage of a longer journey? How, for example, do we know that it was not sent from London, or Brussels, or Berlin, in the first instance, and rebooked at Paris with the object of laying a false scent? With regard to the letter, I understand you did not see the envelope. Therefore it does not seem to be evidence. As for the French paper, Felix had been frequently in France, and he might be responsible for that. The label, again, was a readdressed old one. Might it not therefore have been taken off some quite different package and put on the cask?'

'I admit the evidence is far from conclusive, though it might be said in answer to your first point about the re-addressing of the cask in Paris, that such would involve a confederate here. In any case it seemed to both our Chief and myself that Paris should be our first point of inquiry.'

'But yes, monsieur, in that I entirely agree. I only wished to make the point that you have no real evidence that the solution of the problem lies here.'

'I'm afraid we have not.'

'Well, to proceed. As you have suggested, the first point is to ascertain if anyone resembling the dead woman has disappeared recently. Your doctor says that she has been dead for a week or longer, but I do not think that we can confine our inquiries to that period only. She might have been kidnapped and held a prisoner for a considerable time previous to her death. I should say that it is not likely, but it may have happened.'

He lifted his telephone, pressing another button.

'Bring me the list of disappearances of persons in the Paris area during the last four weeks, or rather' – he stopped and looked at the others – 'the disappearances in all France for the same period.'

In a few seconds a clerk entered with some papers.

'Here are all the disappearances reported during March, monsieur,' he said, 'and here those for April up to the present date. I haven't a return for the last four weeks only, but can get one out at once if you wish.'

'No. These are all right.'

The Chief examined the documents.

'Last month,' he said, 'seven persons disappeared of whom six were women, four being in the Paris area. This month two people have disappeared, both women and both in the Paris area. That is six women in Paris in the last five weeks. Let's see, now,' he ran his fingers down the column, 'Suzanne Lemaître, aged seventeen, last seen – well, it could not be she. Lucille Marquet, aged twenty – no good either. All these are girls under twenty-one, except one. Here, what is this? Marie Lachaise, aged thirty-four, height 172 centimetres – that is about five feet eight in English measure – dark hair and eyes and clear complexion, wife of M. Henri Lachaise, the avocat, of 41 rue Tinques, Boulevarde Arago. Left home on the twenty-ninth ultimo, that is about ten days ago, at three o'clock, ostensibly for shopping. Has not been heard of since. Better take a note of that.'

M. Lefarge did so, and spoke for the first time.

'We shall try it, of course, monsieur, but I don't expect much result. If that woman went out to shop she would hardly be wearing evening dress, as was the corpse.'

'Also,' said Burnley, 'I think we may take it the dead woman's name was Annette B.'

'Probably you are both right. Still, you had better make sure.'

The Chief tossed away the papers and looked at Burnley.

'No other disappearances have been reported, nor have we any further information here that would seem to help. I am afraid we must fall back on our other clues. Let us consider, therefore, where we should start.'

He paused for a few moments and then resumed.

'We may begin, I think, by checking the part of Felix's statement which you, Mr Burnley, have not yet been able to inquire into, and to do so we must interview M. Le Gautier and try to ascertain if he wrote the letter. If he admits it we will be a step farther on, if not, we must find out how far the story of the lottery and the bet is true, and whether the conversation described by Felix actually took place. In this case we must ascertain precisely who were present and overheard that conversation, and would therefore have the knowledge necessary to write that letter. If this does not give us what we want, it may be necessary to follow up each of these persons and try for our man by elimination, A part of that inquiry would be a search for the typewriter used, which, as Mr Burnley points out, is identifiable. Simultaneously, I think we should endeavour to trace the wearing apparel and the cask. What do you think of that, gentlemen, for a rough programme?'

'I don't think we could do better, sir,' returned Burnley as the Chief looked at him, while Lefarge nodded his approval.

'Very well, I would suggest that you and Lefarge go into the matter of the letter tomorrow. Arrange your programme as you think best for yourselves and keep me advised of how you get on. And now as to the clothes. Let me see exactly what you have.'

Burnley spread out the dead woman's clothes and jewellery on a table. The Chief examined them for some minutes in silence.

'Better separate them into three lots,' he said at length, 'the dress, the underclothes, and the trinkets. It will take three to work it properly.' He consulted his card index and picked up the telephone.

'Send Mme. Fumier and Mlles. Lecoq and Blaise here.'

In a few seconds three stylishly dressed women entered. The Chief introduced Burnley and briefly explained the case.

'I want you three ladies,' he said, 'to take one each of these three lots of clothes and trinkets, and find the purchaser. Their quality will give you an idea of the shops to try. Get at it first thing tomorrow, and keep yourselves in constant touch with headquarters.'

When the women had withdrawn with the articles he turned to Burnley, – 'In an inquiry of this sort I like a report in the evenings of progress during the day. Perhaps you and Lefarge wouldn't mind calling about nine tomorrow evening, when we shall have a further discussion. And now it is nearly eight o'clock, so you cannot do anything tonight. You, Mr Burnley, are doubtless tired from your journey and will be glad to get to your hotel. So good night, gentlemen.'

The detectives bowed themselves out. After an exchange of further greetings and compliments, Lefarge said: 'Are you really very tired? Are you game for a short inquiry tonight?'

'Why, certainly. What do you propose?'

'This. Let us cross and get some dinner at Jules' in the Boule Miche. It's on the way to that address the Chief gave us. Then we could go on and see whether the body you found in the cask can be identified as that of Madame Marie Lachaise.'

They strolled leisurely over the Pont St Michel and crossed the Quai into the Boulevard. When Burnley was in London he swore there was no place like that city, but in Paris he never felt so sure. Jove! he was glad to be back. And what luck to have met this good fellow Lefarge again! He felt that in the intervals of business he was going to enjoy himself.

They dined inexpensively but well, sitting over their cigars and liqueur coffee until the clocks struck nine. Then Lefarge made a move.

'I don't like to go to this place too late,' he said. 'Do you mind coming now?'

They took a taxi and, leaving the Luxembourg behind on the left, quickly ran the mile or so to the Boulevard Arago. M. Lachaise received them at once and they stated their melancholy business, showing the photograph of the body. The avocat took it to the light and examined it earnestly. Then he returned it with a gesture of relief.

'Thank God,' he said at length, 'it's not she.'

'The body was clothed in a light pink evening dress, with several diamond rings on the fingers and a diamond comb in the hair.'

'It is not she at all. My wife had no pink dress, nor did she wear a diamond comb. Besides, she left here in an out-of-door walking dress and all her evening things were in her wardrobe.'

'It is conclusive,' said M. Lefarge, and with thanks and compliments they took their leave.

'I thought that would be no good,' said Lefarge, 'but we must do what the Chief says.'

'Of course. Besides, you never know. Look here, old man,' he added, 'I am tired after all. I think, if you don't mind, I'll get away to the hotel.'

'But, of course. Whatever you feel like. Let's stroll to the end of the Boulevard. We can get the Metro across the street at the Avenue d'Orleans.'

They changed at Chatelet and, having arranged to meet next morning, the Inspector took the Maillot train for Concorde, while Lefarge went in the opposite direction to his home near the Place de la Bastille.

10

WHO WROTE THE LETTER?

At ten o'clock next morning Lefarge called for Burnley at the latter's hotel in the rue Castiglione.

'Now for M. Alphonse Le Gautier, the wine merchant,' said the former as he hailed a taxi.

A short drive brought them to the rue de Vallorbes, off the Avenue Friedland, and there they discovered that the gentleman they were in search of was no myth, but a creature of real flesh and blood. He occupied a flat on the first floor of a big corner house, and the spacious approach and elegant furnishing indicated that he was a man of culture and comparative wealth. He had gone, they were told, to his office in the rue Henri Quatre, and thither the two friends followed him. He was a man of about five-and-thirty, with jet black hair and a pale, hawk-like face, and his manner was nervous and alert.

'We have called, monsieur,' said Lefarge, when the detectives had introduced themselves, 'at the instance of M. le Chef de la Sûreté, to ask your assistance in a small inquiry we are making. We want to trace the movements of a gentleman who is perhaps not unknown to you, a M. Léon Felix, of London.'

'Léon Felix? Why, of course I know him. And what has he been up to?'

'Nothing contrary to the law, monsieur,' returned Lefarge with a smile, 'or, at least, we believe not. But unfortunately, in the course of another inquiry a point has arisen which makes it necessary for us to check some statements he has made about his recent actions. It is in this we want your help.'

'I don't think I can tell you much about him, but any questions you ask I'll try to answer.'

'Thank you, M. Le Gautier. Not to waste your time, then, I'll begin without further preface. When did you last meet M. Felix?'

'Well, it happens I can tell you that, for I had a special reason to note the date.' He referred to a small pocket diary. 'It was on Sunday the 14th of March, four weeks ago next Sunday.'

'And what was the special reason to which you refer?'

'This. On that day M. Felix and I made an arrangement to purchase coupons in the Government lotteries. He handed me 500 francs as his share, and I was to add another 500 francs and put the business through. Naturally I noted the transaction in my engagement book.'

'Can you tell me under what circumstances this arrangement came to be made?'

'Certainly. It was the result of an otherwise idle conversation on the lottery system, which took place that afternoon between a number of men, of whom I was one, at the Café Toisson d'Or, in the rue Royale. At the close of the discussion I said I would try my luck. I asked Felix to join me, and he did so.'

'And did you purchase the bonds?'

'I did. I wrote enclosing a cheque that same evening.'

'And I hope your speculation turned out successfully?'

M. Le Gautier smiled.

'Well, I can hardly tell you that, you know. The drawing will not be made till next Thursday.'

'Next Thursday? Then I can only hope you will have luck. Did you write M. Felix that you had actually moved in the matter?'

'No, I took it, that went without saying.'

'So that you have not communicated with M. Felix in any way since last Sunday three weeks?'

'That is so.'

'I see. Now, another point, M. Le Gautier. Are you acquainted with a M. Dumarchez, a stockbroker, whose office is in the Boulevard Poissonière?'

'I am. As a matter of fact he also was present at the discussion about the lotteries.'

'And since that discussion you made a certain bet with him?'

'A bet?' M. Le Gautier looked up sharply. 'I don't understand you. I made no bet.'

'Do you remember having a discussion with M. Dumarchez about criminals pitting their wits against the police?'

'No, I recollect nothing of the kind.'

'Are you prepared, monsieur, to say that no such conversation took place?'

'Certainly, I do say it. And I should very much like to know the purport of all these questions.'

'I am sorry, monsieur, for troubling you with them, and I can assure you they are not idle. The matter is a serious one, though I am not at liberty to explain it fully at present. But if you will bear with me I would like to ask one or two other things. Can you let me have the names of those present at the Toisson d'Or when the conversation about the lotteries took place?'

M. Le Gautier remained silent for some moments.

'I hardly think I can,' he said at last. 'You see, there was quite a fair sized group. Besides Felix, Dumarchez, and myself, I can recollect M. Henri Briant and M. Henri Boisson. I think there were others, but I cannot recall who they were.'

'Was a M. Daubigny one of them?'

'You are right. I had forgotten him. He was there.'

'And M. Jacques Rôget?'

'I'm not sure.' M. Le Gautier hesitated again. 'I think so, but I'm not really sure.'

'Can you let me have the addresses of these gentlemen?'

'Some of them. M. Dumarchez lives five doors from me in the rue de Vallorbes. M. Briant lives near the end of the rue Washington, where it turns into the Champs Élysées. The other addresses I cannot tell you off-hand, but I can help you to find them in a directory.'

'Many thanks. Now, please excuse me for going back a moment. You gave me to understand you did not write to M. Felix on the subject of the lottery?'

'Yes, I said so, I think, quite clearly.'

'But M. Felix states the very opposite. He says he received a letter from you, dated Thursday, 1st April, that is, this day week.'

M. Le Gautier stared.

'What's that you say? He says he heard from me? There must be a mistake there, monsieur, for I did not write to him.'

'But he showed me the letter.'

'Impossible, monsieur. He could not have shown you what did not exist. Whatever letter he may have shown you was not from me. I should like to see it. Have you got it there?'

For answer Lefarge held out the sheet which Felix had given to Burnley during their midnight conversation at the villa of St Malo. As M. Le Gautier read it the look of wonder on his expressive face deepened.

'Extraordinary!' he cried, 'but here is a mystery! I never wrote, or sent, or had any knowledge of such a letter. It's not only a forgery, but it's a pure invention. There's not a word of truth in that story of the bet and the cask from beginning to end. Tell me something more about it. Where did you get it?'

'From M. Felix himself. He gave it to Mr Burnley here, saying it was from you.'

'But, good heavens!' the young man sprang to his feet and began pacing up and down the room, 'I can't understand that. Felix is a decent fellow, and he wouldn't say it was from me if he didn't believe it. But how could he believe it? The thing is absurd.' He paused and then continued. 'You say, monsieur, that Felix said this note was from me. But what made him think so? There's not a scrap of writing about it. It isn't even signed. He must have known anyone could write a letter and type my name below it. And then, how could he suppose that I should write such a tissue of falsehoods?'

'But that is just the difficulty,' returned Lefarge. 'It's not so false as you seem to imagine. The description of the conversation about the lottery and your arrangement with Felix to purchase bonds is, by your own admission, true.'

'Yes, that part is, but the rest, all that about a bet and a cask, is wholly false.'

'But there I fear you are mistaken also, monsieur. The part about the cask is apparently true. At least the cask arrived, addressed as described, and on the day mentioned.'

Again the young merchant gave an exclamation of astonishment.

'The cask arrived?' he cried. 'Then there really was a cask?' He paused again. 'Well, I cannot understand it, but I can only repeat that I never wrote that letter, nor have I the slightest idea what it is all about.'

'It is, of course, obvious, monsieur, as you point out, that anyone could have typed a letter ending with your name. But you will admit it is equally obvious that only a person who knew of your entering the lottery could have written it. You tell us you are not that person, and we fully accept your statement. Who else then, M. Le Gautier, had this information?'

'As far as that goes, anyone who was present at the discussion at the Toisson d'Or.'

'Quite so. Hence you will see the importance of my questions as to who these were.'

M. Le Gautier paced slowly up and down the room, evidently thinking deeply.

'I don't know that I do,' he said at last. 'Suppose everything in that letter was true. Suppose, for arguments sake, I had written it. What then? What business of the police is it? I can't see that the law has been broken.'

Lefarge smiled.

'That ought to be clear enough, anyway. Look at the facts. A cask arrives in London by the I and C boat from Rouen, labelled to a man named Felix at a certain address. Inquiries show that no one of that name lives at that address. Further, the cask is labelled "Statuary," but examination shows that it does not contain statuary, but money, sovereigns. Then a man representing himself as Felix appears, states he lives at the false address, which is untrue, says he is expecting by that boat a cask of statuary, which is also untrue, and claims the one in question. The steamer people, being naturally suspicious, will not give it up, but by a trick Felix gets hold of it, and takes it to quite another address. When questioned by the police he produces this letter to account for his actions. I do not think it surprising that we are anxious to learn who wrote the letter, and if its contents are true.'

'No, no, of course, it is reasonable. I did not understand the sequence of events. All the same, it is the most extraordinary business I ever heard of.'

'It is strange, certainly. Tell me, M. Le Gautier, have you ever had any disagreement with Mr Felix? Can you imagine him having, or thinking he had, any cause of offence against you?'

'Nothing of the kind.'

'You never gave him cause, however innocently, to feel jealousy?'

'Never. But why do you ask?'

'I was wondering whether he might not have played a trick on you, and have written the letter himself.'

'No, no. I'm sure it's not that. Felix is a very straight, decent fellow. He would not do a thing like that.'

'Well, can you think of anyone who might be glad to give you annoyance? What about the men who were present when you discussed the lottery? Or anyone else at all?'

'I cannot think of a single person.'

'Did you tell anyone about this matter of the lottery?'

'No. I never mentioned it.'

'One other question, monsieur, and I have done. Did you at any time borrow £50 or the equivalent of French money from M. Felix?'

'I never borrowed from him at all.'

'Or do you know anyone who borrowed such a sum from him?'

'No one, monsieur.'

'Then, monsieur, allow me to express my regret for the annoyance given, and my thanks for your courteous replies to my questions.' He flashed a glance at Burnley. 'If we might still further inflict ourselves on you, I should like, with your permission, to ask M. Dumarchez to join us here so that we may talk the matter over together.'

'An excellent idea, monsieur. Do so by all means.'

One of the eventualities the colleagues had discussed before starting their morning's work was the possible denial by M. Le Gautier of any bet with M. Dumarchez. They had decided that in such a case the latter must be interrogated before a communication could reach him from Le Gautier. It was with this in view that Lefarge left his friend with the wine merchant, while going himself to interview his neighbour.

As the detective reached the door of the stockbroker's office in the Boulevard Poissonière it opened and a middle-aged gentleman with a long, fair beard emerged.

'Pardon, but are you M. Dumarchez?' asked Lefarge.

'My name, monsieur. Did you wish to see me?'

The detective introduced himself, and briefly stated his business.

'Come in, monsieur,' said the other. 'I have an appointment in another part of Paris shortly, but I can give you ten minutes.' He led the way into his private room and waved his visitor to a chair.

'It is the matter of the bet, monsieur,' began Lefarge. 'The test has failed, and the police have therefore to satisfy themselves that the cask was really sent with the object stated.'

M. Dumarchez stared.

'I do not understand,' he replied. 'To what bet are you referring?'

'To the bet between you and M. Le Gautier. You see, M. Felix's dealings with the cask are the result of the bet, and it must be obvious to you that confirmation of his statement is required.'

The stockbroker shook his head with decision as if to close the conversation.

'You have made some mistake, monsieur. I made no bet with M. Le Gautier and, for the rest, I have no idea what you are speaking of.'

'But, monsieur, M. Felix stated directly that you had bet M. Le Gautier he could not get the cask away. If that is not true, it may be serious for him.'

'I know nothing of any cask. What Felix are you referring to?'

'M. Léon Felix, of St Malo, London.'

A look of interest passed over the stockbroker's face. 'Léon Felix? I certainly know him. A decent fellow he is too. And you mean to say he told you I was mixed up with some matter connected with a cask?'

'Certainly. At least he told my colleague, Mr Burnley, of the London police.'

'My dear monsieur, your colleague must be dreaming. Felix must have been speaking of someone else.'

'I assure you not, monsieur. There is no mistake. M. Felix states the bet arose out of a conversation on the State lotteries, which took place in the Café Toisson d'Or, three weeks ago last Sunday, at which you were present.'

'He is right about the conversation, anyway. I recollect that quite well, but I know nothing whatever of any bet. Certainly, I made none.'

'In that case, monsieur, I have to offer my apologies for having troubled you. I can see a mistake has been made. But before I leave, perhaps you would have the kindness to tell me who else were present on that occasion. Probably I should have gone to one of them.'

After some consideration M. Dumarchez mentioned three names, all of which Lefarge already had in his note-book. Then excusing himself on the ground of his appointment, the stockbroker hurried away, while Lefarge returned to report to Burnley and M. Le Gautier.

During the afternoon the colleagues called on each of the men whose names they had been given as having been present at the Café Toisson d'Or when the lottery discussion took place. M. Briant had gone to Italy, but they saw the others, and in each case the result was the same. All remembered the conversation, but none knew anything of the bet or the cask. Inquiries from the waiters at the Toisson d'Or likewise were without result.

'We don't seem to get much forrader,' remarked Burnley, as the two friends sat over their coffee after dinner that evening. 'I am inclined to believe that these men we have seen really don't know anything about the cask.'

'I agree with you,' returned Lefarge. 'At any rate it shouldn't be difficult to test at least part of their statements. We can find out from the lottery people whether Le Gautier did purchase 1000 francs worth of bonds on Sunday three weeks. If he did, I think we must take it that the story of the conversation in the Toisson d'Or is true, and that he and Felix did agree to go in for it jointly.'

'There can be no reasonable doubt of that.'

'Further, we can find out if the drawing takes place next Thursday. If it does, it follows that all that part of the letter about the winning of the money and the test with the cask is false. If, on the other hand, it has already been made, the letter may conceivably be true, and Le Gautier is lying. But I don't think that likely.'

'Nor I. But I don't quite agree with you about the letter. We already know the letter is false. It said £988 would be sent in the cask, whereas there was a body and £52 10s. But the question of the test is not so clear to me. The cask *did* come as described in the letter, bearing the false address and description, and if it was not so sent for the reason mentioned, what other reason can you suggest?'

'None, I admit.'

'Let us see, then, just what we do know about the writer of the letter. Firstly, he must have known of the conversation about the lottery, and of the arrangement made by Felix and Le Gautier to enter for it. That is to say, he must either have been present in the Toisson d'Or when it took place, or someone who was there must have repeated it to him. Secondly, he must have known all the circumstances of the sending out of the cask, at least as far as the false address and description were concerned. Thirdly, he must have had access to a rather worn typewriter, which we believe could be identified, and fourthly, he must have possessed, or been able to procure French notepaper. So much is certain. We may also assume, though it has neither been proved, nor is it very important, that he could use the typewriter himself, as it is unlikely that such a letter would be done by a typist from dictation.'

'That's true, and so far as I can see, the only man that fills the bill so far is Felix himself.'

'I don't think it was Felix. I believe he was telling the truth all right. But we haven't enough information yet to judge. Perhaps when we follow up the cask we shall be able to connect some of these men we saw today with it.'

'Possibly enough,' answered Lefarge, rising. 'If we are to get to the Sûreté by nine, we had better go.'

'Is it your Chief's habit to hold meetings at nine o'clock? It seems a curious time to me.'

'And he's a curious man, too, First rate at his job, you know, and decent, and all that. But peculiar. He goes away in the afternoons, and comes back after dinner and works half the night. He says he gets more peace then?'

'I dare say he does, but it's a rum notion for all that.'

M. Chauvet listened with close attention to the report of the day's proceedings and, after Lefarge ceased speaking, sat motionless for several seconds, buried in thought. Then, like a man who arrives at a decision he spoke: 'The matter, so far as we have gone, seems to resolve itself into these points. First, did a conversation about the lotteries take place in the Café Toisson d'Or about four weeks ago? I think we may assume that it did. Second, did Felix and Le Gautier agree to enter, and if so, did Le Gautier send a cheque that day? Here we can get confirmation by making inquiries at the lottery offices, and I will send a man there tomorrow. Third, has the drawing taken place? This can be ascertained in the same way. Beyond that, I do not think we can go at present, and I am of opinion our next move should be to try and trace the cask. That line of inquiry may lead us back to one of these gentlemen you have seen today, or may point to someone else whom we may find was present at the Toisson d'Or. What do you think, gentlemen?'

'We had both arrived at the same conclusion, monsieur,' answered Lefarge.

'Well then, you will make inquiries about the cask tomorrow, will you? Good. I will look out for you in the evening.'

PART 2: PARIS

Having arranged eight o'clock at the Gare du Nord for the rendezvous next day, the detectives bid each other good night and went their ways.

11

MM. DUPIERRE ET CIE

The hands of the large clock at the Gare du Nord were pointing to three minutes before eight next morning as Inspector Burnley walked up the steps of the entrance. Lefarge was there before him and the two men greeted each other warmly.

'I have a police box cart here,' said Lefarge. 'Give me your papers and we'll have the cask out in a brace of shakes.'

Burnley handed them over and they went to the luggage bureau. Lefarge's card had a magical effect, and in a very few minutes the sacking-covered barrel had been found and loaded on to the cart. Lefarge instructed the driver.

'I want that taken to a street off the rue de la Convention at Grenelle. You might start now and stop at the Grenelle end of the Pont Mirabeau. Wait there until I come for you. I suppose it will take you an hour or more?'

'It'll take more than an hour and a half, monsieur,' replied the man. 'It is a long way and this cart is very heavy.'

'Very well, just do the best you can.'

The man touched his cap and moved off with his load.

'Are we in any hurry?' asked Burnley.

'No, we have to kill time until he gets there. Why do you ask?'

'Nothing, except that if we have time enough, let's go down directly to the river and take a boat. I always enjoy the Seine boats.'

'As a matter of fact so do I,' replied Lefarge. 'You get the air and the motion is pleasanter and more silent than a bus. They are not so slow either when you consider the stops.'

They took a bus which brought them southwards through the Louvre, and, alighting at the Pont des Arts, caught a steamer going to Suresnes. The morning was fresh and exquisitely clear. The sun, immediately behind them at first, crept slowly round to the left as they followed the curve of the river. Burnley sat admiring perhaps for the fiftieth time the graceful architecture of the bridges, justly celebrated as the finest of any city in the world. He gazed with fresh interest and pleasure also on the buildings they were carried past, from the huge pile of the Louvre on the right bank to the great terrace of the Quai d'Orsay on the left, and from the Trocadero and the palaces of the Champs Élysées back to the thin tapering shaft of the Eiffel Tower. How well he remembered a visit that he and Lefarge had paid to the restaurant on the lower stage of this latter when they lunched at the next table to Madame Marcelle, the young and attractive-looking woman who had murdered her English husband by repeated doses of a slow and irritant poison. He had just turned to remind his companion of the circumstance when the latter's voice broke in on his thoughts.

'I went back to the Sûreté after we parted last night. I thought it better to make sure of the cart this morning, and I also looked up our records about this firm of monumental sculptors. It seems that it is not a very large concern, and all the power is vested in the hands of M. Paul Thévenet, the managing director. It is an old establishment and apparently eminently respectable, and has a perfectly clean record so far as we are concerned.'

'Well, that's so much to the good.'

They disembarked at the Pont Mirabeau and, crossing to the south side and finding a tolerably decent-looking café, sat down at one of the little tables on the pavement behind a screen of shrubs in pots.

'We can see the end of the bridge from here, so we may wait comfortably until the cart appears,' said Lefarge, when he had ordered a couple of bocks.

They sat on in the pleasant sun, smoking and reading the morning papers. Nearly an hour passed before the cart came into view slowly crossing the bridge. Then they left their places at the café and, signing to the driver to follow, walked down the rue de la Convention, and turned into the rue Provence. Nearly opposite, a little way down the street, was the place of which they were in search.

Its frontage ran the whole length of the second block, and consisted partly of a rather ancient-looking four storey factory or warehouse and partly of a high wall, evidently surrounding a yard. At the end of the building this wall was pierced by a gateway leading into the yard, and just inside was a door in the end wall of the building, labelled 'Bureau.'

Having instructed the driver to wait outside the gate, they pushed open the small door and asked to see M. Thévenet on private business. After a delay of a few minutes a clerk ushered them into his room.

The managing director was an elderly man, small and rather wizened, with a white moustache, and a dry but courteous manner. He rose as the detectives entered, wished them good morning, and asked what he could do for them.

'I must apologise for not sending in my card, M Thévenet,' began Lefarge, presenting it, 'but, as the matter in question is somewhat delicate, I preferred that your staff should not know my profession.'

M. Thévenet bowed.

'This, sir,' went on Lefarge, 'is my colleague, Mr Burnley of the London police, and he is anxious for some information, if you would be so kind as to let him have it.'

'I will be pleased to answer any questions I can. I speak English if Mr Burnley would prefer it.'

'I thank you,' said Burnley. 'The matter is rather a serious one. It is briefly this. On Monday last – four days ago – a cask arrived in London from Paris. Some circumstances with which I need not trouble you aroused the suspicions of the police, with the result that the cask was seized and opened. In it were found, packed in sawdust, two things, firstly, £52 10s. in English gold, and secondly the body of a youngish woman, evidently of good position, and evidently murdered by being throttled by a pair of human hands.'

'Horrible!' ejaculated the little man.

'The cask was of very peculiar construction, the woodwork being at least twice as heavy as that of an ordinary wine cask and secured by strong iron bands. And, sir, the point that has brought us to you is that your firm's name was stencilled on it after the words "Return to," and it was addressed on one of your firm's labels.'

The little man sprang to his feet.

'Our cask? Our label?' he cried, in evident astonishment. 'Do I understand you to say, sir, that the cask containing this body was sent out by us?'

'No, sir,' returned Burnley, 'I did not say that. I simply say that it arrived bearing your name and label. I am in total ignorance of how or when the body was put in. That is what I am over from London to investigate.'

'But the thing is utterly incredible,' said M. Thévenet, pacing up and down the room. 'No, no,' he added, with a wave of his hand as Burnley would have spoken, 'I don't mean that I doubt your word. But I cannot but feel that there must be a terrible mistake.'

'It is only right to add, sir,' continued Burnley, 'that I did not myself see the label. But it was seen by the men of the carrying company, and especially by one of their clerks who examined it carefully after suspicion had been aroused. The label was afterwards destroyed by Felix, to whom the cask was addressed.'

'Felix, Felix, the name seems familiar. What was the full name and address?'

'M. Léon Felix, 141 West Jubb Street, Tottenham Court Road, London, WC.'

'Ah, of course,' rejoined M. Thévenet. 'There is, then, really such a man? I rather doubted it at the time, you know, for our advice card of the despatch of the cask was returned marked, "Not known," and I then looked him up in the London directory and could not find him. Of course, as far as we were concerned, we had the money and it did not matter to us.'

Burnley and his colleague sat up sharply.

'I beg your pardon, M. Thévenet,' said Burnley. 'What's that you say? At the time? At what time, if you please?'

'Why, when we sent out the cask. When else?' returned the director, looking keenly at his questioner.

'But, I don't understand. You *did* send out a cask then, addressed to Felix at Tottenham Court Road?'

'Of course we did. We had the money, and why should we not do so?'

'Look here, M. Thévenet,' continued Burnley, 'we are evidently talking at cross purposes. Let me first explain more fully about the label. According to our information, which we have no reason to doubt, the address space had been neatly cut out and another piece of paper pasted behind, bearing the address in question. It seemed to us therefore, that some person had received the cask from you and, having altered the label, packed the body in it and sent it on. Now we are to understand that the cask was sent out by you. Why then should the label have been altered?'

'I'm sure I cannot tell.'

'May I ask what was in the cask when it left here?'

'Certainly. It was a small group of statuary by a good man and rather valuable.'

'I'm afraid, M. Thévenet, I haven't got the matter clear yet. It would oblige us both very much if you would be kind enough to tell us all you know about the sending out of that cask.'

'With pleasure.' He touched a bell and a clerk entered.

'Bring me,' he said, 'all the papers about the sale of that group of Le Mareschal's to M. Felix of London.' He turned again to his visitors.

'Perhaps I had better begin by explaining our business to you. It is in reality three businesses carried on simultaneously by one firm. First, we make plaster casts of well-known pieces. They are not valuable and sell for very little. Secondly, we make monuments, tombstones, decorative stone panels and the like for buildings, rough work, but fairly good. Lastly we trade in really fine sculpture, acting as agents between the artists and the public. We have usually a considerable number of such good pieces in our showroom. It was one of these latter, a 1400 franc group, that was ordered by M. Felix.'

'Felix ordered it?' burst in Burnley, 'but there, pardon me. I must not interrupt.'

The clerk returned at this moment and laid some papers on his principal's desk. The latter turned them over, selected one, and handed it to Burnley.

'Here is his letter, you see, received by us on the morning of the 30th of March, and enclosing notes for 1500 francs. The envelope bore the London postmark.'

The letter was written by hand one on side of a single sheet of paper and was as follows:

141 West Jubb Street,
Tottenham Court Road,
London, WC

29th March, 1912

Messrs Dupierre et Cie,
Rue Provence,
Rue de la Convention,
Grenelle, Paris.

GENTLEMEN

I am anxious to purchase the group of statuary in the left-hand corner back of your Boulevard des Capucines showroom, looking from the street. The group is of three female figures, two seated and one standing. There can be no doubt about the one I mean, as it is the only such in the left of the window.

Please forward immediately to the above address.

I do not know the exact price, but understand it is about 1500 francs. I therefore enclose notes for that sum, and if a balance remains on either side it can be adjusted by letter.

I may say that an unexpected call to England prevented me ordering this in person.

Yours, etc.

LÉON FELIX

Inspector Burnley examined the letter.

'You will allow us to keep this in the meantime, I presume?' he asked.

'Certainly.'

'You said the money was in notes. You mean, I take it, ordinary State paper money whose source could not be traced; not any kind of cheque or draft payable through a bank?'

'Precisely.'

'Well, sir, pardon my interruption.'

'There is little more to add. The group was packed and despatched on the day we received the letter. Its price was, as a matter of fact, only 1400 francs, and the balance of 100 francs was therefore enclosed with it. This was considered as safe as any other way of sending it, as the cask was insured for its full value.'

'The cask? You packed it then in a cask?'

'Yes. We make a special kind of cask in two sizes, very heavy and strong, for sending out such pieces. It is our own idea, and we are rather proud of it. We find it simpler and safer than a crate.'

'We have the cask in a cart outside. Perhaps, if we brought it in, you would be good enough to see if it could be identified, firstly if it is yours, and secondly, if so, if it is the particular one you sent to Felix.'

'Well, you see, unfortunately it was sent from our showrooms in the Boulevard des Capucines. If you have time to take it there I will instruct the manager to assist you in every way in his power. Indeed, I will go with you myself. I shall not be able to rest until the matter is cleared up.'

The detectives thanked him and, while Lefarge was instructing the carter, M. Thévenet procured a taxi and they drove to the Boulevard des Capucines.

12

AT THE GARE ST LAZARE

The showrooms consisted of a small but luxuriously fitted up shop, containing many objects of excellence and value. M. Thévenet introduced the manager, M. Thomas, a young and capable-looking man, who invited them into his office. He did not speak English, and Lefarge carried on the conversation.

'These gentlemen,' said M. Thévenet, 'are making some inquiries about the sale of Le Mareschal's group to Mr Felix of London last week. I want you to tell them all you can, Thomas.'

The young man bowed.

'With pleasure, monsieur.'

In a few words Lefarge put him in possession of the main facts. 'Perhaps,' he continued, if you would be kind enough to tell me all that you know, I could then ask questions on any point I did not understand,'

'But certainly, monsieur. There is not much to tell.' He looked up some memoranda. 'On Tuesday week, the 30th March, we had a phone from the head office saying that M. Le Mareschal's last group, which we had on exhibition in our window, was sold. We were to send it at once to M. Léon Felix, at the London address you know. Also we were to enclose 100 francs, refund of an overpayment of the cost. This was done. The group and the money were duly packed and despatched. Everything was perfectly in order and in accordance with our usual custom. The only remarkable feature in the whole transaction was the absence of a receipt from Felix. I do not think I can recall another instance in which we were not advised of our goods safe arrival, and in this case it was doubly to be expected, owing to the enclosure of money. I might perhaps mention also that on that same Tuesday we had a telephone call from M. Felix, through from London, asking when and by what route we were sending the cask, to which I replied in person.'

The young man paused, and Lefarge asked how the group was packed.

'In a number A cask, our usual practice.'

'We have a cask coming along. It will be here presently. Could you identify it?'

'Possibly I or the foreman might.'

'Well M. Thévenet, I do not think we can get any further till it arrives. There would just be time for *déjeuner*. We hope you and M. Thomas will give us the pleasure of your company.'

This was agreed to, and they lunched at one of the comfortable restaurants on the Boulevard. When they returned to the shop the cart was waiting.

'We had better have him round to the yard,' said M. Thomas. 'If you will go through I shall show him the way.'

The yard was a small open area surrounded by sheds. Into one of these the cart was backed and the cask unpacked. M. Thomas examined it.

'That's certainly one of our casks,' he said. 'They are our own design and, so far as I am aware, are used by no one else.'

'But, M. Thomas,' said Lefarge, 'can you identify it in any special manner? We do not, of course, doubt what you have said, but if it could be established that this particular cask had passed through your yard it would be important. Otherwise, if you judge only by likeness to type, we cannot be sure that someone has not copied your design to try and start a false scent.'

'I see what you mean, but I fear I cannot certify what you want. But I'll call the foreman and packers. Possibly some of them can help you.'

He went into another of the sheds, returning immediately with four men.

'Look at that cask, men,' he said. 'Have any of you ever seen it before?'

The men advanced and inspected the cask minutely, looking at it from all sides. Two of them retreated, shaking their heads, but the third, an elderly man with white hair, spoke up.

'Yes,' he said. 'I packed this cask not a fortnight ago.'

'How are you so certain of that?' asked Lefarge.

'By this, monsieur,' said the man, pointing to the broken stave. 'That stave was split. I remember quite well the shape of the crack. I noticed it, and wondered if I should report it to the foreman, and then I thought it was safe enough and didn't. But I told my mate about it. See here, Jean,' he called to the fourth man, 'is that the crack I showed you some days ago, or is it only like it?'

The fourth man advanced and inspected it in his turn.

'It's the same one,' he said confidently. 'I know, because I thought that split was the shape of my hand, and so it is.'

He placed his hand on the adjoining stave, and there certainly was a rude resemblance in shape.

'I suppose neither of you men remember what you packed in it, or whom it was for?'

'As far as I remember,' said the third man, 'it was a statue of three or four women, but I don't remember who it was for.'

'It wasn't for a man called Felix, of London?'

'I remember the name, but I can't say if it was for him.'

'Thank you. Would you tell me how it was packed? What steadied the group?'

'Sawdust, monsieur, simply sawdust, carefully rammed.'

'Can you tell me if the railway cart took it from here, or how did it go?'

'No, monsieur, it was taken by one of our own motor lorries from the Grenelle works.'

'Did you know the driver?'

'Yes, monsieur, it was Jules Fouchard.'

'I suppose, monsieur,' Lefarge turned to the managing director, 'we could interview this man Fouchard?'

'Why, certainly. M. Thomas will find out where he is.'

'Pardon, messieurs,' interposed the elderly packer, 'but he's here now. Or at least I saw him not ten minutes ago.'

'Good. Then try and find him, and tell him not to go away till we have seen him.'

In a few moments the driver was found and, having asked him to wait outside, Lefarge continued his questions to the packer.

'At what o'clock did the cask leave here?'

'About four. I had it packed and ready by two, but the lorry did not come for a couple of hours after that.'

'Did you see it loaded up?'

'I helped to load it up.'

'Now tell me,' continued Lefarge, 'where was the cask between the time you put the group in and the arrival of the motor?'

'Here, monsieur, in this shed where I packed it.'

'And did you leave it during that time?'

'No, monsieur, I was here all the time.'

'So that – please be very careful about this – no one could have tampered with it in any way up till the time it left the yard?'

'Absolutely impossible, monsieur. It is quite out of the question.'

'Thank you, we are exceedingly obliged to you,' said Lefarge, slipping a couple of francs into the man's hand as he withdrew. 'Now, could I see the lorry driver?'

Jules Fouchard proved to be a small, energetic-looking man, with sharp features and intelligent eyes. He was sure of his facts, and gave his answers clearly and without hesitation.

'M. Fouchard,' began Lefarge, 'this gentleman and I are trying to trace the movements of one of your casks, which I am informed left here by your lorry about four o'clock on Tuesday, the thirtieth of March last. Can you recall the occasion?'

'Permit me to get my delivery book, monsieur.'

He disappeared for a moment, returning with a small, cloth-covered book. Rapidly turning over the pages, he found what he was looking for.

'For M. Léon Felix, 141 West Jubb Street, Tottenham Court Road, London? Yes, monsieur, it was the only cask which left here that day. I took it to the Gare St Lazare, and handed it to the railway officials. Here is their signature for it.'

He passed the book over and Lefarge read the name. 'Thank you. Who is this Jean Duval? I shall probably want to see him and would like to know where to find him.'

'He is a clerk in the departure passenger cloakroom.'

'You left here with the cask, I understand, about four o'clock?'

'About that, monsieur.'

'And what time did you arrive at the Gare St Lazare?'

'Just a few minutes later. I went direct.'

'You didn't stop on the way?'

'No, monsieur.'

'Well now, monsieur, please don't answer till you have considered carefully. Was there any way in which the cask could have been tampered with between the time it was loaded up here and your handing it over to Jean Duval at the Gare St Lazare?'

'None, monsieur. No one could have got on the lorry without my knowledge, much less have done anything to the cask.'

'And I take it from that, it would have been equally impossible to remove it entirely and substitute another?'

'It would have been absolutely out of the question, monsieur.'

After thanking and dismissing the driver, they returned to the manager's room.

'The position, then, seems to be this,' said Lefarge, as they sat down. 'The cask left your yard containing a group of statuary, and it arrived in London containing the dead body of a woman. The change must therefore have been effected along the route, and the evidence of the steamer people seems to narrow it down to between here and Rouen.'

'Why Rouen?' asked both gentlemen in a breath.

'Well, I should have said, perhaps, between here and the time of loading on to the steamer at Rouen wharf.'

'But I am afraid you are making a mistake there,' said M. Thomas, 'the cask went by Havre. All our stuff does.'

'Pardon me, M. Thomas, for seeming to contradict you,' said Burnley, in his somewhat halting French, 'but I am as certain of it as of my presence here now: however the cask may have been sent, it certainly arrived in the London Docks by the Insular and Continental Steam Navigation Company's boat from Rouen.'

'But that is most mysterious,' rejoined Thomas. He struck a bell and a clerk appeared.

'Bring me the railway papers about the sending of that cask to Felix, London, on the thirtieth ultimo.'

'Here you are,' he said to Burnley, when the clerk returned. 'Look at that. That is the receipt from the St Lazare people for the freight on the cask between this and the address in London, per passenger train via Havre and Southampton.'

'Well,' said Burnley, 'this gets me altogether. Tell me,' he added after a pause, 'when Felix telephoned you from London asking when and by what route you were sending the cask, what did you reply?'

'I told him it was crossing on Tuesday night, the 30th March, by Havre and Southampton.'

'We'd better go to St Lazare,' said Lefarge. 'Perhaps M. Thomas will kindly lend us that receipt?'

'Certainly, but you must please sign for it, as I shall want it for my audit.'

They parted with expressions of thanks on the part of the detectives, who promised to keep the others advised of the progress of the inquiry.

A taxi brought them to St Lazare where, at the office of the superintendent of the line, Lefarge's card had the usual magical effect.

'Please be seated, gentlemen,' said the superintendent, 'and let me know what I can do for you.'

Lefarge showed him the receipt.

'The matter is somewhat puzzling,' he said. 'That cask, as you see, was invoiced out via Havre and Southampton on the 30th ultimo, and yet it turned up in London on Monday, the 5th instant, by the Insular and Continental Steam Navigation Company's boat *Bullfinch* from Rouen. The contents of the cask when it left Messrs Dupierre's showroom was a group of statuary, but when it arrived at St Katharine's Docks – well, I may tell you, monsieur, in confidence – it contained the body of a woman – murdered.'

The superintendent gave an exclamation of surprise.

'You see, therefore, monsieur, the necessity of our tracing the cask as privately as possible.'

'I certainly do. If you will wait a few minutes, gentlemen, I can get you part at least of the information you want.'

The few minutes had expanded into nearly an hour before the superintendent returned.

'Sorry to have kept you so long,' he apologised. 'I find that your cask was delivered at our outward passenger cloakroom at about 4.15 p.m. on the 30th ultimo. It remained there until about 7.0 p.m., and during all this time it was under the personal supervision of one of the clerks named Duval, a most conscientious and reliable man. He states it stood in full view of his desk, and it would have been quite impossible for anyone to have tampered with it. He particularly remembers it from its peculiar shape and its weight, as well as because it was an unusual object to send by passenger train. At about 7.0 p.m. it was taken charge of by two porters and placed in the van of the 7.47 p.m. English boat train. The guard of the train was present when they put it into the van, and he should have been there till the train left. The guard is unfortunately off duty at present, but I have sent for him and will get his statement. Once the train left, the cask would simply be bound to go to Havre. If it had not done so with that insurance on it, we should have heard about it. However, I will communicate with our agent at Havre, and I should be able to get definite information in the morning.'

'But, my dear sir,' cried Burnley helplessly, 'I know of my own knowledge that it came by long sea from Rouen. I don't for one moment doubt your word, but there must be a mistake somewhere.'

'Ah,' returned the superintendent, smiling, 'now I come to something that will interest you. The cask we have just spoken of was sent out on the evening of the 30th ult. But I find another cask was despatched three days later, on the 1st instant. It also was addressed to M. Felix at the same London address and sent in by Messrs Dupierre. It was labelled via Rouen and the I and C Company's boat. It went by goods train that night, and I will get our Rouen agent to try and trace it, though, as he would have had no reason to remark it, I doubt if he will be able to do so.'

Burnley swore. 'I beg your pardon, sir, but this gets deeper and deeper. Two casks!' He groaned.

'At least,' said the superintendent, 'it has cleared up your difficulty about how a cask that left by one route arrived by another.'

'It has done that, monsieur, and we are really extremely obliged for all your kindness and trouble.'

'If there is anything else I can do I shall be very pleased.'

'Thank you again. The only other point is to trace the cart that brought the second cask.'

'Ah,' the superintendent shook his head, 'I can't do that for you, you know.'

'Of course not. But perhaps you could get hold of, or put us in a position to get hold of your men who received the cask? We might get some information from them.'

'I shall do what I can. Now, gentlemen, if you will call any time in the morning, I shall let you have any further information I receive.'

The detectives, having thanked him again, bowed themselves out and, strolling up and down the vast concourse, discussed their plans.

'I should like to wire to London now, and also to write by tonight's post,' said Burnley. 'They'll want to get on to tracing that second cask from Waterloo as soon as possible.'

'Well, the ordinary letter boxes are cleared at half-past six, but if you are late you can post in the van of the English mail at the Gare du Nord up till 9.10 p.m., so you have plenty of time for that later. What about sending your wire from here now, and then going to the Hotel Continental to look up your friend Felix?'

Burnley agreed, and when the telegram had been sent they took another taxi and drove to the Continental. Lefarge's card produced immediately a polite and agreeable manager, anxious to assist.

'We are trying to trace a man whom we believe stayed here recently,' explained Lefarge. 'His name was Léon Felix.'

'A rather short and slight man with a black beard and a pleasing manner?' replied the manager. 'Oh yes, I know M. Felix very well, and very pleasant I have always found him. He was here recently. I will inquire the exact dates.'

He disappeared for a few seconds. 'He was here from Saturday, the 13th of March till Monday, the 15th. Then he returned on Friday, the 26th, and left again on the morning of Sunday, the 28th, to catch the 8.20 train for England at the Gare du Nord.'

The two detectives exchanged glances of surprise.

'Could you let me compare his signature in your register with one I have here?' asked Burnley. 'I am anxious to make sure it is the same man.'

'Certainly,' replied the manager, leading the way.

The signature was the same, and, after thanking the manager, they took their departure.

'That's an unexpected find,' Burnley remarked. 'Felix said nothing to me about being here ten days ago.'

'It's a bit suggestive, you know,' returned his companion. 'We'll have to find out what he was doing during the visit.'

Burnley nodded.

'Now for my report, anyway,' he said.

'I think I'll go to the Sûreté and do the same,' answered Lefarge.

They parted, having arranged to meet later in the evening. Burnley wrote a detailed account of his day to his Chief, asking him to have inquiries made at Waterloo about the second cask. Having posted it, he gave himself up to a study of Felix's letter ordering the group of statuary.

It was written on a sheet of the same kind of paper as those of the two typewritten letters received by Felix. Burnley carefully compared the watermarks and satisfied himself on the point. Then, drawing from his pocket the address he had got Felix to write in the house on the Great North Road, he compared them.

The handwriting was the same in each, at least that was his first impression, but on a closer examination he felt somewhat less certain. He was not a handwriting expert, but he had come across a good many of these men, and was aware of some of their methods. He applied those he knew and at last came to the conclusion that Felix had written the order, though a certain doubt remained. He wrote another note to his Chief and enclosed the two letters, asking him to have them compared.

Then he went out to spend the evening with Lefarge.

13

THE OWNER OF THE DRESS

When some time later the two friends met, Lefarge said: 'I saw the Chief, and he's not very satisfied with the way things are going. None of those women have done anything with the clothes. He's got a notion we ought to advertise and he wants us to go there at nine tonight and talk it over.'

Accordingly, at the hour named, they presented themselves at the office in the Sûreté.

'Sit down, gentlemen,' began the Chief. 'I wanted to consult with you about this case. In our efforts to identify the dead woman, which we agreed was our first essential we have unfortunately had no success. Our three women have done exceedingly well as far as covering ground goes, but they have had no luck. You, gentlemen, have found out some important facts, but they have not led in this particular direction. Now, I am inclined to think we ought to advertise and I'd like to hear your views.'

'What particular advertisements do you suggest, sir?' asked Burnley.

'For everything. Advertise, in each case with 100 francs reward, for information about the dress, the underclothes if singular in any way, the rings, the comb, and the body itself.'

There was silence for a few moments, and then Burnley replied hesitatingly: 'We have a bit of prejudice at Scotland

Yard about advertising except in special cases. I think the idea is that it puts people on their guard who might otherwise give themselves away. But in this case it would probably be the quickest way to a result.'

'To me it would seem,' said Lefarge, 'that even if there was a band of persons anxious to hush this murder up, there would also be enough outside that band to answer every one of the advertisements.'

'That is rather my view,' agreed the Chief. 'Take the servants, for example. A woman wearing such clothes is certain to have lived in a house with several servants. Someone of them is bound to read the advertisement and recognise the description. If he or she intends to try for the reward we get the information, if not, he will certainly show the paper to the others, one of whom is almost certain to come. The same thing applies to shop assistants, none of whom could conceivably wish to keep the thing a secret. Yes, I think we'll try it. Will you draft out some forms, something like this, I should imagine. "One hundred francs reward will be paid for information leading to the identification of the body of a lady, believed to have died about the 30th March" – say "died," of course, not "was murdered" – then the description, and "Apply at any Police Station." The others would be for information leading to the identification of the purchaser of the various clothes.'

'I shall have to see the three ladies for a proper description of the clothes,' said Lefarge.

'Of course. I'll send for them.'

M. Chauvet telephoned to the department in question, and, after a delay of a few minutes, the three female detectives came in. With their help the advertisements were drawn up, and when the Chief had read and approved they were telephoned to the principal papers for insertion next day. Special trade journals relating to the millinery and jewellery trades were also supplied with copies for their next issues.

'By the way,' observed M. Chauvet, when the women had left, 'I have had a report about the lottery business. M. Le Gautier is correct on both points. He paid in the cheque on the date stated, and the drawing does not take place till next Thursday. The probabilities seem therefore to point to his being an honest man and having had nothing to do with the letter. And now, with regard to tomorrow. What do you propose?'

'First, monsieur, we thought of going to the Gare St Lazare to see if the superintendent has any further information for us. I thought we should then try and trace back the cask that went via Rouen.'

'Very good. I think I shall try another scent also, though not a very promising one. I shall put on a couple of men to go round the fashionable photographers with that photo of yours, and try if they can find a portrait of the woman. I had rather you could have done it' – he looked at Burnley – 'because you have seen the body, but they may get something. That's all, then, is it not? Good night.'

'Hard lines being done out of our evening,' said Lefarge, when they had left the great man's room. 'I was going to propose the Folies Bergères. It's not too late yet, though. What do you say?'

'I'm on,' answered Burnley, 'but I don't want to stay more than an hour or so. I can always work better on plenty of sleep.'

'Right,' returned Lefarge, and, calling a taxi, the two friends were driven to the famous music hall.

Lefarge called for Burnley the next morning at the latter's hotel, and they made their way to the superintendent's office at the Gare St Lazare.

'Well, gentlemen,' said their friend of the previous afternoon, motioning them to be seated, 'I think I've got the information you want.' He took up some papers. 'I have here the receipt of the Southampton boat people for what we may call number one cask, which was handed them on the arrival of the 7.47 from this station on the night of the 30th ult. Here,' he took up a similar paper, 'I have the receipt of the I and C Steam Navigation Co. at Rouen for cask number two, which left here by goods train on the 1st inst., and was got on board on the 3rd. Finally, our agent at the Goods Station at the rue Cardinet informs me he has found the porters who assisted to unload this number two cask when it arrived. You can see them by going down there now.'

'I can hardly find words to thank you, sir,' said Lefarge, 'your help has been of the utmost value.'

'Delighted, I am sure.'

They parted with mutual compliments, and the detectives took a Ceinture train to Batignoles, and walked down the rue Cardinet to the vast goods station.

They introduced themselves to the agent, who was expecting them, and brought them through long passages and across wide yards alive with traffic to a dock in the side of one of the huge goods sheds for outward bound traffic. Calling up two blue-bloused porters and instructing them to answer the detectives' questions, he excused himself and took his leave.

'Now, men,' said Lefarge, 'we'll be much obliged for some information and there'll be a few francs going if you can give it.'

The men expressed anxiety to supply whatever was needed.

'Do you remember on Thursday week, the 1st instant, unloading a cask labelled for Felix, London, via Rouen and long sea?'

'But yes, monsieur, we remember it,' said the men in chorus.

'You must unload hundreds of casks. How did you come to notice this one so specially?'

'Ah, monsieur,' replied one of the men, 'had monsieur had to lift it himself he also would have noticed it. The weight was remarkable, extraordinary. The shape also was peculiar. In the middle there was no bulge.'

'At what time did it arrive here?'

'Just after six in the evening, monsieur, between five and ten minutes past.'

'It is a good while since then. How do you come to remember the time so exactly?'

'Because, monsieur,' the man smiled, 'we were going off duty at half-past six, and we were watching the time.'

'Can you tell me who brought it to the yard?'

The men shrugged their shoulders.

'Alas! monsieur, we do not know,' the spokesman answered. 'The carter we would recognise if we saw him again, but neither of us know where he lives nor the name of his employers.'

'Can you describe him?'

'But certainly, monsieur. He was a small man, thin and sickly-looking, with white hair and a clean-shaven face.'

'Well, keep a good lookout, and if you see him again find out who he is and let me know. Here is my address. If you do that there will be fifty francs for you.'

Lefarge handed over a couple of five franc pieces and the detectives left, followed by the promises and thanks of the men.

'I suppose an advertisement for the carter is the next scheme,' said Burnley, as they walked back in the Clichy direction,

'We had better report to headquarters, I think,' replied Lefarge, 'and see what the Chief advises. If he approves, we might get our advertisement into tonight's papers.'

Burnley agreed, and when they had had some lunch they rang up the Sûreté from the nearest call office.

'That Lefarge?' was the answer. 'The Chief wants you to return immediately. He's got some news.'

They took the Metro from Clichy to Chatelet and reached the Sûreté as the clocks were striking two. M. Chauvet was in.

'Ah,' he said, as they entered, 'we've had a reply to the dress advertisement. Madame Clothilde's people near the Palais Royal rang up about eleven saying they believed they had supplied the dress. We got hold of Mlle. Lecoq, who was working it, and sent her over, and she returned here about an hour ago. The dress was sold in February to Madame Annette Boirac, at the corner of Avenue de l'Alma and rue St Jean, not far from the American Church. You'd better go round there now and make some inquiries.'

'Yes, monsieur,' said Lefarge, 'but before we go there is this question of the cask,' and he told what they had learnt, and suggested the advertisement about the carter.

M. Chauvet had just begun his reply when a knock came to the door and a boy entered with a card.

'The gentleman's waiting to see you on urgent business monsieur,' he said.

'Hallo!' said the Chief, with a gesture of surprise. 'Listen to this.' He read out the words, "M. Raoul Boirac, rue St Jean, 1, Avenue de l'Alma." This will be Mme. Annette B's husband, I presume. These advertisements are doing well. You had better stop, both of you,' and then to the boy, 'Wait a moment.'

He picked up the telephone, pressing one of the buttons on its stand. 'Send Mlle. Joubert here immediately.'

In a few moments a girl stenographer entered. M. Chauvet pointed to a corner of the room where Burnley had noticed a screen, set back as if to be out of the way.

'I want every word of this conversation, mademoiselle,' said the Chief. 'Please be careful to miss none of it, and also to keep quiet.'

The girl bowed and, having seen her settled behind the screen, the Chief turned to the messenger.

'I'll see him now.'

In a few seconds M. Boirac entered the room. He was a strongly built man of rather under middle age, with thick black hair and a large moustache. On his face was an expression of strain, as if he was passing through a period of acute bodily or mental pain. He was dressed entirely in black and his manner was quiet and repressed.

He looked round the room and then, as M. Chauvet rose to greet him, he bowed ceremoniously. 'M. le Chef de la Sûreté?' he asked, and, as M. Chauvet bowed him to a chair, continued, – 'I have called to see you, monsieur, on a very painful matter. I had hoped to have been able to do so alone,' he paused slightly, 'but these gentlemen, I presume, are completely in your confidence?' He spoke slowly with a deliberate pronunciation of each word, as if he had thought out whether that was the best possible he could use and had come to the conclusion that it was.

159

'If, monsieur,' returned M. Chauvet, 'your business is in connection with the recent unfortunate disappearance of your wife, these gentlemen are the officers who are in charge of the case, and their presence would be, I think, to the advantage of all of us.'

M. Boirac sprang from his chair, deep emotion showing under his iron control.

'Then it is she?' he asked, in a suppressed voice. 'You know? It seemed possible from the advertisement, but I wasn't sure. I hoped – that perhaps – There is no doubt, I suppose?'

'I shall tell you all we know, M. Boirac, and you can form your own conclusions. First, here is a photograph of the body found.'

M. Boirac took the slip of card and looked at it earnestly.

'It is she,' he murmured hoarsely, 'it is she without a doubt.'

He paused, overcome, and, the others respecting his feelings, there was silence for some moments. Then with a strenuous effort he continued, speaking barely above a whisper, – 'Tell me,' his voice shook as he pronounced the words with difficulty, 'what makes her look so terrible? And those awful marks at her throat? What are they?'

'It is with the utmost regret I have to tell you, M. Boirac, that your wife was undoubtedly murdered by strangulation. Further, you must know that she had been dead several days when that photograph was taken.'

M. Boirac dropped into his chair, and sunk his head in his hands.

'My God!' he panted. 'My poor Annette! Though I had no cause to love her, I did, God help me, in spite of everything, I did. I know it now when I have lost her. Tell me,' he continued in a low tone after another pause, 'tell me the details.'

'I fear they are rather harrowing, monsieur,' said the Chief, with sympathetic sorrow in his tone. 'A certain cask was noticed by the London police, a detail, with which I need hardly trouble you, having aroused their suspicions. The cask was seized and opened, and the body was found inside.'

The visitor remained with his face buried in his hands. After a few seconds he raised himself and looked at M. Chauvet.

'Any clue?' he asked, in a choking tone. 'Have you any clue to the villain who has done this?'

'We have a number of clues,' returned the Chief, 'but have not yet had time to work them. I have no doubt that we will have our hands on the murderer shortly. In the meantime, M. Boirac, to make assurance doubly sure, I would be glad if you would see if you can identify these clothes.'

'Her clothes? Oh, spare me that. But there, I understand it is necessary.'

M. Chauvet picked up his telephone and gave directions for the clothes to be sent in. The jewellery was not available, as Mlle. Blaise had taken it in her round of the shops.

'Alas! Yes,' cried M. Boirac sadly, when he saw the dress, 'it is hers, it is hers. She wore it the evening she left. There can be no further doubt. My poor, mistaken Annette!'

'I am afraid, M. Boirac, at the risk of giving you pain, I must ask you to be good enough to tell us all you can about the circumstances of your wife's disappearance. These gentlemen are Mr Burnley of the London police, and M. Lefarge of our own staff, and they are collaborating in the matter. You may speak before them with complete freedom.'

M. Boirac bowed.

'I will tell you everything, monsieur, but you must pardon me if I seem a little incoherent. I am not myself.'

M. Chauvet stepped to a press and took from it a flask of brandy.

'Monsieur,' he said, 'you have our fullest sympathy. Allow me to offer you a little of this.' He poured out a stiff glass.

'I thank you, monsieur,' returned the visitor, as he drank the cordial. It pulled him together, and he became once more the unemotional man of business. He kept himself well in hand and did not, during the telling of his story, allow his emotion to overcome him, though at times it was clear all his powers of self-control were needed. In a stronger voice he began his statement, and his three companions settled themselves more comfortably in their chairs to listen.

14

M. BOIRAC MAKES A STATEMENT

'My name and address you know,' began M. Boirac. 'In business I am the managing director of the Avrotte Pump Construction Co, whose works are situated off the rue Championnet, not far from the Omnibus Co's depot. I am fairly well off, and we lived comfortably, my wife going a good deal into society.

'On Saturday, the 27th ult., this day fortnight, we had a dinner party at the Avenue de l'Alma. Our principal guest was the Spanish ambassador, at whose house my wife had visited when in Madrid the previous year. Among the others was a M. Léon Felix, an old friend of my wife's, who lived in London, and was in some business there. The guests arrived and we sat down to dinner, but unfortunately before the meal was concluded a telephone message came for me from the works to say that a serious accident had happened, and requiring my immediate presence. There was nothing for it but to apologise to my guests and go off at once, which I did, though I promised to return at the earliest possible moment.

'When I reached the works I found that the main bed casting of a new 200-h.p. engine which was being put in during the weekend, had slipped and slewed sideways while being got into place, killing one man and seriously injuring two others. One of the cylinders was fractured, and the whole casting had jammed between the wall and the flywheel pit and could not be got out.

'As soon as I saw how serious things were, I telephoned home to say I would be very late, and that there would be no chance of my returning in time to see my guests. However, we got on much better than I expected, and it was barely eleven when I turned out of the works. Not seeing a taxi, I walked to the Simplon station of the Metro. My route, as you will understand, involved a change of trains at Chatelet and I accordingly alighted there. I had hardly done so when I was clapped on the back by someone, and turning, found an American acquaintance called Myron H. Burton, with whom I had stayed in the same hotel in New York and with whom I had become friendly. We stood in talk for some time, and then I asked him where he was staying, inviting him to put up at my house instead of returning to his hotel. He declined, saying he was going to Orleans by the 12.35 from the Quai d'Orsay, and asked me to go and see him off and have a drink at the station. I hesitated, but remembering I was not expected at home, I agreed and we set off. The night being mild and pleasant we walked along the quais, but when we reached the Pont Royal it was barely a quarter to twelve. Burton suggested continuing our stroll, which we did, going round the Place de la Concorde and the end of the Champs Élysées. Interested in our talk, we forgot the passage of time, and arrived at the Gare Quai d'Orsay with only a minute to spare for my friend to catch his train and, therefore, to his apparent great chagrin, missing the drinks to which he had wished to treat me. I felt wakeful, and began to walk home, but when I had gone about halfway, rain began to fall. I looked for a taxi, but could not see one, and therefore continued my journey on foot, arriving home about one o'clock.

'François, the butler, met me in the hall. He seemed uneasy.

' "I heard the front door bang not ten minutes ago, monsieur," he said, as I took off my wet coat. "I got up to see if anything was wrong."

' "Got up?" I said. "How had you come to go to bed before I returned?"

' "Madame told me to, monsieur, about half-past eleven. She said you would be very late and that she would be sitting up."

' "All right," I said, "where is Madame?"

He hesitated.

' "I don't know, monsieur," he said at length.

' "Don't know?" I said. I was growing angry. "Has she gone to bed?"

' "She has not gone to bed, monsieur," he answered.

'I am not, M. le Chef, an imaginative man, but suddenly a feeling of foreboding swept over me. I hurried into the drawing-room and from that to my wife's small sitting-room. They were both empty. I ran to her bedroom. There was no one there. Then I recollected she had frequently waited for me in my study. I went there to find it also untenanted, and I was just about to withdraw when I saw on my desk a letter which had not been there earlier in the evening. It was addressed to me in my wife's handwriting, and, with a terrible sinking of the heart, I opened it. Here, M. Le Chef, it is.'

It was a short note, written on a sheet of cream-laid notepaper in a woman's hand and without date or address. It read:

I do not ask you to forgive me for what I am doing tonight, Raoul, for I feel it would be quite too much to expect, but I do ask you to believe that the thought of the pain and annoyance it will be bound to give you cuts me to the heart. You have always been just and kind according to your lights, but you know, Raoul, as well as I do, that we have never loved each other. You have loved your business and your art collection, and I have loved – Léon Felix, and now I am going to him. I shall just disappear, and you will never hear of me again. You, I hope, will get your divorce, and be happy with some more worthy woman.

Goodbye, Raoul, and do not think worse of me than you can help.

ANNETTE

M. Boirac bowed his head while the others read this unhappy note. He seemed overcome with emotion, and there was silence in the Chief's room for a few seconds. The sun shone gaily in with never a hint of tragedy, lighting up that bent figure in the armchair, and bringing into pitiless prominence details that should have been cloaked decently in shadow, from the drops of moisture on the drawn brow to the hands clenched white beneath the edge of the desk. Then, as they waited, he pulled himself together with an effort and continued: 'I was almost beside myself from the blow, and yet I instinctively felt I must act as if nothing had happened. I steadied myself and called to François, who was still in the hall: ' "It's all right, François. I've had a note from Madame. She was obliged to go out at a moment's notice to catch the Swiss train. She had a message that her mother is dying."

'He replied in his ordinary tone, but I could see that he did not believe one word. The understanding and the pity in his eyes almost drove me frantic. I spoke again as carelessly as I could, – ' "I wonder had she time to call Suzanne and get properly dressed. You might send her here and then you can get back to bed."

'Suzanne was my wife's maid, and when she came into the study I saw from her startled and embarrassed air that she knew.

' "Suzanne," I said, "Madame has had to go to Switzerland suddenly and unexpectedly. She had to rush off to catch the train without proper time for packing, still, I hope she was able to take enough for the journey?"

'The girl answered at once in a nervous, frightened tone. "I have just been to her room, monsieur. She has taken her fur coat and hat and a pair of walking shoes. The evening shoes she was wearing tonight are there where she changed them. She did not ring for me and I did not hear her go to her room."

'I had become somewhat calmer by this time, and I was thinking rapidly while she spoke.

' "Ah, well," I answered, "you had better pack some of her things tomorrow so that I can send them after her. She will be staying with her mother, and will no doubt be able to borrow what she wants till her own things arrive."

'François was still hanging about the corridor. I sent them both to bed and sat down to try and realise what had taken place.

'I need hardly trouble you with my thoughts. For some days I was half crazed, then I pulled myself together. Suzanne I sent home, saying I had heard from Madame that she was employing one of her mother's maids.'

M. Boirac paused.

'That,' he said at length, 'I think is all I have to tell you, M. le Chef. From that awful evening until I saw your advertisement in the *Figaro* a couple of hours ago, I have not heard a syllable from either my wife or Felix.'

M. Boirac had told his story simply and directly, and his manner seemed to bear the impress of truth. The statement carried conviction to his hearers, who felt their sympathy going out to this man who had acted so loyally to the wife who had betrayed him. M. Chauvet spoke – 'Permit me to express to you, M. Boirac, our deep regret for what has happened and particularly for your having had to come here and make this painful statement. Still more we regret that the terrible *dénouement* should make it almost impossible to keep the matter hushed up. Our search for the murderer has, of course, begun. We shall not detain you any longer, except to ask you to repeat a few names and hours so that we may note them to make your statement complete.'

'I thank you for your courtesy, M. le Chef.'

The Chief continued, – 'There is first of all your address. That we have on your card. Next – I shall put it in question form – What time was dinner?'

'Quarter to eight.'

'And what time did the message come for you from your works?'

'About a quarter to nine.'

'And you arrived there?'

'About nine-fifteen, I should think, I did not look. I walked to the Champs Élysées and took a taxi.'

'You said, I think, that you telephoned home then informing your wife that you could not return until very late?'

'I believe I did say that, but it is not strictly correct. I went to see the damage immediately on arrival, and was occupied there for some time. I should say I telephoned about ten o'clock.'

'But you unexpectedly got away about eleven?'

'That is so.'

'So that you must have met your friend at Chatelet about twenty past eleven?'

'About that, I should think.'

'Now your friend. I should like a note of his name and address.'

'His name I have already given you, Myron H. Burton. His address I unfortunately cannot, as I do not know it.'

'His home address, then?'

'I don't know that, either. I met him in an hotel in New York. We played billiards together a few times and became friendly enough, but not to the extent of exchanging our family histories.'

'When was that, M. Boirac?'

'In the summer of 1908, no, 1909, three years ago.'

'And the hotel?'

'The Hudson View, the one that was burnt out last Christmas.'

'I remember, a terrible business, that. Your friend went by the 12.35 to Orleans. He was staying there I suppose?'

'No, he was changing there and going on, though where he was going to I do not know. He told me this because I remarked on his choosing such a train – it does not get in until about 4.30 – instead of sleeping in Paris and going by an early express that would do the journey in two hours.'

'Oh, well, it is not of much importance. The only other thing, I think, is the name and address of your wife's maid.'

M. Boirac shook his head.

'I'm sorry I can't give you that either. I only know her as Suzanne. But I dare say François or some of the other servants would know it.'

'I shall have, with your permission, to send a man to look over the house, and he can make inquiries. I am sure, M. Boirac, we are extremely obliged to you for your information. And now, what about the formal identification of the body? I have no doubt from what you say it is indeed that of your wife, but I fear the law will require a personal identification from you. Would it be convenient for you to run over to London and see it? Interment has not yet, I understand, taken place.'

M. Boirac moved uneasily. The suggestion was clearly most unwelcome to him.

'I needn't say I would infinitely prefer not to go. However, if you assure me it is necessary, I can have no choice in the matter.'

'I am exceedingly sorry, but I fear it is quite necessary. A personal examination is required in evidence of identification. And if I might make a suggestion, I think that the visit should be made as soon as convenient to you.'

The visitor shrugged his shoulders.

'If I have to go, I may as well do it at once. I will cross tonight and be at Scotland Yard at, say, 11.0 tomorrow. It is Scotland Yard, I suppose?'

'It is, monsieur. Very good. I will telephone to the authorities there to expect you.'

The Chief rose and shook hands, and M. Boirac took his leave. When he had gone, M. Chauvet jumped up and went to the screen.

'Get half a dozen copies of that statement and the questions and answers typed at once, mademoiselle. You can get a couple of the other girls to help you.'

He turned to the two detectives.

'Well, gentlemen, we have heard an interesting story, and, whatever we may think of it, our first business will be to check it as far as we can. I think you had better get away immediately to the Avenue de l'Alma and see this François, if possible before Boirac gets back. Go through the house and get anything you can, especially a sample of the wife's handwriting. Try also and trace the maid. In the meantime, I will set some other inquiries on foot. You might call in about nine tonight to report progress.'

15

THE HOUSE IN THE AVENUE DE L'ALMA

Burnley and Lefarge took the tram along the quais and, dismounting at the Pont Alma, proceeded up the Avenue on foot. The house was a corner one fronting on the Avenue, but with the entrance in the side street. It was set a few feet back from the footpath, and was a Renaissance building of grey rubble masonry, with moulded architraves and enrichments of red sandstone and the usual mansard roof.

The two men mounted the steps leading to the ornate porch. On their right were the windows of a large room which formed the angle between the two streets.

'You can see into that room rather too clearly for my taste,' said Burnley. 'Why, if that's the drawing-room, as it looks to be by the furniture, every caller can see just who's visiting there as they come up to the door.'

'And conversely, I expect,' returned Lefarge, 'the hostess can see her visitors coming and be prepared for them.'

The door was opened by an elderly butler of typical appearance, respectability and propriety oozing out of every pore of his sleek face. Lefarge showed his card.

'I regret M. Boirac is not at home, monsieur,' said the man politely, 'but you will probably find him at the works in the rue Championnet.'

'Thanks,' returned Lefarge, 'we have just had an interview with M. Boirac, and it is really you we wish to see.'

The butler ushered them into a small sitting-room at the back of the hall.

'Yes, messieurs?' he said.

'Did you see an advertisement in this morning's papers for the identification of a lady's body?'

'I saw it, monsieur.'

'I am sorry to say it was that of your mistress.'

François shook his head sadly.

'I feared as much, monsieur,' he said in a low tone.

'M. Boirac saw the advertisement also. He came just now to the Sûreté and identified the remains beyond any doubt. It is a painful case, for I regret to tell you she had been murdered in a rather brutal way, and now we are here with M. Boirac's approval to make some enquiries.'

The old butler's face paled.

'Murdered!' he repeated in a horrified whisper. 'It couldn't be. No one that knew her could do that. Every one, messieurs, loved Madame. She was just an angel of goodness.'

The man spoke with real feeling in his voice and seemed overcome with emotion.

'Well, messieurs,' he continued, after a pause, 'any help I can give you to get your hands on the murderer I'll give with real delight, and I only hope you'll succeed soon.'

'I hope so too, François. We'll do our best anyway. Now, please, will you answer some questions. You remember M. Boirac being called to the works on Saturday the 27th of March, the evening of the dinner party, at about a quarter to nine. That was about the time, wasn't it?'

'Yes, monsieur.'

'He went out at once?'

'He did, monsieur.'

'Then he telephoned at about half-past ten that he could not return until later. Was that about the time?'

'Rather earlier than that, I should think, monsieur. I don't remember exactly, but I should think it was very little, if at all, past ten.'

'About ten, you think? Can you tell me what words he used in that message?'

'He said the accident was serious, and that he would be very late, and possibly might not get back before the morning.'

'You told your mistress, I suppose? Did the guests hear you?'

'No, monsieur, but Madame immediately repeated the message aloud.'

'What happened then?'

'Shortly after that, about 11.0 or 11.15, the guests began to leave.'

'All of them?'

The butler hesitated.

'There was one, a M. Felix, who waited after the others. He was differently situated to them, being a friend of the family. The others were merely acquaintances.'

'And how long did he wait after the others?'

François looked confused and did not immediately reply.

'Well, I don't know, monsieur,' he said slowly. 'You see, it was this way. I happened to have a rather bad headache that evening, and Madame asked me if I was not well – it was just like her to notice such a thing – and she told me to go to bed and not to sit up for Monsieur. She said M. Felix was waiting to get some books and would let himself out.'

'So you went to bed?'

'Yes, monsieur. I thanked her, and went after a little time.'

'About how long?'

'Perhaps half an hour.'

'And had M. Felix gone then?'

'No, monsieur, not at that time.'

'And what happened then?'

'I fell asleep, but woke up suddenly again after about an hour. I felt better and I thought I would see if Monsieur was in and if everything was properly locked up. I got up and went towards the hall, but just as I came to the staircase I heard the front door close. I thought, "That's Monsieur coming in," but there was no sound of anyone moving in the hall and I went down to see.'

'Yes?'

'There was no one there, so I looked into the different rooms. They were all empty, though lighted up. I thought to myself, "This is strange," and I went to find Suzanne, Madame's maid, who was sitting up for her. I asked her had Madame gone to bed, but she said not. "Well," I said, "she's not downstairs. Better go up and see if she's in her room." She went and came down in a moment looking frightened, and said the room was empty, but that Madame's hat and fur coat and a pair of walking shoes were gone. Her evening shoes that she had been wearing were lying on the floor, where she had changed them. I went up myself and we searched around, and then I heard the latch of the front door again and went down. Monsieur was just coming in and, as I took his coat and hat, I told him about hearing the door close. He asked where Madame was, and I answered I did not know. He looked himself, and in the study he found a note which I suppose was from her, for after he had read it he asked no more questions, but told me she had

had to go to Switzerland to her mother, who was ill. But I knew when he got rid of Suzanne two days later that she wasn't coming back.'

'What time did M. Boirac come in?'

'About one o'clock, or a few minutes after.'

'Were his hat and coat wet?'

'Not very wet, monsieur, but he had been evidently walking through rain.'

'You didn't make any further search to see if anything else had been taken, I suppose?'

'Yes. monsieur. Suzanne and I searched the entire house most thoroughly on Sunday.'

'With no result?'

'None, monsieur.'

'I suppose the body could not have been concealed anywhere in the house?'

The butler started as this new idea struck him.

'Why, no, monsieur,' he said, 'it would have been absolutely impossible. I myself looked in every spot and opened everything large enough to contain it.'

'Thank you, I think that's about all I want to know. Can you put me in touch with Suzanne?'

'I believe I can get you her address, monsieur, from one of the parlour maids with whom she was friends.'

'Please do, and in the meantime we shall have a look through the house.'

'You will not require me, monsieur?'

'No, thanks.'

The plan of the downstairs rooms was simple. The hall, which was long and rather narrow, stretched back from the entrance door in the rue St Jean to the staircase in a direction parallel to the Avenue de l'Alma. On the right was the drawing-room, a large apartment in the angle between the two streets, with windows looking out on both. Across the hall, with its door facing that of the drawing-room, was the study, another fine room facing on to the rue St Jean. A small sitting-room, used chiefly by the late Madame Boirac, and the dining-room were situated behind the study and the drawing-room respectively. To the rear of the doors of these latter rooms were the staircase and servants' quarters.

The detectives examined these respective rooms in detail. The furnishing was luxurious and artistic. The drawing-room furniture was Louis Quatorze, with an Aubusson carpet and some cabinets and tables of buhl. There was just enough of good Sèvres and Ormolu, the whole selection and arrangement reflecting the taste of the connoisseur. The dining-room and boudoir gave the same impression of wealth and culture, and the detectives as they passed from room to room were impressed by the excellent taste everywhere exhibited. Though their search was exhaustive it was unfortunately without result.

The study was a typical man's room, except in one respect. There was the usual thick carpet on the floor, the customary book-lined walls, the elaborate desk in the window, and the huge leather armchairs. But there was also what almost amounted to a collection of statuary – figures, groups, friezes, plaques, and reliefs, in marble and bronze. A valuable lot, numerous enough and of sufficient excellence not to have disgraced the art galleries of a city. M. Boirac had clearly the knowledge, as well as the means, to indulge his hobby to a very full extent.

Burnley took his stand inside the door and looked slowly round the room, taking in its every detail in the rather despairing hope that he would see something helpful to his quest. Twice he looked at the various objects before him, observing in the slow, methodical way in which he had trained himself, making sure that he had a clear mental conception of each before going on to the next. And then his gaze became riveted on an object standing on one of the shelves.

It was a white marble group about two feet high of three garlanded women, two standing and one sitting.

'I say,' he said to Lefarge, in a voice of something approaching triumph, 'have you heard of anything like that lately?'

There was no reply, and Burnley, who had not been observing his companion, looked round. Lefarge was on his knees examining with a lens something hidden among the thick pile of the carpet. He was entirely engrossed, and did not appear to have heard Burnley's remark, but as the latter moved over he rose to his feet with a satisfied little laugh.

'Look here!' he cried. 'Look at this!'

Stepping back to the cross wall adjoining the door, he crouched down with his head close to the floor and his eyes fixed on a point on the carpet in a line between himself and the window.

'Do you see anything?' he asked.

Burnley got into the same position, and looked at the carpet.

'No,' he answered slowly, 'I do not.'

'You're not far enough this way. Come here. Now look.'

'Jove!' Burnley cried, with excitement in his tones. 'The cask!'

On the carpet, showing up faintly where the light struck it, was a ring-shaped mark about two foot four inches diameter. The pile was slightly depressed below the general surface, as might have been caused by the rim of a heavy cask.

'I thought so too,' said Lefarge, 'but this makes it quite certain.'

He held out his lens, and indicated the part of the floor he had been scrutinising.

Burnley knelt down and, using the lens, began to push open the interstices of the pile. They were full of a curious kind of dust. He picked out some and examined it on his hand.

'Sawdust!' he exclaimed.

'Sawdust,' returned the other, in a pleased and important tone. 'See here' – he traced a circle on the floor – 'sawdust has been spilled over all this, and there's where the cask stood beside it. I tell you, Burnley, mark my words, we are on to it now. That's where the cask stood while Felix, or Boirac, or both of them together, packed the body into it.'

'By Jove!' Burnley cried again, as he turned over this new idea in his mind. 'I shouldn't wonder if you are right!'

'Of course I'm right. The thing's as plain as a pikestaff. A woman disappears and her body is found packed in sawdust in a cask, and here, in the very house where she vanishes, is the mark of the same cask – a very unusual size, mind you – as well as traces of the sawdust.'

'Ay, it's likely enough. But I don't see the way of it for all that. If Felix did it, how could he have got the cask here and away again?'

'It was probably Boirac.'

'But the alibi? Boirac's alibi is complete.'

'It's complete enough, so far as that goes. But how do we know it's true? We have had no real confirmation of it so far.'

'Except from François. If either Boirac or Felix did it, François must have been in it too, and that doesn't strike me as likely.'

'No, I admit the old chap seems all right. But if they didn't do it, how do you account for the cask being here?'

'Maybe that had something to do with it,' answered Burnley, pointing to the marble group.

Lefarge started.

'But that's what was sent to Felix, surely?' he cried, in surprise.

'It looks like it, but don't say anything. Here's François. Let us ask him.'

The butler entered the room holding a slip of paper which he gave to Lefarge.

'Suzanne's address, messieurs.' Lefarge read:

Mlle. Suzanne Daudet,
rue Popeau, 14B,
Dijon.

'Look here, François,' said the detective, pointing to the marble group. 'When did that come here?'

'Quite recently, monsieur. As you see, Monsieur is a collector of such things, and that is, I think, the latest addition.'

'Can you remember the exact day it arrived?'

'It was about the time of the dinner party, in fact, I remember now distinctly. It was that very day.'

'How was it packed?'

'It was in a cask, monsieur. It was left in here that Saturday morning with the top boards loosened for Monsieur to unpack. He never would trust anyone to do that for him.'

'Was he, then, in the habit of getting these casks?'

'Yes, monsieur, a good many of the statues came in casks.'

'I see. And when was this one unpacked?'

'Two days later, monsieur, on Monday evening.'

'And what happened to the cask?'

'It was returned to the shop. Their cart called for it two or three days later.'

'You don't remember exactly when?'

The butler paused in thought.

'I do not, monsieur. It was on the Wednesday or Thursday following, I believe, but I'm not positive.'

'Thank you, François. There is one other thing I should be greatly obliged if you could do for me. Get me a sample of Madame's writing.'

François shook his head.

'I haven't such a thing, monsieur,' he replied, 'but I can show you her desk, if you would care to look over it.'

They went into the boudoir, and François pointed out a small davenport finished with some delicate carving and with inlaid panels, a beautiful example of the cabinetmaker's art. Lefarge seated himself before it and began to go through the papers it contained.

'Somebody's been before us,' he said. 'There's precious little here.'

He produced a number of old receipted bills and circulars, with some unimportant letters and printed papers, but not a scrap in Madame's handwriting could he discover.

Suddenly François gave an exclamation.

'I believe I can get you what you want, messieurs, if you will wait a moment.'

'Yes,' he said, as he returned a few seconds later, 'this will perhaps do. It was framed in the servants' hall.'

It was a short document giving the work of the different servants, their hours of duty, and other similar information, and was written in the hand, so far as the detectives could recollect, of the letter of farewell to M. Boirac. Lefarge put it away carefully in his notebook.

'Now let us see Madame's room.'

They examined the bedroom, looking particularly for old letters, but without success. Next they interviewed the other servants, also fruitlessly.

'All we want now,' said Lefarge to the old butler, 'is a list of the guests at that dinner, or at least some of them.'

'I can tell you, I think, all of them, monsieur,' returned François, and Lefarge noted the names in his book.

'What time is M. Boirac likely to return?' asked Burnley, when they had finished.

'He should have been here before this, monsieur. He generally gets back by half-past six.'

It was now nearly seven, and, as they waited, they heard his latchkey in the door.

'Ah, messieurs,' he greeted them, 'so you are here already. Any luck?'

'No luck so far, M. Boirac,' replied Lefarge, continuing after a pause: 'There is a point on which we should be obliged for some information, monsieur. It is about this marble group.'

'Yes?'

'Could you tell us the circumstances under which you got it, and of its arrival here?'

'Certainly. I am a collector of such articles, as you must have noticed. Some time ago, in passing Dupierre's in the Boulevard des Capucines, I saw that group and admired it greatly. After some hesitation I ordered it and it arrived – I believe it was the very day of – of the dinner party, either that or the day before – I am not positive. I had the cask containing it brought into the study to unpack myself – I always enjoy unpacking a new purchase – but I was so upset by what had happened I hadn't much heart in doing so. However, on the following Monday evening, to try and distract my thoughts, I did unpack it, and there you see the result.'

'Can you tell me, monsieur,' asked Burnley, 'was M. Felix also interested in such things?'

'He was. He is an artist and painting is therefore his speciality, but he had a good knowledge of sculpture.'

'He wasn't interested in that particular group, I suppose?'

'Well, I can hardly tell you that. I told him about it and described it to him, but, of course, so far as I am aware he had not seen it.'

'Did you happen to mention the price?'

'I did, fourteen hundred francs. That was the thing he specially asked. That, and the shop at which I had bought it. He said he could not afford it then, but that at some time he might try and get another.'

'Well, I think that's all we want to know. Our best thanks, M. Boirac.'

'Good evening, messieurs.'

They bowed themselves out, and, walking to the top of the Avenue, took the Metro to Concorde, from which they passed up the rue Castiglione to the Grands Boulevards to dine and spend the time until they were due back at the Sûreté.

16

INSPECTOR BURNLEY UP AGAINST IT

At nine o'clock that evening the usual meeting was held in the Chief's room at the Sûreté.

'I also have had some news,' said M. Chauvet, when he had heard Burnley's and Lefarge's reports. 'I sent a man up to that pump manufactory and he found out enough to substantiate entirely Boirac's statement of the hours at which he arrived there and left on the night of the accident. There is also a despatch from Scotland Yard. On receipt of Mr Burnley's wire immediate inquiries were made about the cask sent by Havre and Southampton. It appears it arrived all right at Waterloo on the morning after it was despatched from here. It was booked through, as you know, to an address near Tottenham Court Road, and the railway people would in the ordinary course have delivered it by one of their lorries. But just as it was being removed from the van of the train, a man stepped forward and claimed it, saying he was the consignee, that he wished to take it to another address, and that he had a cart and man there for the purpose. He was a man of about medium height, with dark hair and beard, and the clerk thought he was a foreigner, probably French. He gave his name as Léon Felix and produced several envelopes addressed to himself at the Tottenham Court Road address as identification. He signed for, and was handed over the cask, and took it away.

His movements after that were completely lost sight of, and no further traces of him have been discovered. A photo of Felix was shown to the Waterloo people, but while the clerk said it was like the man, neither he nor any of the others would swear to it.

'Inquiries have also been made about Felix. It turns out he is an artist or designer in Messrs Greer and Hood's, the advertisement poster people of Fleet Street. He is not married, but keeps an elderly servant-housekeeper. This woman was on a fortnight's holiday from the 25th of March to the 8th of this month.

'So much for London,' continued M. Chauvet. 'Now, let us see what we have still to do. First, that lady's maid at Dijon must be interviewed. I think, Lefarge, you might do that. Tomorrow is Sunday. Suppose you go tomorrow. You could sleep at Dijon, and get back as early as possible on Monday. Then, Mr Burnley, that matter of the statue sent to M. Boirac must be gone into. Perhaps you would be good enough to make inquiries at Dupierre's on Monday morning, and please keep in touch with me by phone. I will look into some other points, and we shall meet here at the same time that evening.'

The detectives took the Metro at Chatelet, Burnley going west to his hotel in the rue Castiglione, and Lefarge east to the Gare de Lyons.

On Monday morning Burnley called to see M. Thomas at the showroom in the Boulevard des Capucines.

'I'm back again, M. Thomas,' he said, as they greeted one another. He explained what had been learnt about the casks at the Gare St Lazare, continuing, 'So you see, two must have been sent out. Now, can you give me any information about the sending out of the second cask?'

'Absolutely none, monsieur,' returned Thomas, who was evidently amazed at this new development, 'I am quite positive we only sent one.'

'I suppose it's impossible that Felix's order could have been dealt with twice in error, once by you here, and once by the head office in the rue Provence?'

'I should say quite, because they do not stock the good work there, it is all stored and dealt with here. But if you like I'll phone the head office now, and make quite sure.'

In a few minutes there was a reply from M. Thévenet. No cask of any kind had been sent out from the rue Provence establishment on or about the date mentioned, and none at any time to Felix.

'Well, M. Thomas, it's certain, is it not, that one of your casks was sent by Rouen and long sea about the 1st instant. Do you think you could let me have a list of all the casks of that size that were out of your yard on that date? It must have been one of them.'

'Yes, I suppose it must. I think I can give you that information, but it will take some time to get out.'

'I'm sorry for giving you the trouble, but I see no other way. We shall have to follow up each of these casks until we find the right one.'

M. Thomas promised to put the work in hands without delay, and Burnley continued: 'There is another point. Could you tell me something about your dealings with M. Raoul Boirac, of the Avenue de l'Alma, and particularly of any recent sales you made him?'

'M. Boirac? Certainly. He is a very good customer of ours and a really well-informed amateur. For the last six years, since I was appointed manager here, we must have sold him thirty or forty thousand francs worth of stuff. Every month or two he would drop in, take a look round, and select some really good piece. We always advised him of anything new we came across and as often as not he became a purchaser. Of recent sales,' M. Thomas consulted some papers, 'the last thing we sold him was, curiously enough, the companion piece of that ordered by Felix. It was a marble group of three female figures, two standing and one seated. It was ordered on the 25th of March, and sent out on the 27th.'

'Was it sent in a cask?'

'It was. We always use the same packing.'

'And has the cask been returned?'

M. Thomas rang for a clerk and asked for some other papers.

'Yes,' he said, when he had looked over them, 'the cask sent to M. Boirac on the 27th of last month was returned here on the 1st instant.'

'One other point, M. Thomas. How can one distinguish between the two groups, that sent to M. Felix, and that to M. Boirac?'

'Very easily. Both consist of three female figures, but in M. Felix's two were seated and one standing, while in M. Boirac's two were standing and one seated.'

'Thank you very much. That's all I want.'

'Not at all. Where shall I send that list of casks?'

'To the Sûreté, if you please,' and with a further exchange of compliments the two men parted.

Burnley was both mystified and somewhat disappointed by the information M. Thomas had given him. He had been really impressed by Lefarge's discovery that a cask containing sawdust had recently been opened in M. Boirac's study, though he had not admitted it at the time. His friend's strongly expressed opinion that either Felix or Boirac, or both, had at that time packed the body in the cask had seemed more and more likely, the longer he had thought it over. There were, however, difficulties in the theory. First, as he had pointed out to Lefarge, there was the personality of François. He felt he would stake his reputation on François' innocence, and without the butler's co-operation he did not see how the murder could have been carried through. Then, what possible motive could either of the men named have had for desiring the death of the lady? These and other difficulties he had foreseen, but he had not considered them insuperable. Possibly, in spite of them, they were on the right track. But now all hopes of that were dashed. The explanation of M. Boirac of the presence of the cask was complete, and it had been confirmed by François. This perhaps was not conclusive, but M. Thomas had confirmed it also, and Burnley felt the evidence of its truth was overwhelming. The body could not therefore have been packed in the cask, because it had been returned direct from M. Boirac's to the showrooms. Reluctantly he felt Lefarge's theory must be abandoned, and, what was much worse, he had no other to substitute.

Another point struck him. If he could find out the hour at which Felix had reached his hotel on the fatal evening, and his condition on arrival, it might confirm or disprove some of the statements they had heard, Therefore, having phoned to the Sûreté and finding he was not required there, he turned his steps again to the Hotel Continental and asked for the manager.

'I'm afraid I am back to give more trouble, monsieur,' he said, as they met, 'but one point has arisen upon which we want some information.'

'I shall be pleased to assist you as far as I can.'

'We want to know at what hour M. Felix returned to the hotel on the night of Saturday fortnight, the 27th March, and his condition on arrival. Can you get us that?'

'I'll make inquiries. Excuse me a moment.'

The manager was gone a considerable time. When he returned after more than half an hour he shook his head.

'I can't find out,' he said. 'I've asked every one I can think of, but no one knows. One of the hall porters was on duty that evening up till midnight, and he is positive he did not come in before that hour. This is a very reliable man and I think you may take what he says as accurate. The man who relieved him is off duty at present, as is also the night lift boy, and the chambermaid on late duty in M. Felix's corridor, but I will interview them later and let you know the result. I presume that will be time enough?'

'Certainly,' and with thanks Burnley withdrew.

He lunched alone, greatly regretting M. Lefarge's absence, and then called up the Sûreté again. M. Chauvet wanted to speak to him, he was told, and soon he was switched through to the great man's private room.

'There has been another wire from London,' said the distant voice, 'and it seems a cask was sent by passenger train from Charing Cross to Paris via Dover and Calais on Thursday week, the 1st of April, consigned to M. Jaques de Belleville, from Raymond Lemaitre. I think you had better go to the Gare du Nord and find out something about it.'

'How many more casks are we going to find?' thought the puzzled Burnley, as he drove in the direction of the station. As the taxi slipped through the crowded streets he again took stock of his position, and had to admit himself completely at sea. The information they gained – and there was certainly plenty coming in – did not work into a connected whole, but each fresh piece of evidence seemed, if not actually to conflict with some other, at least to add to the tangle to be straightened out. When in England he had thought Felix innocent. Now he was beginning to doubt this conclusion.

He had not Lefarge's card to show to the clerk in the parcels office, but fortunately the latter remembered him as having been with the French detective on the previous call.

'Yes,' he said, when Buruley had explained, in his somewhat halting French, what he wanted, 'I can tell you about that cask.' He turned up some papers.

'Here we are,' he said. 'The cask came off the Calais boat train at 5.45 p.m. on Thursday week, the 1st instant. It was consigned from Charing Cross to M. Jaques de Belleville, to be kept here until called for. He claimed it personally almost immediately after, and removed it on a cart he had brought.'

'Can you describe M. de Belleville?'

'He was of medium height and dark, with a black beard. I did not take special notice of him.'

Burnley produced a photograph of Felix he had received from London.

'Is that the man?' he asked, handing it over.

The clerk scrutinised it carefully.

'I could hardly say,' he replied, hesitatingly, 'it's certainly like my recollection of him, but I am not sure. Remember I only saw him once, and that about ten days ago.'

'Of course, you could hardly be expected to remember. Can you tell me another thing? What time did he take the cask away?'

'I can tell you that because I book off duty at 5.15, and I waited five minutes after that to finish the business. He left at 5.20 exactly.'

'I suppose there was nothing that attracted your attention about the cask, nothing to differentiate it from other casks?'

'As a matter of fact,' returned the clerk, 'there were two things. First, it was exceedingly well and strongly made and bound with thicker iron hoops than any I had previously seen, and secondly, it was very heavy. It took two men to get it from here to the cart that M. de Belleville had brought.'

'You didn't notice any lettering on it, other than the labels?'

'I did,' he answered, 'there was "Return to" in French, English, and German, and the name of a Paris firm.'

'Do you recollect the name?'

The young man paused in thought.

'No, monsieur,' he replied, after a few seconds, 'I regret to say I have quite forgotten it.'

'I suppose you wouldn't recognise it if you heard it? It was not, for example, Messrs Dupierre, the monumental sculptors, of Grenelle?'

The clerk hesitated again.

'Possibly it was, monsieur, but I fear I could not say definitely.'

'Well, I am greatly obliged for what you have told me, any way. Just one other question. What was in the cask?'

'It was invoiced *Statuary*, but of course I did not see it opened, and don't know if the description was correct.'

Burnley thanked the young man and turned out of the great station. Certainly it sounded as if this was a similar cask to that he had taken to Scotland Yard, if it was not the same one. Of course, he had to remember that even if it were one of Messrs Dupierre's, which was not proven, there were a large number of these casks in circulation, and it did not follow that this one was connected with his quest. But the whole circumstances gave him to think, and he felt that his bewilderment was not lessened by the new development. As he walked slowly down the rue de Lafayette towards his hotel, he racked his brains in the endeavour to piece together into a connected whole the various facts he had learnt. He strolled on into the Tuileries and, choosing a quiet spot under a tree, sat down to think the matter out.

And first, as to these mysterious journeyings of casks. He went over the three in his mind. First, there was the cask sent out by Messrs Dupierre on the Tuesday evening after the dinner party, which travelled via Havre and Southampton, and which was received at Waterloo on the following morning by a black-bearded man, believed to have been Felix. That cask was addressed to Felix and it contained a statue. Then there was the second cask, sent out from Paris two days later – on the Thursday evening – which went via Rouen and long sea, and which was undoubtedly received at St Katherine's Docks by Felix. This number two cask contained the body of Madame Annette Boirac. And finally, there was what he might call number three cask, which was sent from London to Paris on that same Thursday, and which was claimed on arrival at the Gare du Nord by a M. Jaques de Belleville. This cask like both the others, was labelled 'Statuary,' but whether that was really its contents was not known.

The Inspector lit one of his strong cigars and puffed thoughtfully, as he turned these journeys over in his mind. He could not but think there was some connection between them, though at first he could not trace it. Then it occurred to him that if they were considered, not in the order of their discovery, but chronologically, some light might be gained. He went over them anew. The first journey was still that from Paris to London via Havre and Southampton, leaving Paris on Tuesday night and arriving at Waterloo on Wednesday morning. The second was now that leaving London on Thursday morning and reaching Paris that afternoon, via Dover and Calais, and the third that from Paris to London via Rouen, leaving on that same Thursday evening, and arriving at St Katherine's Docks on the following Monday. That is, from Paris to London, back from London to Paris, and back again from Paris to London. This seemed to show an element of design. And then a possible connection flashed across his mind. Instead of three casks might there not have been only one? Did the same cask not travel in each case?

The more Burnley thought over this, the more likely it seemed. This would explain M. Thomas' statement that only one cask had been sent out. It would make clear how the cask containing the body had been obtained. It would account for the astonishing coincidence that three casks of this unusual kind had made three such journeys almost at the same time.

Yes, it seemed probable. But if so, at some point in that triple journey the cask must have been opened, the statue removed, and the body substituted. The evidence was overwhelming that the cask had contained a statue when it left the Boulevard des Capucines yard, and that it had not been tampered with till it reached the van of the 7.47 p.m. from the Gare St Lazare to Havre. Further, it had contained the body on arrival at St Katherine's Docks, and here again there was evidence that it could not have been opened in the hold of the *Bullfinch*. Therefore, at some point along the route, Gare St Lazare, Havre, Southampton, Waterloo, Charing Cross, Dover, Calais, Gare du Nord, rue Cardinet goods station, Rouen, the change must have been made. Burnley made a mental note that every part of that journey must be the subject of the closest inquiry.

He went a step further. At the end of each of the three journeys it was met by a middle-sized, black-bearded, French-looking man. In the case of the third journey that man was Felix. In the two earlier, his identity was not definitely known, but he was like Felix. Suppose it was Felix in each case, would not this also tend to prove there was only one cask, and that Felix was sending it backwards and forwards with some design of his own? The Inspector felt sure that he was right so far.

But if Felix had acted in this way, it followed that either he was the murderer and wished to get the body to his house to dispose of it there, or else he was an innocent man upon whom the real criminal wished to plant the corpse. This latter idea had been growing in the Inspector's mind for some time. It seemed to hinge very much on the question, Did Felix know what was in the cask when he met it at St Katherine's Docks? Burnley recalled the scene at Scotland Yard when it was opened. Either Felix was an incomparable actor, or else he did not know. Burnley doubted even whether any acting could have been so realistic. He remembered also that Felix's illness from the shock was genuine. No, he rather believed Felix knew nothing of the corpse and, if so, he must be innocent. The point was one Burnley felt he could not settle alone. They must have medical evidence.

But if Felix was innocent, who was likely to be guilty? Who else could have had any motive to kill this lady? What could that motive have been, in any case? He could not tell. No evidence had yet come to light to suggest the motive.

His thoughts turned from the motive to the manner of the crime. Strangulation was an unusual method. It was, moreover, a horrible method, ghastly to witness and comparatively slow in accomplishment. Burnley could not imagine anyone, no matter how brutal, deliberately adopting it and carrying it out in cold blood. No, this was a crime of passion. Some of the elemental forces of love and hate were involved. Jealousy, most probably. He considered it in his careful, methodical way. Yes, jealousy certainly seemed the most likely motive.

And then another point struck him. Surely strangulation would only be adopted, even in the heat of passion, if no other method was available. If a man about to commit a murder had a weapon in his hand, he would use it. Therefore, thought Burnley, in this case the murderer could have had no weapon. And if he had no weapon, what followed from that? Why, that the crime was unpremeditated. If the affair had been planned, a weapon would have been provided.

It seemed, therefore, probable that the crime was not deliberate and cold-blooded. Someone, when alone with Madame, had been suddenly and unexpectedly roused to a pitch of furious, overmastering passion. And here again, what more likely to cause this passion than acute jealousy?

The Inspector lit another cigar, as he continued his train of thought. If the motive was what he suspected, who would be a likely person to feel jealousy in reference to Madame? A former lover, he thought. So far they knew of none, and Burnley took a mental note that inquiries must be made to ascertain if such existed. Failing a former lover, the husband immediately came into his mind, and here he seemed on firmer ground. If Madame had had an understanding with Felix, and Boirac had come to know of it, there was the motive at once. Jealousy was what one would naturally expect Boirac to feel under such circumstances. There was no doubt that, so far as the facts had as yet come to light, Boirac's guilt was a possibility they must not overlook.

The Inspector then turned his thoughts to a general review of the whole case. He was a great believer in getting things on paper. Taking out his notebook, he proceeded to make a list of the facts so far as they were known, in the order of their occurrence, irrespective of when they were discovered.

First of all was the dinner party at M. Boirac's, which took place on Saturday evening, the 27th March. At this Felix was present, and, when Boirac was called away to his works, he remained behind, alone with Madame Boirac, after the other guests had left. He was alone with her from 11.0 p.m. till at least 11.30, on the evidence of François. About one in the morning, François heard the front door close, and, coming down, found that both Felix and Madame had disappeared. Madame had changed her shoes and taken a coat and hat. On Boirac's return, a few minutes later, he found a note from his wife stating that she had eloped with Felix. Felix was believed to have gone to London next day, this having been stated by the manager of the Hotel Continental, as well as by Felix to his friend Martin outside his house when Constable Walker was listening in the lane. On that Sunday or the Monday following, a letter, apparently written by Felix, was posted in London. It contained an order on Messrs Dupierre to send a certain group of statuary to that city. This letter was received by the firm on Tuesday. On the same day, Tuesday, the statue was packed in a cask and despatched to London via Havre and Southampton. It reached Waterloo on the following morning, and was removed from there by a man who claimed to be Felix, and probably was. The next morning, Thursday, a similar cask was despatched from

Charing Cross to the Gare du Nord in Paris, being met by a man giving his name as Jaques de Belleville, but who was probably Felix. The same evening, some fifty minutes later, a similar cask was delivered at the goods station of the State Railway in the rue Cardinet, for despatch to London via Rouen and long sea. Next day, Friday, Felix stated he received a typewritten letter purporting to be from Le Gautier, telling about the lottery and the bet, stating the cask was being sent by long sea, and asking him to get it to his house. On the following morning, Saturday, he had a card from the same source, saying the cask had left, and on Monday, the 5th of April, he got the cask from the *Bullfinch* at St Katherine's Docks, and took it home.

Burnley's list then read as follows:

Saturday, March 27 – Dinner at M. Boirac's. Madame disappears.

Sunday, March 28 – Felix believed to cross to London.

Monday, March 29 – Felix writes to Dupierre, ordering statue.

Tuesday, March 30 – Order received by Dupierre. Statue despatched via Havre and Southampton.

Wednesday, March 31 – Cask claimed at Waterloo, apparently by Felix.

Thursday, April 1 – Cask sent from Charing Cross. Cask met at Gare du Nord. Cask delivered at rue Cardinet goods station for despatch to London.

Friday, April 2 – Felix receives Le Gautier's letter.

Saturday, April 3 – Felix receives Le Gautier's card.

Monday, April 5 – Felix meets cask at docks.

Some other points he added below, which did not fall into the chronological scheme.

1. The typescript letter produced by Felix purporting to be from Le Gautier about the lottery, the bet, and the test with the cask, and the typescript slip in the cask about the return of a £50 loan, were done by the same machine, on the same paper.
2. The letter from Felix to Dupierre, ordering the statue was written on the same paper as the above, pointing to a common origin for the three.

Pleased with the progress he had made, Burnley left his seat under the tree and strolled back to his hotel in the rue Castiglione to write his daily report to Scotland Yard.

17

A COUNCIL OF WAR

At nine that evening, Inspector Burnley knocked at the door of the Chief's room in the Sûreté. Lefarge was already there, and, as Burnley sat down, M. Chauvet said: 'Lefarge is just going to tell his adventures. Now, Lefarge, if you please.'

'As arranged on Saturday,' began the detective, 'I went to Dijon yesterday and called on Mlle. Daudet in the rue Popeau. She seems a quiet, reliable girl, and, I think, truthful. She corroborated M. Boirac's and the butler's statements on every point, but added three details they omitted. The first was that Mme. Boirac took a wide-brimmed hat, but no hatpins. This seemed to strike the girl as very strange, and I asked why. She said because the hat was useless without the pins, as it would not stay on. I suggested the lady must have been so hurried she forgot them, but the girl did not think that possible. She said it would have taken no appreciable time to get the pins, as they were stuck in the cushion at Madame's hand, and that a lady would put in hatpins quite automatically and as a matter of habit. In fact, had they been forgotten, the loose feel of the hat, even in the slight air caused by descending the stairs, would have at once called attention to the omission. She could offer no explanation of the circumstance. The second detail was that Madame took no luggage – not even a handbag with immediate necessaries for the night. The third seems more important still. On the morning of the dinner party Madame sent Suzanne to the Hotel Continental with a note for Felix. Felix came out and instructed her to tell Madame he had her note and would come.'

'A curious point, that about the pins,' said the Chief, and, after a few moment's silence, he turned to Burnley and asked for his report. When this had been delivered and discussed he went on: 'I also have some news. There has been a telephone call from the manager of the Hotel Continental. He says it can be established beyond doubt that Felix returned to the Hotel at 1.30 on Sunday morning. He was seen by the hall porter, the lift boy, and the chambermaid, all of whom are agreed on the time. All three also agree that he was in a quite normal condition, except that he was in a specially good humour and seemed pleased about something. The manager points out, however, that he was habitually good-humoured, so that there may be nothing remarkable about this.'

M. Chauvet took some cigars from a drawer and, having selected one, passed the box to the others.

'Help yourselves, gentlemen. It seems to me that at this stage we should stop and see just where we stand, what we have learnt, if we have any tenable theory, and what still remains to be done. I am sure each of us has already done this, but three minds are better together than separate. What do you say, Mr Burnley?'

'An excellent idea, monsieur,' returned the Inspector, congratulating himself on his cogitations earlier in the day.

'Perhaps you would tell us how you approached the problem, and we shall add our ideas as you go on?'

'I started, monsieur, with the assumption that the murder was the central factor of the whole affair, and the other incidents merely parts of a design to get rid of the body and divert suspicion.'

'I fancy we are all agreed there, eh, Lefarge?'

The Frenchman bowed, and Burnley continued: 'I thought then of the method of the murder. Strangulation is such a brutal way of killing that it seemed the work either of a maniac, or a man virtually mad from passion. Even then it would hardly have been used if other means had been available. From that I argued the crime must have been unpremeditated. If it had been planned, a weapon would have been provided.'

'A good point, Mr Burnley. I also had come to the same conclusion. Please continue.'

'If this was so, it followed that some person, when alone with Mme. Boirac, had suddenly been overcome with absolute, blind passion. What, I asked myself, could have aroused this?

'A love affair, causing hate or jealousy, naturally suggested itself, but I could not fit it in. Who could have felt these passions?

'Considering Felix first, I did not see how he could experience either hate or jealousy against a woman who had eloped with him. It is true, a lover's quarrel might have taken place, resulting in something approaching temporary hatred, but it was inconceivable this would be bitter enough to lead to such a climax. Jealousy, I did not believe could be aroused at all. It seemed to me that Felix would be the last man in the world to commit the crime.

'Then it occurred to me that hate and jealousy would be just what one might expect to find in Boirac's case. If he were guilty, the motive would be obvious. And then, when

M. Lefarge discovered yesterday that a cask similar to that in which the body was found had been unpacked in Boirac's study, I felt sure this was the solution. However, since hearing the explanation of the presence of that cask, I admit I am again in doubt.'

'I agree with all you say, Mr Burnley, except that we should remember that the passions of hate and jealousy could only arise in Boirac's mind in a certain circumstance, namely, that he was aware his wife had eloped, or was about to elope, with Felix. If he were in ignorance of that, it is obvious he could have had no such feelings.'

'That is so, sir. Yes, it would only be if he knew.'

'And then, again, it would only be if he really loved his wife. If not, he might he vastly annoyed and upset, but not enough to throttle her in the blind passion we have spoken of. If they were not on good terms, or if there was some other woman in Boirac's life, he might even view her action with delight, as a welcome relief, particularly as there were no children to complicate the question of a divorce.' The Chief looked inquiringly at his companions.

'I agree with that too, sir,' said Burnley, answering the look.

'And I, monsieur,' added Lefarge.

'So then, we have reached this point. If Boirac was in love with his wife, and if he knew she had eloped or was about to do so, he would have had a motive for the crime. Otherwise, we can suggest no motive at all, either for him, or Felix, or anybody else.'

'Your last words, monsieur, open up possibilities,' observed Lefarge. 'Might it not have been some other person altogether? I do not see that we are limited to Felix or Boirac. What about Le Gautier, for instance, or someone we have not yet heard of?'

'Quite so, Lefarge. That is undoubtedly a possibility. There are others, François, the butler, for example, into whose actions we must inquire. The possibility of Madame's having had some former lover must not be forgotten either. But I think we should make up our minds about these two men before we go farther afield.'

'There is another point,' resumed Burnley. 'The medical evidence shows that only a short time can have elapsed between the time Madame left her house and the murder. We assume, on the hotel manager's testimony, Felix went to London the morning after the dinner party. If so, did Madame accompany him? If the former, it points to Felix, and if the latter, to Boirac.'

'I think we can deduce that,' said Lefarge.

'And how?'

'In this way, monsieur. Leave aside for a moment the question of the identity of the murderer, and consider how he got the body into the cask. This cask we have traced fairly well. It was packed in the showrooms in the Boulevard des Capucines, and in it was placed a statue. Then it travelled to Waterloo, and the evidence that it was not tampered with *en route* is overwhelming. Therefore the body was not in it when it arrived at Waterloo. Then, for twenty-two hours, it disappeared. It reappeared at Charing Cross, for it is too much to suppose there are really two casks in question, and travelled back to Paris, and again it is quite impossible that it could have been interfered with on the journey. At Paris it left the Gare du Nord at 5.20, and disappeared again, but it turned up at the State Railway goods station at 6.10 p.m. the same evening, and returned to London by long sea. On arrival in London it contained the body. It is certain the change was not made during any of the three journeys, therefore it must have been done during those disappearances in London or Paris.

'Of these disappearances, take that in Paris first. It lasted fifty minutes, and, during that time, the cask was conveyed between the Gare du Nord and the rue Cardinet goods station on a horse cart. How long, monsieur, should that journey have taken?'

'About fifty minutes, I should think,' returned the Chief.

'I thought so too. That is to say, the whole time of the disappearance is accounted for. We may reckon, also, it would take some considerable time to open, unpack, repack, and close the cask, and it seems to me it would have been utterly impossible for it to have *both* been opened and to have made that journey in the time. It made the journey, therefore it wasn't opened. Therefore the body must have been put into it in London.'

'Excellent, Lefarge. I believe you are right.'

'There is a further point, monsieur. If my suggestion is correct, it definitely proves Madame Boirac went to London while alive, because her dead body obviously could not have been brought there. If we consider this in relation to the point about the medical evidence raised by Mr Burnley, I think we shall be forced to conclude she crossed with Felix on Sunday.'

'It certainly sounds probable.'

'If she crossed with Felix, it seems almost certain that he is the guilty man. But there are a good many other things that point to Felix. Suppose for a moment he is guilty, and picture him faced with the question of how to dispose of the body. He wants a receptacle to remove it in. It suddenly occurs to him that only a few hours before he has seen the very thing. A cask for statuary. And, fortunately for him, he has not only seen it, but he has learnt where to get a similar cask. What does he do? He proceeds to get that similar cask. He writes to the firm who use them, and he orders just such a piece of statuary as will ensure his getting the kind of cask he wants.'

'What about the false address?'

'Of that, monsieur, I cannot suggest the explanation, but I presume it was with some idea of covering his tracks.'

'Please continue.'

'I suggest, then, that he got the cask on arrival in London, brought it to St Malo, unpacked and probably destroyed the statue, packed the body, took the cask to Charing Cross and sent it to Paris, travelling over in the same train himself. In Paris he got a cart, and took it from the Gare du Nord to the rue Cardinet goods station, travelled back to London, and met the cask at St Katherine's Docks on the following Monday.'

'But what was the object of all these journeys? If his purpose was to get rid of the body, why would he first get rid of it, and then arrange an elaborate scheme to bring it back again?'

'I saw that difficulty, monsieur,' admitted Lefarge, 'and I cannot explain it, though I would suggest it was for the same purpose as the false address – in some way to divert suspicion. But more than that, monsieur. We have evidence that the black-bearded man who met the cask on its various journeys was like Felix. But we have so far found no other black-bearded man in the entire case. It seems to me, therefore, it must have been Felix.'

'If M. Lefarge's theory is correct,' interposed Burnley, 'the letter about the bet must have been written by Felix. In this case, could this letter and the journeys of the cask not have been devised with the object of throwing suspicion on Le Gautier?'

'Or on Boirac?" suggested the Chief.

'Boirac!' cried Lefarge, with a rapid gesture of satisfaction. 'That was it, of course! I see it now. The whole of the business of the letter and the cask was a plant designed by Felix to throw suspicion on Boirac. What do you think, monsieur?'

'It certainly presents a working theory.'

'But why,' queried the Englishman, 'should Le Gautier's name be brought in? Why did he not use Boirac's?'

'It would have been too obvious,' returned Lefarge, delighted with the rapid strides his theory was making. 'It would have been crude. Felix would argue that if Boirac had written that letter, he would never have signed it himself. It was a subtle idea introducing Le Gautier's name.'

'If Felix did it,' Burnley continued, 'it would certainly clear up the difficulty of the authorship of the letter. He is the only man we have discovered so far that would have had the necessary knowledge to write it. He was present at the Café Toisson d'Or, and had joined with Le Gautier in the lottery, and therefore knew that part of it. The discussion about criminals evading the police and the bet between Le Gautier and Dumarchez, neither of which we believe took place, he could have invented to account for the receipt of the cask, and finally, he would naturally know the details about the last journey of the cask, since he himself arranged them.'

'Quite so,' cried Lefarge eagerly, 'it all works in. I believe we are beginning to see light. And we must not forget Suzanne's evidence about the note. It is clear Madame and Felix had an understanding for that night. At least, we know of messages passing between them and the reply of Felix points to an assignation.'

'An important point, certainly. And yet,' the Chief objected, 'there are difficulties. That singular point about the hatpins, for example. What do you make of that, Lefarge?'

'Agitation, monsieur. I would suggest that this lady was so excited at the action she was about to take that she hardly knew what she was doing.'

The Chief shook his head.

'I don't know that that is very satisfactory,' he said.

'Might it not, as also the fact that she took no luggage, mean that she never left the house at all? That she was murdered that same evening of the dinner party, and the hat and coat removed to make a false scent? I suppose you have considered that?'

Burnley answered at once.

'I thought of that first of all, monsieur, but I dismissed it as impossible for the following reasons. First, if she was murdered on Saturday night, what was done with the body? It could not have been put into the cask in the study, as I had thought at first, for that was full. The statue was not unpacked till two nights later, on Monday. We know, indeed, it was not put into the cask, for that was returned direct to Messrs Dupierre's and found to be empty. Secondly, it could not have been hidden anywhere else in the house, for François and Suzanne made a thorough search on the Sunday, and the corpse would have been too big a thing for them to have overlooked. Further, if she was murdered in the house, either Felix, Boirac, or some third person or persons must have done it. Felix could hardly be the man, as I do not see how he could have removed the body without a confederate, and we have not found such. Boirac would perhaps have had more chances of disposing of the body, though I do not see how, but he had a complete alibi. Lastly, I felt strongly that François, the butler, was to be believed. I could not imagine him party to the murder, and I did not see how it could have been done at the time you suggest without his knowledge.'

'That certainly seems probable. In fact, when you add it to M. Lefarge's point that the body must have been put into the cask in London, it seems to me almost conclusive.'

'I also feel sure it could not have been done then,' observed Lefarge, 'though I don't agree with Mr Burnley that Boirac's alibi is good.'

'Well now, I was rather inclined to accept the alibi,' said M. Chauvet. 'What part of it do you consider doubtful, Lefarge?'

'All of it from the time Boirac left the works. We don't know whether that American exists at all. As far as I can see, the whole thing may be an invention.'

'That is quite true,' admitted the Chief, 'but it didn't seem to me so very important. The crucial point, to my mind, is the hour at which Boirac says he returned home – a few minutes past one. That is confirmed by François and by Suzanne, and I think we may accept their statement. But we have a further rather convincing incident. You may recollect Boirac stated that when he was halfway home from the Gare Quai d'Orsay it began to rain? You very properly tried to check even so small a point by asking François if his master's coat was wet. He replied that it was. Now, I made inquiries, and I find that night was perfectly fine till almost one o'clock, when a thick, wetting rain began to fall. We know, therefore, quite definitely that Boirac was out until the time he said. Therefore he could not have done the deed before 1.15. Also, we know that he could not have done it after that hour, because the lady was gone, and also the butler and maid were about. Therefore, if Boirac did it at all, it must have been after that night.'

'That seems unquestionable, monsieur,' said Lefarge, 'and when you add to that the fact that we have, so far at any rate, been quite unable to connect Boirac with the letter or the cask, and that we are practically certain Madame travelled to London, I think he may almost be eliminated from the inquiry. What do you say, Burnley?'

'Well, I think it's a little too soon to eliminate anyone from inquiry. I confess that point of motive struck me as being very strong against Boirac.'

'That also, by the way, seems to show the deed was not done by Boirac that night,' the Chief went on. 'Your point is that he killed his wife because she had run away with Felix. But if he came home and found her there, she obviously *hadn't* run away. Hence the motive, for that night at least, falls to the ground.'

The three men laughed, and M. Chauvet resumed: 'Now, to sum up our present position. We know that Mme. Boirac was murdered between 11.30 p.m. on the Saturday of the dinner-party, and the following Monday evening, when the letter purporting to be from Felix and ordering the statue, was written. Obviously only Felix, Boirac, or some third person could be guilty. There is not, so far, a scintilla of evidence of any third person being involved, therefore it almost certainly was one of the other two. Taking Boirac first, we find that under certain circumstances he would have had a motive for the crime, but we have not yet been able to obtain any evidence that these circumstances existed. Apart from this, we can find nothing whatever against him. On the other hand, he has established a strong alibi for the only time during which, so far as we can now see, he could have committed the crime.

'Against Felix there are several suspicious circumstances. Firstly, it is proved he received a note from Madame, presumably arranging a meeting. Then we know he took advantage of the husband's absence on the night of the dinner to have a private interview with her. That went on from 11.0 till at least 11.30, and there is reason to believe, though not proof, till 1.0. Then we believe Madame went to London, either actually with Felix, or at the same time. We conclude that for three reasons. First, she wrote to her husband that she had done so. The value of this evidence will, of course, depend on the opinion of our handwriting experts, whose report on the genuineness of this letter we have not yet received. Second, she could not have remained in the house, either alive or dead, as it was thoroughly searched by the servants, who found no trace of her. Neither could her body have been put in the cask in the study, for that contained the statue, and was not unpacked till the following Monday evening. Third, it is certain from the journeyings of the cask that the body was put into it in London, for the simple reason that it could not have been done anywhere else. Therefore she must have travelled to that city.

'Further, the letter presumed to be written to Felix by Le Gautier could be reasonably accounted for if Felix himself wrote it as a blind to cover his actions with the cask, should such be discovered. It is clear that it was written with some such purpose, as half of it – all about the bet and the test – is entirely untrue, and evidently invented to account for the arrival of the cask. Now, we may take it, Le Gautier did not write that letter. On the other hand, Felix is the only man we have yet found who had sufficient information to do so.

'Again, we know that a black-bearded man like Felix arranged the journeys of the cask. So far, Felix himself is the only black-bearded man we have found. On the other hand we have two strong points in Felix's favour. First, we have not been able to prove motive, and second, his surprise when the body was found in the cask appears to have been genuine. We have undoubtedly a good deal of evidence against Felix, but we must note that not only is this evidence circumstantial, but there is also evidence in his favour.

'The truth is, in my opinion, that we have not yet sufficient information to come to a conclusion, and I fear it will take a lot of work to get it. Firstly, we must definitely prove the authorship of that letter about the lottery and the bet. And here, it seems to me, the tracing of that typewriter is essential. This should not be so difficult, as I think we may take it that the author used the typewriter himself. Therefore, only machines to which the possible writers could have had access need be examined. I will send a man tomorrow to get samples from all the machines Boirac could have used, and if that produces nothing, he can do the same in connection with Le Gautier, Dumarchez, and the other gentlemen whose names we have. I presume, Mr Burnley, your people will take similar action with regard to Felix?'

'I expect they have done so already, but I will write tonight and make sure.'

'I consider that a vital point, and the next is almost equally important. We must trace Felix's movements from the Saturday night till the Thursday evening when the cask containing the body was despatched from Paris. Further, we must ascertain by direct evidence, if Madame travelled with him to London.

'We must similarly trace the movements of Boirac for the same period. If none of these inquiries help us, other points would be the confronting of Felix and Boirac with the various luggage clerks that did business with the black-bearded man with the cask, in the hope that some of them might possibly identify him. The tracing of the carters who brought the cask to and from the various stations might or might not lead us to the men from whom they got their instructions. An exhaustive inquiry into the past life of Mme. Boirac and all the suspected men is also likely to be necessary. There are several other directions in which we can prosecute inquiries, but I fancy the above should give us all we want.'

The discussion was carried on for some time longer, various points of detail being more fully gone into. Finally, it was arranged that on the following morning Burnley and Lefarge should begin the tracing of Felix's movements from the night of the dinner party until he left French soil, after which Burnley would continue the quest alone, while Lefarge turned his attention to ascertaining Boirac's movements during the crucial period.

18

LEFARGE HUNTS ALONE

At nine o'clock next morning the two colleagues met at the hotel in the rue Castiglione. They had discussed their plan of campaign before separating the previous evening, and did not waste time getting to work. Calling a taxi, they drove once more to the Hotel Continental and asked for their old friend the manager. In a few minutes they were ushered into the presence of that urbane and smiling, but somewhat bored official.

'We are exceedingly sorry to trouble you again, monsieur,' apologised Lefarge, 'but the fact is we find we require some more information about your recent visitor, M. Felix. If you can help us to obtain it, you will greatly add to our already large debt of gratitude.'

The manager bowed.

'I shall be delighted to tell you anything I can. What is the point in question?'

'We want to trace M. Felix's movements after he left here. You have already told us he went to catch the 8.20 English boat train at the Gare du Nord. We wondered if he really did travel by it. Can you help us to find out?'

'Our bus meets all the incoming boat trains, but attends only those outward bound by which visitors are travelling. If you will pardon me a moment, I will ascertain if it ran that day. It was Sunday, I think?'

'Sunday, the 28th March.'

The manager was absent for a few moments, returning with a tall young man in the uniform of a porter.

'I find the bus did run on the day in question, and Karl, here, went with it. He may be able to answer your questions.'

'Thank you, monsieur.' Lefarge turned to the porter. 'You went to the Gare du Nord on Sunday, the 28th March, with some passengers for the 8.20 English boat train?'

'Yes, monsieur.'

'How many passengers had you?'

The porter considered.

'Three, monsieur,' he replied at length.

'Did you know who they were?'

'Two of them I knew, monsieur. One was M. Leblanc, a gentleman who had stayed in the hotel for over a month. The second was M. Felix, who has been a constant visitor for years. The third was an English gentleman, but I do not know his name.'

'Did these gentlemen converse together while in the bus?'

'I saw M. Felix speaking to the Englishman as they were leaving the bus, otherwise I cannot say.'

'Did they go by the 8.20?'

'Yes, monsieur. I put their luggage into the carriages, and I saw all three in the train as it was starting.'

'Was M. Felix alone?'

'He was, monsieur.'

'Did he meet or speak with a lady at the station?'

'I do not think so, monsieur. Certainly I did not see a lady.'

'Did he seem anxious or perturbed?'

'Not at all, monsieur. He was just as usual.'

'Thank you, I am exceedingly obliged.'

Some silver changed hands, and Karl withdrew.

'That is very satisfactory information, M. le Directeur. The only other point I want is the names and addresses of the two other occupants of the bus.'

These were ascertained with some slight difficulty – M. Guillaume Leblane, rue Verte, Marseilles, and Mr Henry Gordon, 327 Angus Lane, Sauchiehall Street, Glasgow – and the detectives bowed themselves out with compliments and thanks.

'That's a piece of luck,' remarked Lefarge, as they drove towards the Gare du Nord. 'Those men may have seen Felix at other stages of the journey, and we may be able to trace him the whole way.'

They spent the morning in the great station, interviewing ticket examiners and other officials, but without success. No one had seen either of the travellers.

'The boat is more likely,' observed Burnley. 'If he is a constant traveller, some of the stewards will certainly know him.'

Taking the 4.0 p.m. train, they reached Boulogne as dusk was falling, and began their inquiries at the pier. Finding the *Pas de Calais*, which had made the run in which they were interested, would not leave till noon next day, they turned their steps to the local police station. There they saw the men who had been on duty when the boat left on the Sunday in question, but here again without getting any information. Then they went on board the steamer and sought the chief steward.

'I know that gentleman, yes,' he said when, after introducing themselves, Lefarge showed him Felix's photograph. 'He crosses frequently, once or twice a month,

I should say. He is a M. Felix, but I cannot say where he lives, nor do I know anything else about him.'

'What we want to find out, monsieur, is when he last crossed. If you can tell us that, we shall be extremely obliged.'

The official considered.

'I am afraid I could hardly be sure of that. He crossed both ways fairly lately. I should say about ten days or a fortnight ago, but I'm not sure of the exact date.'

'We think he crossed on Sunday, the 28th March. Can you think of anything that would confirm whether it was this date?'

'No, I cannot. You see there would be nothing to record it. We could not now trace the ticket he held, and there is no way in which the identity of our passengers is ascertained and noted. Speaking from memory, I should say that the date you mention is about correct, but I could not be sure.'

'Is there anyone on board who might be able to help us?'

'I'm really very sorry, monsieur, but I don't think there is. The captain, or one of the officers, might know him; I could not say.'

'Well, just one other question, monsieur. Was he travelling alone?'

'I think so. No, wait a minute, was he? I believe, now that you mention it, there was a lady with him. You will understand I was not noticing particularly, as my mind was occupied with my work, but it's like a dream to me, I saw him talking to a lady on the promenade deck.'

'You could not describe her?'

'I could not, monsieur. I cannot be even positive she was there at all.'

Seeing there was nothing further to be learnt, they thanked the chief steward courteously. Then, remaining on board, they interviewed everyone they could find, whom they thought might be able to give them information. Of all they spoke to, only one, a waiter, knew Felix, and he had not seen him on the occasion in question.

'That's no good, I'm afraid,' said Burnley, as they walked to an hotel. 'I believe that steward did see a woman, but he would be useless as a witness.'

'Quite. I don't fancy you'll get much at Folkestone either.'

'Most unlikely, I should say, but I can but try. I think I'll probably run up to Glasgow and see that man that travelled in the bus with him. He might know something.'

'If not, I'll see the other – the one who lives in Marseilles.'

A few minutes before twelve next day saw the detectives strolling along the wharf beside the English boat.

'Well,' said Lefarge, 'our ways part here. There is no use in my going to Folkestone, and I'll take the 2.12 back to Paris. We have had a pleasant inquiry, and I'm only sorry we have not had a more definite result.'

'We're not done with it yet,' returned the Englishman. 'I expect we'll get it pretty square before we stop. But I'm really sorry to say "Goodbye," and I hope we may be working together again before long.'

They parted with mutual assurances of goodwill, Burnley expressing his appreciation of the kindly treatment he had received in Paris, and Lefarge inviting him back to spend his next holidays in the gay capital.

We may accompany Lefarge on his return journey to Paris, and follow him as he endeavours to trace the movements of M. Boirac from the Saturday night of the dinner-party to the following Thursday evening, when the cask containing the body was despatched to London from the State Railway goods station in the rue Cardinet.

He reached the Gare du Nord at 5.45 p.m., and immediately drove to the Sûreté. M. Chauvet was in his office, and Lefarge reported his movements since they parted.

'I had a telephone call from Scotland Yard yesterday,' said the Chief. 'It seems Boirac turned up at eleven as arranged. He definitely identified the body as that of his wife, so that point is settled.'

'Has he returned yet, do you know, monsieur?'

'I have not heard. Why do you ask?'

'I thought if he was still away I might take the opportunity of pumping François about his movements since the murder.'

'A good idea. We can find out at once.'

M. Chauvet turned over the pages of his telephone directory and, having found what he wanted, gave a call.

'Hallo! Is that M. Boirac's? – Is M. Boirac at home? – About seven o'clock? Ah, thank you. I'll ring up again later. – No, don't mind. It's of no consequence.'

He replaced the receiver.

'He's crossing by the 11.0 from Charing Cross, and will be home about seven. If you were to call about half-past six, which is the hour at which he usually returns, your visit would not be suspicious, and you could have a chat with François.'

'I shall do that, monsieur,' and with a bow the detective withdrew.

The clocks had just finished chiming the half-hour after six when Lefarge presented himself at the house in the Avenue de l'Alma. François opened the door.

'Good evening, M. François. Is M. Boirac at home?'

'Not yet, monsieur. We expect him in about half an hour. Will you come in and wait?'

Lefarge seemed to consider, and then, – 'Thanks. I think I will.'

The butler preceded him to the small sitting-room into which he had shown the two detectives on their first call.

'I heard at the Sûreté that M. Boirac had gone to London to identify the body. You don't know, I suppose, if he was able to do so?'

'No, monsieur. I knew he had gone to London, but I did not know for what purpose.'

The detective settled himself in a comfortable chair and took out a cigarette case.

'Try one of these. They're special Brazilian cigarettes. I suppose we may smoke here?'

'Certainly, monsieur. I thank you.'

'It's a long way over from London. I don't envy Monsieur his journey. You've been, I suppose, monsieur?'

'Twice, monsieur.'

'Once is all right to see the place, but after that – no, thank you. But I suppose M. Boirac is used to it? They say you can get used to anything.'

'I should think he must be. He travels a lot. London, Brussels, Berlin, Vienna – he had been at them all to my knowledge in the last two years.'

'I'm glad it's he and not I. But I should think this unhappy event would take away his love for travelling. I should imagine he would want to stay quiet in his own home and see no one. What do you think, M. François?'

'Well, he hasn't anyway, or else he can't help himself. This is the second journey he's made since then'

'You surprise me. Or rather, no, you don't. I suppose we shouldn't be talking about what doesn't concern us, but I would be willing to lay a napoleon I could tell you where the first journey was to and what it was for. It was to see the Wilson Test. Am I not right?'

'The Wilson Test, monsieur? What is that?'

'Have you never heard of the Wilson Test? Wilson is the head of a great firm of English pump manufacturers, and each year a reward of over 10,000 francs is offered by them for any pump that can throw more water than theirs. A test is held every year, and the last one took place on Wednesday. M. Boirac would naturally be interested, being head of a pump manufactory himself. He would go to the Test.'

'I'm afraid you would have lost your money, then, monsieur. He was away on Wednesday right enough, but I happen to know he went to Belgium.'

'Well,' said Lefarge, with a laugh, 'I'm glad we didn't bet, anyway. But,' he added, in a changed tone, 'maybe I'm right after all. Maybe he went from Belgium to London, or vice versa. Was he long away?'

'He could not have done that, monsieur. He was only away two days, Wednesday and Thursday.'

'It ought to be a lesson to me. I'm always too ready to bet on an unsupported opinion,' and Lefarge led the conversation on to bets he had won and lost, till François excused himself to prepare for his master's arrival.

Shortly after seven M. Boirac came in. He saw Lefarge at once.

'I don't wish to trouble you after your journey, monsieur,' said the latter, 'but some further points have arisen in this unhappy business, and I would be obliged if you could kindly give me an appointment at whatever time would suit you.'

'No time like the present. If you will excuse me for an hour till I change and get some dinner, I shall be at your service. You have dined, I suppose?'

'Yes, thank you. If, then, I may wait here for you, I would be glad to do so.'

'Then come into the study. You'll perhaps find something to read in these bookcases.'

'I thank you, monsieur.'

The hands of the clock on the study chimneypiece were pointing to half-past eight when M. Boirac re-entered. Sinking into an easy chair, he said: 'Now, monsieur, I am at your service.'

'The matter is a somewhat difficult one for me to approach, monsieur,' began Lefarge, 'in case it might seem to you that we had suspicions which we do not really entertain. But, as a man of the world, you will recognise that the position of the husband in unhappy affairs such as this must inevitably be made clear. It is a matter of necessary routine. My Chief, M. Chauvet, has therefore placed on me the purely formal, but extremely unpleasant duty of asking you some questions about your own movements since the unhappy event.'

'That's rather roundabout. Do you mean that you suspect me of murdering my wife?'

'Certainly not, monsieur. It is simply that the movements of *everyone* in a case like this must be gone into. It is our ordinary routine, and we cannot consult our inclination in carrying it out.'

'Oh, well, go ahead. You must, of course, do your duty.'

'The information my Chief requires is a statement from you of how you passed your time from the night of the dinner party until the evening of the following Thursday.'

M. Boirac looked distressed. He paused before replying, and then said in an altered tone: 'I don't like to think of that time. I passed through a rather terrible experience. I think I was temporarily insane.'

'I still more regret that I must persevere in my question.'

'Oh, I will tell you. The seizure, or whatever it was, is over and I am myself again. What happened to me was this.

'From the Saturday night, or rather Sunday morning, when I learnt that my wife had left me, I was in a kind of dream. My brain felt numb, and I had the curious feeling of existing in some way outside of and apart from myself. I went as usual to my office on Monday, returning home at my ordinary time in the evening. After dinner, in the hope of rousing myself, I unpacked the cask, but even that failed to excite my interest or lighten my depression. On the following morning, Tuesday, I again went to the office at my customary time, but after an hour of effort I found I could no longer concentrate my mind on my work. I felt that at all costs I must be alone so as to relax the strain of pretending nothing had happened. Still like a man in a dream, I left the office and, going down into the street, entered a Metro station. On the wall my eye caught sight of the notice, "Direction Vincennes," and it occurred to me that the Bois de Vincennes would be the very place for me to go. There I could walk without fear of meeting any of my acquaintances. I accordingly took the train there, and spent the morning pacing the more sequestered paths. The physical exercise helped me, but as I grew tired my mood changed. A great longing for human sympathy took possession of me, and I felt I must confide in someone, or go mad. I thought of my brother Armande, and felt sure I would get the sympathy I wanted from him. He lived not far from Malines, in Belgium, and I determined to go and see him at once. I lunched at a little café at Charenton, and from there telephoned to the office and to my house that I was going to Belgium for a couple of days. I instructed François to pack a handbag of necessaries and leave it immediately at the cloakroom at the Gare du Nord, where I should call for it. While sitting at lunch it occurred to me that if I went by the 4.5 p.m. train – the first I could get – I would not arrive at my destination till the middle of the night, so I decided I would wait till the evening train and see my brother the following day. Accordingly, I went for a long walk up the Seine, returning by a local train to the Gare du Lyon. I dined at a café in the Place de la Bastille, and finally went to the Gare du Nord, got my bag, and left by the 11.20 for Brussels. I slept well in the train and breakfasted in one of the cafés off the Place du Nord. About eleven I left for Malines, walking the four miles to my brother's house for the sake of the exercise. But when I reached it I found it empty, and then I recollected, what had entirely slipped my memory, that my brother had spoken of a business trip to Stockholm, on which he was going to take his wife. I cursed my forgetfulness, but my mind was in such a state I hardly realised my loss of time and money. Walking slowly back to Malines, I considered returning to Paris that evening. Then I thought I had had enough travelling for one day. It was pleasant in the afternoon sun, and I let the time slip away, returning to Brussels about six. I dined at a café in the Boulevard Anspach, and then, thinking I would try and distract my thoughts, decided I would turn in for a couple of hours to a theatre. I telephoned to the Hôtel Maximilian, where I usually stayed, to reserve a room, and then I went to Berlioz's *Les Troyens* at the Théâtre de la Monnaie, getting to my hotel about eleven. That night I slept well and next day my brain seemed saner and better. I left Brussels by the 12.50 from the Gare du Midi, arriving at Paris about five. Looking back on that abortive journey is like remembering a nightmare, but I think the solitude and the exercise really helped me.'

When M. Boirac ceased speaking, there was silence for a few moments, while Lefarge, in just the same painstaking way that Burnley would have adopted, went over in his mind what he had heard. He did not wish to question M. Boirac too closely lest, in the unlikely event of that gentleman proving guilty, he should put him on his guard; but he was anxious to miss no detail of the statement, so that he might as far as possible check it by independent testimony. On the whole, he thought the story reasonable, and, so far, he could see no internal reason for doubting it. He would, therefore, get a few details made clearer and take his leave.

'Thank you, M. Boirac. Might I ask a few supplementary questions? At what time did you leave your office on Tuesday?'

'About nine-thirty.'

'What café did you lunch at in Charenton?'

'I don't remember. It was in a street about halfway between the station and the steamboat wharf, a rather poor place with an overhanging, half-timbered front.'

'And what time was that?'

'About one-thirty, I think. I am not sure.'

'And from where did you telephone to your house and office?'

'From the same café.'

'About what time?'

'About an hour later, say half-past two.'

'Now, the café in the Place de la Bastille. Which one was it?'

'I am not very certain. I think it was at the corner of the rue St Antoine. At all events it faced up the rue de Lyon.'

'And you were there about what time?'

'Eight-thirty, I should say.'

'Did you get your bag at the Gare du Nord?'

'Yes, it was waiting for me at the left luggage office.'

'Did you have a sleeping berth on the train?'

'No, I travelled in an ordinary first-class compartment.'

'Was there anyone else in it?'

'Three other men. I did not know any of them.'

'Now, all that day, Tuesday, did you meet anyone who knew you, or who could confirm your statement?'

'Not that I can remember, unless the waiters at the cafés could do so.'

'On the next day, Wednesday, from where did you telephone to the Hôtel Maximilian?'

'From the café where I dined. It was in the Boulevard Anspach, just before it opens into the Place Brouckère. I don't recall the name.'

'What time was the message sent?'

'Just before dinner, about seven, I should say.'

The detective stood up and bowed.

'Well, M. Boirac, accept my thanks for your courtesy. That is all I want to know. Good night, monsieur.'

The night being fine, Lefarge walked slowly to his home near the Place de la Bastille. As he paced along he thought over the statement he had just listened to. If it was true, it appeared at first sight entirely to clear M. Boirac from suspicion. If he was in Paris on Monday he could not have sent the letter to Dupierre ordering the statue. That was received on Tuesday morning, and must therefore have been posted in London the previous day. If he was at Brussels and Malines, he obviously could not have met the cask in London. The first thing would therefore be to test the statement by independent inquiries. He reviewed it again in detail, taking a mental note of all the points on which confirmation should be obtainable.

First of all, it should be easy to find out whether he really was in Paris up till Tuesday evening. François and the other servants could tell him this with regard to Sunday, Sunday night, and Monday night, and the office staff at the pump manufactory could testify to Monday and Tuesday morning. The servants could also tell whether he unpacked the statue on Monday evening. There was then the question of the time he left his office on Tuesday; that could easily be ascertained. With regard to the restaurant at Charenton, M. Boirac would be a well-dressed and striking luncher at a place in such a locality, and would therefore undoubtedly have been specially noticed. If he really did lunch there, confirmation should be easily obtainable, particularly as the episode of the telephone would further call attention to the visit. The receipt of these telephone messages should also be easy to substantiate, as well as the leaving of the luggage at the Gare du Nord. Confirmation from the Gare du Nord cloakroom attendant, as well as from the waiters in the restaurant in the Place de la Bastille, could hardly be expected, owing to the larger number of strangers these men served, but both places would be worth trying. Inquiries at Malines might prove Boirac's visit, and certainly would show whether he had a brother there, as well as whether the house was locked up on the day in question. The staff in the Hôtel Maximilian in Brussels would know whether or not he was there on the Wednesday night, and could tell about the receipt of the telephone message booking the room. Finally, it would be worth finding out if Berlioz's *Les Troyens* was really given on that evening at the Théâtre de la Monnaie.

As Lefarge thought over the matter, he saw that the statement was one which admitted of a good many tests, and he felt that, if it stood those he had enumerated, it might be fully accepted.

19

THE TESTING OF AN ALIBI

The Seine was looking its best on the following morning, as Lefarge boarded an east-bound steamer at the Pont des Artes, behind the Louvre. The day was charming, the air having some of the warmth and colouring of summer, without having lost the clear freshness of spring. As the boat swung out into the current, the detective recalled the last occasion on which he had embarked at this same pier – that on which he and Burnley had gone downstream to Grenelle to call on M. Thévenet at the statuary works. This time the same quest took him in the opposite direction, and they passed round the Ile de la Cité, along the quais, whose walls are topped by the stalls of the book-vendors of the Latin Quarter, past the stately twin towers of Notre Dame, and under the bridge of the Metropolitaine opposite the Gare d'Austerlitz. As they steamed up the broad river the buildings became less and less imposing, till before they had covered the four miles to the suburb of Charenton, where the Marne pours its waters into the Seine, trees and patches of green had begun to appear.

Landing at Charenton, which was as far as the steamer went, Lefarge strolled up the street in the direction of the station, looking for a restaurant with an overhanging, half-timbered front. He had not to make a long search. The largest and most pretentious café in the street answered the description and, when he saw telephone wires leading to it, he felt it was indeed the one he sought. Entering, he sat down at one of the small marble-topped tables and called for a bock.

The room was fair-sized, with a bar at one corner, and a small dancing stage facing the door. But for the detective, it was untenanted. An elderly, white-moustached waiter passed back and forward from some room in the rear.

'Pleasant day,' said Lefarge, when this man came over with his bock. 'I suppose you don't get busy till later on?'

The man admitted it.

'Well I hear you give a very good lunch, anyway,' continued the detective. 'A friend of mine lunched here some days ago and was much pleased. And he's not so easy to satisfy either.'

The waiter smiled and bowed.

'We try to do our best, monsieur. It is very gratifying to learn that your friend was satisfied.'

'Did he not tell you so? He generally says what he thinks.'

'I am not sure that I know your friend, monsieur. When was he here?'

'Oh, you'd remember him right enough if you saw him. There he is.' Lefarge took a photograph of Boirac from his pocket and handed it over.

'But yes, monsieur. Quite well I remember your friend. But,' he hesitated slightly, 'he did not strike me as being so much pleased with the lunch as you suggest. I thought indeed he considered the restaurant not quite – ' He shrugged his shoulders.

'He was not very well, but he was pleased right enough. It was last Thursday he was here, wasn't it?'

'Last Thursday, monsieur? No, I think it was earlier. Let me see, I think it was Monday.'

'I made a mistake. It was not Thursday. I remember now it was Tuesday he said. Was it not Tuesday?'

'Perhaps it was, monsieur, I am not certain; though I rather think it was Monday.'

'He telephoned to me that day from Charenton – I think he said from here. Did he telephone from here?'

'Yes, monsieur, he made two calls. See, there is the telephone. We allow all our patrons to use it.'

'An excellent idea. I am sure it is much appreciated. But there was an unfortunate mistake about the message he sent me. It was making an appointment, and he did not turn up. I am afraid I misunderstood what he said. Could you hear the message? Perhaps, if so, you would tell me if he spoke of an appointment on last Tuesday?'

The waiter, who up to then had been all smiles and amiability, flashed a suspicious little glance at the detective. He continued to smile politely, but Lefarge felt he had closed up like an oyster in his shell, and when he replied: 'I could not hear, monsieur. I was engaged with the service,' the other suspected he was lying.

He determined to try a bluff. Changing his manner and speaking authoritatively, though in a lower tone, he said: 'Now, look here, *garçon*. I am a detective officer. I want to find out about those telephone messages, and I don't want to have the trouble of taking you to the Sûreté to interrogate you.' He took out a five-franc piece. 'If you can tell me what he said, this will be yours.'

A look of alarm came into the man's eyes. 'But, monsieur –' he began.

'Come now, I am certain you know, and you've got to tell. You may as well do it now and get your five francs, as later on at the Sûreté and for nothing. What do you say now? Which is it to be?'

The waiter remained silent, and it was obvious to Lefarge that he was weighing his course of action. His hesitation convinced the detective that he really did know the messages, and he determined to strike again.

'Perhaps you are doubtful whether I really am from the Sûreté,' he suggested. 'Look at that.'

He displayed his detective's credentials, and the sight seemed to bring the other to a decision.

'I will tell you, monsieur. He first called up someone that I took to be his valet, and said he was going unexpectedly to Belgium, and that he wanted something left at the Gare du Nord for him – I did not catch what it was. Then he called up some other place and gave the same message, simply that he was going to Belgium for a couple of days. That was all, monsieur.'

'That's all right, *garçon*. Here's your five francs.'

'A good beginning,' thought the detective, as he left the café and, turning his back on the river, passed on up the street. There could be no doubt that Boirac really had lunched at Charenton as he said. It was true the waiter thought he had been there on Monday, whereas Boirac had said Tuesday, but the waiter was not certain, and, in any case, the mistake would be a very easy one to make. Besides, the point could be checked. He could find out from M. Boirac's chief clerk and butler on what day they received their messages.

He walked to Charenton Station, and took a train to the Gare du Lyon. Hailing a taxi, he was driven to the end of the rue Championnet, the street in which was situated the pump factory of which M. Boirac was managing director. As he left the motor and began strolling down the footpath, he heard the clocks chiming the half-hour after eleven.

The pump factory had not a very long frontage on the street, but, glancing in through an open gateway, Lefarge saw that it stretched a long way back. At one side of the site was a four-storey block of buildings, the door of which bore the legend, 'Bureau au Deuxième Étage.' The detective strolled past with his head averted, looking round only to make sure there was no other entrance to the works.

Some fifty yards or more beyond the factory, on the opposite side of the street, there stood a café. Entering in a leisurely way, Lefarge seated himself at a small marble-topped table in the window, from where he had a good view of the office door and yard gate of the works. Ordering another bock, he drew a newspaper from his pocket and, leaning back in his chair, began to read. He held it carefully at such a level that he could keep an eye over it on the works entrance, while at any moment raising it by a slight and natural movement would screen him from observation from without. So, for a considerable time he sipped his bock and waited.

Several persons entered and left the works, but it was not till the detective had sat there nearly an hour and had consumed two more bocks, that he saw what he had hoped for. M. Boirac stepped out of the office door and, turning in the opposite direction, walked down the street towards the city. Lefarge waited for five minutes longer, then, slowly folding up his paper and lighting a cigarette, he left the café.

He strolled a hundred yards farther from the works, then crossed and turning, retraced his steps and passed in through the door from which the managing director had emerged. Handing in his private card, he asked for M. Boirac.

'I'm sorry, monsieur,' replied the clerk who had come forward, 'but he has just gone out. I wonder you didn't meet him.'

'No,' said Lefarge, 'I must have missed him. But if his confidential clerk is in, perhaps he could see me instead? Is he here at present?'

'I believe so, monsieur. If you will take a seat, I'll inquire.'

In a few moments the clerk returned to say that M. Dufresne was in, and he was shown into the presence of a small, elderly man, who was evidently just about to leave for lunch.

'I rather wanted to see M. Boirac himself, monsieur,' said Lefarge, when the customary greetings had passed. 'It is on a private matter, but I think I need hardly wait for M. Boirac, as you can probably tell me what I want to know, if you will be so kind. I am, monsieur, a detective officer from the Sûreté' – here he produced his official card – 'and my visit is in connection with some business about which we are in communication with M. Boirac. You will readily understand I am not at liberty to discuss its details, but in connection with it he called recently at the Sûreté and made a statement. There were, unfortunately, two points which he omitted to tell us and which we, not then understanding they were relevant, omitted to ask. The matter is in connection with his recent visit to Belgium, and the two points I wanted to ask him are, first, the hour he left the office here on that Tuesday, and second, the hour at which he telephoned to you from Charenton that he was making the journey. Perhaps you can tell me, or would you prefer I should wait and see M. Boirac himself?'

The chief clerk did not immediately reply, and Lefarge could see he was uncertain what line he should take. The detective therefore continued: 'Pray do not answer me if you feel the slightest hesitation. I can easily wait, if you would rather.'

This had the desired effect and the clerk answered: 'Certainly not, monsieur, if you do not wish to do so yourself. I can answer your questions, or at least one of them. The other I am not so sure of. I received the telephone message from M. Boirac from Charenton at about quarter before three. That I am sure of as I particularly noted the time. As to when M. Boirac left here that morning, I cannot be so definite. He asked me at nine o'clock to draft a rather difficult reply to a letter and to take it in to him when ready. It took me half an hour to compose, as several figures had to be got out to make the matter clear. I took it in at 9.30 and he had then gone.'

'That was on the Tuesday, wasn't it?'

'Yes, on the Tuesday.'

'And it was on the Friday morning M. Boirac returned?'

'That is so, monsieur.'

Lefarge rose.

'A thousand thanks, monsieur. I am very grateful to you for saving me a long wait.'

He left the office and, walking to the Simplon station of the Metropolitaine, took the train for the centre of the town. He was pleased with his progress. As in the earlier stages of the inquiry, information was coming in rapidly. At first he was inclined to think he had already got enough to confirm the first portion of Boirac's statement, then his training reasserted itself, and he decided to go back to the house in the Avenue de l'Alma, and if possible get François' corroboration. He therefore alighted at Chatelet and took the Maillot train to Alma, walking down the Avenue.

'Ah, M. François,' he began, when the butler opened the door. 'Here I am back to trouble you again. Can you spare me a couple of minutes?'

'Certainly, monsieur. Come in.'

They went to the same small sitting-room and Lefarge produced his Brazilian cigarettes.

'How do you like them? 'he asked, as the butler helped himself. 'Some people think they're too strong, but they suit me down to the ground. Like strong whiffs, only without the cigar flavour. I won't keep you a moment. It's just about that bag of M. Boirac's you took to the Gare du Nord last Tuesday. Tell me, were you followed to the station?'

'Followed, monsieur? I? Why no, certainly not. At least not that I know of.'

'Well, did you observe at the left luggage office a rather tall man, dressed in grey and with a red beard?'

'No,' he answered, 'I saw no one answering to the description.'

'At what hour did you leave the bag in?'

'About 3.30, monsieur.'

Lefarge affected to consider.

'Perhaps it's my mistake,' he said at last. 'It was on Tuesday, wasn't it?'

'On Tuesday. Yes monsieur.'

'And M. Boirac sent his telephone call about two, did he not? I think he said about two.'

'It was later, monsieur. It was nearer three. But, monsieur, you fill me with curiosity. How, if I may ask, did you know I took Monsieur's bag to the station?'

'He told me last night. He happened to mention he had unexpectedly gone to Belgium, and that you had taken his bag to the left luggage office.'

'And the man with the red beard?'

Lefarge, having got his information, was not much troubled to justify his little ruse.

'One of our detectives. He has been on a case of theft of valuable luggage. I wondered if you had seen him. By the way, did M. Boirac bring back the bag with him? *It* wasn't stolen?'

Lefarge smiled, and the butler, politely presuming this was meant for a joke, smiled also.

'It was not stolen, monsieur. He brought it back all right.'

So far so good. M. Boirac had then, beyond any doubt or question, telephoned about 2.45 on Tuesday and had instructed the butler to take his bag to the Gare du Nord, as he had said. Further, he had called there himself and got the bag. So much was certain. But the statement he made of his movements on Sunday and Monday, and the unpacking of the cask on Monday night still remained to be tested. Lefarge spoke again: 'While I'm here, M. François, I wonder would you mind checking one or two dates for my report?' He pulled out his notebook. 'I will read out and perhaps you would please say if the items are correct. Saturday, 27th March, the day of the dinner party.'

'Correct, monsieur.'

'Sunday, 28th, nothing special occurred. M. Boirac unpacked the cask in the evening.'

'That's not right, monsieur. It was on Monday the cask was unpacked.'

'Ah, Monday.' Lefarge pretended to correct his notes. 'Monday evening, of course. M. Boirac was at home on Sunday night, but he did not unpack it till Monday. That's right, I think?'

'That's right.'

'Then on Tuesday he went to Belgium, and returned home on Thursday evening?'

'Correct, monsieur.'

'Thanks very much. I'm glad you noticed that slip. I've got it right now, I think.'

He remained conversing for a few minutes, making himself agreeable to the old man and telling him some of the adventures he had met with during his career. The more he saw of François, the more he came to respect him, and he felt increasingly certain the old man's statement was to be believed and that he would not lend himself to anything dishonourable.

As if to balance the successes of the morning, during the whole of the afternoon Lefarge drew blank. After leaving the house in the Avenue de l'Alma, he questioned the clerks in the left luggage office at the Gare du Nord. Here he could get no information at all. No one remembered François putting in the bag, nor Boirac claiming it, nor could any record of the bag itself be turned up. Again, in the Place de la Bastille, where he spent some hours interviewing the waiters in the various restaurants, both in the Place itself and close by in the diverging streets, no better luck attended his efforts. He could find no trace of Boirac's having dined in any of them.

All the same he was well satisfied with his day's work. The information he had got was definite and valuable, in fact, he thought it conclusively established the truth of Boirac's statement, at least in as far as Tuesday was concerned. If he could do as well in connection with the Wednesday and Thursday, he thought the manufacturer's alibi would stand, and his innocence of the murder must then be admitted.

To carry on the inquiry, he would have to visit Brussels, and he accordingly telephoned to the Gare du Nord engaging a berth on the 11.20 p.m. sleeping car train that night. Then, after calling up the Sûreté, he turned his steps homewards to dine and have a rest till it was time to start.

He made a comfortable journey, and, having breakfasted in one of the cafés in the Place du Nord in Brussels, took an early train to Malines. He presented himself at the post office and asked if he could be directed to the residence of M. Armande Boirac. The clerk knew the name, though he was not certain of the address, but after inquiries at two or three of the principal shops, the detective found one at which M. Boirac dealt.

'Yes, monsieur, it's a good four miles out on the Louvain road. A large white house with a red roof, standing in trees on the right-hand side, immediately beyond a crossroads. But I think M. Boirac is from home, if you wanted to see him.'

'I did wish to see him,' returned Lefarge, 'but I dare say Mme. Boirac would see me instead.'

'I fear she is also away, monsieur. At least, I can only tell you what I know. She came in here about a fortnight ago, indeed, I remember now it was just this day fortnight, and said: "Oh, Laroche," she said, "you need not send anything for two or three weeks, till you hear from me again. We are going away and are shutting up the house. So, monsieur, I don't think you'll see either of them if you go out.'

'I am greatly obliged to you, monsieur. I wonder if you could still further add to your kindness by informing me of M. Boirac's place of business, where I might get his address. He is in business, I suppose?'

'He is a banker, monsieur, and goes frequently to Brussels, but I don't know in which bank he is interested.

But if you go across the street to M. Leblanc, the avocat, I expect he could tell you.'

Lefarge thanked the polite shopman and, following his advice, called on the avocat. Here he learnt that M. Boirac was one of the directors of a large private bank, the Crédit Mazières, in the Boulevard de la Senne, in Brussels.

He was half tempted to return at once to the capital, but a long experience had convinced him of the folly of accepting *any* statement without investigation. To be on the safe side, he felt he should go out and see for himself if the house was indeed empty. He therefore hired a small car and drove out along the Louvain road.

The day was bright and sunny, though with a little sharpness in the air, and Lefarge enjoyed the run through the pleasant Belgian country. He hoped to get his work finished by the afternoon, and, in that case, he would go back to Paris by the night train.

About fifteen minutes brought them to the house, which Lefarge immediately recognised from the shopman's description. A glance showed it was empty. The gates of the avenue were fastened with a padlock and chain, and, through the surrounding trees, the window shutters could be seen to be closed. The detective looked about him.

Alongside the road close to the gates were three cottages, occupied apparently by peasants or farm labourers. Lefarge stepped up to the first of these and knocked.

'Good morning,' he said, as a buxom, middle-aged woman came to the door. 'I have just come from Brussels to see M. Boirac, and I find the house is locked up. Can you tell me if there is a caretaker, or anyone who could tell me where M. Boirac is to be found?'

'I am the caretaker, monsieur, but I do not know M. Boirac's address. All he told me before he left was that any letters sent to the Crédit Mazières in Brussels would be forwarded.'

'He has not then been gone long, I suppose?'

'A fortnight today, monsieur. He said he would be away three weeks, so if you could call in about a week, you should see him.'

'By the way, a friend of mine was to call on him here last week. I am afraid he must have missed him also. You did not see my friend?' He showed her Boirac's photograph.

'No, monsieur, I did not see him.'

Lefarge thanked the woman and, having walked round to two or three of the other neighbouring houses and asked the same questions without result, he re-entered the car and was driven back to Malines. From there he took the first train to Brussels.

It was close on two o'clock when he entered the ornate portal of the Crédit Mazières, of which M. Boirac was a director. The building was finished with extraordinary richness, no expense having been spared in its decoration. The walls of the vast public office were entirely covered with choice marbles – panels of delicate green separated by pilasters and cornice of pure white. The roof rose into a lofty dome of glass which filled the building with a mellow and pleasant light. 'No want of money here,' Lefarge thought, as he approached the counter and, handing in his card, asked to see the manager.

He had to wait for some minutes, then, following a clerk along a corridor decorated in the same style as the office, he was ushered into the presence of a tall, elderly gentleman with clean-shaven features and raven black hair, who was seated at a large roll-top desk.

Having exchanged greetings, Lefarge began: 'I wonder, monsieur, if you would be so very kind as to tell me whether the M. Armande Boirac who is a member of your board, is the brother of M. Raoul Boirac, the managing director of the Avrotte Pump Construction Company of Paris? I went to Malines this morning to see M. Armande, but he was from home, and I do not wish to spend time in finding out his address and communicating with him, unless he really is the man I seek.'

'Our director, monsieur,' replied the manager, 'is a brother of M. Raoul. Though I don't know the latter personally, I have heard our M. Boirac speak of him. I can also give you M. Armande's present address, if you require it.'

'I am exceedingly obliged, monsieur, and should be most grateful for the address.'

'It is Hôtel Rydberg, Stockholm.'

Lefarge noted it in his book and, with further thanks, left the bank.

'Now for the Théâtre de la Monnaie,' he thought. 'It is just round the corner.'

He crossed the Place de Brouckère, and turned into the Place de la Monnaie. The box office of the theatre was open, and he interviewed the clerk, learning that Berlioz's *Les Troyens* was given on the Wednesday night in question, as stated by M. Boirac. But a search for that gentleman's name through the list of that evening's bookings was unproductive, though, as the clerk pointed out, this did not mean that he was not present, but only that he had not reserved a seat.

Lefarge's next visit was to the Hôtel Maximilian. It was a large modern building occupying a complete block of the Boulevard Waterloo, not far from the Porte Louise. A polite clerk came to the bureau window to attend to him.

'I am expecting to meet a M. Boirac here,' Lefarge began. 'Can you tell me if he is in the hotel?'

'M. Boirac?' repeated the clerk, doubtfully, 'I do not think we have anyone of that name here at present.' He turned over a card index on the desk. 'No, monsieur, he has not come yet.'

Lefarge took out a photograph.

'That is he,' he said, 'a M. Raoul Boirac, of Paris.'

'Oh, to be sure,' returned the clerk, 'I know that gentleman. He has frequently stayed with us, but he is not here at present.'

The detective began to turn over the leaves of his pocket-book as if looking for something.

'I hope I haven't made a mistake in the date,' he said. 'He wasn't here recently by any chance, was he?'

'He was here, monsieur, quite lately – last week in fact. He spent one night.'

Lefarge made a gesture of annoyance.

'I've missed him!' he exclaimed 'As sure as fate I've missed him. Can you tell me what night he was here?'

'Certainly, monsieur.' He turned up some papers. 'He was here on Wednesday night, the 31st March.'

'I've missed him. Now, isn't that too bad? I must have mistaken the date.' The detective stood apparently considering.

'Did he mention my name – Pascal, Jules Pascal?'

The clerk shook his head.

'Not to me, monsieur.'

Lefarge continued, as if to himself: 'He must have come through from Paris that night.' And then to the clerk: 'You don't remember, I suppose, what time he arrived?'

'Yes, I do. It was late in the evening, about eleven, I should think.'

'Rather a chance coming at that hour, wasn't it? He might easily have found you full?'

'Oh, he had reserved his room. Earlier in the evening he telephoned up from a restaurant in the Boulevard Anspach that he was coming.'

'Was that before five? I was to meet him about five.'

'Not so early, I think. More like half-past seven or even eight, as well as I can remember.'

'Well, I can't understand it at all. But I mustn't be wasting your time. I'll write a note and, if he should turn up again, perhaps you would be kind enough to give it to him? I'm much obliged to you, I'm sure.'

Lefarge was an artist in his profession. He never made an impersonation without carrying through the details in the most thorough manner possible. He therefore wrote a note to M. Boirac in an assumed hand, regretting having missed him and carefully explaining some quite imaginary business. Having signed it 'Jules Pascal' with a flourish, and left it with the clerk, he took his leave.

As he passed out of the Boulevard Waterloo to return to the old town, the clocks were striking six. He had completed his errand and he was tired, though well satisfied with its result. He would rest in a picture house for an hour or two, then have a leisurely dinner and catch the midnight train for Paris.

Sitting over his coffee in a quiet corner of one of the large restaurants in the Boulevard du Nord, he reviewed once more M. Boirac's statement, ticking off in his mind the various items he had been able to check. On Saturday night Madame had disappeared. On Sunday and Sunday night Boirac was at his home. Monday he spent at his office, and that night he was again at home. On that same Monday evening he had unpacked the statue from the cask. Tuesday morning saw him in his office at the usual hour, but he had

243

left again between nine o'clock and half-past. About 1.30 that same day he had lunched at Charenton, and shortly after 2.30 had telephoned to François and to his office. François had taken his bag to the Gare du Nord about 3.30, and Boirac had got it from there, as he had brought it back with him from Belgium. He had telephoned to the Hôtel Maximilian about 7.30 or 8.0 on the Wednesday, and had slept there that night. Next day he had returned to Paris, reaching his house in the evening. Further, it was true that his brother lived at Malines and that his house had been shut up on the Wednesday in question, also that Berlioz's *Les Troyens* was given on the night he said.

So much was absolute bedrock fact, proved beyond any doubt or question. Lefarge then turned his mind to the portions of Boirac's statement which he had not been able to verify.

He could not tell whether the manufacturer had walked in the Bois de Vincennes before lunching at Charenton, nor if he had gone up the Seine after it. He could not trace his having dined in any of the cafés of the Place de la Bastille. He had not proved that he went to Malines or called at his brother's house, nor did he know if he had been present at the opera in Brussels.

As he considered the matter, he came to the conclusion that in the nature of things he could hardly have expected to confirm these points, and he also decided they were not essential to the statement. All the essentials – Boirac's presence at Charenton and in Brussels – particularly in Brussels – he had proved up to the hilt. He therefore came to the deliberate conclusion that the pump manufacturer's statement was true. And if it was true M. Boirac was innocent of the murder, and if he was innocent – Felix...

Next day he made his report to M. Chauvet at the Sûreté.

20

SOME DAMNING EVIDENCE

When Burnley left Lefarge on the pier at Boulogne, he felt as if he was losing a well-tried friend. Not only had the Frenchman, by his kindliness and cheerful companionship, made Burnley's stay in the French capital a pleasant one, but his skill and judgment had been a real asset in the inquiry.

And how rapidly the inquiry had progressed! Never before could Burnley recall having obtained so much information on any case in so short a time. And though his work was by no means complete, he was yet within reasonable distance of the end.

After an uneventful crossing he reached Folkestone and immediately went to the police station. There he saw the men who had been on duty when the *Pas de Calais* had berthed on the Sunday in question. But his inquiries were without result. No one resembling either Felix or Mme. Boirac had been observed.

He next tried the Customs officials, the porters who had taken the luggage from the boat, and the staff at the Pier Station. No information was forthcoming.

'H'm. Means going to Glasgow, I suppose,' he thought and, turning into the telegraph office on the platform he sent a wire:

Henry Gordon, 327 Angus Lane, Sauchiehall Street, Glasgow. Could you see me if I called at ten tomorrow. Reply Burnley, Scotland Yard.

Then he set off to walk to the Town Station to catch the next train for London.

At New Scotland Yard he had an interview with his Chief, to whom he recounted the results of the consultation in the Sûreté, and his movements during the past two days, explaining that he proposed to go on to Glasgow that night if Mr Gordon could see him the next morning. Then he went home for an hour's rest. Ten o'clock saw him back at the Yard, where a telegram from Mr Gordon was awaiting him. 'Can see you tomorrow at the hour named.'

'So far, so good,' he thought, as he called a taxi and was driven to Euston, where he caught the 11.50 express for the north. He usually slept well in trains, and on this occasion he surpassed himself, only waking when the attendant came round half an hour before they were due in Glasgow.

A bath and breakfast at the Central Hotel made him feel fresh and fit as he sallied forth to keep his appointment in Angus Lane, Sauchiehall Street. Ten o'clock was chiming from the city towers as he pushed open the office door of No. 327, which bore the legend, 'Mr Henry Gordon, Wholesale Tea Merchant.' That gentleman was expecting him, and he was ushered into his private room without delay.

'Good morning, sir,' he began, as Mr Gordon, a tall man with small, fair side whiskers, and two very keen blue eyes, rose to meet him. 'I am an Inspector from Scotland Yard, and I have taken the liberty of making this appointment to ask your help in an inquiry in which I am engaged.'

Mr Gordon bowed.

'Well, sir, and what do you wish me to do?'

'To answer a few questions, if you don't mind.'

'I shall be pleased if I am able.'

'Thank you. You were in Paris recently, I believe?'

'That is so?'

'And you stayed at the Hôtel Continental?'

'I did.'

'Can you tell me what day you left to return to England?'

'Yes, it was Sunday, the 28th of March.'

'You drove, if I am not mistaken, from the hotel to the Gare du Nord in the hotel bus?'

'I did.'

'Now, Mr Gordon, can you recollect what, if any, other persons travelled with you in the bus?'

The tea merchant did not immediately reply.

'I did not specially observe, Mr Inspector. I am not sure that I can tell you.'

'My information, sir, is that three gentlemen travelled by that bus. You were one, and the man I am interested in was another. I am told that he conversed with you, or made at least one remark as you were leaving the bus at the station. Does this bring the circumstance to your mind?'

Mr Gordon made a gesture of assent.

'You are correct. I recall the matter now, and the men too. One was small, stout, clean-shaven, and elderly, the other younger, with a black pointed beard and rather foppishly dressed. They were both French, I took it, but the black-bearded man spoke English excellently. He was talkative, but the other hadn't much to say. Is it the bearded man you mean?'

For answer Burnley held out one of Felix's photographs.

'Is that he?'

'Yes, that's the man sure enough. I remember him perfectly now.'

'Did he travel with you to London?'

'He didn't travel with me, but he got to London all right, for I saw him twice again, once on the boat and once as I was leaving the station at Charing Cross.'

Here was definite evidence anyway. Burnley congratulated himself and felt glad he had not delayed making this visit.

'Did he travel alone?'

'So far as I know. He certainly started alone from the Hotel.'

'And he didn't meet anyone *en route* that you saw?'

'When I saw him on the boat he was talking to a lady, but whether they were travelling together or merely chance acquaintances I couldn't say.'

'Was this lady with him in London?'

'Not that I saw. He was talking to a man on the platform as I drove out. A tall young fellow, dark and rather good-looking.'

'Would you know this young man again if you saw him?'

'Yes, I think so. I got a good look at his face.'

'I should be obliged if you would describe him more fully.'

'He was about five feet eleven, or six feet in height, rather thin and athletic-looking. He had a pale complexion, was clean-shaven except for a small black moustache, and was rather French-looking. He was dressed in some dark clothes, a brown overcoat, I fancy, but of that I'm not sure. I imagined he was meeting your friend, but I had really no definite reason to think so.'

'Now, the lady, Mr Gordon. Can you describe her?'

'No, I'm afraid I can't. She was sitting beside him and I did not see her face.'

'Can you tell how she was dressed?'

'She wore a reddish brown fur coat, sable, I fancy, though I'm not certain.'

'And her hat? You didn't notice anything special about that.'

'No, nothing.'

'It hadn't, for example, a wide brim?'

'A wide brim? Not that I noticed. But it may have had.'

'Was it windy where they were sitting?'

'Every place was windy that day. It was an abominable crossing.'

'So that if it had had a wide brim, the lady would have had difficulty in keeping it on?'

'Possibly,' replied Mr Gordon a trifle dryly, 'but you probably can form an opinion on that as well as I.'

Burnley smiled.

'We Scotland Yard people like to know everything,' he said. 'And now, Mr Gordon, I have to express my thanks for your courtesy and help.'

'That's all right. Would it be indiscreet to ask the reason of these queries?'

'Not at all, sir, but I fear I am not at liberty to give you much information. The man with the pointed beard is suspected of having decoyed a French lady over to England and murdered her. But, you will understand, it is so far only a matter of suspicion.'

'Well, I should be interested to hear how it turns out.'

'I am afraid you will hear, sir. If this man is tried, I expect your evidence will be required.'

'Then for both our sakes I hope your case will not go on. Good day, Mr Burnley. Glad to have met you.'

There being nothing to keep him in Glasgow, the Inspector returned to the Central and took the midday London express. As it thundered southwards across the smiling country, he thought over the interview he had just had. He could not help marvelling again at the luck that had pursued his efforts ever since the inquiry began. Nearly every one he had interviewed had known at least something, if not always exactly what he wanted. He thought how many thousands of persons crossed the Channel each week whose journey it would be absolutely impossible to trace, and here, in the one instance that mattered, he had found a man who had been able to give him the very information he needed. Had Felix not gone in the bus, had Mr Gordon not been so observant, had the circumstances not fallen out precisely as they did, he might never have ascertained the knowledge of Felix's movements that day. And the same applied all through. Truly, if he did not get a complete case it would be his own fault.

And yet the evidence was unsatisfactory. It was never conclusive. It had a kind of thus-far-and-no-farther quality which always pointed to a certain thing, but stopped short of certainty. Here there was a strong presumption that Mme. Boirac had crossed with Felix, but no proof. It might, however unlikely, have been someone else. Nearly all the evidence he had got was circumstantial, and he wanted certainty.

His mind switched over to the case itself. He felt the probability of Felix's guilt had been somewhat strengthened. Mr Gordon's statement was entirely consistent with that hypothesis. One would naturally expect the journey to be carried out just as it had been. In Paris, the lovers would be careful not to be seen together. At a station like the Gare du Nord, where acquaintances of both might easily be present, they would doubtless ignore each other's existence. On the boat they would probably risk a conversation, particularly as the deck was almost deserted owing to the weather, but in London, especially if Felix expected someone to meet him, they would follow their Paris plan and leave the station separately. Yes, it certainly worked in.

The Inspector lit one of his strong cigars and gazed with unseeing eyes at the flying landscape as he continued his ruminations. On arrival in London what would be their next step? Felix, he expected, would shake off his friend, meet Madame at some prearranged spot, and in all probability take her to St Malo. Then he recalled that the housekeeper had been granted a holiday, and they would doubtless arrive to find a house without food or fire, empty and cheerless. Therefore would they not go to an hotel? He thought it likely, and he began to plan a possible future step, a visit to all the probable hotels. But while speculating on the best to begin with, it occurred to him that if Felix had really committed the murder it must, almost certainly, have been done at St Malo. He could not conceive it possible at an hotel. Therefore probably they did go to the villa after all.

He went a step further. If the murder had taken place at St Malo, the cask must have been packed there. He recalled the traces this operation had left in Boirac's study. Surely some similar indications must have been left at the villa? If the cask had stood on a carpet or even possibly a linoleum, he might expect marks of the ring. And if not, there was the sawdust. He did not believe every trace of sawdust could have been removed.

It had been his intention in any case to search the house, and he took a mental note when doing so to look with special care for any such traces. This search, he decided, should be his next business.

On the following morning, therefore, he set out for St Malo with his assistant, Sergeant Kelvin. As they drove, he explained his theory about the unpacking of the cask, and pointed out what, if this had been done, they might expect to find.

The house was empty as, owing to Felix still being in hospital, the housekeeper's leave had been extended. Burnley opened the door with a key from Felix's bunch and the two men entered.

Then took place a search of the most meticulous thoroughness. Burnley began in the yard and examined each of the outhouses in turn. These had concrete floors and marks of the cask itself were not to be expected, but they were carefully brushed and the sweepings examined with a powerful lens for traces of sawdust. All their contents were also inspected, Felix's two-seater, which was standing in the coach house, receiving its full share of attention. Then the searchers moved to the house, one room after another being gone over in the same painstaking way, but it was not till they were doing Felix's dressing-room that Burnley made his first discovery.

Several of Felix's suits were hanging in a press, and in the right-hand side pocket of one of the coats – that of a blue lounge suit – there was a letter. It was crumpled and twisted, as if thrust carelessly into the pocket. Burnley did not at first notice anything interesting or important about it, till, reading it for the second time, it flashed across his mind that here, perhaps, was the very thing for which they had been searching – the link in that chain of evidence against Felix which up to then had been missing.

The letter was written on a sheet of rather poor quality notepaper in a woman's hand, rather uneducated both as to calligraphy and diction – such a letter, thought Burnley, as might be written by a barmaid or waitress or shopgirl. There was no water or other distinctive mark on it. It bore no address, and ran as follows:

Monday

MY DEAREST LÉON,

It is with a heavy heart I take up my pen to write these few lines. What has happened to you, dearest? Are you ill? If you are, I will come out to you, no matter what happens. I can't go on without you. I waited in all yesterday hoping you would come, same as I waited in all the Sunday before, and every night of the week, but you didn't come. And the money is nearly done, and Mrs Hopkins says if I can't pay next week I'll have to go. I've sometimes thought you were tired of me and weren't going to come back at all, and then I thought you weren't that sort, and that you were maybe ill or away. But do write or come, for I can't go on any longer without you.

Your heartbroken

EMMIE.

When Burnley glanced over this melancholy epistle it seemed at first merely to indicate that Felix was no better than he might be, and it was not till he had read it again that its immense significance struck him. What if this paper supplied the motive of the murder? What if it had opened to Mme. Boirac a chapter in Felix's life which otherwise would have remained closed, and which he intended should remain closed? As Burnley thought over it he believed he could at least dimly reconstruct the scene. Felix and Madame had arrived at St Malo, and then in some way, by some act of extraordinary carelessness on Felix's part, she had got hold of the letter. A quarrel would be inevitable. What would Felix do? Probably first snatch the letter from her and thrust it into his pocket out of sight. Then, perhaps, try to pacify the angry lady, and, finding this impossible, the quarrel would get worse and worse till finally in a paroxysm of passion he would seize her throat and choke out her life. The murder committed, he would be so upset that he would quite probably forget all about the letter. The oversights of criminals were notorious.

The more the Inspector considered the matter, the more likely his theory seemed. But here again he had to recognise it was entirely surmise. No proof that this had taken place was forthcoming. It was another case of the thus-far-and-no-farther evidence he had been deploring in the train. At all events it suggested another line of inquiry. This girl must be found and the relations between her and Felix gone into. Burnley foresaw much arduous work in front of him.

At length he put the letter away in his notebook, and the search continued. Finally, as it was beginning to get dusk, every room had been done except the study where Felix and the Inspector had had their midnight discussion.

'I think we had better come back tomorrow,' said Burnley. 'No use in searching by lamplight.'

Accordingly, the next morning saw them again at work. They crawled over the floor so as to get every part of the carpet between themselves and the light, but could find no impressions. They peered with their lenses in the pile of the carpet, they felt between the arms and seats of the padded leathern chairs, all to no purpose. And then Burnley made his second discovery.

Between the study and the dining-room adjoining there was a door, evidently unused, as it was locked and the key was gone. On the study side this door was covered by a heavy curtain of dark green plush. In front of the curtain, and standing with its back to it, was a small chair whose low, leather-padded back formed a half-circle with the arms. In his anxiety to leave no part of the carpet unexamined, Burnley had moved this chair aside.

As he stooped at the place where the chair had been, a bright object sticking to the curtain caught his eye. He looked more closely. A small, slightly bent, gold safety-pin, bearing a tiny row of diamonds, was caught in the braid at the top of the hem. The point had not penetrated, and the pin fell to the floor when Burnley touched the plush.

He picked it up.

'That's rather a fine thing even for a natty boy like Felix,' he said as he showed it to Kelvin. And then he stood quite still as it flashed across his mind that here, perhaps, was another link in the chain that was being forged about Felix – a link possibly even more important than any of the foregoing. What if it did not belong to Felix at all? It looked too dainty and delicate for a man's use. What if it was a lady's? And, most important question of all, what if that lady was Mme. Boirac? If this proved true, his case was complete.

Dropping into the armchair he had occupied on the occasion of his midnight interview with Felix, he considered the possibilities opened up by this new discovery, endeavouring to evolve some theory of how a pin or brooch belonging to the deceased lady could have been dropped where he found this one. As he did so, a picture of what might have happened gradually grew in his mind. Firstly, he thought it likely that a lady in evening dress would wear

255

such a pin, and it might easily be at her neck or shoulder. And if she had sat in that chair with her back to the curtain, and anyone had caught her by the throat and forced her head backwards, what could be more likely than that the pin should be pulled out in the struggle? And if it were pulled out it almost certainly would drop where or whereabouts he found it.

The Inspector recognised again that this was all surmise, but it was strengthened by the fact that the pin was undoubtedly bent as if it had been pulled out of something without being unhooked. The more he thought over it the more likely his idea seemed. At all events it would be easy to test it. Two points suggested themselves to his mind which would settle it conclusively.

First, if the pin was Madame's, the maid Suzanne would recognise it. The arrangement of the diamonds made it quite distinctive. The girl would also know if Madame wore it on the night of the dinner party. Secondly, if it was pulled out of Madame's dress, the latter would probably be torn or at least marked. Both these points could easily be ascertained, and he decided he would write to Paris about them that night.

He put the brooch into a pocket case, and, getting up, resumed his search of the study. For a time he pursued his labours without result, and then he made another discovery which struck him as being of even greater importance than that of the pin. He had completed his examination of the furniture, and now, for over an hour, had been seated at Felix's desk going through drawer after drawer, reading old letters and examining the watermarks of papers and the alignment of typewritten documents. Felix evidently had some of the defects of the artistic temperament, for his papers were jumbled together without any attempt at filing or classification – accounts, receipts, invitations, engagements, business letters – all were thrust higgledy-piggledy into the first drawer that came handy. But Burnley had methodically gone through every one without finding anything of interest. None of the papers had the watermark of that ordering the statue from Dupierre, none of the typewriting had the defective letters of that ostensibly from Le Gautier to Felix. The Inspector had just reflected that he had only to go through the half-dozen shelves of books and his work would be done, when he made his third find.

On the desk lay a number of sheets of blotting paper folded pamphlet-wise, it being evidently Felix's custom to blot his wet papers between two of the leaves. Following his usual routine, the Inspector fetched a mirror from the bathroom, and with its aid examined the sheets from each edge in turn. At the fourth of these sheets he stopped suddenly with a little gesture of triumph, for there, clearly revealed in the mirror, were some words he had seen before:

.s .. .s th. .... s . c .. ... l... .. t.. ......
    .le... fo.wa.. ..med....ly to ..e ..ove .dd.ess
      I do ..t kn.w th. e.a.t pric., but ..der.t..d .t is
about 1500 francs. I therefore enclose notes for that

It was the bottom of the first page of the letter ordering the statue from Dupierre! Here was certainty: here, at last, proofs of the most complete kind! Felix had ordered the statue and like a fool had blotted his letter and omitted to destroy the blotsheet!

The Inspector chuckled with content at his find. Felix had ordered the statue. That was now certain. And if he had done so he was responsible for its first journey, and therefore undoubtedly for its second and third. In fact, it was now evident he had arranged all the movements of the cask, and, if so, he must unquestionably have put in the body, and if he put in the body he must be the murderer.

Then there was the further point, about the paper. The paper on which this letter had been written was the same as that on which the letter about the lottery and the bet was typed. Felix had stated he had received this letter by post, but at the.discussion in M. Chauvet's office the probability that he himself was the author had been recognised. This probability was now strengthened by finding he had had in his possession the peculiar French paper which had been used.

Truly these three discoveries, the letter signed 'Your heartbroken Emmie,' the bent brooch on the curtain, and the tell-tale impression on the blotting paper seemed to the Inspector entirely to settle the question of Felix's guilt.

On the other hand he had failed to find any trace of the unpacking of the cask, and his search had been so thorough that he almost felt impelled to the conclusion that it had not been there at all. And then a possible explanation struck him. Suppose Felix had got a cart and brought the cask to St Malo intending to remove it again the following morning. Where would he put it for the night? It was too heavy to move by himself, and he would not want to have a helper. What then would he do? Why, leave it on the cart, of course! His obvious plan would be to stable the horse and open the cask where it stood – on the cart. And if he dropped some sawdust in the process, the wind would see to that. There would be none left now.

He felt sure he was on the right track, and then he had a further idea. If a horse was stabled at the villa all night, some traces should surely be visible. He went to the yard again and began a new quest. But this time he had no luck. He was forced to conclude no horse had been kept.

The possibility that the carter might have left his vehicle and taken the horse away with him for the night next occurred to him, but he thought that unlikely, and left the question undecided in the meantime.

On his return to Scotland Yard, the Chief heard his story with close attention, and was much impressed by his discoveries. He gave his views at some length, ending up: 'We shall send the pin over to Paris and see if that girl identifies it. Indeed, whether or not, I think we have a sufficient case against Felix to go into court. By the way, I don't think I told you I sent a man to his firm, the poster people, and found that he was absent on holidays during the week the cask was travelling backwards and forwards to Paris. This, of course, is not evidence against him, but it works in with our theory.'

Two days later a wire came from M. Chauvet –

Suzanne Daudet identifies pin as Madame's property.

'That settles it,' said the Chief, and a warrant was made out for Felix's arrest, so soon as he should be well enough to leave the hospital.

PART 3

London and Paris

21

A NEW POINT OF VIEW

Of the millions who unfolded their papers a few mornings after the events described in the last chapter, there were few but felt a thrill of excitement as their eyes fell on the headlines, 'The Cask Mystery. Arrest of Léon Felix.' Though by no means all the facts discovered by the police had become public, enough had leaked out to arouse a keen and general interest. The tragic circumstances of the case, no less than the baffling mystery in which it was shrouded, intrigued the popular imagination and, though the police were early credited with having the usual clue and the customary arrest was stated to be imminent, none outside the official ranks had any real idea in what direction suspicion was tending.

But to none of those millions did the news come with such a sense of personal shock and affront as to our old acquaintance, Dr William Martin, of The Elms, near Brent village, on the Great North Road. Dr Martin, it will be remembered, was the man who, on the night on which Constable Walker watched from behind his tree, called at St Malo and insisted on Felix accompanying him home to play bridge. The two men were close friends. Many an afternoon they had spent together on the banks of a neighbouring trout stream, many an evening had slipped rapidly away round the doctor's billiard table. And with

Martin's family also Felix was a favourite. No member of it but was pleased to welcome the Frenchman to the house, or but had some special confidence to share with him.

At first Dr Martin could hardly believe his eyes as they rested on the fatal headlines. That Felix, his friend, his trusted companion, should be arrested! And for murder! The thought was so incredible, so utterly horrible, he could not take it in. But, unlike the nightmare to which he compared it, the idea had permanence. Though his thoughts might wander, it was always there, grim and terribly definite, for them to return to.

He began to think over his friend's circumstances. Felix had always been reticent about his life, but to the doctor he had seemed a lonely man. He lived alone, and Martin had never known him to have visitors staying in the house. Nor could the doctor recall the Frenchman's ever having spoken of relatives. 'Who,' he wondered, 'will help him now?'

But with so kindly and warm-hearted a man as Dr Martin, such a question could not long remain unanswered. 'I must go and see him,' he thought. 'I must find out who is going to act for him. If he has no one, then I must do the best I can myself.'

But a practical difficulty arose. How were orders to visit prisoners obtained? The doctor did not know. For a man of his age and standing he was singularly ignorant of legal matters. But when such came his way he invariably adopted the same simple expedient. He 'saw Clifford.' This difficulty he would meet in the same way. He would 'see Clifford.'

'Clifford'– otherwise John Wakefield Clifford, senior partner of Messrs Clifford and Lewisham, Solicitors, Grey's Inn – was Martin's man of business, friend, and crony. The chance that they took the same weekly half-holiday had thrown them together on the links, and they had followed up the acquaintanceship by occasional visits at each other's houses. Mr Clifford was an almost startling contrast to the breezy doctor. Small, elderly, and rather wizened, with white hair and moustache, and dressed always with meticulous care, he seemed the embodiment of conventional propriety. His manner was precise and dry, but the fortunate gift of a sense of humour saved him from becoming dull.

He was a fine lawyer. His admirers, who were many, held that an opinion from him was as good as Counsel's any day, and knew that, beneath the keenness which made him so formidable an opponent, there lay a deep vein of very real human kindness.

A press of unavoidable business kept Martin at work till the afternoon, but three o'clock saw him ascending the stairs of Messrs Clifford and Lewisham's office.

'How are you, Martin?' the senior partner greeted him. 'I am glad to see you. This is an unexpected pleasure.'

'Thanks, old chap,' returned the doctor, accepting the cigarette the other offered, and sinking back into a deep, leather-lined armchair. 'But I'm afraid there won't be much pleasure about my visit. It's business, and nasty business at that. Have you a few minutes to spare?'

The little man bowed gravely.

'Certainly,' he said, 'I am at your service.'

'It's about that neighbour of mine, Léon Felix,' went on the doctor, plunging without further preamble into his subject. 'You saw he was arrested last night on a charge of murdering the woman whose body was found in the cask? You know about it?'

'I read the account in this morning's paper. And so Felix was a neighbour of yours?'

'Yes, and a close friend. He was in and out of the house like one of the family.'

'Indeed? I am sorry to hear that.'

'Yes I thought a good deal of him and I'm naturally upset. We all are, as a matter of fact. I wanted your advice as to what could be done for him.'

'You mean with regard to his defence?'

'Yes.'

'Have you seen him since his arrest?'

'No. That's one of the things I wanted to ask you about. I am not quite sure how you get an order.'

'That can be obtained where a sufficient reason for its application can be shown. I understand, then, that you are unaware of his own plans for his defence?'

'Yes. My idea was to see him and talk the thing over, and, unless he has made some other arrangement, to ask you to undertake it.'

The lawyer nodded slowly. Martin's suggestion was eminently satisfactory to him. Apart from the mere money involved, this case, from its unusual and dramatic nature, promised to be at least one of the most famous of the year. He decided that if it came his way he would attend to it personally, and see that no stone was left unturned to secure an acquittal.

'If you put the case in our hands,' he replied at length, 'quite apart from our personal friendship, you may depend on our doing our utmost for your friend. But I am afraid it will be an expensive business. We shall have to retain counsel, perhaps two or even three men, and their fees are not negligible. Then, as you can imagine' – Mr Clifford gave a wintry little smile – 'we also have to live, or at all events we think so. There will unquestionably be expense in hunting up witnesses, a private detective may have to be employed, in short, the defence of a big case means heavy outlay. Now, can your friend meet this? What are his circumstances financially?'

'I think he is all right,' answered Martin, 'but, in any case, the money will be my affair. Felix may pay what he can. I shall be responsible for the rest.'

Clifford looked at the speaker keenly.

'Very handsome of you, Martin, I'm sure.' He hesitated a moment as if about to continue the subject, then, with a change of manner, he went on: 'I think, in that case, you should see Felix and ascertain his plans. If you can spare the time now, I shall go with you to Bow Street and try and procure for you an immediate visiting order. If, after your conversation, you find you require our assistance, we shall be very pleased to take up the case; if not, you are perfectly free to go elsewhere. Is that agreed?'

'Thank you, Clifford. That's all right. Nothing could be better.'

After introducing his prospective client to the authorities at the famous police station, the lawyer excused himself on the ground of another engagement, while Martin sat down to await the order. The formalities took some time, and it was not till nearly five that the door of Felix's cell opened to admit his friend.

'Martin!' cried the unhappy inmate, springing up and seizing his visitor's hand in both his own. But this is good of you! I hardly dared to expect you.'

'Couldn't see a pal in a hole without butting in,' answered the doctor gruffly, somewhat affected by the warmth of the other's welcome. 'You're a nice one, getting yourself into such a mess, eh? What have you been up to that's raised this dust?'

Felix passed his hand wearily over his forehead.

'My God, Martin,' he groaned, 'I don't know. I'm absolutely at sea. I know no more about the wretched business than you do. The proceedings today were purely formal, so that the evidence against me – whatever it can be – did not come out. I can't conceive what they have got hold of, that has made them suspect me.'

'I've heard nothing about the case at all. I just came along to see you when I saw what had happened.'

'Martin, I can never thank you! I can never repay you! I thought of writing to you today to ask your help, and I should probably have done it tomorrow. But you can't think what it means to me, your coming without being asked. It means, for one thing, that you don't believe this abominable charge? Doesn't it?'

'Well, naturally. You keep your heart up and don't get flustered. You've got some friends left still. All the family are upset about the thing. The mater's shocked, and so are the boys. They all say for you to cheer up, and that the mistake is sure to be put right soon.'

'God bless them for that,' cried Felix, rising and pacing the cell in evident emotion. 'Tell them – how much I appreciate – what all their thought means to me.'

'Rot!' said the doctor shortly. 'What would you expect? But now, I have only a minute or two here, and what I want to ask you is this, what plans have you made for your defence?'

'Defence? None, I fear. I just haven't been able to think about it. I haven't an idea who to turn to, or what to do. What would you advise?'

'Clifford.'

'Eh? What? I don't follow.'

'Employ Clifford, of Clifford and Lewisham. He's a dry stick, but as clever as they're made, and a good sort, He's your man.'

'I don't know him. Do you think he would take up the case?'

'Sure. Fact is, I went round to ask him how I could get an order to see you – I know him pretty well – and I pumped him. The firm would take it on if they were asked, but that means himself, and you couldn't have a better man.'

'Martin, you put new life into me! God bless you for all you're doing! Will you arrange it with him? But, wait a minute, can I afford it? Are his fees very high?'

'What can you afford?'

'Oh, I don't know. Say a thousand pounds.'

'More than enough. I shall arrange it with him at once.'

The friends conversed for some minutes, and then a warder opened the door of the cell. Martin's time was up. He left Felix cheered by the promise of a further visit, and with tears of thankfulness glistening in his eyes.

Determined to lose no time in completing his work, Martin returned direct to the offices of Messrs Clifford and Lewisham. But there the days work was over, and all but one or two junior clerks had already left. The doctor therefore made an appointment for the next day and, with a glow of righteous self-satisfaction, went home to tell his family what he had done.

On the following afternoon he again found himself in the solicitor's office.

'Now,' said Mr Clifford, when it had been definitely agreed that his firm was to take up the case, 'I have to warn you that proceedings will be slow. First, the prosecution will make up their case – get depositions of the evidence, you know, and so on – and that will take time. We, of course, shall also immediately start work, but it is improbable we shall make much headway till we learn the full evidence against us. Additional time will therefore be required for the preparation of the defence. If Felix is returned for trial – and I fear from what I have heard, he will be – weeks and months will probably elapse before both sides are ready. You and I shall therefore require to exercise patience.'

'I can believe it,' muttered the doctor. 'You lawyers take the devil of a time over everything.'

'We can't cover our mistakes like you, so we have to be careful,' retorted the lawyer with his dry, wintry smile.

Martin smote his thigh.

'Ha! Ha!' he laughed. 'That's good. You had me there. But I mustn't be wasting your time. There were some things you wanted to speak to me about?'

'Yes,' admitted Clifford, 'a couple of points. Firstly, I propose to retain Heppenstall – you know, Lucius Heppenstall, the KC. He may want one or two juniors. I suppose that is all right?'

'Of course. You know what is best to be done.'

'The other point is that I want you to tell me everything you possibly can about Felix.'

'As a matter of fact,' returned Martin, 'I can't tell you very much. I was just thinking over what I knew of him, and I was amazed it was so little. We became acquainted about four years ago. Felix had just taken St Malo, an empty house a couple of hundred yards from my own, and the first thing he did was to go and get pneumonia. I was called in, but the attack was bad, and for a time it was touch and go with him. However, he pulled through, and, during his convalescence, we became very good friends. When he came out of the hospital I invited him to my house for a week or two – he had only a not very satisfactory house-keeper at St Malo – and the family took to him, till he became quite like one of ourselves. Since then he has been in and out like a pet dog. He dines quite often, and, in return, insists on taking the boys to the theatre, and the mater when she'll go.'

'He lives quite alone, you say?'

'Quite, except for the housekeeper.'

'And you haven't met any of his people?'

'None. I've never even heard of his people. I don't think he has any. If he has, he never speaks of them.' Martin hesitated for a moment, then went on: 'It may be my fancy, but it has struck me that he seems to avoid women, and the only cynical remarks I have heard him make have been at their expense. I have often wondered if he has had some love disappointment, But he has never hinted at such a thing.'

'How does he live?'

'He is an artist. He designs for some poster firm in the City, and he draws for the better-class magazines. I do not know if he has private means, but he seems to do well enough.'

'Do you know anything about this extraordinary business of the cask?'

'No, except this. On – let me see, what night was it? Monday, I think – yes, Monday, the 5th of April, a couple of friends turned in, and we wanted a rubber of bridge. I went round to St Malo to see if Felix would make a fourth. That was about 8.30 o'clock. At first he hesitated, but afterwards he agreed to come. I went in and waited while he changed. The study fire had just been freshly lighted and the room, and indeed the whole house, was cold and cheerless. We played bridge till nearly one. The next thing we heard was that he was in St Thomas' Hospital, prostrated from a mental shock. Not professionally, but as a friend, I went to see him, and then he told me about the cask.'

'And what did he tell you?'

'He said he had had a letter saying a cask of money was being sent him – he will tell you the details himself – and that he had just got this cask from the steamer and brought it to St Malo when I called on that Monday evening. The reason he hesitated about leaving home was that he was on tenterhooks to unpack the cask.'

'Why did he not tell you about it?'

'I asked him that, and he said he had had trouble with the steamer people about getting it away, and he did not want anyone to know where the cask was, lest it should get round to these steamer folk. But I would rather he would tell you about that himself.'

'I shall ask him, but I want to hear from you anything you know personally about it.'

'Well, there is nothing more than that.'

'Can you tell me anything of his friends?'

'Nothing. I think only twice in all the years I have known him have I met acquaintances of his, in each case artists who were looking at the paintings in his studio, and who I know did not stay the night. Whom he met during the day I can't tell.'

The lawyer sat silent for some minutes.

'Well,' he said at length, 'I think that is all we can do today. I'll let you know how things go on, but, as I warned you before, the business will be slow.'

With a hearty handshake and a word of thanks the doctor took his leave, while Clifford sat down to write to Heppenstall, KC, to know if he would take up the case.

– 22 –

FELIX TELLS A SECOND STORY

The next day Mr Clifford was occupied with various technical formalities, and in obtaining from the authorities such information as was then available about the case, and it was not till the following morning he set out to make the acquaintance of his client. He found him seated in his cell, his head on his hands, and an expression of deep gloom upon his face. The two men talked generalities for some time, and then the lawyer came to business.

'Now, Mr Felix,' he said, 'I want you please to tell me everything you know of this unhappy affair – everything, no matter how seemingly minute or unimportant. Remember – I cannot impress it on you too strongly – for a man in your position it is suicidal to withhold information. Keep nothing back. Your confidence will be as safe as the confessional. If you have made mistakes, done foolish things, or criminal things, or even – forgive me – if you have committed the crime you are charged with, tell me the whole truth. Else I shall be a blind man leading the blind, and we shall both have our fall.'

Felix rose to his feet.

'I will do so, Mr Clifford. I will keep nothing back. And first, before we go on to the details, one point must be settled.' He raised his hand. 'I swear to you, in the presence of Almighty God, in whom I believe, that I am innocent of this crime.' He sat down and then continued: 'I don't ask you if you believe me; I am willing to leave that till afterwards, but I want now, at the commencement of our intercourse, to put that fact as it were on record. I absolutely and categorically deny all knowledge of this hateful and ghastly crime. Now let us get on.'

'I am glad you have made this statement and in this way, Mr Felix,' said the lawyer, who was impressed by his client's manner and earnestness. 'Now, please, begin at the beginning and tell me with all the detail you can, what you know of the matter.'

Felix had the gift of narration, and, apart from the appeal to Clifford's professional instincts, he held the lawyer enthralled as he related the strange story of his experiences.

'I hardly know where to begin,' he said. 'The first thing directly bearing on the affair was a meeting between myself and some friends at the Café Toisson d'Or in Paris, but before I come to that I think I ought to explain just who I am and how I, a Frenchman, come to be living in London. I think this is necessary, as the question of my previous knowledge of poor Annette Boirac is certain to come up. What do you say, Mr Clifford?'

'Necessary to tell this?' thought the lawyer, to whom the fact that Felix had had knowledge of the dead woman came as an ugly discovery. 'Why, my good fellow, no other point in the whole case is likely to be more important for you.' But aloud he only said: 'Yes, I consider it most necessary.'

'Very good, then. As I said, I am a Frenchman, and I was born in Avignon in 1884. I was always keen on drawing, and, as my teachers thought there was promise in my work, I early moved to Paris and entered the *atelier* of M. Dauphin. I studied there for several years, living in a small hotel off the Boule Miche. My parents were both dead, and

I had inherited a little money – not much, but enough to live on.

'Amongst those working at the art school was a young fellow called Pierre Bonchose. He was some four years my junior, and was an attractive and thoroughly decent chap. We became close friends, eventually sharing the same room. But he was not much good at his work. He lacked perseverance, and was too fond of supper parties and cards to settle down seriously to paint. I was not, therefore, surprised when one day he told me he was fed up with art, and was going into business. It seemed he had applied to an old friend of his father's, the senior partner of Messrs Rôget, the wine exporters of Narbonne, and had been offered a position in that firm, which he had decided to accept.

'But a month or two before he left Paris he had introduced to the *atelier* a new pupil, his cousin, Mlle. Annette Humbert. They seemed more like brother and sister than cousins, and Bonchose told me that they had been brought up together, and had always been what you English call "pals." This, Mr Clifford, was none other than the unfortunate young lady who afterwards became Mme. Boirac.

'She was one of the loveliest girls that ever breathed. From the first moment I saw her I admired her as I had never before admired anyone. As Fate would have it we were both making certain pastel studies and, being thus thrown together, we became interested in each other's work. The inevitable happened, and I fell deeply in love with her. She did not discourage me, but, as she was kind and gracious to everyone, I hardly dared to hope she could care for me. At last, to make a long story short, I took my courage in both hands and proposed, and I could hardly believe my good fortune when she accepted me.

'It then became necessary for me to approach her father. M. Humbert came of an old and distinguished family, endowed with much pride of birth. He was well off, though not rich, and lived almost in state in his old château at Laroche, occupying a leading position in the local society. To broach such a subject to him would have been an ordeal for anyone, but for me, who lacked so many of the social advantages he possessed, it was a veritable nightmare. And my forebodings were not disappointed. He received me courteously, but scouted my proposal. Mlle. Humbert was too young, she did not yet know the world nor her own mind, he had other plans for her future, and so on. Also, he delicately indicated that my social standing and means hardly fitted me to enter a family of such age and traditions as his own.

'I need not try to describe the effect this decision had upon both of us, suffice it to say that Annette, after a stormy scene, submitted to her father's authority, leaving the art school and going for an indefinite visit to an aunt in the southern provinces. I, finding life without her insupportable in my old haunts, also left Paris, and, coming to London, obtained a position as artist with Messrs Greer and Hood, the advertisement poster printers of Fleet Street. What with their salary and my spare time drawings for *Punch* and other papers, I soon found myself in receipt of over a thousand a year, and then realised one of my ambitions and moved to a small villa in the suburbs, buying at the same time a two-seater to take me to and from my work. This villa, St Malo, was situated near Brent, on the Great North Road. Here I settled down, alone except for an elderly housekeeper. I fitted up a large attic as a studio where I began studies for a picture I had in mind.

'But before I had been a month in my new home, I developed a nasty attack of pneumonia. Martin, who was the nearest doctor, was called in, and so began the friendship from which your presence here today has resulted.

'I lived a somewhat humdrum existence for some two years, and then one morning I had a pleasant surprise in the shape of a visit from my old friend, Pierre Bonchose. He explained that, having done pretty well in business, he had been sent to represent permanently his firm in London. He also told me that after a year of what he called "sulking" his cousin Annette had, at her father's desire, married a M. Boirac, a wealthy manufacturer, that he had seen her coming through Paris, and that she appeared to be quite happy.

'Bonchose and I resumed our former intimacy, and, during the next summer, that is, two years ago, we had a walking tour through Cornwall. I mention this because of an incident which occurred near Penzance, and which profoundly modified our relations. While bathing in a deserted cove of that rocky coast, I was caught in an off-shore current and, in spite of all my efforts, found myself being carried out to sea. Bonchose, hearing my shouts, swam out after me and at the imminent risk of his own life assisted me back into still water. Though he made light of the matter, I could not forget the danger he had faced to save me, and I felt I had incurred a debt which I should be glad of an opportunity to pay.

'But though, as I have said, I had settled down in London, I did not by any means entirely desert Paris. First at long intervals, but afterwards more frequently, I ran over to see my friends and to keep myself in touch with artistic circles in France. About eight months ago, on one of these visits, it happened that I dropped into an exhibition of the work of a famous sculptor, and there I incidentally came across a man whose conversation interested me extremely. His hobby was statuary, and he was clearly an expert in his subject. He told me he had amassed one of the largest private collections in the world, and as we became more intimate he invited me to dine that evening and see it. I went, and, on arrival he introduced me to his wife. You can imagine my feelings, Mr Clifford, when I found she was none other than Annette. Acting on the impulse of the moment, we met as strangers, though I am sure that, had M. Boirac not been so full of his collection, he must have noticed our embarrassment. But as we sat at dinner I found that, after the first shock of recognition, her presence left me cold. Though I still profoundly admired her, my infatuation had passed away, and I realised that whatever love I might have had for her was dead. And from her manner I felt sure her feelings towards myself had undergone a similar change.

'M. Boirac and I became good friends over his collection, and, on his invitation, I several times repeated my call during subsequent visits to Paris.

'That, Mr Clifford, is all of what I may call my preliminary history. I am afraid it is rather involved, but I have tried to make it as clear as I could.'

The lawyer bowed gravely.

'Your statement is perfectly clear. Pray proceed.'

'I come now,' went on Felix, 'to the events connected with the cask and therefore apparently with the tragedy. I think it will be better to tell you these in their chronological order, even though this makes my story seem a little disconnected?'

Again Mr Clifford inclined his head and the other resumed: 'On Saturday, 13th March, I crossed to Paris for the weekend, returning the following Monday morning. On the Sunday afternoon I happened to drop into the Café Toisson d'Or in the rue Royale and there found a group of men, with most of whom I was acquainted. They were talking about the French Government lotteries, and in the course of conversation one of them, a M. Alphonse Le Gautier, said to me, "Why not have a little flutter with me?" I ridiculed the idea at first, but afterwards agreed to enter a thousand francs jointly with him. He undertook to arrange the matter, the profits, if any, being halved between us. I paid him over my five hundred francs and, believing it was the last I should hear of the affair, dismissed it from my mind.

'A week after my return to England I had a visit from Bonchose. I saw at once he was in trouble and after a while it all came out. It seemed he had been losing heavily at cards, and to meet his liabilities he had gone to money-lenders, who were now pressing him for repayment. In answer to my questions, he explained that he had paid off all his loans with the exception of one for £600. That sum he was utterly unable to raise, and if he failed to procure it before the 31st, that was, in about a week, he was a ruined man. I was much annoyed, for I had helped him out of similar scrapes twice before, on each of which occasions he had given me his word not to play again. I felt I could not go on throwing good money after bad, and yet because of our friendship and the debt I owed him for saving my life, I could not see him go to the wall. Divining what was in my mind, he assured me he had not come to beg, saying that he realised I had already done more for him than he deserved. Then he said he had written to Annette telling her the circumstances, and asking, not for a gift, but for a loan on which he would pay four per cent interest. I talked to him seriously, offering no help, but asking him to keep me advised of how things went on. But though I did not tell him, I decided I would pay the £600 rather than see him stuck.

' "I am going to Paris on Friday," I ended up, "and hope to dine at the Boirac's on Saturday. If Annette speaks to me on the subject, I shall tell her you are making an unholy mess of things."

' "Don't put her against helping me," he pleaded. I said I would not influence her at all, and then he asked me when I was returning, so that he could meet me and hear what had been said. I told him I would cross by Boulogne on Sunday.

'That weekend, a fortnight after the meeting in the Café Toisson d'Or, I was again in the French capital. On the Saturday morning as I sat in the Hotel Continental meditating a visit to M. Dauphin's *atelier*, a note was handed to me. It was from Annette, and in it she said she wanted to speak to me in private, asking if I could come at 7.30 that night, instead of the dinner hour of 7.45, and requiring a verbal reply. I gave the necessary assurance to the messenger, who proved to be Annette's maid, Suzanne.

'I reached the Boirac's house at the appointed hour, but I did not see Annette. As I entered, M. Boirac was passing through the hall, and, seeing me, he invited me into his study to look at an engraving which had been sent him on approval. Naturally, I could not refuse. We went to the study and examined the picture. But there was another object in the study which I also saw and commented on.

Standing on the carpet was a large cask, and, Mr Clifford, you will hardly believe me when I tell you it was either the identical cask which was sent me containing poor Annette's body, or else one so similar as to be indistinguishable!'

Felix paused to let this significant statement, as he evidently considered it, sink into the lawyer's mind. But the latter only bowed and said: 'Pray proceed. Mr Felix, with your statement.'

'I was interested in the cask, as it seemed an unusual object to find in a study. I asked Boirac about it, and he explained that he had just purchased a piece of statuary, and that the cask was simply the special kind of packing case in which it had been sent home.'

'Did he describe the statue?' asked the lawyer, interrupting for the first time.

'No, except to say it was a fine group. He promised to show it to me on my next visit.'

'Did he tell you from whom he had purchased it, or what price he had paid?'

'Neither; the matter was only referred to incidentally as we were leaving the room.'

'Thank you. Pray continue.'

'We then went to the salon, but, as several visitors had already arrived, I could not, at that time, get a private word with Annette.

'The dinner was an important social affair, the Spanish Ambassador being the principal guest. Before it was over M. Boirac was called from the house, owing to an accident having taken place at his works. He apologised for leaving, promising to return speedily, but after a time a telephone message came to say the accident had been more serious than he had supposed, and he would be detained till very late or even all night. The guests began to leave about eleven, but, in obedience to a sign from Annette, I remained till all had gone. Then she told me she had received a letter from Bonchose which had much upset her. She did not mind his having got into difficulties – indeed, she thought a fright would do him good; but she was really troubled lest he might become a confirmed gambler. She wished for my candid opinion of him.

'I told her exactly what I thought; that there wasn't a bit of real harm in him, but that he had got into a bad set and that his only chance was to break with it. She agreed with me, saying he should not be helped until this breach had actually been made. We then discussed where the money was to come from. She, it appeared, could lay her hands on only £300, and, as she felt M. Boirac would disapprove, she did not wish to ask him for the remainder. She therefore proposed to sell a couple of her jewels – her own private property – and she asked me to undertake the matter for her. But I could not bring myself to agree to this, and I said that if she would advance the £300 she had, I would find the balance. At first she would not hear of it, and we had quite a heated argument. Finally I carried my point, and she went upstairs and brought down the money. I took my leave immediately afterwards, promising to let her know how the matter ended. She was much affected, for she was sincerely attached to him. The next day, Sunday, I returned to London.'

'I think you said, Mr Felix,' interrupted Clifford, 'that the last of the guests left at eleven?'

'Yes, about then.'

'And at what time did you yourself leave?'

'About quarter to twelve.'

'Then your conversation lasted about three-quarters of an hour. Now, did anyone see you leave?'

'No one except Annette. She came to the door with me.'

'You returned to your hotel, I suppose?'

'Yes.'

'At what hour did you reach it?'

'About half-past one, I should say.'

'From Madame's house to the Hôtel Continental is about fifteen minutes' walk. What, then, did you do in the interval?'

'I felt wakeful, and thought a stroll would be pleasant. I walked across Paris; to the Place de la Bastille by the Rue de Rivoli, and back to the hotel by the Grands Boulevards.'

'Did you meet anyone you knew?'

'No, not that I can recall.'

'I am afraid this is important, Mr Felix. Think again. Is there no one that could testify to meeting you on this walk? No waiter or other official, for example?'

'No,' said Felix, after a pause, 'I don't think I spoke to a soul, and I certainly did not enter a café.'

'You say you returned to London next day. Did you meet anyone on the journey you knew?'

'Yes, but it will be no help to me. I met Miss Gladys Devine on the Folkestone boat. But she cannot confirm this. As you must know, she died suddenly a week later.'

'Miss Gladys Devine? Not the celebrated Miss Devine, the actress?'

'The same. I have met her at supper parties in Paris.'

'But you must be able to get confirmation of that? So well-known a lady would be recognised wherever she went. But perhaps you visited her private cabin?'

'No, I saw her on the boat deck. She was sitting in the shelter of one of the funnels. I joined her for about half an hour.'

'But somebody must have seen you?'

'Possibly, but possibly not. You see, it was horribly rough. Almost everyone was sick. People, anyway, weren't walking about.'

'What about her maids?'

'I did not see them.'

'Now, Mr Felix, what you must think over when I leave you is, first, what evidence can we get confirming your statement of how you spent your time between 11.0 and 1.30 on the Saturday night? and second, who saw you with Miss Devine on the Folkestone boat? In the meantime, please continue your statement.'

'Bonchose met me at Charing Cross. He was keen to know how I had fared. We drove to his rooms, where I told him the whole thing. I said I would hand him the £600 on condition he broke finally with his gambling friends. He assured me the breach had already been effected, and I therefore gave him the money. We then drove to the Savoy and, after a rather early dinner, I left him and went home.'

'At what hour?'

'About 8.30.'

'How did you go?'

'I took a taxi.'

'From where?'

'The Savoy commissionaire called it.'

'Yes?'

'The next thing was I received an astonishing letter, and Felix went on to tell the lawyer about the typewritten letter signed 'Le Gautier,' his preparations to obtain the cask, his visit to St Katherine's Docks, his interviews with the clerk, Broughton, and the manager of the dock office, his ruse to get the I and C's notepaper, the forging of the letter to Harkness, the removal of the cask to St Malo, his dining at Dr Martin's, the midnight interview with Burnley, the disappearance of the cask, its final recovery, its unpacking, and the discovery of its terrible contents. 'That, Mr Clifford,' he ended up, 'is every single thing I know about the affair, good, bad, or indifferent.'

'I congratulate you on the clear way you have made your statement.' returned the solicitor. 'Now, excuse me while I think if there is anything further I want to ask you.'

He slowly turned over the rather voluminous notes he had taken.

'The first point,' he went on at length, 'is the question of your intimacy with Madame Boirac. Can you tell me how many times you saw her since her marriage?'

Felix considered.

'About half a dozen, I should say, or perhaps eight or even nine. Not more than nine certainly.'

'Excepting on the night of the dinner, was her husband present on all these occasions?'

'Not all. At least twice I called in the afternoon and saw her alone.'

'I think I need hardly ask you, but answer me fully all the same. Were there at any time any tender or confidential passages between you and Madame?'

'Absolutely none. I state most positively that nothing passed between us which Boirac might not have seen or heard.'

Again Clifford paused in thought.

'I want you now to tell me, and with the utmost detail, exactly how you spent the time between your leaving Bonchose after dinner on the Sunday night of your return from Paris, and your meeting the cask at St Katherine's Docks on the following Monday week.'

'I can do so easily. After leaving Bonchose I drove out to St Malo, as I told you, arriving about 9.30. My housekeeper was on holidays, so I went straight over to Brent village and arranged with a charwoman to come in the mornings and make my breakfast. This woman had acted in a similar capacity before. I myself was taking a week's holidays, and each day I passed in the same manner. I got up about half-past seven, had breakfast, and went to my studio to paint. The charwoman went home after breakfast, and I got my own lunch. Then I painted again in the afternoon, and in the evening went into town for dinner and usually, but not always, a theatre. I generally got back between eleven and twelve. On Saturday, instead of painting all day, I went into town and arranged about meeting the cask.'

'Then at ten o'clock on Wednesday you were painting in your studio?'

'That is so, but why that day and hour?'

'I will tell you later. Now, can you prove that? Did anyone call in the studio, or see you there?'

'No one, I'm afraid.'

'What about the charwoman? What is her name, by the way?'

'Mrs Bridget Murphy. No, I don't think she could tell where I was. You see, I practically did not see her at all. My breakfast was ready when I came down, and when I had finished I went direct to the studio. I don't know when she went home, but I should think it was fairly early.'

'What time did you breakfast?'

'Eight nominally, but I wasn't always very punctual.'

'Do you remember, and have you any way of proving, what time you had breakfast on this particular Wednesday?'

Felix thought over the question.

'No,' he answered, 'I don't think so. There was nothing to distinguish that morning from the others.'

'The point is important. Perhaps Mrs Murphy would remember?'

'Possibly, but I hardly think so.'

'No one else could prove it? Were there no callers? No tradesmen's messengers?'

'None. One or two people rang, but I didn't bother. I was expecting no one, and I just let them ring.'

'An unfortunate omission. Now, tell me, where did you dine in town and spend the evenings?'

'I'm afraid a different restaurant each night, and naturally a different theatre.'

By dint of further questions Clifford obtained a list of all the places his client had visited during the week, his intention being to go round them in turn in search of material to build up an alibi. He was very disappointed with all he had heard, and the difficulties of his task seemed to be growing, He continued his examination.

'Now, this typewritten letter, signed Le Gautier. Did you believe it was genuine?'

'I did. I thought the whole thing absurd and annoying, but I did not doubt it. You see, I had actually entered for the lottery with Le Gautier, and fifty thousand francs was the sum we would have made, had we been lucky. I did think at first it was a practical joke on Le Gautier's part, but he is not that kind of man, and I at last concluded it was genuine.'

'Did you write or wire to Le Gautier?'

'No. I got the letter late one evening on my return home. It was too late to do anything then, but I intended to wire next morning that I would go over, and not to send the cask. But next morning's post brought a card, also typewritten, and signed "Le Gautier," saying the cask had

287

actually been despatched. I forgot to mention that in my statement.'

Clifford nodded and again referred to his notes.

'Did you write a letter to Messrs Dupierre of Paris, ordering a statue to be sent to you, to the West Jubb Street address?'

'No.'

'Do you recollect the blotter on your study desk at St Malo?'

'Why, yes,' returned Felix, with a look of surprise.

'Did you ever let that blotter out of your possession?'

'Not to my knowledge.'

'Did you ever take it to France?'

'Never.'

'Then how, Mr Felix,' asked the lawyer slowly, 'how do you account for the fact that the blotted impression of such a letter, in your handwriting, was found on the blotter?'

Felix sprang to his feet.

'What?' he cried. 'What's that you say? A letter in my handwriting? I don't believe it! It's impossible!'

'I have seen it.'

'You have seen it?' The speaker moved excitedly about the cell, gesticulating freely. 'Really, Mr Clifford, this is too much. I tell you I wrote no such letter. You are making a mistake.'

'I assure you, Mr Felix, I am making no mistake. I saw not only the impression on your pad, but also the original letter itself, which had been received by Messrs Dupierre.'

Felix sat down and passed his hand across his brow, as if dazed.

'I cannot understand it. You can't have seen a letter from me, because no such exists. What you saw must have been a forgery.'

'But the impression on the blotter?'

'Good Heavens, how do I know? I tell you I know nothing about it. See here,' he added, with a change of tone, 'there's some trick in it. When you say you've seen these things I'm bound to believe you. But there's a trick. There must be.'

'Then,' said Clifford, 'if so, and I'm inclined to agree with you, who carried out the trick? Someone must have had access to your study, either to write the letter there, or to abstract your blotter or a page of it which could afterwards be replaced. Who could that have been?'

'I don't know. Nobody – or anybody. I can think of no one who would do such a thing. When was the letter written?'

'It was received by Dupierre on Tuesday morning, 30th March. It bore a London postmark, therefore it must have been posted on Sunday night or Monday. That would be either the day or the day after you returned to London, after the dinner.'

'Anyone could have got into the house while I was away. If what you say is true, someone must have, but I saw no traces.'

'Now, M. Felix, who is Emmie?'

Felix stared.

'Emmie?' he said. 'I don't understand. Emmie what?'

Clifford watched the other keenly as he replied, – 'Your heartbroken Emmie.'

'My dear Mr Clifford, I haven't the slightest idea what you're talking about. "Your heartbroken Emmie?" What under the sun do you mean?'

'It should be clear enough, Mr Felix. Who was the girl that wrote to you recently imploring you not to desert her, and who signed herself, "Your heartbroken Emmie"?'

Felix gazed at his visitor in amazement.

'Either you're mad or I'm mad,' he said slowly. 'I have had no letter from any girl asking me not to desert her, and I have had no letter on any subject from anyone signing herself Emmie. Really, I think you might explain yourself.'

'Now tell me something else, Mr Felix. You possess, I understand, two navy-blue suits?'

The astonishment on the artist's face did not lessen as he assented.

'I want to know now when you last wore each of those suits.'

'As it happens, I can tell you. One of them I wore on my Paris trip and again on the following Saturday when I went to town to arrange about the cask, as well as on the Monday and following days till I went to hospital. I am wearing it today. The other blue suit is an old one, and I have not had it on for months.'

'I'll tell you now why I ask. In the coat pocket of one of your blue suits, evidently, from what you tell me, the old one, was found a letter beginning, "My dearest Léon," and ending," Your heartbroken Emmie," and in it the writer said – but here, I have a copy of it, and you may read it.'

The artist looked over the paper as if in a dream. Then he turned to the other.

'I can assure you, Mr Clifford,' he said earnestly, 'that I am as much in the dark as you about this. It is not my letter. I never saw it before. I never heard of Emmie. The whole thing is an invention. How it got into my pocket I cannot explain, but I tell you positively I am absolutely ignorant of the whole thing.'

Clifford nodded.

'Very good. Now there is only one other thing I want to ask you. Do you know the round-backed, leather-covered armchair which stood before the plush curtain in your study?'

'Yes.'

'Think carefully, and tell me who was the last lady to occupy it.'

'That doesn't require much thought. No lady has ever sat in it since I bought it. Very few ladies have been in St Malo since I took it, and these without exception were interested in art and were in the studio only.'

'Now, don't be annoyed, Mr Felix, when I ask you once more, did Madame Boirac ever sit in that chair?'

'I give you my solemn word of honour she never did. She was never in the house, and I believe I am right in saying she was never in London.'

The lawyer nodded.

'Now I have another unpleasant thing to tell you. Caught in the hem of that curtain and hidden by the chair, a pin was found – a diamond safety pin. That pin, Mr Felix, was attached to the shoulder of Madame Boirac's dress on the night of the dinner party.'

Felix, unable to speak, sat staring helplessly at the lawyer. His face had gone white, and an expression of horror dawned in his eyes. There was silence in the dull, cheerless cell, whose walls had heard so many tales of misery and suffering. Clifford, watching his client keenly, felt the doubts which had been partly lulled to rest, again rising. Was the man acting? If so, he was doing it extraordinarily well, but... At last Felix moved.

'My God!' he whispered hoarsely. 'It's a nightmare! I feel helpless. I'm in a net, and it is drawing close round me. What does it mean, Mr Clifford? Who has done this thing? I didn't know anyone hated me, but someone must.' He made a gesture of despair. 'I'm done for. What can help me after that? Can you see any hope, Mr Clifford? Tell me.'

But whatever doubts the lawyer felt he kept to himself.

'It is too soon to come to any conclusion,' he answered in a matter-of-fact tone. 'In cases of difficulty such as this, I have frequently known some small fact to come out, perhaps accidentally, which has cleared up the whole affair. You must not despair. We are only at the beginning. Wait for a week or two, and then I'll tell you what I think.'

'Bless you, Mr Clifford. You put heart into me. But this matter of the pin. What can it mean? There is some terrible conspiracy against me. Can it ever be unravelled?'

The lawyer rose.

'That's what we have to try and do, Mr Felix. I'm afraid I must be off now. Do as I say, keep up your heart, and if you can think of any evidence supporting your statements, let me know.'

Having shaken hands, Mr Clifford withdrew.

23

CLIFFORD GETS TO WORK

When Clifford had finished dinner that evening, he went to his study, and, drawing a large armchair up to the fire, for the evenings were still cold, he lit a cigar and composed himself to master the details of his new case. To say that he was disappointed with Felix's statement would not be to give a true indication of his state of mind. He was woefully chagrined. He had hoped and expected that his client would tell him something that would instantly indicate the line the defence should take, and instead of that he was puzzled to know where any defence at all was to come from.

And the more he thought over it, the worse the outlook seemed. He went over the facts in order, marshalling them in his mind and weighing the bearing of each on the question of Felix's innocence or guilt.

There was first of all the fundamental question of what had taken place in the house in the Avenue de l'Alma between 11.0 p.m. and 1.15 a.m. on the night of the dinner party. At 11.0 Annette Boirac was alive and well; at 1.15 she had disappeared. Felix was the last person, so far as was known, to see her alive, and it was not unreasonable to have expected him to have thrown some light on her fate. But he hadn't.

It was true he had explained the motive for his interview with Madame. Confirmation of the truth of this, Clifford thought, should be obtainable from an investigation of the affairs of Bonchose. But even if it was established, he did not see how it would help his client. It would not prove him innocent. Indeed, it might be argued that this very discussion had been the indirect cause of the elopement, if such took place. It had given Felix an opportunity to see Madame alone which otherwise he might not have had. And who could tell what dormant passions that private interview might not have aroused? No. There was no help here.

And the remainder of Felix's statement was equally unfruitful. He had said that after conversing with the lady till 11.45 p.m., he had walked about Paris till half-past one. But by a singular coincidence he had not been seen leaving the house, he had not met anyone he knew, and he had not been anywhere he was known. Was this, Clifford wondered, so singular a coincidence? Might it not simply mean that Felix's story was untrue?

Then he remembered the closing of the front door. François had heard it shut at 1.0 a.m. If Felix left at 11.45, who shut it? As far as he could see, either Felix must be lying when he said he left at 11.45, or else Madame must have gone out by herself at the later hour. But the lawyer did not know which of these had happened, and the worst of it was there seemed no way of finding out.

Equally useless for the defence was Felix's identification of the fur-coated lady on the Folkestone boat. Even had this been Miss Devine, it did not prove Madame Boirac was not a traveller. Might not Felix, travelling with Madame, have seen the actress on board, her subsequent death suggesting his story? No, even if he could prove all that the artist had said about the crossing, it would not help matters.

But Felix's failure to find an alibi for himself was much more serious. Clifford had confidently expected a defence along these lines, and he was more than disappointed. He ran over the facts. The location of the man or men who had arranged the journeys of the cask was known at two periods; on the Wednesday at 10.0 a.m. at Waterloo, and on the Thursday at 5.15 p.m. at the Gare du Nord. Clifford got out his Continental Bradshaw. To have been in Paris at the time named, a Londoner must have left by the 9.0 a.m. from Charing Cross on Thursday, and he could not have arrived back before 5.35 on Friday morning. Therefore Felix had only to prove an alibi at 10.0 on Wednesday morning, or between 9.0 on Thursday morning and 5.35 on Friday morning, and the greatest part of the case against him would be met. But this was just what he could not do.

Clifford turned to his notes of the artist's statement. According to it, at 10.0 am. on Wednesday, Felix had been painting in his studio. But the chance of the housekeeper's absence and the peculiar arrangement under which the charwoman got breakfast prevented this being proved. And like an idiot, Felix had heard people ringing at the door, and, because he did not wish to be disturbed, had not opened it. One of those callers might have saved him now.

And then, with regard to Thursday and Thursday night. To have caught the 9.0 a.m. from Charing Cross, Felix must have left St Malo at not later than 8.5. According to his statement, his breakfast was left ready for him at 8.0, and there certainly would not have been time for him to eat it. But there was nothing to prevent him having in two or three minutes dirtied the plates and carried away some food, to give the impression he had had his meal. Here there was hope of help from the charwoman. Clifford could not decide the point till he had interviewed her.

He turned back to his notes. After breakfast, Felix, according to his statement, had painted without ceasing, except for a cup of cocoa at lunch time, until half-past six. He had then changed and gone to town, dining alone at the Gresham. Though he had seen no one he knew at the famous restaurant, there was a chance that a waiter or commissionaire or other official might have recognised him. He had left about nine and, feeling tired, he had returned straight home. There, no one could know of his presence till 7.30 the next morning, when Mrs Murphy would expect to hear him answer her knock.

But if he had been to Paris, meeting the cask at the Gare du Nord, he could have been home equally at 7.30 a.m. Therefore the evidence of his answering the knock would be immaterial. Certainly if Felix were telling the truth, the manner in which confirmation was eluding him was most unfortunate. But was Felix telling the truth?...

Then there were those three discoveries of Burnley at St Malo, the 'Emmie' letter, the impression on the blotsheet, and the pin. Any one of these alone would have been highly damaging to Felix's case; the three together seemed overwhelming. And yet Felix had not attempted a word of explanation. He had simply denied knowledge of all three. If the accused man could not explain these damaging facts, how was Clifford to set about it?

But nothing in the whole affair depressed the lawyer so much as the admissions Felix had made about his previous relations with Madame Boirac. It was, of course, true that Felix, a stranger introduced into the Boirac household, might have fallen in love with Madame and persuaded her to elope with him. But if Felix, instead of being a stranger, could be shown to have been not only desperately in love with, but actually formerly engaged to the mistress of the house, how tremendously the probabilities of such an elopement would be strengthened. What a picture a clever counsel could draw of this lady, tied to a man whom perhaps she detested, and with whom life in such case must have been an endless misery, brought unexpectedly in touch with the man of her real choice... And her lover, his crushed-down feelings swelling up at the unlooked-for meeting, seeing her languishing in this bondage... Why, the elopement would be amply accounted for. To Clifford it seemed that if the Crown got hold of the facts he had learnt, Felix was a doomed man. Indeed, the more he himself thought of the affair, the more doubtful of the artist's innocence he became. As far as he could see, Felix had only one uncontrovertible point in his favour – his surprise on seeing the cask opened. And this would prove a matter of medical testimony, and no doubt there would be contradictory evidence... The lawyer could see very little light even here.

And then he reminded himself it was not his business to try Felix. Innocent or guilty, he, Clifford, was there to do the best he could for him. But what form was that best to take?

Till the morrow had dawned he sat smoking in his chair, turning the case over in his mind, looking at the problem from every point of view, still without much result. But though he could not yet see the line his defence should follow, he was clear enough about his immediate next step. Obviously he must first see Bonchose, Mrs Murphy, and the other persons of whom Felix had spoken, not only to test the latter's story, but also in the hope of learning some new facts.

Accordingly, next morning saw the lawyer ascending the steps of the house in Kensington in which the apartments of Mr Pierre Bonchose were situated. But here he met with a disappointment. Mr Bonchose had gone to the south of France on business and would not be home for three or four days.

'That explains why he has made no attempt to see Felix since his arrest,' said the lawyer to himself, as he turned away and hailed a taxi with the idea of a call on the charwoman.

An hour later he reached the small village of Brent, on the Great North Road, and was directed to Mrs Murphy's cottage. The door was opened by a woman who had been tall, but was now shrunken, her sharp, careworn features and grey hair indicating that her life had been a struggle against odds.

'Good morning,' began the lawyer, courteously raising his hat. 'You are Mrs Murphy?'

'I am, sir,' returned the woman, 'and would you come in?'

'Thank· you.' He followed her into the small, poorly-furnished living-room, and sat cautiously down on the somewhat dilapidated chair she pulled forward.

'You know, I suppose,' he went on, 'that your neighbour, Mr Felix of St Malo, has been arrested on a very serious charge?'

' 'Deed then, I do, sir. And sorry I was to hear of it. A fine, decent man he was too.'

'Well, Mrs Murphy, my name is Clifford, and I am the lawyer who is going to defend Mr Felix. I wondered if you would be good enough to answer some questions, to help me in his defence?'

'I would, sir, be glad to do it.'

'You managed the house for him recently, while his housekeeper was away?'

'I did, sir.'

'And when did Mr Felix ask you to do that?'

'On Sunday evening, sir. I was just thinking of going to bed when he came to the door.'

'Now tell me, please, exactly what you did each day at St Malo.'

'I went in the mornings, sir, and lit the fire and got his breakfast. Then I did out his room and washed up and left his lunch ready. He got his own lunch himself in the middle of the day, and went into London for dinner at night.'

'I see. At what hour did you reach the house in the mornings?'

'About seven o'clock. I called him at half-past seven and he had his breakfast at eight.'

'And about what hour did you leave?'

'I could hardly be sure, sir. About half-past ten or eleven, or maybe later.'

'Can you remember the Wednesday of that week? I suppose you were at St Malo at ten o'clock?'

'I was, sir. I was never left by ten any morning.'

'Quite so. Now what I want to know is this: on that Wednesday morning was Mr Felix in the house at ten o'clock?'

'So far as I know, he was, sir.'

'Ah, but I want to be sure. Can you say positively he was there?'

'Well, not to be certain, sir, I couldn't.'

'Now Thursday, Mrs Murphy. Did you see Mr Felix on Thursday?'

The woman hesitated.

'I saw him two or three mornings,' she said at last, 'but I couldn't be sure whether it was on Thursday. It might have been, though.'

'You couldn't tell me at what hour he took his breakfast that morning?'

'Well, I could not, sir.'

It was evident to Clifford that Mrs Murphy, though an intelligent woman, would be no use to him as a witness. He remained at her house for a considerable time, and was very probing and painstaking in his questions. But all to no purpose. While she corroborated what Felix had stated about his household arrangements, she dashed any hope the lawyer might have had of establishing an alibi.

By the time he again reached the city it was one o'clock. He decided he would lunch at the Gresham, and pursue his investigations among the staff.

The head waiter, with whom he began, could not himself give any information, but he took Felix's photo round among his men, and at last found one who had seen the artist. Felix, it appeared from this man's statement, had dined there one evening some five or six weeks previously. The man, an Italian, remembered him because he had at first supposed him to be a compatriot. But, unfortunately, he could not fix the date, and no one else, so far as Clifford could learn, had seen the artist at all. Clifford had regretfully to admit that this evidence, like Mrs Murphy's, was useless. In the lawyer's private judgment it undoubtedly tended to confirm Felix's statement, and he found himself more and more inclined to believe the Frenchman. But a personal impression was one thing, and evidence in a court of law another.

On reaching his office, he wrote to Bonchose, asking him to call on urgent business immediately on his return to London.

The next day saw him again at Brent village. Felix had stated he had gone by train to town each evening of the fateful week, and it had occurred to the lawyer that possibly some of the railway officials might have noticed him travelling. He made exhaustive inquiries and at last found a ticket collector who volunteered some information. Felix, said this man, was a regular traveller. He went to town each morning by the 8.57 and returned at 6.5 each evening. But the collector had noticed that for some days he had not travelled by these trains, but had instead gone up by the evening trains leaving Brent at either 6.20 or 6.47. The collector went off duty at seven o'clock, so he could not tell anything about Felix's return. Nor could anyone else, so far as Clifford could ascertain. But unfortunately the collector could not state how long it was since the artist had changed his habits, still less could he say if he travelled up to town on the Thursday evening in question.

Clifford then strolled to St Malo in the hope of finding it was overlooked by some other house, the occupants of which might have seen the artist on the fateful Thursday. But here again he was disappointed. There was no house in the immediate vicinity.

Puzzled as to his next step, the lawyer returned to his office. He found pressing business of another kind awaiting him, and for the remainder of that day, as well as the next two, he was too fully occupied to turn his attention seriously to the murder case.

On the morning of the fourth day there was a letter from Mr Lucius Heppenstall, KC. It was written from Copenhagen, and the barrister explained that he was in

Denmark on business and hoped to be back in about a week, when he and Clifford could meet and go into the case together.

Hardly had Clifford finished reading the letter when a young man was announced. He was tall and slight, with dark hair and eyes, a small black moustache and a short, hooked nose, which gave him something of the appearance of a hawk.

'Bonchose,' said Clifford to himself, and he was not mistaken.

'You had not heard of Mr Felix's arrest?' he asked, as he waved his visitor to an armchair and held out his cigarette case.

'Not a word,' replied Bonchose, speaking good English, but with a foreign accent. He had a quick, vivacious manner, and moved sharply, as if on wires. 'I cannot tell you how utterly surprised and shocked I was to get your note. But the thing is perfectly absurd – outrageous! Anyone that knew Felix would know he could not commit such a crime. It is surely a misunderstanding that a very short time will clear up?'

'I fear not, Mr Bonchose; I very much fear not. Unfortunately, the case against your friend is strong. The evidence is admittedly circumstantial, but it is strong for all that. Indeed, to be perfectly candid with you, I do not for the moment see any good line of defence.'

The young man made a gesture of amazement.

'You horrify me, sir,' he cried; 'absolutely horrify me. You surely do not mean to suggest there is any chance of a conviction?'

'I am sorry to say that I do. There is a very great chance – unless a good deal more comes to light than we know at present.'

'But this is awful!' He wrung his hands. 'Awful! First it was poor Annette and now Felix! But you don't mean that nothing can be done?' There was real concern and anxiety in the young man's tone.

Mr Clifford was satisfied. This man's affection for and belief in his friend were genuine. Felix could not be altogether a villain to inspire such friendship. The lawyer changed his tone.

'No, Mr Bonchose,' he answered. 'I do not mean that. All I mean is that the fight will not be easy. Mr Felix's friends will have to put their backs into it. And it is to begin that fight I asked you to call here as soon as you returned.'

'I got back early this morning, and I was here before your office opened. Take that as the measure of my willingness to help.'

'I do not doubt it, Mr Bonchose. And now I want you please to tell me everything you can about Mr Felix, and your own life, where it has touched his. Also about your unhappy cousin, the late Madame Boirac.'

'I shall do so, and if at any point I am not clear, please ask me questions.'

Beginning by explaining who he and Annette really were – children of a younger daughter and the eldest son respectively of the late M. André Humbert of Laroche – he gave an account of their childhood, their early love of art, their moving to M. Dauphin's school in Paris, the meeting with Felix, and the latter's love for Annette. Then he told of his move to the wine merchant's firm at Narbonne, his being sent to London, his joy at again meeting Felix, his weakness for cards, the help Felix had given him, and the recent serious money difficulties into which he had fallen. He recounted his having written on the matter to Annette, the hope expressed to Felix that he would see her on the subject, his meeting the artist at Charing Cross on the Sunday evening of his return to London, their dinner together, the receipt of the £600, and finally Felix's departure in a taxi for St Malo.

His whole statement, thought Clifford, was singularly like those of Mrs Murphy, the Gresham waiter, and the ticket-collector at Brent Station, in that, while it confirmed what Felix had said and strengthened the lawyer's growing belief in the artist's innocence, it was of very little use for the trial. It was true that he, Clifford, was now in a position to prove most of Felix's statement, but the worst of it was that most of Felix's statement might be proved without proving Felix's innocence. So much so, indeed, that Clifford could not yet quite banish the suspicion that the whole thing was prearranged.

He questioned Mr Bonchose exhaustively, but without learning anything fresh. His visitor had not seen the artist on the Wednesday or Thursday, and could not help towards the alibi. Finding that nothing was to be gained by further conversation, Clifford bowed the young man out, having promised to let him know how things progressed.

24

MR GEORGES LA TOUCHE

Some days later Mr Clifford and Mr Lucius Heppenstall, KC – who were close personal friends – dined together at the former's residence, intending afterwards to have a long chat over the case. Mr Heppenstall had returned from Denmark rather earlier than was expected, and had already studied the documents received from the prosecution, as well as Clifford's notes of what he had learnt. The two men had together interviewed Felix and Bonchose and some other small inquiries had been made, the only point of importance discovered being that the late Miss Devine had crossed from Calais to Folkestone on the Sunday in question and had been alone on deck, both her maids having been helplessly ill. The meeting on this evening was to formulate a policy, to decide on the exact line which the defence should take.

The difficulty of this decision was felt by both men to be considerable. In their previous cases there had nearly always been an obvious defence. Frequently two distinct lines, or even three, had been possible, the problem then being the selection of the best. But here their difficulty was to find any defence at all.

'The first thing we must settle,' said Heppenstall, throwing himself into an easy chair, 'is whether we are going to assume this fellow Felix innocent or guilty. What is your own private opinion?'

Clifford did not speak for a few moments.

'I hardly know what to think,' he answered finally. 'I must admit that Felix's manner and personality impresses me favourably. He certainly told his story in a convincing way. Then these people that we have recently seen confirm a great deal of what he said. Further, they evidently like and believe in him. Look at Martin, for example. He is a noisy, blustering fellow, but he is no fool. He knows Felix well, and he believes in him to the extent of offering to guarantee our fees to get him off. All that must count for something. Then there is nothing inherently impossible in his story. It all might have happened just as he says. And lastly, his admitted shock when the cask was opened seems strongly in his favour.'

'But?'

'But? Well, there is all the rest of the case.'

'Then you have no private opinion?'

'Not definitely. My opinion inclines towards innocence, but I am by no means sure.'

'I rather agree with you,' remarked the KC. Then, after a pause, 'I have been thinking this thing over and I don't for the life of me see a chance of clearing him on the evidence. It is too strong. Why, if it is true, it is overpowering. It seems to me our only hope is to deny the evidence.'

'To deny it?'

'To deny it. You must admit that Felix is either guilty or the victim of a plot.'

'Of course.'

'Very well. Let us stick to that. The evidence is not genuine because Felix is the victim of a plot. How does that strike you?'

'Well, you know, I shouldn't be at all surprised if that was the actual fact. I've thought over it a good deal, and the more I think the more I begin to doubt those things that were found at St Malo. That letter from Emmie, the marks on the blotting paper, and the diamond pin, they all strike me as being a little too conclusive to be natural. Their very comprehensiveness suggests selection. Then typewritten letters anyone can produce. No, I shouldn't wonder if you're on the right track.'

'I think it's our best defence, anyway.'

'I think it's our only defence. But, mind you, it's an easy theory to suggest, but a mighty hard one to establish.'

'There's only one way,' Heppenstall declared, pouring himself out some whisky from the jar at his elbow, 'we must suggest the real murderer.'

'If we must find the real murderer we may as well let the case alone. If Scotland Yard and the Sûreté couldn't get him, we are not likely to.'

'You haven't quite got me. I don't say we must find him. It will be enough to suggest him. All we have to do is to show that some other person had a motive for Madame's death, and could have murdered her and carried out the plot against Felix. A doubt would then arise as to which of the two was guilty, and, if that doubt was strong enough, Felix would get the benefit of it.'

'But that makes our problem no easier. The difficulty still lies in the finding of this other person.'

'We can only try; it may lead to something. Our first question then is: If Felix is innocent, who might be guilty?'

There was silence for several seconds, then Heppenstall spoke again.

'Who, perhaps I should say, is least unlikely to be guilty?'

'I think there can be only one answer to that,' returned Clifford. 'In the very nature of the case a certain suspicion must attach to Boirac. But the police were fully alive to that. From all we hear, they went into it thoroughly and came to the conclusion he was innocent.'

'It depended on an alibi. But you know as well as I do alibis can be faked.'

'Undoubtedly, but they concluded this one wasn't. We don't know the exact details, but it seems to have been fully tested.'

'At all events, from the information available, I think we may assume that if Felix is innocent, Boirac is guilty. There is no suggestion of any third party being involved. If, then, we can show that Boirac had a motive for the crime, and that he could have committed it and made the plant, that's all we want. We have not to prove him guilty.'

'I suppose that is so. Then our next point is: What might have been Boirac's motive?'

'That's not hard to find. If Boirac found his wife was carrying on with Felix, it might explain his desire to kill her.'

'Yes, and it would give a two-fold reason for his working for Felix's conviction; first, self-defence by shifting over the suspicion, and, second, revenge on the man who had spoilt his home.'

'Quite. I think a plausible motive might be built up. Next let us ask, When was the body put in the cask?'

'The police say in London, because there was no opportunity elsewhere.'

'Yes, and to me it seems a quite sound deduction. Now, if that is true, it follows that if Boirac killed his wife, he must have travelled here to do it.'

'But the alibi?'

'Leave the alibi for a moment. Our defence must be that Boirac followed his wife to London and murdered her there. Now can we suggest possible details? He would arrive at his house on that Sunday morning and find his wife gone, and a letter from her saying she had eloped with Felix. What, then, would he do?'

Clifford leant forward to stir the fire.

'I have thought over that,' he said somewhat hesitatingly, 'and I have worked out a possible theory. It is, of course, pure guesswork, but it fits a number of the facts.'

'Let's hear it. Naturally our theories at present can only be guesswork.'

'I imagined Boirac, then, mad with his discovery on the Sunday morning, sitting down and working out a plan for vengeance. He perhaps goes on that morning to the Gare du Nord, and possibly sees them start. He follows them to London. Or, at least, he sees and follows Felix. Madame may have gone by another route. By the time he finds they have reached St Malo his plan is worked out. He learns they are alone in the house, and he watches till he sees them go out. Then he enters by, say, an open window, and, sitting down at Felix's desk, he forges a letter to Dupierre, ordering the companion statue to that he has already purchased. He does this in order to obtain a cask in which to pack Madame's body, as he intends to murder her. To throw suspicion on Felix, he copies the artist's handwriting and dries it on his blotting paper. For the same reason he signs it with Felix's name. But he does not give Felix's address, as he wants to get the cask himself.'

'Good!' interjected Heppenstall.

'He then comes away with his letter, posts it, telephones to Paris to know when and by what route the cask is being sent, and arranges a carter to meet it and bring it near, but not to, St Malo, instructing the carter to await him. Meantime, by some letter or telegram or other trick, he gets Felix out of the way, leaving Madame alone in the house. He rings, she opens the door, he forces his way in, and, in that little round-backed chair in the study, he throttles her. The pin falls out of the neck of the dress and lies unnoticed. Then he goes back to the carter and brings the cask into the yard. He sends the carter to the nearest inn for his dinner, unpacks and destroys the statue, and packs the body. By this time the carter has returned, and Boirac has him remove the cask, giving him instructions to send it to Paris next morning. To compromise Felix still further he has prepared the Emmie note, and he shoves this into the pocket of Felix's clothes.'

'Good,' said Heppenstall again.

'He goes himself to Paris, gets hold of the cask at the Gare du Nord and sends it to Felix from the rue Cardinet Goods Station. He works out a tricky letter which will have the effect of making Felix claim the cask. Felix does so, and the police get on his track.'

'By George, Clifford, you haven't been idle. I shouldn't wonder if you are pretty near the thing. But if all that had taken place at St Malo, do you think Felix wouldn't have said something about it?'

'I think he would have. On the other hand, he may have wanted to save Madame's memory, and if so, he obviously couldn't mention it.'

'What about the charwoman?'

'Well, that is another difficulty. But I think a clever woman could have hidden her traces.'

'The theory accounts for a great many things, and I think we must adopt it as a basis for investigation. Let us now see what it involves.'

'It involves Boirac having been in London on the Sunday night or Monday after the dinner party to learn what had taken place and to write his letter, and again on the Wednesday to commit the murder and arrange about the cask.'

'Quite. It seems to me, then, our first business is definitely to find out where Boirac was on these dates.'

'He satisfied the police he was in Paris and Belgium.'

'I know, but we agreed alibis could be faked. We'd better have the thing gone into again.'

'It will mean a detective.'

'Yes, and what about La Touche?'

'La Touche is the best man we could have, of course, but he's fairly expensive.'

Heppenstall shrugged his shoulders.

'Can't help that,' he said. 'We must have him.'

'Very well. I'll ask him to meet us – shall I say at three tomorrow?'

'That will suit me.'

The two men continued discussing the affair until the clock struck twelve, when Heppenstall made a move to return to town.

Mr Georges La Touche was commonly regarded as the smartest private detective in London. Brought up in that city, where his father kept a small foreign book store, he learnt till he was twelve the English language and ideas. Then, on the death of his English mother, the family moved to Paris, and Georges had to adjust himself to a new environment. At twenty, he entered Cook's office as a courier, and, learning successively Italian, German, and Spanish, he gradually acquired a first-hand acquaintance-ship with Middle and South-Western Europe. After some ten years of this work he grew tired of the constant travelling, and, coming to London, he offered his services to a firm of well-known private detectives. Here he did so well that, on the death of the founder some fifteen years later, he stepped into his place. He soon began to specialise in foreign or international cases, for which his early training peculiarly fitted him.

But he was not much in appearance. Small, sallow, and slightly stooped, he would have looked insignificant only for the strength of the clear-cut features and the intelligence of the dark, flashing eyes. Years of training had enabled him to alter his expression and veil these tell-tale signs of power, and he had frequently found the weak and insipid impression thus produced, an asset in allaying the suspicions of his adversaries.

His delight in the uncommon and bizarre had caused him to read attentively the details of the cask mystery. When, therefore, he received Clifford's telephone asking him to act on behalf of the suspected man, he eagerly agreed, and cancelled some minor engagements in order to meet the lawyers at the time appointed.

The important question of fees having been settled, Clifford explained to the detective all that was known of the case, as well as the ideas he and Heppenstall had evolved with regard to the defence.

'What we want you to do for us, Mr La Touche,' he wound up, 'is to go into the case on the assumption that Boirac is the guilty man. Settle definitely whether this is a possible theory. I think you will agree that this depends on the truth of his alibi. Therefore, test that first. If it cannot be broken down, Boirac cannot be guilty, and our line of defence won't work. And I need hardly say, the sooner you can give us some information the better.'

'You have given me a congenial task, gentlemen, and if I don't succeed it won't be for want of trying. I suppose that is all today? I'll go over these papers and make the case up. Then I fancy I had best go to Paris. But I'll call in to see you, Mr Clifford, before I start.'

La Touche was as good as his word. In three days he was again in Clifford's room.

'I've been into this case as far as is possible this side of the Channel, Mr Clifford,' he announced. 'I was thinking of crossing to Paris tonight.'

'Good. And what do you think of it all?'

'Well, sir, it's rather soon to give an opinion, but I'm afraid we're up against a tough proposition.'

'In what way?'

'The case against Felix, sir. It's pretty strong. Of course, I expect we'll meet it all right, but it'll take some doing. There's not much in his favour, if you think of it.'

'What about the shock he got when the cask was opened? Have you seen the doctor about it?'

'Yes. He says the thing was genuine enough, but. sir, I'm afraid that won't carry us so far as you seem to think.'

'To me it seems very strong. Look at it this way: the essence of a shock is surprise; the surprise could only have been at the contents of the cask; therefore Felix did not know the contents; therefore he could not have put the body in; therefore surely he must be innocent?'

'That sounds all right, sir, I admit. But I'm afraid a clever counsel could upset it. You see, there's more than surprise in a shock. There's horror. And it could be argued that Felix got both surprise and horror when the cask was opened.'

'How, if he knew what was in it?'

'This way, sir. What was in it was hardly what he was expecting. It might be said that he put in the body as he had seen the lady alive. But she had been dead for a good many days when the cask was opened. She would look a very different object. He would be filled with horror when he saw her. That horror, together with the fact that he would be all keyed up to act surprise in any case, would produce the effect.'

Clifford had not thought of this somewhat gruesome explanation, and the possibility of its truth made him uncomfortable. If the strongest point in Felix's favour could be met as easily as this, it was indeed a black lookout for his client. But he did not voice his doubts to his visitor.

'If you can't get enough to support the defence we suggest,' he said, 'we must just try some other line.'

'I may get what you want all right, sir. I'm only pointing out that the thing is not all plain sailing. I'll cross, then, tonight, and I hope I may soon have some good news to send you.'

'Thank you. I hope so.'

The two men shook hands, and La Touche took his leave. That night he left Charing Cross for Paris.

25

DISAPPOINTMENT

La Touche was a good traveller, and usually slept well on a night journey. But not always. It sometimes happened that the rhythmic rush and roar through the darkness stimulated rather than lulled his brain, and on such occasions, lying in the wagon-lits of some long-distance express, more than one illuminating idea had had its birth. Tonight, as he sat in the corner of a first-class compartment in the Calais-Paris train, though outwardly a lounging and indolent figure, his mind was keenly alert, and he therefore took the opportunity to consider the business which lay before him.

His first duty obviously was to retest Boirac's alibi. He had learnt what the authorities had done in the matter, and he would begin his work by checking Lefarge's investigation. For the moment he did not see how to improve on his *confrère's* methods, and he could only hope that some clue would present itself during his researches, which his predecessor had missed.

So far he was in no doubt as to his proceedings, for this inquiry into Boirac's alibi had been directly asked for by his employers. But, after that, he had been given a free hand to do as he thought best.

He turned to what he considered the central feature of the case – the finding of the body in the cask – and began to separate in his mind the facts actually known about it from those assumed. Firstly, the body was in the cask when the latter reached St Katherine's Docks. Secondly, it could not have been put in during the journey from the rue Cardinet Goods Station. So much was certain. But the previous step in the cask's journey was surmise. It was assumed that it had been taken from the Gare du Nord to the rue Cardinet on a horse-cart. On what was this assumption founded? Three facts. First, that it left the Gare du Nord on a horse-cart; second, that it reached the rue Cardinet in the same manner; and third, that such a vehicle would have occupied about the time the trip had actually taken. The assumption seemed reasonable, and yet... He had to remember that they were up against a man of no ordinary ability, whoever he might be. Might not the cask have been taken by the first horse-cart to some adjoining house or shed where the body could have been put in, then sent by motor-lorry to some other shed near the Goods Station and there transferred to a horse-cart again? This undoubtedly seemed far-fetched and unlikely, nevertheless, the facts were not known, and, he thought, they should be. He must find the carter who brought the cask to the Goods Station. Then he would be certain where the body was put in, and therefore whether the murder was committed in London or Paris.

He noted a third point. The various letters in the case – and there were several – might or might not be forgeries, and if the former, it was obviously impossible for him to say offhand who had written them. But there was one letter which could not be a forgery – at least in a certain sense. The Le Gautier letter which Felix said he had received was done on a typewriter which could be identified. It was hardly too much to assume that the man who typed that letter was the murderer. Find the typewriter, thought La Touche, and the chances are it will lead to the guilty man.

A further point struck him. If Boirac were guilty, might he not even yet give himself away? The detective recalled case after case in his own experience in which a criminal had, after the crime, done something or gone somewhere that had led to his arrest. Would it be worthwhile having Boirac shadowed? He considered the question carefully and finally decided to bring over two of his men for this purpose.

Here, then, were four directions in which inquiries might be made, of which the first three at least promised a certain and definite result. As the train slackened speed for the capital, he felt his work was cut out for him.

And then began a period of tedious and unprofitable work. He was very efficient, very thorough and very pertinacious, but the only result of all his painstaking labours was to establish more firmly than ever the truth of Boirac's statements.

He began with the waiter at Charenton. Very skilfully he approached the subject, and, painting a moving picture of an innocent man falsely accused of murder, he gradually enlisted the man's sympathy. Then he appealed to his cupidity, promising him a liberal reward for information that would save his client, and finally he soothed his fears by promising that in no case should any statement he might make get him into trouble. The waiter, who seemed a quiet, honest man, was perfectly open, and readily replied to all La Touche's questions, but except on one point he stoutly adhered to his previous statement to Lefarge. M. Boirac – whom he identified unhesitatingly from a photograph – had lunched in the café about 1.30, and had then telephoned to two separate places – he had heard the two numbers asked for. As before, he made the reservation that he was not certain of the day of the week, his impression having been that it was Monday and not Tuesday, but he stated that in this he might easily be mistaken. There was no shaking his evidence, and La Touche was strongly of the opinion that the man was speaking the truth.

But as well as repeating his statement to Lefarge, the waiter added one item of information that seemed important. Asked if he could not recall either of the numbers demanded, he now said he recollected the last two figures of one of them. They were 45. They caught his attention because they were the café's own telephone number – Charenton 45. He could not recall either the previous figures of the number nor yet the division. He had intended to tell this to Lefarge, but being somewhat upset by the detective's call, the point had slipped his memory, and it was only when thinking the matter over afterwards it had occurred to him.

For La Touche to look up the telephone directory was the work of a few seconds. The number of Boirac's house in the Avenue de l'Alma did not suit, but when he looked up the Pump Construction Office he found it was Nord 745.

Here was fresh confirmation. It was obvious the waiter could not have invented his tale, and La Touche left utterly convinced that Boirac had indeed lunched at the café and sent the messages.

As he was returning to the city it occurred to him that perhaps the waiter's impression was really correct and that Boirac had been in the café on Monday afternoon instead of Tuesday. How was this point to be ascertained?

He recollected how Lefarge had settled it. He had interviewed the persons to whom Boirac had spoken, the butler and the head clerk, and both were certain of the date. La Touche decided he must follow Lefarge's example.

Accordingly he called at the house in the Avenue de l'Alma and saw François. He was surprised to find the old man genuinely grieved at the news of Felix's arrest. Few though the occasions had been in which the two had met, something in the personality of the former had in this case, as in so many others, inspired attachment and respect. La Touche therefore adopted the same tactics as with the waiter, and, on his explaining that he was acting for the suspected man, he found François anxious to give all the help in his power.

But here again all that La Touche gained was confirmation of Boirac's statement. François recollected the telephone message, and he was sure Boirac had spoken. He positively recognised the voice and equally positively he remembered the day. It was Tuesday. He was able to connect it with a number of other small events which definitely fixed it.

'Lefarge was right,' thought the detective, as he strolled up the Avenue de l'Alma. 'Boirac telephoned from Charenton at 2.30 on Tuesday. However, I may as well go through with the business.'

He turned his steps therefore towards the head office of the Avrotte Pump Construction Company. Repeating Lefarge's tactics, he watched till he observed Boirac leave. Then he entered the office and asked if he could see M. Dufresne.

'I am afraid not, monsieur. I believe he has gone out,' answered the clerk who had come over to attend him. 'But if you will take a seat for a moment I shall ascertain.'

La Touche did as he was asked, looking admiringly round the large office with its polished teak furniture, its rows of vertical file cabinets, its telephones, its clicking typewriters, and its industrious and efficient-looking clerks. Now La Touche was not merely a thinking machine. He had his human side, and, except when on a hot scent, he had a remarkably quick eye for a pretty girl. Thus it was that as his eye roamed inquisitively over the room, it speedily halted at and became focused on the second row of typists, a girl of perhaps two or three-and-twenty. She looked, it must be admitted, wholly charming. Small, dark, and evidently vivacious, she had a tiny, pouting mouth and an adorable dimple. Plainly dressed as became her business like surroundings, there was, nevertheless, a daintiness and chicness about her whole appearance that would have delighted an even more critical observer than the detective. She flashed an instantaneous glance at him from her dark, sparkling eyes, and then, slightly elevating her pert little nose, became engrossed in her work.

'I am sorry, monsieur, but M. Dufresne has gone home slightly indisposed. He expects to be back in a couple of days, if you could conveniently call again.'

La Touche hardly felt a proper appreciation of the clerk's promptness, but he thanked him politely and said he would return later. Then, with a final glance at an averted head of dark, luxuriant hair, he left the office.

The chief clerk's absence was a vexatious delay. But, though it would hold up his work on the alibi for a day or two, he might begin on one of the other points which had occurred to him during the journey to Paris. There was, for example, the tracing of the carter who brought the cask from the Gare du Nord to the rue Cardinet. He would see what could be done on that.

Accordingly he went out to the great Goods Station and, introducing himself to the agent in charge, explained his errand. The official was exceedingly polite, and, after some delay, the two porters whom Burnley and Lefarge had interviewed some weeks before were ushered into the room. La Touche questioned them minutely, but without gaining any fresh information. They repeated their statement that they would recognise the carter who had brought the cask were they to see him again, but were unable to describe him more particularly than before.

La Touche then went to the Gare du Nord. Here he was fortunate in finding the clerk who had handed over the cask to the black-bearded Jacques de Belleville. But again he was disappointed. Neither the clerk nor any of the other officials he interviewed recollected the carter who had taken the cask, and none therefore could say if he was like the man who delivered it at the Goods Station.

Baffled on this point, La Touche turned into a café, and, ordering a bock, sat down to consider his next step. Apparently Lefarge had been right to advertise. He recollected from the report he had had from the authorities that all the advertisements had appeared in, among other papers, *Le Journal*. He determined he would see those advertisements in the hope of discovering why they had failed.

He accordingly drove to the office of the paper and asked leave to look over the files. A slight research convinced him that the advertising had been thoroughly and skilfully done. He took copies of each fresh announcement – there were nearly a dozen. Then, returning to his hotel, he lay down on his bed and looked them over again.

The paragraphs varied in wording, type, and position in the columns, but necessarily they were similar in effect. All asked for information as to the identity of a carter who, about six o'clock on Thursday, the 1st of April, had delivered a cask at the rue Cardinet Goods Station. All offered a reward varying from 1000 to 5000 francs, and all undertook that the carter would not suffer from the information being divulged.

After a couple of hours hard thinking La Touche came to the conclusion that the advertising had been complete. He saw no way in which he could improve on what Lefarge had done, nor could he think of anything in the announcements themselves which might have militated against their success.

To clear his brain he determined to banish all thoughts of the case for the remainder of the day. He therefore went for a stroll along the boulevards, and, after a leisurely dinner, turned his steps towards the Folies Bergères, and there passed the evening.

On his way home it occurred to him that while waiting to interview M. Dufresne at the office of the Pump Construction Company be might run over to Brussels and satisfy himself as to that part of Boirac's alibi. Accordingly, next morning saw him entrained for the Belgian capital, where he arrived about midday. He drove to the Hôtel Maximilian, lunched, and afterwards made exhaustive inquiries at the office. Here he saw copies of the visitors' returns which every Belgian hotel must furnish to the police, and satisfied himself absolutely that Boirac had been there on the date in question. As a result of Lefarge's inquiries the clerk recollected the circumstances of the pump manufacturer's telephone, and adhered to his previous statement in every particular. La Touche took the afternoon train for Paris considerably disappointed with the results of his journey.

On the chance that the chief clerk might be back at work, he returned next day to the pump works. Again he watched till Boirac had left and again entered and asked for M. Dufresne. The same prompt clerk came forward to speak to him, and, saying that M. Dufresne had returned that morning, once more asked him to be seated while he took in his card. La Touche then suddenly remembered the girl he had so much admired, but whose existence he had forgotten since his last visit. He glanced across the room. She was there, but he could not see her face. Something had evidently gone wrong with the splendid-looking machine which she – La Touche whimsically wondered why you did not say 'played' or 'drove' – and she was bending over it, apparently adjusting some screw. But he had no time to pursue his studies of female beauty. The prompt clerk was back at his side almost immediately to say that M. Dufresne could see him. He accordingly followed his guide to the chief clerk's room.

M. Dufresne was quite as ready to assist him as had been his other informants, but he could tell him nothing the detective did not already know. He repeated his statement to Lefarge almost word for word. He was sure M. Boirac had telephoned about 2.30 on the Tuesday – he unmistakably recognised his voice, and he was equally certain of the date.

La Touche regained the street and walked slowly back to his hotel. It was beginning to look very much as if the alibi could not be broken, and he was unable for the moment to see his next step in the matter. Nor had any information resulted from the labours of Mallet and Parol, the two men he had brought over to shadow Boirac. Up to the present the latter had been most circumspect, not having been anywhere or done anything in the slightest degree suspicious. As La Touche wrote a detailed report of his proceedings to Clifford, he felt for the first time a distinct doubt as to the outcome of his investigations.

26

A CLUE AT LAST

La Touche, having finished his report, put on his hat and sallied forth into the rue de la Fayette. He intended after posting his letter to cross to the south side and spend the evening with some friends. He was not in an agreeable frame of mind. The conclusion to which he was apparently being forced would be a disappointment to Clifford, and, if the theory of Boirac's guilt broke down, he saw no better than the solicitor what defence remained.

He sauntered slowly along the pavement, his mind brooding almost subconsciously on the case. Then, noticing a letter box on the opposite side of the street, he turned to cross over. But as he stepped off the pavement an idea flashed into his mind and he stopped as if shot. That typewriter the pretty girl in Boirac's office had been using was a *new machine*. La Touche was an observant man, and he had noted the fact, as he habitually noted small details about the objects he saw. But not until this moment did he realise the tremendously suggestive deduction which might be made from that fact. Lefarge, in his search for the machine on which the Le Gautier letter had been typed, had obtained samples from all the typewriters to which Boirac, so far as he could ascertain, had access. But what if that new machine replaced an old? What if that old machine had typed the Le Gautier letter and had been then got rid of so that samples taken by suspicious detectives might be supplied from some other typewriter? Here was food for thought. If he could prove anything of this kind he need have no fear of disappointing his employer. He put the report back in his pocket till he could adjust himself to this new point of view.

And then he had a revulsion of feeling. After all, offices must necessarily procure new typewriters, and there was no reason in this case to suppose a machine had been purchased otherwise than in the ordinary course of business, and yet – the idea was attractive.

He decided he might as well make some inquiries before forwarding his report. It would be a simple matter to find out when the new machine was purchased, and, if the date was not suspicious, the matter could be dropped.

He considered the best way of ascertaining his information. His first idea was to meet the typist and ask her the direct question. Then he saw that if her answer supported his theory, not only would further inquiries be necessary, but no hint that these were being made must reach Boirac. It might therefore be better to try diplomacy.

To La Touche diplomatic dealing was second nature, and he was not long in devising a plan. He looked at his watch. If was 5.15. If he hurried he might reach the pump works before the pretty typist left.

From the window of the café which had so often served in a similar capacity, he watched the office staff take their departure. For a long time his victim did not appear, and he had almost come to the conclusion she must have gone, when he saw her. She was with two other girls, and the three, after glancing round the street, tripped off daintily citywards.

When they had gone a fair distance La Touche followed. The girls stood for a moment at the Simplon Station of the Metro, then the pretty typist vanished down the steps, while the others moved on along the pavement. La Touche sprinted to the entrance and was in time to see the grey dress of the quarry disappearing down the passage labelled Porte d'Orléans. He got his ticket and followed to the platform. There was a fairly dense crowd, and, after locating mademoiselle he mingled with it, keeping well back out of sight.

A train soon drew up and the girl got in. La Touche entered the next carriage. Standing at the end of his vehicle he could see her through the glass between the coaches without, he felt sure, being himself visible. One, two, five stations passed, and then she got up and moved towards the door ready to alight. La Touche did the same, observing from the map in the carriage that the next station was not a junction. As the train jerked and groaned to a standstill he leaped out and hurried to the street. Crossing rapidly, he stopped at a kiosk and asked for an evening paper. Bending over the counter of the stall, he saw her emerge up the steps and start off down the street. He remained on the opposite side, cautiously following until, after about two blocks, she entered a small, unpretentious restaurant.

'If she is going to dine alone,' thought La Touche, 'I am in luck.'

He waited till she would have probably reached her second or third course and then entered the building.

The room was narrow, corresponding to the frontage, but stretched a long way back, the far end being lighted with electric lamps. A row of marble-topped tables stretched down each side, with six cane chairs at each. Mirrors framed in dingy white and gold lined the walls. At the extreme back was a tiny stage on which an orchestra of three girls was performing.

The place was about half-full. As La Touche's quick eye took in the scene, he noticed the typist seated alone at a table three or four from the stage. He walked forward.

'If mademoiselle permits?' he murmured, bowing, but hardly looking at her, as he pulled out a chair nearly opposite her and sat down.

He gave his order and then, business being as it were off his mind, he relaxed so far as to look around. He glanced at the girl, seemed suddenly to recognise her, gave a mild start of surprise and leant forward with another bow.

'Mademoiselle will perhaps pardon if I presume,' he said, in his best manner, 'but I think we have met before or, if not quite, almost.'

The girl raised her eyebrows but did not speak.

'In the office of M. Boirac,' went on the detective. 'You would not, of course, notice, but I saw you there busy with a fine typewriter.'

Mademoiselle was not encouraging. She shrugged her shoulders, but made no reply. La Touche had another shot.

'I am perhaps impertinent in addressing mademoiselle, but I assure her no impertinence is meant. I am the inventor of a new device for typewriters, and I try to get opinion of every expert operator I can find on its utility. Perhaps mademoiselle would permit me to describe it and ask hers?'

'Why don't you take it to some of the agents?' She spoke frigidly.

'Because, mademoiselle,' answered La Touche, warming to his subject, 'I am not quite certain if the device would be sufficiently valuable. It would be costly to attach and no firm would buy unless it could be shown that operators wanted it. That is what I am so anxious to learn.'

She was listening, though not very graciously. La Touche did not wait for a reply, but began sketching on the back of the menu.

'Here,' he said, 'is my idea,' and he proceeded to draw and describe the latest form of tabulator with which he was acquainted. The girl looked at him with scorn and suspicion.

'You're describing the Remington tabulator,' she said coldly.

'Oh, but, pardon me, mademoiselle. You surely don't mean that? I have been told this is quite new.'

'You have been told wrongly. I ought to know, for I have been using one the very same, as what you say is yours, for several weeks.'

'You don't say so, mademoiselle? That means that I have been forestalled and all my work has been wasted.'

La Touche's disappointment was so obvious that the girl thawed slightly.

'You'd better call at the Remington depot and ask to see one of their new machines. Then you can compare their tabulator with yours.'

'Thank you, mademoiselle, I'll do so tomorrow. Then you use a Remington?'

'Yes, a No. 10.'

'Is that an old machine? Pardon my questions, but have you had it long?'

'I can't tell you how long it has been at the office. I am only there myself six or seven weeks.'

Six or seven weeks! And the murder took place just over six weeks before! Could there be a connection, or was this mere coincidence?

'It must be a satisfaction to a man of business,' La Touche went on conversationally, as he helped himself to wine, 'when his business grows to the extent of requiring an additional typist. I envy M. Boirac his feelings when he inserted his advertisement nearly as much as I envy him when you applied.'

'You have wasted your envy then,' returned the girl in chilly and contemptuous tones, 'for you are wrong on both points. M. Boirac's business has not extended, for I replaced a girl who had just left, and no advertisement was inserted as I went to M. Boirac from the Michelin School in the rue Scribe.'

La Touche had got his information; at least, all he had expected from this girl. He continued the somewhat one-sided conversation for some minutes, and then with a courteous bow left the restaurant. He reached his hotel determined to follow the matter up.

Accordingly, next morning saw him repeating his tactics of the previous evening. Taking up his position in the restaurant near the Pump Works shortly before midday, he watched the staff go for *déjeuner*. First came M. Boirac, then M. Dufresne, and then a crowd of lesser lights – clerks and typists. He saw his friend of the night before with the same two companions, closely followed by the prompt clerk. At last the stream ceased, and in about ten minutes the detective crossed the road and once more entered the office. It was empty except for a junior clerk.

'Good morning,' said La Touche affably. 'I called to ask whether you would be so good as to do me a favour. I want a piece of information for which, as it may give you some trouble to procure, I will pay twenty francs. Will you help me?'

'What is the information, monsieur?' asked the boy – he was little more than a boy.

'I am manager of a paper works and I am looking for a typist for my office. I am told that a young lady typist left here about six weeks ago?'

'That is true, monsieur; Mlle. Lambert.'

'Yes, that is the lady's name,' returned La Touche, making a mental note of it.

'Now,' he continued confidentially, 'can you tell me why she left?'

'I think she was dismissed, monsieur, but I never really understood why.'

'Dismissed?'

'Yes, monsieur. She had some row with M. Boirac, our managing director. I don't know – none of us know – what it was about.'

'I had heard she was dismissed, and that is why I was interested in her. Unfortunately my business is not for the moment as flourishing as I should wish. It occurred to me that if I could find a typist who had some blot on her record, she might be willing to come to me for a smaller salary than she would otherwise expect. It would benefit her as well as me, as it would enable her to regain her position.'

The clerk bowed without comment, and La Touche continued: 'The information I want is this. Can you put me in touch with this young lady? Do you know her address?'

The other shook his head.

'I fear not, monsieur. I don't know where the lives.'

La Touche affected to consider.

'Now, how am I to get hold of her?' he said. The clerk making no suggestion, he went on after a pause: 'I think if you could tell me just when she left it might help me. Could you do that?'

'About six weeks ago. I can tell you the exact day by looking up the old wages sheets if you don't mind waiting. Will you take a seat?'

La Touche thanked him and sat down, trusting the search would be concluded before any of the other clerks returned. But he was not delayed long. In three or four minutes the boy returned.

'She left on Monday, the 5th of April, monsieur.'

'And was she long with you?'

'About two years, monsieur.'

'I am greatly obliged. And her Christian name was?'

'Éloise, monsieur. Éloise Lambert.'

'A thousand thanks. And now I have just to beg of you not to mention my visit, as it would injure me if it got out that my business was not too flourishing. Here is my debt to you.' He handed over the twenty francs.

'It is too much, monsieur. I am glad to oblige you without payment.'

'A bargain is a bargain,' insisted the detective, and, followed by the profuse thanks of the young clerk, he left the office.

'This grows interesting,' thought La Touche, as he once more emerged into the street. 'Boirac dismisses a typist on the very day the cask reaches St Katherine's Docks. Now, I wonder if that new typewriter made its appearance at the same time. I must get hold of that girl Lambert.'

But how was this to be done? No doubt there would be a record of her address somewhere in the office, but he was anxious that no idea of his suspicions should leak out, and he preferred to leave that source untapped. What, then, was left to him? He could see nothing for it but an advertisement.

Accordingly, he turned into a café and, calling for a bock, drafted out the following: 'If Mlle. Éloise Lambert, stenographer and typist, will apply to M. Georges La Touche, Hôtel Suisse, rue de La Fayette, she will hear something to her advantage.'

He read over the words and then a thought struck him, and he took another sheet of paper and wrote: 'If Mlle. Éloise Lambert, stenographer and typist, will apply to M. Guillaume Faneuil, Hôtel St Antoine, she will hear something to her advantage.'

'If Boirac should see the thing, there's no use in my shoving into the limelight,' he said to himself. 'I'll drop Georges La Touche for a day or two and try the St Antoine.'

He sent his advertisement to several papers, then, going to the Hôtel St Antoine, engaged a room in the name of M. Guillaume Faneuil.

'I shall not require it till tomorrow,' he said to the clerk, and next day he moved in.

During the morning there was a knock at the door of his private sitting-room, and a tall, graceful girl of about five-and-twenty entered. She was not exactly pretty, but exceedingly pleasant and good-humoured looking. Her tasteful, though quiet, dress showed she was not in need as a result of losing her situation.

La Touche rose and bowed.

'Mlle. Lambert?' he said with a smile. 'I am M. Faneuil. Won't you sit down?'

'I saw your advertisement in *Le Soir*, monsieur, and – here I am.'

'I am much indebted to you for coming so promptly, mademoiselle,' said La Touche, reseating himself, 'and I shall not trespass long on your time. But before explaining the matter may I ask if you are the Mlle. Lambert who recently acted as typist at the Avrotte Works?'

'Yes, monsieur. I was there for nearly two years.'

'Forgive me, but can you give any proof of that? A mere matter of form, of course, but in justice to my employers I am bound to ask the question.'

An expression of surprise passed over the girl's face.

'I really don't know that I can,' she answered. 'You see, I was not expecting to be asked such a question.'

It had occurred to La Touche that in spite of his precautions Boirac might have somehow discovered what he was engaged on, and sent this girl with a made up story. But her answer satisfied him. If she had been an impostor she would have come provided with proofs of her identity.

'Ah, well,' he rejoined with a smile, 'I think I may safely take the risk. May I ask you another question? Was a new typewriter purchased while you were at the office?'

The surprise on the pleasant face deepened.

'Why, yes, monsieur, a No. 10 Remington.'

'And can you tell me just when?'

'Easily. I left the office on Monday, 5th April, and the new machine was sent three days earlier – on Friday, the 2nd.'

Here was news indeed! La Touche was now in no doubt about following up the matter. He must get all the information possible out of this girl. And the need for secrecy would make him stick to diplomacy.

He smiled and bowed.

'You will forgive me, mademoiselle, but I had to satisfy myself you were the lady I wished to meet. I asked you these questions only to ensure that you knew the answers. And now I shall tell you who I am and what is the business at issue. But first, may I ask you to keep all I may tell you secret?'

His visitor looked more and more mystified as she replied, 'I promise, monsieur.'

Then I may say that I am a private detective, employed on behalf of the typewriter company to investigate some very extraordinary – I can only call them frauds, which have recently been taking place. In some way, which up to the present we have been unable to fathom, several of our machines have developed faults which, you understand, do not prevent them working, but which prevent them being quite satisfactory. The altering of tensions and the slight twisting of type to put them out of alignment are the kind of things I mean. We hardly like to suspect rival firms of practising these frauds to get our machines into disfavour, and yet it is hard to account for it otherwise. Now, we think that you can possibly give us some information, and I am authorised by my company to hand you one hundred francs if you will be kind enough to do so.'

The surprise had not left the girl's face as she answered: 'I should have been very pleased, monsieur, to tell you all I knew without any payment, had I known anything to tell. But I am afraid I don't.'

'I think, mademoiselle, you can help us if you will. May I ask you a few questions?'

'Certainly.'

'The first is, can you describe the machine you used prior to the purchase of the new one?'

'Yes, it was a No. 7 Remington.'

'I did not mean that,' answered La Touche, eagerly noting this information, 'I knew that, of course, as it is this No. 7 machine I am inquiring about. What I meant to ask was, had it any special marks or peculiarities by which it could be distinguished from other No. 7's?'

'Why, no, I don't think so,' the girl answered thoughtfully. 'And yet there were. The letter S on the S-key had got twisted round to the right and there were three scratches here' – she indicated the side plate of an imaginary typewriter.

'You would then be able to identify the machine if you saw it again?'

'Yes, I certainly should.'

'Now, mademoiselle, had it any other peculiarities – defective letters or alignment or anything of that kind?'

'No, nothing really bad. It was old and out of date, but quite good enough. M. Boirac, of course, thought otherwise, but I maintain my opinion.'

'What did M. Boirac say exactly?'

'He blamed me for it. But there wasn't anything wrong, and if there had been it wasn't my fault.'

'I am sure of that, mademoiselle. But perhaps you would tell me about it from the beginning?'

'There's not much to tell. I had a big job to do – typing a long specification of a pumping plant for the Argentine, and when I had finished I left it as usual on M. Boirac's desk. A few minutes later he sent for me and asked how I came to put such an untidy document before him. I didn't see anything wrong with it and I asked him what he complained of. He pointed out some very small defects – principally uneven alignment, and one or two letters just a trifle blurred. You really would hardly have seen it. I said that wasn't my fault, and that the machine wanted adjustment. He said I had been striking while the shift key was partly moved, but, M. Faneuil, I had been doing nothing of the kind. I told M. Boirac so, and he then apologised and said I must have a new machine. He telephoned there and then to the Remington people, and a No. 10 came that afternoon.'

'And what happened to the old No. 7?'

'The man that brought the new one took the old away.'

'And was that all that was said?'

'That was all, monsieur.'

'But, pardon me, I understood you left owing to some misunderstanding with M. Boirac?'

The girl shook her head.

'Oh, no,' she said, 'nothing of the sort. M. Boirac told me the following Monday, that is, two days after the typewriter business, that he was reorganising his office and would do with a typist less. As I was the last arrival, I had to go. He said he wished to carry out the alterations immediately so that I might leave at once. He gave me a month's salary instead of notice, and a good testimonial which I have here. We parted quite friends.'

The document read:

I have pleasure in certifying that Mlle. Éloise Lambert was engaged as a stenographer and typist in the head office of this company from August, 1910 till 5th April, 1912, during which time she gave every satisfaction to me and my chief clerk. She proved herself diligent and painstaking, thoroughly competent in her work, and of excellent manners and conduct. She leaves the firm through no fault of her own, but because we are reducing staff. I regret her loss and have every confidence in recommending her to those needing her services.

(Signed) RAOUL BOIRAC,
Managing Director.

'An excellent testimonial, mademoiselle,' La Touche commented. 'Pray excuse me for just a moment.'

He stepped into the adjoining bedroom and closed the door. Then taking a sample of Boirac's writing from his pocket-book, he compared the signature with that of the testimonial. After a careful scrutiny he was satisfied the latter was genuine. He returned to the girl and handed her the document.

'Thank you, mademoiselle. Now, can you recall one other point? Did you, within the last three or four weeks, type a letter about some rather unusual matters – about someone winning a lot of money in the State Lottery and about sending this packed in a cask to England?'

'Never, monsieur,' asserted the typist, evidently completely puzzled by the questions she was being asked. La Touche watched her keenly and was satisfied she had no suspicion that his business was other than he had said. But he was nothing if not thorough, and his thoroughness drove him to make provision for suspicions which might arise later. He therefore went on to question her about the No. 7 machine, asking whether she had ever noticed it had been tampered with, and finally saying that he believed there must have been a mistake and that the machine they had discussed was not that in which he was interested. Then, after obtaining her address, he handed her the hundred francs, which, after a protest, she finally accepted.

'Now, not a word to anyone, if you please, mademoiselle,' he concluded, as they parted.

His discoveries, to say the least of it, were becoming interesting. If Mlle. Lambert's story was true – and he was strongly disposed to believe her – M. Boirac had acted in a way that required some explanation. His finding fault with the typist did not seem genuine. In fact, to La Touche it looked as if the whole episode had been arranged to provide an excuse for getting rid of the typewriter. Again, the manufacturer's dismissal of his typist at a day's notice was not explained by his statement that he was about to reorganise his office. Had that been true he would have allowed her to work her month's notice, and, even more obviously, he would not have immediately engaged her successor. As La Touche paid his bill at the hotel he decided that though there might be nothing in his suspicions, the matter was well worth further investigation. He therefore called a taxi and was driven to the Remington typewriter depot.

'I want,' he said to the salesman who came forward, 'to buy a second-hand machine. Can you let me see some?'

'Certainly, monsieur. Will you step this way?'

They went to a room at the back of the building where were stored a vast assemblage of typewriters of all sizes and in all states of repair. La Touche, inquiring as to prices and models, moved slowly about, running his quick eye over the machines, looking always for one with a twisted S-key. But, search as he would, he could not find what he wanted. Nor could he find any No. 7's. These machines were all more modern.

He turned at last to the shopman.

'These are all rather expensive for me. I should explain that I am the principal of a commercial school, and I merely want a machine on which beginners could learn the keys. Any old thing would do, if I could get it cheap. Have you any older machines?'

'Certainly, monsieur, we have several quite good No. 7's and a few No. 5's. Come this way, please.'

They went to a room devoted to more antiquated specimens. Here La Touche continued his investigations, searching always for the twisted S.

At last he saw it. Not only was the letter turned to the right, but on the side plate were the three scratches mentioned by Mlle. Lambert.

'I think that one would suit,' he said. 'Could you get it down and let me have a look at it?'

He went through the pretence of examining it with care.

'Yes,' he said, 'this will do if it works all right. I should like to try it.'

He put in a sheet of paper and typed a few words. Then, drawing out his work, he examined the letters and alignment.

As he looked at it even his long experience scarcely prevented him giving a cry of triumph. For, to the best of his belief, this was the machine on which the Le Gautier letter had been typed!

He turned again to the shopman.

'That seems all right,' he said. I'll take the machine, please.'

He paid for it and obtained a receipt. Then he asked to see the manager.

'I'm going to ask you, monsieur,' he said, when he had drawn that gentleman aside, 'to do me a rather unusual favour. I have just bought this machine, and I want you to see it before I take it away, and, if you will be so kind, to give me some information about it. I shall tell you in confidence why I ask. I am a detective, employed on behalf of a man charged with a serious crime, but who I believe is innocent. A certain letter, on the authorship of which his guilt largely depends, was written, if I am not mistaken, on this machine. You will forgive me if I do not go into all the particulars. An adequate identification of the typewriter is obviously essential. I would therefore ask you if you would be kind enough to put a private mark on it. Also, if you would tell me how it came into your possession, I should be more than obliged.'

'I shall do what you ask with pleasure, monsieur,' returned the manager, 'but I trust I shall not be required to give evidence.'

'I do not think so, monsieur. I feel sure the identity of the machine will not be questioned. I make my request simply as a matter of precaution.'

The manager, with a small centre punch, put a few 'spots' on the main frame, noting the machine's number at the same time.

'Now you want to know where we got it,' he went on to La Touche. 'Excuse me a moment.'

He disappeared to his office, returning in a few minutes with a slip of paper in his hand.

'The machine was received from the Avrotte Pump Construction office' – he referred to the paper – 'on 2nd April last. It was supplied to the firm several years earlier, and on the date mentioned they exchanged it for a more up-to-date machine, a No. 10.'

'I am extremely obliged, monsieur. You may trust me to keep you out of the business if at all possible.'

Calling a taxi, La Touche took the machine to his hotel in the rue de La Fayette. There he typed another sample, and, using a powerful lens, compared the letters with the photographic enlargements he had obtained of the Le Gautier type. He was satisfied. The machine before him was that for which he had been in search.

He was delighted at his success. The more he thought of it, the more certain he felt that Boirac's fault-finding was merely an excuse to get rid of the typewriter. And the manufacturer had dismissed Mlle. Lambert simply because she knew too much. If inquiries were made in the office, he would be safer with her out of the way.

And as to Boirac's deeper object? So far as the detective could see, there could be only one explanation. Boirac knew the Le Gautier letter was done on that machine. And if he knew, did it not follow that he had sent the letter to Felix? And if he had sent the letter, must he not be guilty? To La Touche it began to look like it.

Then a further point struck him. If Boirac were guilty, what about the alibi? The alibi seemed so conclusive. And yet, if he were innocent, what about the typewriter? There seemed to be no escape from the dilemma, and La Touche was horribly puzzled.

But as he thought over the matter he began to see that the discovery of the typewriter did not so greatly help his client after all. Though at first sight it had seemed to indicate Boirac's guilt, second thoughts showed him that the manufacturer could make a very good case for himself. He could stick to the story told by Mlle. Lambert – that the type was in point of fact not good enough for his work. He could say plausibly enough that for some time he had wanted a machine with a tabulator, and that the bad alignment had only brought the matter to a head. Then, with regard to the typist. Though the girl seemed quiet and truthful, goodness only knew what she might not be holding back. On her own showing she had had exchanges of opinion with her employer, and she might have been very impertinent. At all events, Boirac could give his own version of what took place and no one would know the truth. Further, he could account for his testimonial by saying that while he disliked the girl and wished to be rid of her, he did not want to injure her permanently. He might even admit falsely telling the girl he was going to reorganise his office in order to smooth over her leaving.

With regard to the Le Gautier letter, Boirac could simply deny knowledge, and La Touche did not see how he could be contradicted. It could even be argued that Felix might have bribed a clerk to copy the letter for him on that machine so as to throw suspicion on Boirac. If Felix were guilty, it would be a likely enough move.

At last La Touche came to the definite conclusion that he had not enough evidence either to convict Boirac or dear Felix. He *must* do better. He *must* break the alibi and find the carter.

– 27 –

LA TOUCHE'S DILEMMA

That night La Touche could not sleep. The atmosphere was sultry and tense. Great masses of blue-black clouds climbing the south-western sky seemed to promise a storm. The detective tossed from side to side, his body restless, his mind intently awake and active. And then an idea suddenly occurred to him.

He had been mentally reviewing the wording of the various advertisements Lefarge had inserted for the carter. These, he recollected, were all to the effect that a reward would be paid for information as to the identity of the carter who had delivered the cask at the rue Cardinet Goods Station. Who, he thought, in the nature of things could answer that? Only, so far as he could see, two people – the carter himself and the man who engaged him. No one else would know anything about the matter. Of these, obviously the latter was not going to give the affair away. Nor would the carter if the other paid him well or had some hold over him. This, thought La Touche, may be why these advertisements have all failed.

So far he had got when his illuminating idea struck him. The fault of these advertisements was that they had appealed to the wrong people. Instead of appealing to the carter, could his associates not be approached? Or rather his employer, for it was obvious that neither Boirac nor

Felix could be his employer, except in the case of this one job. He jumped out of bed, turned on the light, and began to draft a circular letter.

DEAR SIR, *he wrote,*
An innocent man is in danger of conviction on a murder charge for want of certain evidence. This could be supplied by a carter – a clean-shaven, sharp-featured man with white hair. If you have (or had last March) such a man in your employment, or know of such, I most earnestly beg you to advise me. I am a private detective, working on behalf of the accused man. I guarantee no harm to the carter. On the contrary, I am willing to pay all men who answer the description five francs if they will call on me here any evening between 8.0 and 10.0, as well as 500 francs to the man who can give me the information I require.

Repeating the manoeuvre he had employed in the case of the advertisement for Mlle. Lambert, La Touche did not add his own name and address. He signed the note Charles Epée, and headed it Hôtel d'Arles, rue de Lyon.

Next morning he took his draft to a manufactory of office supplies and arranged for copies to be made and posted to the managers of all the carting establishments in Paris, the envelopes being marked 'confidential.' Then he went on to the rue de Lyon, and, in the name of Charles Epée, engaged a room at the Hôtel d'Arles.

Taking the Metro at the Place de la Bastille, he returned to the goods station in the rue Cardinet. There, after a considerable delay he found his two friends, the porters who had unloaded the cask on that Thursday nearly two months before. Explaining that he expected the carter he was in search of to call at his hotel on some evening in the early future, he offered them five francs a day to sit in his room between 8.0 and 10.0 p.m. to identify the man, should he arrive. To this the porters willingly agreed. That evening they had their first meeting, but without success. No clean-shaven, white-haired, sharp-featured carters turned up.

When La Touche returned to his rue de La Fayette hotel he found a letter from Clifford. The police had made two discoveries. The first La Touche had realised they were bound to make sooner or later. They had learnt of Felix's identity with the art school student who had been in love with the late Mme. Boirac, and of the short-lived engagement between the two. All the assistance which these facts gave the prosecution was therefore now at the disposal of the authorities.

The second piece of information was that Inspector Burnley had found the carter who had taken the cask from Waterloo on the Wednesday morning of the fateful week and delivered it at Charing Cross next morning, for, it seemed, both these jobs had been done by the same man.

It appeared that about 7.30 on the Tuesday evening of that week a dark, foreign-looking man with a pointed black beard had called at the office of Messrs Johnson, the large carting agents in Waterloo Road, and had hired a dray and man for the two following days, as well as the use of an empty shed for the same period. He had instructed the carter to meet him at Waterloo Station at 10.0 next morning, Wednesday. There, on the arrival of the Southampton boat train, he had claimed the cask and had it loaded up on the dray, as was already known. The vehicle had been taken to the shed, where it had been left, the horse having been sent back to the stable. The black-bearded man had told the driver he might take the remainder of the day as a holiday, but that he wanted him to return on the following morning, Thursday, take the cask to Charing Cross, and there book it to Paris. He had handed him the amount of the freight as well as ten shillings for himself. Upon the man asking where in Paris the cask was to be sent, the other had told him he would leave it properly addressed. This he had done, for next morning the cask had a new label, bearing the name of Jaques de Belleville, Cloakroom, Gare du Nord. The carter had then left the black-bearded man in the shed with the cart and cask. Next morning he had booked the latter to Paris.

Asked if he could identify the black-bearded man, the carter said he believed he could. But he failed to do so. On being taken to see Felix, he stated the artist was like the dark foreigner, but he would not swear he was the same man.

This news interested La Touche greatly, and he sat smoking into the small hours seeing how far he could work these new facts into the theories of the crime which he and Clifford had discussed. If the prosecution were correct, Felix must have been the man who called at the cartage establishment at 7.30 on Tuesday evening. He would therefore have had undisputed possession of the cask from about 11.0 a.m. on the Wednesday until, say, 7.0 on the following morning, and there were two obvious ways in which he could have put in the body. Either he could have procured another horse and taken the cask to St Malo, where, in the privacy of the walled yard, he could have removed the statue and substituted the body, returning the cask to the shed by the same means, or he could have hidden the body in his two-seater and run it to the shed, making the exchange there. Unfortunately, La Touche saw, the facts he had just learnt would fit in only too well with the theory of Felix's guilt.

On the other hand they supplied another period for which an alibi might be found for the artist – 7.30 on the Tuesday night. But, remembering his own and Clifford's researches into the manner in which Felix spent that week, La Touche was not hopeful of help here.

The detective then turned his thoughts to Clifford's theory of Boirac's guilt. And immediately he saw how the news crystallised the issue of the alibi. Up to the present the alibi had been considered as a whole, the portions which had been tested and those which had not, alike included. Generally speaking, it had been argued that if Boirac was in Paris and in Belgium during the fateful days, he could not have been in London. But now here was a direct issue between definite hours. At 7.30 on the Tuesday evening the bearded man was at Johnson's in the Waterloo Road. At 2.30 that same day Boirac was at Charenton. La Touche looked up his Continental Bradshaw. A train arrived at Victoria at 7.10, which would just enable a traveller from Paris to reach the carting contractor's at the hour named. But that train left Paris at 12.0 noon. Therefore it was utterly and absolutely out of the question that Boirac could be the man. But then there was the typewriter…

La Touche was back on the horns of the old dilemma. If Boirac was guilty, how did he work the alibi? If innocent, why did he get rid of the typewriter? He almost writhed in his exasperation. But it only made him more determined than ever to reach a solution, cost him what it might of labour and trouble.

The next evening he set off to the Hôtel d'Arles in the rue de Lyon, to await with the goods yard porters the coming of sharp-featured carters with white hair.

A number of replies to his circular had come in. Some were merely negative, the recipients having written to say that no carter answering to the description was known to them. Others stated they knew men of the type required, mentioning names and addresses. La Touche made lists of these, determining to call on any who did not come to see him at the hotel.

While he was engaged in this work his first visitor was announced. This man was clean-shaven and white-haired, but the sharpness of his features was not much in evidence. The porters immediately gave the prearranged sign that this was not the man, and La Touche, handing him his five francs, bowed him out, at the same time noting him 'Seen' on his list.

After he left came another and another, till before ten o'clock they had interviewed no less than fourteen men. All these more or less completely answered the description, but all the porters instantly negatived. The following evening eleven men called, and the next four, with the same result.

On the third day there was another letter from Clifford. The lawyer wrote that he had been greatly struck by the intelligence of the carter who had carried about the cask in London. Surprised at so superior a man holding such a position, he had brought him to his house in the hope of learning his history. And there he had made a discovery of the highest importance, and which, he thought, would lead them direct to the end of their quest. The carter, John Hill, had been quite ready to tell his story, which was as follows: Until four years previously Hill had been a constable in the Metropolitan police. He had a good record, and, he had believed, a future. Then he had had an unfortunate difference with his superior officer. Hill did not give the particulars, but Clifford understood it was a private matter and concerned a girl. But it led to a row during hours of duty, in which Hill admitted having entirely forgotten himself. He had been dismissed, and, after a long and weary search, could find no better job than that he now held.

'But,' wrote Clifford, 'it's an ill wind, etc. This curious history of Hill's is the thing that will settle our case. He has been trained in observation, and he observed something about the man with the cask that will definitely settle his identity. When he was paying him he noticed on the back of the first joint of his right forefinger, a small scar as if from a burn. He says he is sure of this mark and could swear to it. I asked him had he told the police. He said not, that he didn't love the police, and that he had answered what he had been asked and nothing more. When he understood I was acting against the police he volunteered the information, and I could see that he would be glad to give evidence that would upset their conclusions.'

Clifford had then done the obvious thing. He had gone to inspect Felix's finger, and he had found there was no mark on it.

At first to La Touche this seemed the end of the case. This man's evidence definitely proved Felix innocent. His next business would be to examine Boirac's hand, and, if the mark was there, the matter was at an end.

But as he thought over it he saw that this was indeed far from being the fact. There was still the alibi. As long as that stood, a clever counsel would insist on Boirac's innocence. To a jury the thing would be conclusive. And this ex-policeman's evidence could be discredited. In fact, the very thing that had enabled them to get hold of it – the man's dislike of the official force – would minimise its value. It would be argued that Hill had invented the scar to upset the police case. By itself, a jury might not accept this suggestion, but the alibi would give it weight, in fact, would make it the only acceptable theory.

However, the next step was clear. La Touche must see Boirac's hand, and, if there was a scar, Hill must see it too.

About eleven o'clock therefore, the detective hailed a taxi with an intelligent-looking driver. Having reached the end of the rue Championnet he dismounted, explaining to the man what he wanted him to do. A few moments later found him once more seated in the window of the café, his eyes fixed on the Pump Construction office across the street. The taxi in accordance with orders, drove slowly about, ready to pick him up if required.

About quarter to twelve, Boirac came out and began walking slowly citywards. La Touche quietly followed, keeping at the other side of the street, the taxi hovering close behind. Then the detective congratulated himself on his foresight, for, on Boirac's reaching the end of the street, he hailed another taxi, and, getting in, was driven rapidly off.

It was the work of a couple of seconds for La Touche to leap into his car and to instruct his driver to follow the other vehicle.

The chase led down to the Grands Boulevards to Bellini's in the Avenue de l'Opera. Here Boirac entered, followed by his shadower.

The great restaurant was about three parts full, and La Touche from the door was able to see Boirac taking his seat in one of the windows. The detective dropped into a place close to the cash desk, and, ordering table d'hôte lunch, insisted on getting the bill at once, on the grounds that his time was limited and that he might have to leave before finishing. Then he ate a leisurely lunch, keeping an eye on the manufacturer.

That gentleman was in no hurry, and La Touche had spent a long time over his coffee before the other made a move. A number of people were leaving the restaurant and there was a very short queue at the cash desk. La Touche so arranged his departure that he was immediately behind Boirac in this queue. As the manufacturer put down his money La Touche saw his finger. The scar was there!

'Here at last is certainty,' thought the detective, as he drew back out of the other's sight. 'So Boirac is the man after all! My work is done!'

And then the annoying afterthought arose. Was his work done? Was the proof he had got of Boirac's guilt sufficient? There was still the alibi. Always that alibi loomed in the background, menacing his success.

Though La Touche had now no doubt Boirac was the man the carter saw, he felt it would be more satisfactory if the two could be brought together in the hope of getting direct evidence of identity. As time was of value he called up Clifford and rapidly discussed the point. It was agreed that, if possible, Hill should be sent to Paris by that evening's train. A couple of hours later there was a telegram from the solicitor that this had been arranged.

Accordingly, next morning La Touche met the English boat train at the Gare du Nord and welcomed a tall, dark man with a small, close-cut moustache. As they breakfasted, the detective explained what he wished done.

'The difficulty is that you must see Boirac without his seeing you,' he ended up, 'we do not want him to know we are on his trail.'

'I understand that, sir,' returned Hill. 'Have you any plan arranged for me?'

'Not exactly, but I thought if you were to make up with a false beard and wear glasses he wouldn't spot you. You could dress differently also. Then I think you might lunch in the same restaurant and come out behind him and see his hand when he's paying same as I did.'

'That would do, sir, but the worst of it is I don't know my way about either in Paris or in a restaurant of that class.'

'You can't speak any French?'

'Not a word, sir.'

'Then I think I had better ask my man, Mallet, to go with you. He could keep you straight, and you needn't talk at all.'

Hill nodded his head.

'A good idea, sir.'

'Come, then, and let me get you a rig-out.'

They drove to shop after shop till the ex-policeman was supplied with new clothes from head to foot. Then they went to a theatrical property maker, where a flowing black beard and long moustache were fitted on. A pair of clear glass pince-nez completed the purchases. When, an hour later, Hill stood in La Touche's room dressed up in his new disguise, no one who had known him before would have recognised the ex-policeman, still less the London carter.

'Capital, Hill,' said La Touche. 'Your own mother wouldn't know you.'

The detective had sent a wire for his assistant, and Mallet was waiting for them. La Touche introduced the two men and explained his plans.

'We haven't much more than time,' said Mallet, 'so if you're ready, Hill, we'll go on.'

In something under three hours they returned. The expedition had been a complete success. They had gone direct to Bellini's, preferring to take the risk that the manufacturer did not lunch at the same place each day, rather than that of following him again. And they were not disappointed. Towards twelve, Boirac had entered and taken his seat at what was probably the same table in the window. On his rising to leave, they had repeated La Touche's manoeuvre and Hill, just behind him when he was paying, had seen his finger. Instantly he had identified the scar. Indeed, before seeing it he had been sure from Boirac's build and way of moving he was the man they sought.

In the evening, La Touche gave Hill a good dinner, paid him well, and saw him off by the night train to London. Then he returned to his hotel, lit a cigar, and lay down on his bed to wrestle again with the problem of the alibi.

He now knew that the alibi was faked. Boirac, beyond question, had been in London at 7.30 on the Tuesday evening. Therefore he could not have been at Charenton at 2.0. That was the ever-recurring difficulty, and he could see no way out.

He took a piece of paper and wrote down the hours at which they definitely knew the manufacturer's whereabouts. At 7.30 on Tuesday evening he was in London at Johnson's carting establishment in Waterloo Road. From 10.0 till 11.0 next morning, Wednesday, he was with Hill, getting the cask from Waterloo to the shed. He could not have left London in the interval, so this meant that he must have been in the English capital from 7.30 o'clock on Tuesday evening till 11.0 on Wednesday morning. Then he was at the Hôtel Maximilian in Brussels at 11.0 on that same Wednesday evening. So much was certain beyond doubt or question.

Did these hours work in? On Tuesday, frankly, they did not. What about Wednesday? Could a man who was in

London at 11.0 in the morning be in Brussels at 11.0 the same evening? La Touche got his Continental Bradshaw. Here it was. London depart 2.20 p.m.; Brussels arrive 10.25 p.m. That seemed all right. A traveller arriving by that train would reach the Hôtel Maximilian 'about 11.0.' Then La Touche remembered that Boirac's account of how he spent this day had not been substantiated. He had told Lefarge he had gone to his brother's house at Malines, having forgotten that the latter was in Sweden. No confirmation of that statement was forthcoming. Neither the caretaker nor anyone else had seen the manufacturer. La Touche was not long in coming to the conclusion he had never been there at all. No, he had crossed from London by the 2.20.

Then the detective recalled the telephone. A message had been sent by Boirac from one of the cafés in the old towns asking the hotel clerk to reserve a room. That call had been received about eight o'clock. But at eight o'clock Boirac was not in the old town. He was on his journey from London.

La Touche took up his Bradshaw again. Where would a traveller by the 2.20 p.m. from Charing Cross be at eight o'clock? And then like a flash he understood. The boat arrived at Ostend at 7.30 p.m. and the Brussels train did not leave until 8.40. He had telephoned from Ostend!

So that was it! A simple plan, but how ingenious! And then La Touche remembered that Lefarge had been quite unable to confirm the statement that Boirac had dined at the café in the Boulevard Anspach, or had been present at *Les Troyens* in the Théâtre de la Monnaie. No. He was on the right track at last.

The Wednesday was now accounted for, but there still remained the terrible difficulty of the Tuesday. What about the café at Charenton?

And then La Touche got another of his inspirations. He had solved the Wednesday telephone trick. Could that on Tuesday be explained in the same way?

He had already noted that a traveller by the train leaving Paris at 12.0 noon and arriving at Victoria at 7.10 could just reach Waterloo Road by 7.30. Thinking again over the point, he suddenly saw the significance of the hour of the call at the carting establishment. It was late. A man wishing to do business there would have gone earlier, had he been able. But this man was not able. He had only reached the city at 7.10.

He turned back to the telephone calls. Where, he asked himself with growing excitement, would a passenger by the 12.0 noon from Paris be at 2.30? And then he was dashed with disappointment. That train did not reach Calais till 3.31 p.m., and at 2.30 it must have been running at full speed somewhere between Abbeville and Boulogne. Boirac could not have telephoned from the train. Therefore he could not have travelled by it.

La Touche had hoped to find that, adopting the same manoeuvre on each day, the manufacturer had telephoned from some station *en route*, presumably Calais. But that apparently was not so. At the same time, the detective could not but feel he was getting near the truth.

He looked at the timetable again. The train in question reached Calais at 3.31 and the boat left at 3.45. That was a delay of 14 minutes. Would there be time, he wondered, to make two long-distance calls in 14 minutes? Hardly, he thought. He considered what he himself would do if confronted with Boirac's problem.

And then suddenly he saw it. What could be more obvious than to go by an earlier train and to break the journey at Calais? How would this timetable work?

Paris	dep.	9.50 a.m.
Calais	arr.	1.11 p.m.
Calais	dep.	3.45 p.m.
Victoria	arr.	7.10 p.m.

If Boirac had done that he would have had over two and a half hours in Calais, which would have given him the opportunity he required. La Touche believed he had reached the solution at last.

But Boirac had been actually seen telephoning from Charenton. For a moment the detectives spirits fell. But he felt he must be right so far. Some explanation of the difficulty would occur to him.

And it did. The waiter had believed Boirac was there on *Monday*. And he must have been! In some way he must have faked the telephoning. There could be nothing else for it.

Another point occurred to him. Surely, he thought, the telephone operator always mentions the name of the calling town in inter-urban calls? If Boirac had called up his office from Calais, would not the operator have said, 'Calais wants you'? If so, how had the manufacturer been able to deceive his butler and chief clerk?

This was undoubtedly a difficulty. But he put it on one side as he began to think how this new theory could be tested.

First he would go again to the Charenton waiter and explain the importance of settling the day on which Boirac lunched. Perhaps the man would now be able to recall some circumstance which would make this clear. Next he would find out from François and Dufresne whether any phrase such as 'Calais wants you' had been used by the telephone operator. This inquiry, he noted, must be made with great skill, so as to avoid rousing Boirac's suspicions should either man repeat the conversation. From the telephone central at Calais, if not at Paris, he could doubtless find if calls were made from the former town to the latter at the hour in question, and he might also find that someone answering to the description of Boirac had made those calls. Finally, it might be possible at Ostend to get information about the Brussels call.

Inquiries on these points should reveal enough to either confirm or disprove his theory.

The next morning therefore saw La Touche again in the café at Charenton in conversation with the waiter.

'The point as to which day the gentleman was here has become important,' he explained, 'and I shall hand you another twenty francs if you can settle it.'

The man was evidently anxious to earn the money. He thought earnestly for some time, but at last had to confess he could recall nothing fixing the date.

'Do you remember what he had to eat? Would that help you?' asked the detective.

The waiter shook his head after consideration.

'Or any little matter of a clean cloth or napkin or anything of that kind? No? Or any other person who was in at the same time, or to whom you may have spoken on the subject?'

Again the man shook his head. Then suddenly a look of satisfaction passed over his face.

'But yes, monsieur,' he said eagerly, 'I remember now. What you have just asked me brings it to my mind. M. Pascot lunched also when the gentleman was here, and he noticed him and asked me if I knew who he was. M. Pascot may be able to tell us.'

'Who is M. Pascot?'

'The apothecary, monsieur. From a dozen doors up the street. He comes here sometimes when Madame goes shopping to Paris. If you like, monsieur, I will go with you to him and we can inquire.'

'I should be greatly obliged.'

A walk of a few yards brought them to the chemist's shop. M. Pascot was a large, bald-headed man, with a high colour and a consequential manner.

'Good day, M. Pascot,' the waiter greeted him deferentially. 'This gentleman is a friend of mine, a detective, and he is engaged on an inquiry of much importance. You remember that man with the black beard who was lunching in the café the last day you were in? He was sitting at the little table in the alcove and then he began telephoning. You remember? You asked me who he was.'

'I remember,' rumbled the apothecary in a deep bass voice, 'and what of him?'

'My friend here wants to find out what day he was at the café, and I thought perhaps you would be able to tell him?'

'And how should I be able to tell him?'

'Well, M. Pascot, you see it was on the same day that you were with us, and I thought maybe you would be able to fix that date, the day Madame was in Paris – you told me that.'

The pompous man seemed slightly annoyed, as if the waiter was taking a liberty in mentioning his personal concerns before a stranger. La Touche broke in with his smooth suavity.

'If, M. Pascot, you could do anything to help me, I should be more than grateful. I should explain to you that I am acting on behalf of an innocent man,' and he drew a pathetic picture of the evil case in which Felix found himself, ending up by delicately insinuating that a reward for suitable information was not out of the reckoning.

M. Pascot thawed.

'Permit me to consult Madame, monsieur,' he said, and with a bow he withdrew. In a few moments he reappeared.

'I can recollect the date now, monsieur. Madame had occasion to go to Paris to see her solicitor on business, and a note of the date was kept. It was Monday, the 29th of March last.'

'I cannot say, monsieur, how obliged I am to you,' said La Touche in heartfelt tones, and, by a sort of legerdemain, of which both participants remained profoundly unconscious, a twenty-franc bill passed from hand to hand. La Touche was extraordinarily pleased. He had broken the alibi.

Leaving the apothecary and waiter bowing and smiling as a result of their *douceurs*, La Touche turned his steps to the pier and took a river steamer to the Pont de l'Alma. Walking up the Avenue, he rang at Boirac's, and was soon closeted with François in his little room.

'About that telephone message we were talking of the other day. M. François,' he remarked casually, when they had conversed on general subjects for some minutes, 'I wasn't quite certain where you said M. Boirac was speaking from. My first recollection was that you said Calais; then I wondered if it was not Charenton. I have to make a report on my proceedings and I would like to get it as correct as possible.'

The butler looked surprised and interested.

'It is curious, monsieur, that you should ask me that, for I don't remember mentioning anything about it. I also thought at first it was Calais. I thought the operator said

"Calais wants you," and I was surprised, for I did not know M. Boirac intended to leave Paris. But I was wrong, for when M. Boirac began to speak I asked him the direct question. "You are speaking from Calais?" I said. "No," he answered, "from Charenton." I am sure now it was my mistake and that what I thought was Calais was really Charenton. I am not very quick and on the telephone these names sound very much alike. Strange your making the same mistake.'

'It is curious,' admitted La Touche, 'almost like one of those extraordinary cases of thought transference you read of. However, I am obliged for your confirmation that it was Charenton,' and he diverted the conversation into other channels.

His next visit was to the Telephone Central. Here at first they were not keen to give him any information, but on producing his card and confidentially explaining his business to the head of the department, he obtained what he wanted. Inquiries were made from Calais by wire, and after a considerable delay he was informed that at 2.32 and 2.44 on the Tuesday in question calls were made on Paris. The demand came from the public call office and were for the following numbers: Passy 386 and Nord 745. When La Touche found from the directory that these numbers were those of M. Boirac's house and office respectively, he could hardly refrain from laughing aloud.

'How, I wonder,' he thought, 'did Lefarge neglect so obvious a check on the Charenton messages?' Then it occurred to him that probably only inter-urban calls were so noted.

The proof of his theory seemed so complete he did not think it necessary to make inquiries at Ostend. Indeed, he believed his task was at last accomplished, and he began to consider an immediate return to London.

28

THE UNRAVELLING OF THE WEB

When La Touche solved the problem of how Boirac had faked his alibi, his first impression was that his work was done. But, as had happened so often before, second thoughts showed him that this was hardly the case. Though he had established Boirac's guilt to his own satisfaction, he doubted if he could prove it in court, and, indeed, the whole matter was still far from clear.

He felt that if he could only find the carter who had brought the cask to the rue Cardinet he would reach certainty on at least some of the points which were puzzling him. He therefore decided to concentrate once more on this problem.

Since the sending out of his circular to the managers of the various carting establishments in the city, he had interviewed no less than twenty-seven more or less clean-shaven, white-haired, and sharp-featured carters. But all to no purpose. The man he wanted was not among them. And as answers to practically all his circulars had been received, he had reluctantly come to the conclusion his plan had failed.

That evening, when Mallet called to make his customary report on Boirac's doings, the two men discussed the matter, and it was a remark dropped by his assistant that turned La Touche's thoughts to a point he had previously overlooked.

'Why do you think he was employed by a cartage contractor?' Mallet had asked, and La Touche had been going to reply with some asperity that cartage contractors were not uncommonly found to employ carters, when the pertinence of the other's question struck him. Why, Indeed? Of the thousands of carters in Paris, only a small proportion were employed by cartage firms. By far the greater number worked for specific businesses. Might not the man who brought the cask to the goods station belong to this class, and if so, might not this account for the failure of the original advertisements? If a carter were bribed to use his employer's vehicle for his own gain he would not afterwards give the fact away. And to La Touche it seemed that such a move would be just what might be expected from a man of Boirac's mentality.

But if this theory were correct; if the carter had thus been bound over to silence, how was the man to be discovered and the truth wrung from him?

La Touche smoked two cigars over this problem, and then it occurred to him that the method he had already adopted was sound as far as it went. It merely did not go far enough.

The only way in which he could ensure finding his hypothetical carter would be to send a circular to every employer in Paris. But that was too large an order.

That night, he discussed the matter with the two porters, whom he found intelligent men and keenly interested in the inquiry. He made them describe the kind of cart the cask was brought in, then with a directory he marked off the trades in which the employment of such a vehicle was likely. When he had finished, though some thousands of names were included, he did not think the number overwhelming.

For a considerable time he pondered the question of advertising his circular in the press. At last he decided he could not do so, as if Boirac saw it he would doubtless take precautions to prevent the truth becoming known. La Touche therefore returned to the office of the Business Supplies Company and instructed them to send his circular to each of the thousands of employers in the selected trades, they tabulating the replies and giving him the summary. Though he was by no means sanguine of the success of this move, he felt it offered a chance.

For the next three evenings La Touche and the porters had a busy time. White-haired carters turned up at the Hôtel d'Arles literally in dozens, till the management threatened an ejectment and talked of a claim for fresh carpets. But all was fruitless. The man they wanted did not appear.

On the third day, amongst other letters sent on from the Business Supplies Company, was one which immediately interested La Touche.

'In reply to your circular letter of the 18th inst.,' wrote Messrs Corot, Fils, of the rue de Rivoli, 'we have a man in our employment who, at the end of March, answered your description. His name is Jean Dubois, of 18b rue de Falaise, near Les Halles. About that time, however, he ceased shaving and has now grown a beard and moustache. We have asked him to call with you.'

Was it, thought La Touche, merely a coincidence that this clean-shaven carter should begin to grow a beard immediately after the delivery of the cask? When two more days passed and the man did not turn up, La Touche determined to call on him.

Accordingly the next evening he arranged for Mallet and one of the porters to deal with the men at the Hôtel d'Arles, while he himself in company with the other porter set out to find Dubois. The rue de Falaise turned out to be a narrow, dirty street of high, sombre buildings, with the word slum writ large across their grimy frontages. At 18b, La Touche ascended and knocked at a ramshackle door on a dark stone landing. It was opened by a slatternly woman, who stood, silently waiting for him to speak, in the gloom of the threshold. La Touche addressed her with his usual suavity.

'Good evening, madame. Is this where M. Jean Dubois of Messrs Corot, Fils lives?'

The woman signified assent, but without inviting her visitor in.

'I have a little job for him. Could I see him, please?'

'He's not in, monsieur.'

'That's unfortunate for me and for him too, I fancy. Can you tell me where I should find him?'

The woman shrugged her shoulders.

'I cannot tell, monsieur.' She spoke in a dull, toneless way, as if the struggle for existence had sapped away all her interest in life.

La Touche took out a five-franc piece and pushed it into her hand.

'You get hold of him for me,' he said, 'I want this little job done and he could do it. It'll get him into no trouble, and I'll pay him well.'

The woman hesitated. Then, after a few seconds, she said: 'If I tell you where he is, will you give me away?'

'No, on my honour. We shall have found him by accident.'

'Come this way, then, monsieur.'

She led them down the stairs and out again into the dingy street. Passing along it like a furtive shadow she turned twice, then halted at the corner of a third street.

'Down there, monsieur,' she pointed. 'You see that café with the coloured glass windows? He'll be in there,' and without waiting for an acknowledgment she slipped away, vanishing silently into the gloom.

The two men pushed open the café door and entered a fairly large room dotted with small marble tables, with a bar in one corner and a dancing stage at the back. Seating themselves unostentatiously at a table near the door they called for drinks.

There were some fifteen or twenty men and a few women in the place, some reading the papers, some playing dominoes, but most lounging in groups and talking. As La Touche's keen eye ran over the faces, he soon spotted his man.

'Is that he, Charcot?' he asked, pointing to a small, unhealthy-looking fellow, with a short, untidy, white beard and moustache.

The porter looked cautiously. Then he assented eagerly.

'It's the man, monsieur, I believe. The beard changes him a bit, but I'm nearly sure it's he.'

The suspect was one of those on the outskirts of a group, to whom a stout, fussy man with a large nose was holding forth on some socialistic subject. La Touche crossed over and touched the white-haired man on the arm.

'M. Jean Dubois?'

The man started and an expression of fear came into his eyes. But he answered civilly enough.

'Yes, monsieur. But I don't know you.'

'My name is La Touche. I want a word or two with you. Will you have a drink with me and my friend here?'

365

He indicated the porter, Charcot, and they moved over. The fear had left Dubois' eyes, but he still looked uneasy. In silence they sat down.

'Now, Dubois, what will you take?'

When the carter's wants were supplied, La Touche bent towards him and began speaking in a low tone: 'I dare say, Dubois, you already guess what I want, and I wish to say before anything else that you have nothing to fear if you are straight with me. On the contrary, I will give you one hundred francs if you answer my questions fully. If not – well, I am connected with the police, and we'll become better acquainted.'

Dubois moved uneasily as he stammered: 'I don't know what you mean, monsieur.'

'So that there shall be no mistake, I shall tell you. I want to know who it was engaged you to take the cask to the rue Cardinet goods station.'

La Touche, who was watching the other intently, saw him start, while his face paled and the look of fear returned to his eyes. It was evident he understood the question. That involuntary motion had given him away.

'I assure you, monsieur, I don't know what you mean. What cask are you referring to?'

La Touche bent closer.

'Tell me, do you know what was in that cask? No? Well, I'll tell you. There was a body in it – the body of a woman – a murdered woman. Did you not guess that from the papers? Did you not realise that the cask you carried to the station was the one that all the papers have been full of? Now, do you want to be arrested as an accessory after the fact in a murder case?'

The man was ghastly, and beads of perspiration stood on his forehead. In a trembling voice he began again to protest his ignorance. La Touche cut him short.

'Chut, man! You needn't keep it up. Your part in the thing is known, and if it wasn't you would soon give it away. Dubois, you haven't red enough blood for this kind of thing! Be guided by me. Make a clean breast of it, and I'll give you the hundred francs, and, what's more, I'll do my best to help you out of your trouble with your employers. If you don't, you'll have to come along now to the Sûreté. Make up your mind quickly what you're going to do.'

The man, evidently panic-stricken, remained silent.

La Touche took out his watch.

'I'll give you five minutes,' he said, and, leaning back in his chair, he lit a cigar.

Before the time was up the man spoke.

'If I tell you everything will you not arrest me?'

His fright was pitiable.

'Certainly not. I don't want to do you any harm. If you give me the information you go free with a hundred francs in your pocket. But if you try to deceive me, you can explain your position tomorrow to the examining magistrate.'

The bluff had its effect.

'I'll tell you, monsieur. I'll tell you the whole truth.'

'Good,' said La Touche, 'then we had better move to a more private place. We'll go to my hotel, and you, Charcot' – he turned to the porter – 'get away back to the rue de Lyon and tell M. Mallet and your friend the man's found. Here's what I owe you and a trifle more.'

Charcot bowed and vanished, while La Touche and the carter, getting out into one of the larger streets, drove to the rue de la Fayette.

'Now, Dubois,' said the detective, when they were seated in his room.

'I'm going to tell you the gospel truth, monsieur,' began the carter, and from his earnest, anxious manner La Touche believed him. 'And I'm not going to deny that I was in the wrong, even if I do get the sack over it. But I was fair tempted, and I thought it was an easy way to earn a bit of money without doing anyone any harm. For that's the fact, monsieur. What I did, did no harm to anyone.

'It was on Monday, monsieur, Monday the 29th March, that I was out at Charenton delivering goods for Messrs Corot. I stopped at a café there for a glass of beer. While I was drinking it a man came up to me and asked was that my cart? I said I was in charge of it, but it belonged to Messrs Corot. "I want a little job done with a cart," he says, "and it's not convenient for me to go into Paris to an agent's, and if you would save me the trouble by doing it for me I'll pay you well." "I couldn't do that, monsieur," I says, "for if my employers got to know they'd give me the sack." "But how would they know?" he asks, "I wouldn't tell them, and I guess you wouldn't either." Well, monsieur, we talked on, and first I refused, but afterwards I agreed to do it. I admit I was wrong using the cart like that, but he tempted me. He said it would only take about an hour, and he would give me ten francs. So I agreed.'

'What was this man like?'

'He was a middle-sized man, monsieur, with a black pointed beard, and very well dressed.'

'And what did he want you to do?'

'On the next Thursday afternoon at half-past four I was to go to an address he gave me and load up a cask, and bring it to the corner of the rue de la Fayette, close to the

Gare du Nord. He said he would meet me there and tell me where to take it.'

'And did he?'

'Yes. I got there first and waited about ten minutes, and then he came up. He took the old label off the cask and nailed on another he had with him. Then he told me to take the cask to the State Railway Goods Station in the rue Cardinet and book it to London. He gave me the freight as well as the ten francs for myself. He said he should know if the cask did not get to London, and threatened that if I played any tricks he would inform Messrs Corot what I had done.'

This statement was not at all what La Touche had expected, and he was considerably puzzled.

'What was the address he gave you at which you were to get the cask?'

'I forget the exact address. It was from a large corner house in the Avenue de l'Alma.'

'What?' roared La Touche, springing excitedly to his feet. 'The Avenue de l'Alma, do you say?' He laughed aloud.

So this was it! The cask that went to St Katherine's Docks – the cask containing the body – had gone, not from the Gare du Nord, but direct from Boirac's house! Fool that he was not to have thought of this! Light was at last dawning. Boirac had killed his wife – killed her in her own house – and had there packed her body in the cask, sending it direct to Felix. At long last La Touche had got the evidence he wanted, evidence that would clear Felix – evidence that would bring Boirac to the scaffold!

He was thrilled with his discovery. For a moment the whole affair seemed clear, but once again second thoughts showed him there was a good deal still to be explained.

However, once he had got rid of this Dubois, he would see just where he stood.

He questioned the carter exhaustively, but without gaining much further information. That the man had no idea of the identity of his seducer was clear. The only name he had got hold of was that of Dupierre, for Boirac had instructed him to say at his house that he had called for Messrs Dupierre's cask. Asked if he had not seen the advertisements of rewards for the information he had now given, the man said he had, but that he was afraid to come forward. First he feared he would lose his job if the matter came to his employer's ears, and then the very fact that so large a reward was offered had frightened him, as he assumed he had unwittingly helped with some crime. He had suspected the matter was one of robbery until he saw of the discovery of the cask in the papers. Then he had at once guessed that he had assisted a murderer to dispose of his victim's body, and he had lived in a veritable nightmare lest his share in the business should be discovered. Failing to get anything further out of him, La Touche finally dismissed him somewhat contemptuously with his hundred francs. Then he settled himself to try and puzzle out his problem.

And first as to the movements of the cask. It had started from Boirac's house; how did it get there? Clearly from Dupierre's. It must have been the cask in which Boirac's statue had been sent home. That cask, then, left Dupierre's on the Saturday of the dinner party, reaching Boirac's house the same day. It lay there until the following Thursday. During that time the statue was taken out and the body substituted. The cask then travelled to London, was taken by Felix to St Malo, and finally got into the hands of the police at Scotland Yard.

But then, what about the cask which was met at Waterloo and sent back from London to the Gare du Nord?

This, La Touche saw, must have been a different cask, and there must therefore have been two moving about, and not one as they had believed. He tried to follow the movements of this second cask. It left Dupierre's on the Tuesday evening, reached Waterloo on the following morning and on the next day, Thursday, was sent back to Paris, reaching the Gare du Nord at 4.45 p.m. It had always been assumed this cask went from there to the rue Cardinet Goods Station. This was now proved to have been an error. Where, then, did it go?

Like a flash La Touche saw. It had gone from the Gare du Nord to Dupierre's. He looked up his chronology of the case. Yes, a cask had been received by Dupierre on that Thursday evening, but they had believed it had come from Boirac's house. And then the whole diabolical plot began dimly to appear, as La Touche endeavoured to picture the scene which had probably taken place.

Boirac, he conjectured, must have discovered his wife had eloped with Felix, Mad with jealousy and hatred he kills her. Then, cooling down somewhat, he finds himself with the body on his hands. What is he to do with it? He thinks of the cask standing in the study. He sees that a better receptacle for getting the body out of the house could hardly be devised. He therefore unpacks the statue and puts in the body. The question then arises, where is he to send it? A horrible idea occurs to him. He will wreak his vengeance on Felix by sending it to him. And then a second idea strikes him. If he could arrange that the police would find the body in Felix's possession, would the artist not then be suspected and perhaps executed? Truly a ghastly vengeance! Boirac then types the Le Gautier letter, and sends it to Felix with the idea of making the artist act in so suspicious a way that the police will interfere and find him with the body.

So far La Touche felt his surmises had a ring of probability, but he was still puzzled about the second cask. But, as he turned the matter over in his mind, he gradually began to see light here too.

Boirac had received a cask from Dupierre with his statue. But as it had gone to Felix he had no empty cask to send back in its place to the sculptors. He must return them an empty cask, or else suspicion falls on him at once. Where is he to get it?

And then La Touche saw that the whole business of the second cask must have been arranged simply to meet this difficulty. Boirac must have ordered it, forging Felix's handwriting. La Touche recollected that order was written on the same paper as the Le Gautier letter, suggesting a common origin for both. Boirac met it in London, took it to the shed, there removed and destroyed the statue, and had the cask returned to Paris. At the Gare du Nord he doubtless changed the labels, so that when it reached Dupierre's it bore that with the address of his own house. The other label he must have altered from the Waterloo route to that of long sea. This would account for Dubois' statement that Boirac had changed the labels when he met him in the rue de la Fayette, as well as for the curious faking of that described by the clerk Broughton.

The more La Touche pondered over this theory, the more satisfied he became that he had at last reached the truth. But he had to admit that even yet there were several points he could not understand. When did the murder take place, and where? Did Madame really elope with Felix, and, if so, did her husband bring her back alive or dead?

How did the impression of the letter ordering the second statue come to be on Felix's blotting paper? If Madame was murdered in Paris, how did the jewelled pin reach St Malo?

But in spite of these and other difficulties, La Touche was more than pleased with his progress, and, as very late he went to his bedroom, he felt a short investigation should be sufficient to test his theory, as well as to clear up all that still remained doubtful.

29

A DRAMATIC DÉNOUEMENT

Three days after the finding of the carter, Dubois, and La Touche's discovery of what he believed was the true solution of the mystery, he received a letter which interested him considerably. It came by post to his hotel, and was as follows:

Rue St Jean 1,
Avenue de L'Alma

26th May, 1912

DEAR MONSIEUR,

In connection with your calls hére and inquiries into the death of my late mistress, I have just by accident hit on a piece of information which I am sure would be of value to you. It explains the closing of the front door which, you will recollect, I heard about 1.0 a.m. on the night of the dinner party. I think it will have the effect of entirely clearing your client, though I am afraid it does not point to anyone else as the murderer. M. Boirac is dining out tonight and most of the servants are attending the marriage festivities of one of the housemaids; the house is therefore unprotected, and I cannot leave it to call on you, but if you could see your way to call here any time during the evening, I shall tell you what I have learnt.

Yours respectfully,

HENRI FRANÇOIS.

'Extraordinary,' thought La Touche, 'how, when you get some information about a case, more nearly always comes in. Here I worked for ages on this case without getting any forrader, and François made no discoveries to encourage me. Now, when I have almost solved it and it no longer matters, he comes forward with his help. I suppose it's the inverse of misfortunes never coming singly.'

He looked at his watch. It was just five o'clock. M. Boirac might not leave home till nearly eight. If he went a few minutes past that hour he could see François and hear his news.

He wondered what the butler could have discovered. If it really did what he claimed – explained the closing of the front door, that would necessarily clear up much that was still doubtful about the events of that tragic night.

Suddenly an idea flashed into his mind. Was the letter genuine? He had never seen the butler's handwriting, and therefore could form no opinion from its appearance. But was the whole thing *likely*? Could it possibly be the work of Boirac? Might not the manufacturer have discovered that he, La Touche, was on his trail, and might not this be a trap? Could it be an attempt to lure him into a house in which he and his information would be at the manufacturer's mercy?

This was a sinister idea, and he sat pondering its possibility for some minutes. On the whole, he was disposed to reject it. Any attempt on his life or liberty would be exceedingly risky for Boirac. If he really knew what had come out, his game would surely be to collect what money he could and disappear while there was yet time. All the same La Touche felt he should neglect no precaution for his own safety.

He went to the telephone and called up the house in the Avenue de l'Ama.

'Is M. François there?' he asked, when he had got through.

'No, monsieur,' was the reply. 'He has gone out for the afternoon. He will be in about 7.30.'

'Thank you. Who is speaking, please?'

'Jules, monsieur, the footman. I am in charge till M. François returns.'

This was unsatisfactory, but quite natural and unsuspicious. La Touche felt fairly satisfied, and yet, almost against his will, a doubt remained. He thought he might be better with company, and made another call.

'That you, Mallet? Which of you is off duty? You? Well, I want your company tonight on a short excursion. Will you call round for dinner here at seven and we can go on afterwards?'

When Mallet arrived, La Touche showed him the letter. The subordinate took precisely the same view as his chief.

'I don't think it's a plant,' he said, 'but with Boirac you can't be too careful. I should bring your John Cockerill, or whatever you use, if I were you.'

'I'll do so,' said the other, slipping an automatic pistol into his pocket.

They reached the house in the Avenue de l'Alma about 8.15, and La Touche rang. To their surprise and disappointment the door was opened by no less a person than Boirac himself. He seemed to be on the point of going out, as he wore his hat and a dark, caped overcoat which, open at the front, showed his evening dress. Round his right hand was tied a bloodstained handkerchief. He appeared annoyed and as if his temper might give way at any minute. He looked inquiringly at the detectives.

'Could we see M. François, monsieur,' asked La Touche politely.

'If you don't mind waiting a few minutes, certainly,' answered Boirac. 'I was just going out when I cut my hand and I had to send him for a doctor to stop the bleeding. He will be back in a moment. If you like to wait, you can do so in his room – the fourth door on the right.'

La Touche hesitated a moment. What if it was a plant after all? Finding Boirac here alone was certainly suspicious. But the cut at least was genuine. La Touche could see the red stain slowly spreading across the handkerchief.

'Well, messieurs, I'm sorry I can't hold the door open. Kindly either come in and wait, or, if you prefer it, call back later on.'

La Touche made up his mind. They were armed and on their guard. As he entered the hall his left hand in his overcoat pocket crept to the handle of his magazine pistol, and he quietly covered the manufacturer.

The latter closed the front door behind them and led the way to François' room. It was in darkness, but Boirac, entering before the others, turned on the light.

'Come in and be seated, gentlemen, if you please,' he said. 'I should like a word with you before François returns.'

La Touche did not at all like the turn affairs were taking. Boirac's conduct seemed to him to grow more and more suspicious. Then he reflected again that they were two to one, were armed, and keenly on their guard, and that there could be no cause for uneasiness. Besides, there could be no trap. Boirac had preceded them into the room.

The manufacturer pulled together three chairs.

'If you would kindly be seated, gentlemen, I would tell you what I want you to know.'

The detectives obeyed, La Touche still keeping his pistol turned on his host.

'Gentlemen,' went on the latter, 'I owe you both a very full apology for having played a trick on you, but I am sure, when I have explained the extraordinary circumstances in which I am placed, you will hold me, if not justified, at least excused. And first, I must tell you that I know who you are, and on what business you came to Paris.'

He paused for a moment. Then, the others not replying, he continued: 'I happened to notice your advertisement, M. La Touche, for Mlle. Lambert, and it set me thinking. And when I found, M. Mallet, that you and your friend were shadowing me, I thought still more. As a result of my cogitations I employed a private detective, and learnt from him the identity of both of you and what you were engaged on. When I learnt that you had found Mlle. Lambert, I guessed you would soon discover the typewriter, and sure enough, my detective soon after reported that you had purchased a second-hand No. 7 Remington. Then I had the carter, Dubois, shadowed, and I thus learnt that you had discovered him also. I have to compliment you, M. La Touche, on the cleverness with which you found out these matters.'

Again he paused, looking inquiringly and somewhat hesitatingly at the others.

'Pray proceed, M. Boirac,' said La Touche at last.

'First, then, I offer you my apologies for the trick played you. I wrote the note which brought you here. I feared if I wrote in my own name you would suspect some trick on my part and refuse to come.'

'Not unnaturally a suspicion of the kind did enter our minds,' answered La Touche. 'It is but fair to tell you, M. Boirac, that we are armed' – La Touche withdrew his automatic pistol from his pocket and laid it on a table at his hand – 'and if you give either of us the slightest cause for anxiety, we shall fire without waiting to make inquiries.'

The manufacturer smiled bitterly.

'I am not surprised at your suspicions. They are reasonable, though absolutely unfounded, and your precautions cannot therefore be offensive to me. As I try to do everything thoroughly, I may admit this cut on my hand was also faked. I simply squeezed a tube of liquid red paint on to the handkerchief. I did it to account for my being alone in the hall when you arrived, which I thought necessary, lest you might refuse to enter.'

La Touche nodded.

'Pray proceed with your statement,' he said again.

For a man of his years, Boirac looked strangely old and worn. His black hair was flecked with white, his face drawn and unhappy and his eyes weary and sombre. Though he had been speaking quietly enough, he seemed deeply moved and at a loss how to proceed. At last, with a gesture of despair, he went on: 'What I have to say is not easy, but, alas, I deserve that. I may tell you at once without any beating about the bush – I brought you here tonight to make my confession. Yes, gentlemen, you see before you the miserable, guilty man. I killed her, gentlemen. I did it that awful night of the dinner party. And since then I have never known one moment's ease. What I have suffered no living being could describe. I have been in hell ever since. I have aged more in these last few weeks than in ten years of ordinary life. And now, when to the gnawings of remorse the certainty of the result of your researches is looming before me – I can bear it no longer. The suspense must end. Therefore, after much thought I have decided to make my confession.'

That the man was in earnest and his emotion genuine La Touche could no longer doubt. But his suspicions still remained. He asked a question.

'Why have you brought us here to tell us, M. Boirac? Surely the obvious thing would have been for you to go to the Sûreté and see M. Chauvet.'

'I know. I should have done that. But this was easier. I tell you, gentlemen, it is bad enough to have to say this to you here, sitting quietly in my own house. There – with several and perhaps stupid officials, with typists – I just couldn't face it. What I want you to do is this. I will tell you everything. Any questions you ask I will answer. Then I don't want to be bothered with it again. All I now hope for is that the end will come quickly. You do what is necessary and at the trial I will plead guilty. You will agree?'

'We will hear what you have to say.'

'For that, at least, I am grateful.' He pulled himself together with an obvious effort and continued in a low tone, without showing very evident traces of emotion.

'My statement, I fear, will be a long one, as I must tell you all that occurred from the beginning, so that you may understand what led up to this awful consummation. A great part of it you already know – how my wife and Felix fell in love at the art school, and how her father refused his consent to their marriage, then how I, too, fell a victim and asked her hand; how my suit was looked upon with favour and I was misled both by herself and her father about what had taken place at the art school, and how, in short, we were married. And you know, too, I imagine, that our marriage from the first was a failure. I loved Annette intensely, but she never cared for me. We needn't go into it, but I soon saw that she had only married me in a fit of despair at her engagement being broken off. She did me the gravest wrong, though I admit I don't think she meant or realised it. We drifted farther and farther apart, till life together became insupportable. And then I met Felix and asked him to the house, not knowing till weeks later that he was the man who had been in love with my wife at the art school. But you must not think I have anything to say against the honour of either of them. My wife spoiled my life it is true, but she did not elope with Felix, nor did he, so far as I know, ask her to. They were good friends, but, to the best of my belief, nothing more. That is the smallest and the only reparation I can make them, and I make it unreservedly.

'But with me, alas, it was different. Baulked of any chance of happiness in my home through my wife's wicked action – I say it advisedly – her wicked action in marrying me while she loved another, I succumbed to the temptation to look elsewhere for happiness. I met, quite by accident, someone with whom I could have been happy. You will never learn who she was or how I managed to meet her without being suspected – it is enough to say that things reached such a pass that this woman and I found we could no longer go on in the way we were, meeting by stealth, seeing each other only with carefully thought out precautions. The situation was intolerable and I determined to end it. And it was on the evening of the dinner party that I first saw the way.

'But here, before I go on to tell you the events of that terrible night, lest you might try to find this woman and saddle her with a part of the responsibility for what followed, let me tell you that here again I lost. The week after I destroyed my soul with the ghastly crime of which I will tell you, she got a chill. It turned to pneumonia, and in four days she was dead. I saw the judgment of Heaven beginning. But that is for me alone. Her name, at any rate, is safe. You will never find it out.'

Boirac's voice had fallen still lower. He spoke in a sort of toneless, numb way, as if mechanically, and yet his hearers could see that only his iron control prevented a breakdown.

'On that night of the dinner party,' he resumed, 'I met Felix accidentally in the hall on his arrival, and brought him into my study to see an etching. It is true we there spoke of the cask which had just arrived with my group, but I gave him no information such as would have enabled him to obtain a similar one.

'All that has been found out of the events of that evening up to the time that I left the works is true. It is true I thought at first I would be kept till late, and afterwards got away comparatively early. I actually left the works about eleven, took the Metro and changed at Châtelet, as I said, but from there my statement to the police was false. No American friend clapped me on the back as I alighted there, nor did such a man exist at all. My walk with him to the Quai d'Orsay, our farther stroll round the Place de la Concorde, his going by train to Orléans, and my walk home – all these were pure inventions on my part, made to account for my time between eleven-fifteen and one. What really happened during this time was as follows: I changed at Châtelet, taking the Maillot train for Alma, and walked home down the Avenue. I must have reached my house about twenty minutes or a quarter to twelve.

'I took out my latchkey as I mounted the steps, and then I noticed that one of the slats of the venetian blind of the drawing room window looking out towards the porch had caught up at one end, and a long, thin, triangular block of light shone out into the night. It was just on the level of my eyes and involuntarily I glanced through. What I saw inside stiffened me suddenly and I stood looking. In an armchair in the farther part of the room sat my wife, and bending closely over her, with his back towards me, was Felix. They were alone, and, as I watched, a plan entered my mind, and I stood transfixed with my pulses throbbing. Was there something between my wife and Felix? And if not, would it not suit my purpose to assume there was? I continued looking in and presently Felix rose to his feet and they began talking earnestly, Felix gesticulating freely, as was his habit. Then my wife left the room, returning in a few moments and handing him a small object. It was too far off to see what it was, but it seemed like a roll of banknotes. Felix put it carefully in his pocket and then they turned and walked towards the hall. In a few seconds the door opened and I shrank down into the shadows below the window sill.

' "Oh, Léon," I heard my wife's voice, and it seemed charged with emotion. "Oh, Léon, how good you are! How glad I am you have been able to do this!"

'Felix's voice showed that he also was moved.

' "Dear lady, is it not such happiness to me? You know I am always at your service."

'He moved down the steps.

' "You'll write?"

' "Immediately," he answered, and was gone.

'As the door closed, a furious passion of hate burned up in me for this woman who had ruined my life – who had not only ruined it, but who was still blocking out any chance of happiness I might have had. And also I furiously and jealously hated Felix for being the cause, however innocent, of my loss. And then suddenly I felt as if – perhaps I should say I felt that – a devil had entered and taken possession of me. I became deadly cold and I had the strange feeling that I myself was not really there, but that I was watching someone else. I slipped out my key, noiselessly opened the door, and followed my wife into the drawing-room. Her calm, nonchalant walk across the room roused me to still wilder fury. How well I knew her every motion. This was the way she would have turned to greet me when I arrived from the works, with cold politeness – when it might have been so different...

'She reached her chair in the corner of the room and tuned to sit down. As she did so she saw me. She gave a little scream.

' "Raoul, how you startled me," she cried. "Have you just arrived?"

'I threw off my hat and she saw my face.

' "Raoul," she cried again, "what's the matter? Why do you look like that?"

'I stood and looked at her. Outwardly I was calm, inwardly my blood whirled like molten metal through my veins and my mind was a seething fire.

' "Nothing really," I said, and someone else seemed to be speaking in a voice I had never heard before, a hoarse, horrible voice. "Only a mere trifle. Only Madame entertaining her lover after her husband has come home."

'She staggered back as if from a blow and collapsed into her chair, and turned her now pallid face to me.

' "Oh!" she cried in a trembling, choking voice, "Raoul, it's not true! It's not true, Raoul, I swear it! Don't you believe me, Raoul?"

'I stepped close to her. My hate swelled up in a blinding, numbing, overwhelming passion. It must have shown in my eyes, for a sudden fear leapt into hers.

'She tried to scream, but her dry throat produced only a piteous little cry. Her face had grown ghastly. Drops of sweat grew on her brow.

'I was close by her now. Instinctively my hands went out. I seemed to feel her slender neck between them, with my thumbs pressing... She read my purpose, for a hideous terror shone in her eyes. Dimly I was conscious of her hands tearing at my face...

'I stopped. My brain was numb. I seemed to see myself from a great distance standing looking at her. She was dead. I hated her more than ever. I was glad to see her dead, to watch that horror still lingering in her eyes. And he? How I hated him, he who had lost me my love and spoilt my life. I would go now. I would follow him and I would kill him. Kill him as I had killed her. I stumbled blindly to find the door.

'And then the devil that possessed me suggested another plan. He had wanted her. Well, he would get her. If he couldn't have her alive, he could have the next best thing. He could have her dead.'

M. Boirac paused. He had been speaking in a high-pitched voice and gesticulating as if overwhelmed with excitement. He seemed unconscious of his hearers, as if, carried away by his recollections, he was mentally living over again the awful scene, passing once more through the frenzy of that terrible time. Then, after a few moments' silence he pulled himself together and went on in a more normal tone.

'I determined to send the body to Felix, not only to satisfy my hate, but in the hope that his efforts to get rid of it would bring suspicion of the murder on him. Where, I wondered, could I get a receptacle in which to send it? And then it occurred to me that in the study adjoining was the cask that had just arrived with my statue. It was large, strongly made and bound with iron. It would suit my purpose admirably.

'I crossed to the study and unpacked the group. Then quite coolly I carried the body in and placed it in the cask. The idea that I must divert suspicion from myself grew in my mind, and I therefore took off my wife's evening shoes as their presence would tend to show she had not left the house. I filled up the cask with sawdust, ramming it tight. The body being so much larger than the group, there was a lot of sawdust over. This I swept up with the clothes brush from the hall and put in a handbag, which I locked. Finally I replaced the wooden top of the cask loosely as before, though still strongly enough not to come out if the cask was moved. When I had finished no one would have suspected that anything had been tampered with.

'It was my intention to create the impression that my wife had gone away with Felix. To this end two things appeared immediately necessary. Firstly, such of her outdoor clothes as she probably would have worn must disappear. I accordingly picked up the group and her shoes and went to her room. There I threw the shoes down carelessly before a chair, as if she had changed them. I took her fur coat, a hat, and a pair of walking shoes, and, with the group, carried them to my dressing-room. The only place I could think of for hiding them was in a couple of empty portmanteaux, so I packed the group in one and the clothes in another, carefully locking both.

'The second point was to produce a letter purporting to be from my wife to myself, in which she would say she loved Felix and had gone away with him. I had not time to write one then, but for temporary purposes I put an old letter of my own into a new envelope, addressing it to myself as best I could in my wife's hand. This I left on my desk.

'I had already spent over three-quarters of an hour and it was nearly one. I took a final look round to see that nothing had been forgotten, and was just leaving the drawing-room when my eye caught a glint of light from the carpet immediately behind the chair in which my wife had died. I stepped over and saw it was a brooch which had evidently been torn from her dress during the struggle. I broke out into a cold sweat as I thought how nearly I had missed it, and realised that its discovery by someone else might have disproved my story and brought me to the scaffold. With no clear idea except to hide it, I put it in my waistcoat pocket, took my hat, and, letting myself out, drew the door sharply behind me. After strolling as far as the Champs Élysées and back, I re-entered with my key. As I had hoped and intended, the shutting of the front door had been heard, and I found the butler obviously uneasy at my wife's disappearance. I endeavoured to confirm his suspicions that she had gone away with Felix, and, as you know, completely succeeded.

'Most of that night I spent in my study working out my plans. There was first of all the cask. A cask had been sent me by Dupierre, and it was obvious I must return them an empty one against it or I would give myself away. Where was this empty one to come from?

'It was clear to me that I must get a precisely similar cask to return, and the only way I could do so would be to order another group, in the hope that it would be sent packed in the same way. But obviously I could not have this group sent to me. The idea then occurred to me that I must write in some imaginary name ordering the statue to be delivered at some place such as a station cloak room, to be kept till called for. There I could get it without letting my identity become known.

'But this plan did not please me. I was afraid the police would be able to trace me. I thought over it again, and then I saw that if I ordered it in Felix's name it would meet the case. It would account for his getting the cask I was sending him, and he would not be believed when he denied ordering it. But I couldn't give Felix's name and address, for then he might get both casks, and I would be as badly fixed as ever. Finally I worked out the plan you know. I forged an order in Felix's hand for the companion group to my own to be sent to Felix at an imaginary address, made a tracing of it, left the letter in Dupierre's letter box on Monday night, telephoned them on Tuesday morning ascertaining by what route and train they were sending the group, went to London, met it and had it left in a shed there, all as you must have learnt.'

'A moment, please,' interrupted La Touche. 'You are going a little too quickly for me. You say you made a tracing of your forged order for the companion group and left the letter in Dupierre's letter box. I don't quite understand that.'

'Oh, you hadn't found that out, had you not? I will explain. I was in Paris, you see, when I forged the letter. But Dupierre must believe it came to him from London, or his suspicions would be aroused. I met the difficulty by sticking on the envelope a cancelled stamp from a letter I had received from London, copying the remainder of the postmark with a little lampblack. Then I went down to Grenelle in the middle of Monday night and dropped the letter into Dupierre's box. He would find it next morning all correct with its English stamp, cancelled in a London office.'

In spite of their loathing for this callous and cynical criminal, La Touche and Mallet could not but be impressed by the cleverness of the trick. All the detectives concerned had argued that as the order for the statue had been received apparently from London on Tuesday, it must have been posted there on Monday, and that as Felix was there and Boirac in Paris, the former must have posted it. But how simply they had been duped! Truly, thought the detectives with unwilling admiration, Boirac had deserved to succeed.

'But the tracing?' persisted La Touche.

'I thought that not only must Dupierre believe the letter came from London, but some definite proof that Felix had written it must be provided. I did it in this way. After I had written the letter I made a careful tracing of it on a bit of tracing paper. As you probably know, I visited St Malo when in London, and there, with Felix's pen and ink, I retraced over the writing and blotted it. This gave the impression.'

Again his hearers had to admit a rueful admiration for the ingenious ruse. The finding of the impression had seemed so conclusive, and – it was only a trick. And what a simple trick – when you knew it!

'That is quite clear, thank you,' said La Touche.

'I met the cask in London and brought it to the shed,' went on the manufacturer. 'There, after dismissing the carter, I opened the cask, took out the statue, packed it in a portmanteau I had with me, took the label off the cask and put it carefully in my pocket, replacing it with one addressed to Jacques de Belleville at the Gare du Nord. As you know, this Jacques de Belleville was myself.

'As you found Dubois, the carter, you will have learnt the method by which I exchanged the casks, sending that containing the body from my house to Felix, while the other, which I had emptied in London, went back to Dupierre. You understand that part of it?'

'Perfectly.'

'So much then for the getting of the body to Felix. But it was my desire not only to give him the shock of opening the cask and discovering it; I wished also to make the police suspicious so that he would be watched and his attempts to get rid of the corpse discovered. In this case I intended he should be charged with the murder, incidentally clearing me. To ensure this result I set myself to construct such evidence as would weave a net round him from which he would be unable to escape. Gradually the details of my plan arranged themselves in my mind.

'Firstly, it was necessary that I should really have the letter of farewell, the envelope of which I had prepared, and which I had pretended to find on going to my study. Collecting a number of specimens of my wife's handwriting from her davenport, I forged the letter I showed to the French police. Putting it away for future use, I burnt the specimens to prevent them from being compared with the forgery.

'The problem of getting Felix to meet the cask which I intended to send him, and while doing so to attract the attention of the police, then occupied my thoughts. After much consideration I decided on the plan you know. It happened that some three weeks previously I had been seated in the Café Toisson d'Or, when a bad neuralgic headache had come on, and I had moved into an alcove to be as private as possible. While there I had seen Felix come in and begin talking to a group of men. I had not made myself known, as I was in considerable pain, but I had overheard their conversation and learnt the arrangement Felix and his friend Le Gautier had made about the lottery. This I now decided to use, and I drafted a letter to Felix purporting to come from Le Gautier, mentioning this matter of the lottery to make it seem genuine. I also drafted a slip about money I intended to send in the cask. The contents of this letter and slip you know. These I put away in my pocket-book, to be used later.

'The next evening, Monday, I pretended to unpack the cask. I brought the group I had taken out of it on the previous Saturday from the portmanteau in which I had hidden it, and placed it on the table in my study. On the floor, about the cask, I sprinkled some of the sawdust from the handbag. By this manoeuvre I hoped if suspicion arose it would be argued that as the cask was not unpacked till Monday night, the body could not have been put into it on the night of the dinner. As you know, this ruse also succeeded. I also took the label off the cask and put it in my pocket.

'Opening the cask again, I put in £52 10s. in English gold, to correspond with my slip. I hoped that, if the police got hold of the cask, they would assume that Felix had put in this money in order to strengthen his story that the cask had been sent to him. I put in sovereigns instead of French gold with the intention of making this theory more likely, as I hoped it would be argued that Felix in his agitation had overreached himself, and forgotten from what country the cask was supposed to be coming.

'Calling François, I told him I had unpacked the statue, and when Messrs Dupierre sent for the cask he was to give it to them. Then, informing him that I would be from home for a couple of nights, I left next morning by the early train for London.

'On the Monday I had purchased a false beard and arranged to get myself up to resemble Felix, and I wore this disguise all the time till my return. I brought with me on the journey the portmanteau containing my wife's clothes, and, on board the boat, from a quiet place on the lower deck, slipped these articles overboard without being observed. On arrival in London I arranged with a carting firm to carry about the cask on the next two days, as you already know. I then went out to St Malo, Felix's house, which I found after some judicious inquiries. A careful reconnoitre showed me it was unoccupied. I tried round the windows and had the luck to find one unhasped. Opening it, I crept into the house and went to the study. There by the light of an electric torch I carefully inked over the tracing I had made of the forged letter ordering the cask, and blotted it on Felix's pad. This, I felt sure, would be found, and would seem to prove that he had written the order.

'I had foreseen that it would be argued that Felix must be innocent because not only would he have no motive to murder my wife, but also he would naturally be the last man in the world to do such a thing. It was necessary for me, therefore, to provide a motive. For this purpose I had written a letter purporting to be from a girl whom Felix had wronged. Having crumpled this letter I put it into the side pocket of one of Felix's coats. I hoped this would be found, and that it would be argued that my wife had got hold of it and that there had been a quarrel which led to her death. Crumpling it was to suggest Felix had snatched it from her, thrust it into his pocket and forgotten it.

'As I stood in the study a further idea occurred to me. I had thought of a use for a brooch that had dropped from my wife's clothes. It had fallen just behind the chair she had been sitting in, and I thought if I placed it on the floor behind a chair in this room, it would suggest she had been murdered here. My eye fell on a chair with a low back, standing in front of a curtain, and I saw at once it would suit my purpose. I dropped the brooch behind it and it caught on the braid at the bottom of the curtain. There it was hidden from casual inspection by the chair, but I knew the police would not overlook it. I withdrew without disturbing anything or leaving traces, closed the window, and returned to the city.

'Such was my plot, and, but for your cleverness, it would have succeeded. Is there any other point on which you are not clear?'

'Only one, I think,' answered La Touche. 'You were heard to telephone on the Monday from the café at Charenton to your butler and chief clerk. They received their messages on the Tuesday from Calais. How did you manage that?'

'Easily. I never telephoned on Monday at all. I slipped a tiny wooden wedge into the instrument to prevent the hook rising when I lifted off the receiver. No call was therefore made on the exchange, though I went through the form of speaking. Any other point?'

'I do not think so,' returned La Touche, who again could not but feel a kind of rueful admiration for this ingenious ruffian. 'Your statement has been very complete.'

'It is not quite complete,' M. Boirac resumed. 'There are two more points of which I wish to speak. Read that.'

He took a letter from his pocket and handed it to La Touche. Both men leant a little forward to look. As they did so there was a slight click and the light went out. What sounded like Boirac's chair was heard falling.

'Hold the door!' yelled La Touche, springing to his feet and fumbling for his electric torch. Mallet leaped for the door, but, tripping over the chair, missed it. As La Touche flashed on his light they could see it closing. There was a low, mocking laugh. Then the door slammed and they heard the key turn in the lock.

La Touche fired rapidly through the panels, but there was no sound from without. Then Mallet flung himself on the handle. But at his first touch it came off. The holes for the screws had been enlarged so that they had no hold.

The door opened inwards, and presented to the imprisoned men a smooth, unbroken surface, with nothing on which to pull. To push it through towards the hall was impossible, as it shut solidly against the frame. Their only hope seemed to split it, but as they gazed at its solid oak timbers this hope died.

'The window,' cried La Touche, and they swung round. The sashes opened readily, but outside were shutters of steel plate, closely fastened. Both men shoved and prised with all their might. But Boirac had done his work well. They were immovable.

As they stood panting and baffled, Mallet's eye caught the switch of the electric light. It was off. He clicked it on. Though no answering flood of light poured down, he noticed something that interested him.

'Your torch, La Touche!' he cried, and then he saw what it was, tied to the switch was a length of fisherman's gut. Practically invisible, it passed down the wall and through a tiny hole in the floor. Anyone pulling it from below would switch off the light.

'I don't understand,' said La Touche. 'That means he had a confederate?'

'No!' cried Mallet, who had been looking about with the torch. 'See here!'

He pointed to the chair Boirac had occupied and which now lay on its side on the floor. Fastened to the left arm was another end of gut which also entered a hole in the floor.

'I bet those are connected!'

Their curiosity temporarily overcame their fears. La Touche turned on the switch and Mallet, pulling the gut at the arm of the chair, heard it click off again.

'Ingenious devil,' he muttered. 'It must go round pulleys under the floor. And now he has cut off the current at the meter.'

'Come on, Mallet,' La Touche called. 'Don't waste time. We must get out of this.'

Together they threw themselves on the door with all the weight of their shoulders. Again they tried, and again, but to no purpose. It was too strong.

'What does it mean, do you think?' panted Mallet.

'Gas, I expect. Perhaps, charcoal.'

'Any use shouting at the window?'

'None. It's too closely shuttered, and it only opens into a courtyard.'

And then suddenly they perceived a faint odour which, in spite of their hardened nerves, turned their blood cold and set them working with ten times more furious energy at the door. It was a very slight smell of burning wood.

'My God!' cried Mallet, 'he's set the house on fire!'

It seemed impossible that any door could withstand so furious an onslaught. Had it opened outwards, hinges and lock must long since have given way, but the men could not make their strength tell. They worked till the sweat rolled in great drops down their foreheads. Meanwhile the smell increased. Smoke must be percolating into the room.

'The torch here,' cried La Touche suddenly.

Taking his pistol, he fired a number of shots on the bolt of the lock.

'Don't use them all. How many have you?'

'Two more.'

'Keep them.'

The lock seemed shattered, but still the door held. The men's efforts were becoming frenzied when Mallet had an idea. Along the farther wall of the room stood a heavy, old-fashioned sofa.

'Let's use the couch as a battering-ram.'

The room was now thick with smoke, biting and gripping the men's throats. Hampered by coughing and bad light, they could not work fast. But at last they got the couch across the room and planted end on to the door. Standing one at each side, they swung it back and then with all their strength drove it against the timber. A second time they drove, and a third, till at the fourth blow there was a sound of splitting wood, and the job was done.

Or so they thought. A moment later they found their mistake. The right bottom panel only was gone.

'The left panel! Then the bar between!'

Though the men worked feverishly, their operations took time. The smoke was now increasing rapidly. And then suddenly La Touche heard a terrible, ominous sound. Crackling was beginning somewhere not far off.

'We haven't much time, Mallet,' he gasped, as the sweat poured down his face.

Desperately they drove the couch against the bar. Still it held. The terrible fear that the couch would come to pieces was in both their hearts.

'The torch!' cried Mallet hoarsely. 'Quick, or we're done!'

Drawing his magazine pistol and holding it close to the door, he fired its full charge of seven shots at the vertical bar. La Touche instantly grasped his idea, and emptied his two remaining shots at the same place. The bar was thus perforated by a transverse line of nine holes.

There was a singing in the men's ears and a weight on their chests as, with the energy of despair, they literally hurled the heavy couch against the weakened bar. With a tearing sound it gave way. They could get through.

'You for it, Mallet! Quick!' yelled La Touche, as he staggered drunkenly back. But there was no answer. Through the swirling clouds the detective could see his assistant lying motionless. That last tremendous effort had finished him.

La Touche's own head was swimming. He could no longer think connectedly. Half unconsciously he pulled the other's arms to the hole. Then, passing through, he turned to draw his *confrère* out. But the terrible roaring was swelling in his ears, the weight on his chest was growing insupportable, and a black darkness was coming down over him like a pall. Insensible, he collapsed, half in and half out of the doorway.

As he fell there was a lurid flicker and a little dancing flame leaped lightly from the floor.

30

CONCLUSION

When La Touche's senses returned he found himself lying in the open air, with Farol, his other assistant, bending over him. His first thought was for his companion in misfortune.

'Mallet?' he whispered feebly.

'Safe,' answered Farol, 'We got him out just in time.'

'And Boirac?'

'The police are after him.'

La Touche lay still. He was badly shaken. But the fresh air rapidly revived him, and he was soon able to sit up.

'Where am I?' he asked presently.

'Just round the corner from Boirac's. The firemen are at work.'

'Tell me about it.'

Farol's story was short. It seemed that Boirac had returned home that afternoon about three. Shortly after, the detective had been surprised to observe a regular exodus of servants from the house. Cabs and taxis took away two men and four women, all with luggage. Lastly, about four o'clock, came François, also with luggage, and with him Boirac. François closed and locked the door, handing the key to his master. The two then shook hands and, stepping into separate vehicles, were driven away. It was evident the house was being closed for a considerable period.

Farol, entering the taxi he kept in waiting, followed. They drove to the Gare St Lazare, where the manufacturer dismissed his vehicle and entered the station. But instead of taking a ticket, he simply walked about the concourse and in a few minutes left by another door. Travelling by the Metro, he reached Alma Station, walked down the Avenue, and, with a hurried look round, re-entered his house. To Farol it was obvious that something was in the wind. He withdrew to some distance and watched.

His surprise at these strange proceedings was not lessened when he saw La Touche and Mallet drive up to the door and ring. He hurried forward to warn them, but before he could do so the door opened and they disappeared within. Growing more and more anxious, Farol waited till, after a considerable time, he saw Boirac leave the house alone. Now certain that something was wrong, he decided he must let the manufacturer go, while he telephoned his suspicions to the Sûreté. A car with some men was sent immediately, and they drove up to the door just as Farol returned to it on foot. Smoke was beginning to issue from the upper windows, and one man was sent for the fire brigade, while the others attempted to break into the house. In this they succeeded only after considerable trouble. Through the smoke they saw La Touche's body lying half in the hall and half in François' room. Only just in time they got the men out, the back of the hall being a sheet of flame before they reached the open air.

'We better go to the Sûreté,' said La Touche, who, by this time, had practically recovered.

Twenty minutes later M. Chauvet was in possession of the facts, and operations for the tracing of Boirac had begun.

La Touche then confidentially told the Chief all that he had learnt about the mystery. M. Chauvet was utterly astounded, and chagrined beyond measure at the blunder he and his men had fallen into.

'Clever devil!' he exclaimed. He knew that nothing but the absolute truth would put you off your guard. But we'll get him, M. La Touche. He can't get out of the city. By now, every route will be barred.'

The Chief's prophecy was fulfilled earlier than even he expected. Only an hour later they had news. Evidently believing himself secure in the destruction of the only two men who, so far as he was aware, knew enough to convict him, Boirac, after setting the house on fire, had gone openly to his club. A detective who went there to make inquiries, found him calmly sitting smoking in the lounge. He had, it appeared, made a desperate effort to escape arrest, and attempted to shoot the officer. Then, seeing it was all up with him, he turned the revolver upon himself, and, before he could be stopped, shot himself through the head.

So perished one of the most callous and cold-blooded criminals of the century.

In a curious manner Felix received his reparation. Heppenstall, who had learnt to respect and appreciate his client, engaged him to paint a portrait of his wife. While thus occupied the artist made the acquaintance of the KC's daughter. The two young people promptly fell in love. Six months later they were quietly married, and, his bride bringing a not inconsiderable dot, Felix threw up his appointment and moved to a new St Malo on the sunny shores of the Mediterranean. Here he divided his attention between his young wife and the painting of that master-piece which had so long remained an unattainable dream.

Freeman Wills Crofts

The Box Office Murders

A London box office clerk falls under the spell of a mysterious trio of crooks. Assisted by a helpful solicitor who directs her to Scotland Yard, she tells Inspector French the story of the Purple Sickle. But when her body is found floating in Southampton Water the next day, French discovers that similar murders have taken place and determines to learn the trio's secret and run them to ground...

The Hog's Back Mystery

Several local residents have disappeared in suspicious circumstances at The Hog's Back ridge in Surrey. When a doctor vanishes, followed by a nurse with whom he was acquainted, Inspector French deduces murder, but there are no bodies. Can he eventually prove his theory and show that murder has been committed?

'As pretty a piece of work as Inspector French has done...on the level of Mr Crofts' very best; which is saying something.'

E C Bentley in the *Daily Telegraph*

Freeman Wills Crofts

Inspector French's Greatest Case

A head clerk's corpse is discovered beside the empty safe of a Hatton Garden diamond merchant. There are many suspects and a multitude of false clues to be followed before a tireless investigator is called in to solve the crime. This is a case for Freeman Wills Crofts' most famous character – Inspector French.

Man Overboard!

In the course of a ship's passage from Belfast to Liverpool, a man disappears and his body is later picked up by Irish fishermen. Although the coroner's verdict is suicide, murder is suspected. Inspector French co-operates with Superintendent Rainey and Sergeant McClung once more to determine the truth, whatever the cost...

'To me, Inspector French is the most human sleuth to be found in the detective novels of today.'

Punch

FREEMAN WILLS CROFTS

MYSTERY IN THE CHANNEL

The cross-channel steamer *Chichester* stops halfway to France. A motionless yacht lies in her path and when a party clambers aboard it finds a trail of blood and two dead men. Chief Constable Turnbill has to call on the ever-reliable Inspector French for help in solving the mystery of the *Nymph*.

MYSTERY ON SOUTHAMPTON WATER

The Joymount Rapid Hardening Cement Manufacturing Company is in serious financial trouble. Two young company employees hatch a plot to break into a rival works on the Isle of Wight to find out their competitor's secret for undercutting them. But the scheme does not go according to plan and results in the death of a night watchman, theft and fire. Inspector French is brought in to solve the baffling mystery.

OTHER TITLES BY FREEMAN WILLS CROFTS AVAILABLE DIRECT FROM HOUSE OF STRATUS

Quantity		£	$(US)	$(CAN)	€
	THE 12.30 FROM CROYDON	6.99	12.95	19.95	13.50
	THE AFFAIR AT LITTLE WOKEHAM	6.99	12.95	19.95	13.50
	ANTIDOTE TO VENOM	6.99	12.95	19.95	13.50
	ANYTHING TO DECLARE?	6.99	12.95	19.95	13.50
	THE BOX OFFICE MURDERS	6.99	12.95	19.95	13.50
	CRIME AT GUILDFORD	6.99	12.95	19.95	13.50
	DEATH OF A TRAIN	6.99	12.95	19.95	13.50
	DEATH ON THE WAY	6.99	12.95	19.95	13.50
	THE END OF ANDREW HARRISON	6.99	12.95	19.95	13.50
	ENEMY UNSEEN	6.99	12.95	19.95	13.50
	FATAL VENTURE	6.99	12.95	19.95	13.50
	FEAR COMES TO CHALFONT	6.99	12.95	19.95	13.50
	FOUND FLOATING	6.99	12.95	19.95	13.50
	FRENCH STRIKES OIL	6.99	12.95	19.95	13.50
	GOLDEN ASHES	6.99	12.95	19.95	13.50
	THE GROOTE PARK MURDER	6.99	12.95	19.95	13.50
	THE HOG'S BACK MYSTERY	6.99	12.95	19.95	13.50
	INSPECTOR FRENCH AND THE CHEYNE MYSTERY	6.99	12.95	19.95	13.50

ALL HOUSE OF STRATUS BOOKS ARE AVAILABLE FROM GOOD BOOKSHOPS OR DIRECT FROM THE PUBLISHER:

Internet: www.houseofstratus.com including synopses and features.

Email: sales@houseofstratus.com
info@houseofstratus.com
(please quote author, title and credit card details.)

OTHER TITLES BY FREEMAN WILLS CROFTS AVAILABLE DIRECT FROM HOUSE OF STRATUS

Quantity		£	$(US)	$(CAN)	€
☐	INSPECTOR FRENCH AND THE STARVEL TRAGEDY	6.99	12.95	19.95	13.50
☐	INSPECTOR FRENCH'S GREATEST CASE	6.99	12.95	19.95	13.50
☐	JAMES TARRANT, ADVENTURER	6.99	12.95	19.95	13.50
☐	A LOSING GAME	6.99	12.95	19.95	13.50
☐	THE LOSS OF THE JANE VOSPER	6.99	12.95	19.95	13.50
☐	MAN OVERBOARD!	6.99	12.95	19.95	13.50
☐	MANY A SLIP	6.99	12.95	19.95	13.50
☐	MURDERERS MAKE MISTAKES	6.99	12.95	19.95	13.50
☐	MYSTERY IN THE CHANNEL	6.99	12.95	19.95	13.50
☐	MYSTERY OF THE SLEEPING CAR EXPRESS	6.99	12.95	19.95	13.50
☐	MYSTERY ON SOUTHAMPTON WATER	6.99	12.95	19.95	13.50
☐	THE PIT-PROP SYNDICATE	6.99	12.95	19.95	13.50
☐	THE PONSON CASE	6.99	12.95	19.95	13.50
☐	THE SEA MYSTERY	6.99	12.95	19.95	13.50
☐	SILENCE FOR THE MURDERER	6.99	12.95	19.95	13.50
☐	SIR JOHN MAGILL'S LAST JOURNEY	6.99	12.95	19.95	13.50
☐	SUDDEN DEATH	6.99	12.95	19.95	13.50

ALL HOUSE OF STRATUS BOOKS ARE AVAILABLE FROM GOOD BOOKSHOPS OR DIRECT FROM THE PUBLISHER:

Tel:	**Order Line** 0800 169 1780 (UK) 800 724 1100 (USA) **International** +44 (0) 1845 527700 (UK) +01 845 463 1100 (USA)
Fax:	+44 (0) 1845 527711 (UK) +01 845 463 0018 (USA) (please quote author, title and credit card details.)
Send to:	**House of Stratus Sales Department** **Thirsk Industrial Park** **York Road, Thirsk** **North Yorkshire, YO7 3BX** **UK**

House of Stratus Inc.
2 Neptune Road
Poughkeepsie
NY 12601
USA

PAYMENT

Please tick currency you wish to use:

☐ £ (Sterling)   ☐ $ (US)   ☐ $ (CAN)   ☐ € (Euros)

Allow for shipping costs charged per order plus an amount per book as set out in the tables below:

CURRENCY/DESTINATION

	£(Sterling)	$(US)	$(CAN)	€(Euros)
Cost per order				
UK	1.50	2.25	3.50	2.50
Europe	3.00	4.50	6.75	5.00
North America	3.00	3.50	5.25	5.00
Rest of World	3.00	4.50	6.75	5.00
Additional cost per book				
UK	0.50	0.75	1.15	0.85
Europe	1.00	1.50	2.25	1.70
North America	1.00	1.00	1.50	1.70
Rest of World	1.50	2.25	3.50	3.00

PLEASE SEND CHEQUE OR INTERNATIONAL MONEY ORDER
payable to: HOUSE OF STRATUS LTD or HOUSE OF STRATUS INC. or card payment as indicated

STERLING EXAMPLE

Cost of book(s):.................... Example: 3 x books at £6.99 each: £20.97
Cost of order: .... Example: £1.50 (Delivery to UK address)
Additional cost per book:............. Example: 3 x £0.50: £1.50
Order total including shipping:.......... Example: £23.97

VISA, MASTERCARD, SWITCH, AMEX:

☐ ☐ ☐ ☐ ☐ ☐ ☐ ☐ ☐ ☐ ☐ ☐ ☐ ☐ ☐ ☐ ☐ ☐ ☐ ☐

Issue number (Switch only):

☐ ☐ ☐

Start Date: **Expiry Date:**

☐ ☐ / ☐ ☐   ☐ ☐ / ☐ ☐

Signature: _____

NAME: _____

ADDRESS: _____

COUNTRY: _____

ZIP/POSTCODE: _____

Please allow 28 days for delivery. Despatch normally within 48 hours.

Prices subject to change without notice.
Please tick box if you do not wish to receive any additional information. ☐

House of Stratus publishes many other titles in this genre; please check our website (**www.houseofstratus.com**) for more details.